POWER STRUGGLE

by
Doug Farren

PublishAmerica
Baltimore

© 2004 by Doug Farren.
All rights reserved. No part of this book may be reproduced, stored in a retrieval system or transmitted in any form or by any means without the prior written permission of the publishers, except by a reviewer who may quote brief passages in a review to be printed in a newspaper, magazine or journal.

First printing

ISBN: 1-4137-4550-4
PUBLISHED BY PUBLISHAMERICA, LLLP
www.publishamerica.com
Baltimore

Printed in the United States of America

To my wife, Cheryl, for her love and help in making this book a reality. Without her this book may never have been published. To my dad, Ron, who got me interested in science fiction. To my late mother, Geraldine Busse, who would have been proud to see this book published.

Chapter 1

This is how life was meant to be enjoyed, thought Ken as he stretched out on the deck of his eight meter sailboat. The pleasure craft was drifting aimlessly, the only sound being the gentle slap of the waves as they caressed the side of the ship. Ken was watching a spectacular sunset and enjoying every minute of it. The sun appeared as a gigantic reddish-orange ball sitting on top of the water's surface. As he watched, it slowly sank lower.

The stars were beginning to peek through the darkening sky. As Ken tried to make out the constellations, an insect buzzed near his right ear. He ignored it, hoping it would go away. Instead, it got closer and the buzzing louder. As he reached up to brush the offending insect away, the dream faded into oblivion. The buzz of the ship's com system continued, announcing the fact that someone was determined to interrupt the Captain's sleep.

Captain Ken Stricklen shook his head to clear away the last vestiges of the dream before hitting the acknowledge button. "Stricklen," he said not bothering to hide his annoyance. "What is it?"

"Sorry to disturb you sir," replied a voice that Ken identified as belonging to his executive officer. "We have picked up an unusual gravitational anomaly which I believe you should take a look at."

"Gravitational anomaly? What is so unusual about this anomaly that warrants my personal attention at this time of the morning?" Ken was obviously upset. Being the captain of an Alliance heavy cruiser, he was used to being awakened in the middle of the night, but this sounded like a problem his XO could handle.

"Well sir, it's difficult to describe. It's a pulsating gravitational field of very high strength. We are unable to identify a source."

"So catalog it and let someone else worry about it."

Stricklen was all set to go back to sleep when the XO argued, "We are also picking up some faint energy readings. I really think you should see this. A course correction to investigate might be in order."

Ken knew his executive officer quite well and when his XO suggested a course correction he knew it must be something more than just the standard uncataloged gravitational anomaly. "All right. Give me a few minutes," his voice clearly implying that this anomaly had better be worth it. "What the hell time is it anyway?"

"Zero four fifteen, sir." The circuit went dead with a barely audible click.

Ken ordered the lights to half intensity and swung his legs over the side of the bunk. He passed his hand over the stubble on his chin then began the morning ritual of getting into his uniform. Fifteen minutes later he stood in front of a full length mirror.

Captain Ken Stricklen, Commanding officer of the Alliance heavy-cruiser *Komodo Dragon*, checked over his 165 centimeter, 63.5 kilogram reflection. The space-black uniform fit snugly on his trim figure. At thirty-nine, he still looked and felt as if he was in his late twenties. The only adornment on the uniform was a small starburst on his upper right chest signifying his rank of captain. He had combed his jet-black hair but left the stubble on his face. He rubbed it again and thought, *Perhaps I'll grow a beard*, knowing in his heart that it would never happen. Casting his brown eyes one last time over his reflection, Ken headed for the bridge.

"Captain on the bridge!" Doug Scarboro announced as the door hissed open. The XO turned toward his Captain and, in an overly polite tone of voice, said, "Good morning, sir."

Ken suppressed a non-professional reply, instead opting for a simple nod. A cup of steaming coffee was waiting for him in the holder near the captain's chair. Reaching for it he said, "Show me what you have Doug."

The *Dragon's* executive officer was a vastly different individual than his CO. His 82 kilogram mass towered 196 centimeters above the deck. The top of his head was covered by a wild tangle of deep red hair. His blue eyes seemed to peer directly into a person's soul but his jovial attitude kept people at ease. Doug had served as Ken's XO for the last three years and they had become good friends.

The Captain settled into his chair as Doug keyed a request into the ship's computer system. A display screen came to life and a pattern of lines appeared. "This is the gravitational anomaly I mentioned," Doug said. "It is very regular and repeats every 2.16 minutes. We have a fix on its location to within 500 million klics."

Doug touched a key and the primary navigational display, a large globe nearly three meters in diameter located near the center of the circular bridge, displayed a three-dimensional map of the surrounding space. A thin green line indicated the *Dragon's* course. Off to one side a red dot slowly pulsed. "Whatever is generating it is located here at a distance of 0.43 lights.

POWER STRUGGLE

Preliminary analysis puts its mass equivalence at about 30 billion metric tons."

Ken's coffee cup stopped halfway to his lips. "Thirty BILLION? Nobody can generate a gravity field like that! Even if you could, why would you want to? Why is it pulsating?"

Another graph appeared on the display in front of them at Doug's request. Pointing to one of the lines, he said, "This is a faint energy pulse we have also detected from the same point in space. It occurs in synch with the gravity field. The energy spectrum is unlike anything we have ever seen before. Whatever it is, it's not natural—the computer confirms it. I would like to investigate."

The Captain took a long drink from his coffee as he considered this request. The *Komodo Dragon* was en route to a remote mining station to investigate why all contact had suddenly been lost. Three times in the recent past, remote outposts had been attacked by an unknown assailant near this area of space. In each attack there were no survivors. Every outpost had been totally destroyed, and no evidence of who the attackers were or why they had attacked had been found. The *Dragon's* mission was to determine what had happened to this outpost and, if possible, to extract any survivors if an attack had occurred and any could be found. The Captain decided that he could let nothing interfere with that mission.

"I will not deviate from our primary mission," he replied. "Deploy a probe to investigate. By the way, what is our ETA to Mintaka?"

The XO did not even bother to look up the answer. Instead, he simply glanced at his wrist-com and replied, "We should be there in about eighteen hours. Still no contact."

"Very well. I'm going to get some breakfast. Go ahead and deploy the probe. I'll relieve you when I get back." Without waiting for a reply, Stricklen walked off the bridge.

On his way to the mess hall he felt the soft thump through the deck plating as the probe was ejected from its launch bay. The mess hall was deserted and any meals would have to be self-serve. At this time of the morning the only people awake were those standing watch. Ken fixed himself a simple breakfast and sat down to enjoy it. As he was finishing, the call to reveille sounded. Soon the ship would be awake and the quiet he was savoring would be broken. Before the crowd arrived, the Captain returned to the bridge.

After receiving an update from Doug, Ken relieved him and took his customary seat in the captain's chair. The XO stated that he was going to get some breakfast and then retire for a few hours. Ken was soon immersed in the daily routine of commanding a starship. The probe, even though it was traveling at more than 200 times the speed of light, would require over seventeen hours to reach the area of the anomaly. The *Komodo Dragon* was traveling at over 2300c toward an encounter with the unknown. By the time the probe reached its target it would be so far behind the *Dragon* that communications would have a time lag of about one hour even at the phenomenal FTL communication speed of 38,600c. The probe quickly made its way into an unimportant corner of Ken's mind.

* * * * *

The buzz of the intercom interrupted Stricklen's concentration. Setting down the report he had been preparing for sector command he acknowledged the call. "We'll be dropping to sublight in about ten minutes, Sir. You asked to be informed." The voice was that of Commander Stiles, the weapons officer who was standing his normal bridge watch.

"Very well—I'll be right there," Ken replied.

A moment later he strode onto the bridge. "Captain on the bridge!" Stiles announced.

Stricklen surveyed the bridge seeing at a glance that all was well, "What is our status Mr. Stiles?" he asked, indicating that he was ready to relieve the watch.

"We are approaching Mintaka at 56c and decelerating due to gravitational interference. Fusion reactor three is being restarted following a routine maintenance shutdown. All other systems are green."

Stricklen listened to the ship's status while his seasoned eyes scanned the bridge taking in additional data. When Stiles had finished, Ken looked at him and said, "Very well, I relieve you."

With the formalities of turnover completed, Ken took his position in the command chair and punched up several displays. The *Komodo Dragon* was being forced to slow down as it entered the gravity-well of the Mintaka system's sun. Faster-than-light drive fields worked directly upon the fabric of space itself. Any distortion of that fabric, such as a gravitational field, affected the drive's ability to maintain the ship's super-luminal velocity. The intricately interlaced fields of force had to be precisely matched to the ever-changing structure of space. Too great a mismatch and the complex structure of the drive fields would collapse and the ship would return to normal space.

POWER STRUGGLE

As the gravitational warping of space grew worse, more and more power had to be poured into the drive fields to keep them properly synchronized. Eventually, the generator's power limit was reached and the ship had no choice but to slow down. Slower FTL speeds required a less complex and less power-hungry field structure. Ken was looking at a display showing the critical engine parameters for the ship's Kauffman stardrive.

Suddenly, without any warning to the bridge crew, Ken's hand reached out and touched the battle stations alarm button. The crew, knowing their Captain as they did, were probably expecting the alarm but, never-the-less, Ken wanted to surprise them as much as possible. The alarm klaxon sounded throughout the ship.

As the crew raced to their assigned stations, the *Dragon's* master computer exerted its will on the various parts of the ship which it controlled. Environmental systems split into many separate isolated sections; weapon systems powered themselves up; standby systems switched from inactive to active; the power grid re-aligned itself into a more reliable configuration; unnecessary systems were shutdown.

Stricklen watched as the indicators around the bridge shifted. Four minutes after he had initiated battle stations, the XO reported from combat control that the ship was ready. Ken was very satisfied – four minutes was a good time. "Communications, any contact with Mintaka?" he asked.

"No sir, all channels are clear with the exception of standard telemetry data from probe one."

Ken had almost forgotten about the probe, since it had yet to report anything. Being that it still had nothing to report, he promptly put it out of his mind. Instead, he concentrated upon the situation at hand. The Captain had decided to put the ship at battle stations because there was a very real possibility that if Mintaka had been attacked, the attackers could still be in the area. As the *Komodo Dragon* plunged deeper into the planetary system's gravity well, it slowed ever more quickly. The ship's detectors were flung out to their maximum range looking for anything that could become a threat. Ken watched the numerous displays showing the Kauffman drive's power usage and the relative amount of spacial warp that the drive had to contend with as they both approached critical values. Eventually, a point was reached where the ship could no longer maintain the complex Kauffman stardrive fields.

A single tone sounded throughout the ship followed by the voice of the helmsman. "FTL dropout in fifteen seconds," he calmly announced. The seconds ticked by, then a minor flurry of activity occurred on the bridge.

"Disengaging stardrive, sublight engines on-line, drive field synchronization in progress," the helm announced. "We made break-out at 8.64 megaklics from Mintaka. Correcting for intra-system intrinsic velocity differential and setting course for Mintaka at max acceleration."

"Defense shield grid up and stable," said the weapon's officer. "All weapon systems fully charged and active."

"Initiating sweep of the system," the XO reported from his station in the combat control center. "No targets identified at this time."

"Very well," Stricklen replied. "Coms, I want continuous attempts to contact Mintaka on all channels. Also, send out a general call to see if there might have been any miners out in the system doing surveys. Let me know the moment you hear anything. Helm, what's our ETA?"

"ETA about 1.4 hours at max acceleration. We should be within detail scan range of the planet in about forty minutes," came the near instant reply.

Stricklen pushed a button on his console which opened a channel to Doug Scarboro in combat control. Once the connection had been established, Ken said, "Doug, as soon as you can, I want a series of probes sent out to perform a detailed search of the planet. Mintaka is a mining world and there may have been several geological expeditions away from the primary mining sites at the time of the attack. If there are survivors, they could be anywhere on the planet."

"I take it you are assuming they were attacked?" Doug asked.

"I am working under that assumption until proven otherwise. Use the probes to scan the surface and keep our main detectors watching our back."

"Yes sir," Scarboro replied and the connection snapped.

Ken was on his third cup of coffee when the first direct detailed scan of the main mining site came in. Doug's face appeared on one of the numerous miniature monitors on the Captain's console. "First scan is in Sir—you were right, they were attacked. I'll send the pictures up to the bridge."

The main monitor switched from a tactical display to a highly enhanced view of what used to be a mining town. Where over 1600 people had once lived and worked there now existed a landscape pockmarked with craters and ruined land. Large scars from energy weapons were visible and, according to the false color image, several areas still had higher than normal temperatures. It was impossible to tell if any man-made structures had ever existed.

Ken slammed his fist on the armrest of his chair. "Who the hell would attack an unarmed mining site on a worthless planet?" he said in a low steady voice to no one in particular. "What about the other mines Doug?"

"This picture is a computer generated image based upon long-range scans made from the ship. We were lucky in that the main mining site was on the side of the planet facing us when we came within range. As soon as the other sites are visible to our scanners I will be able to answer your question."

"Where are the probes?"

"Twenty probes with search capability were launched about ten minutes ago," Doug replied. They will be within scanning range in another fifteen minutes."

As the *Dragon* continued to approach Mintaka, the continuing search revealed nothing but destruction. Each mining site had been blasted into oblivion. When the probes reached the planet, they sent back detailed views of the destruction. In all his years in the Alliance military, Ken had never seen such complete and total devastation. As time slowly trickled by, their hopes of locating any survivors sank lower and lower.

"Captain," the communication station announced. "Report coming in from probe one. The source of the gravitational anomaly has been found. It's a ship Sir!"

Taking his eyes off a view of yet another a destroyed mining site, Ken turned to the communications station and asked, "What kind of ship?"

The junior officer punched in a command on his console and the main viewer shifted to show a spacecraft of a type unknown to Ken. One side of the screen displayed the ship's statistics. Length – 850 meters; Width – 280 meters; Height – 160 meters; Mass – unknown; Type – unknown; Origin – unknown. The ship was slowly rotating as if it had lost stability control. As Ken watched, a badly damaged area came into view.

"Do we have any additional data on the ship?" Stricklen asked.

"Yes sir, the computer has been analyzing it."

Ken touched a button and spoke, "Dragon – identify the ship that is currently being scanned by probe one."

A soft, almost boyish sounding voice replied, "The ship is unidentifiable. It is drifting in space and appears to be unpowered, although at least one power source is known to be operating within the ship. Microstructure analysis indicates that the ship has been adrift for at least several thousand years. A more accurate determination of its age will become available after all data has been received. The ship has been preliminarily classified as a cargo vessel similar to an Alliance heavy cargo carrier. Additional information will have to wait until the probe data can be further analyzed."

"A thousand year old derelict with something still operating onboard?"

exclaimed the Captain. "Another damn mystery! I hate mysteries."

"Captain!" yelled the communicator. "A signal has been detected from the planet – possibly a survivor!"

Stricklen forgot about the probe and its mystery ship. "On speaker!" Ken almost shouted out the order.

A loud static-filled hiss issued from the speakers. The crackles and pops indicated extreme amplification. After a few seconds a faint voice was heard. "... ee nothing. What ab ..." The entire bridge crew burst into cheers of joy.

"Quiet!" Stricklen yelled out. "Can you get a fix on the source of that signal?"

The communicator turned to his console and spoke softly to the computer. After listening to the reply he announced, "Probe 9 picked it up sir. Computer estimates the signal to originate about 300 klics Southwest of the OM-3 mining area. The probe is continuing to close in on the signal's location. Probe 5 is being redirected to assist in triangulating their exact location."

The static continued for a moment, then – "The rover has ... CRACKLE-POP-POP ... ay supply. Unless ... POP-HISS ... or we're screwed." The signal was getting stronger and clearer as the probe homed in on it.

"Wilks," Stricklen called the communicator by name. "Can you route a transmission through the probe on the same frequency the survivor is using?"

"Yes sir! Just one moment... Ready on com channel three."

The Captain selected com channel three and said, "This is Captain Ken Stricklen of the Alliance heavy-cruiser *Komodo Dragon*. We are about to orbit Mintaka. If you receive this signal please reply."

There was a moment of silence then a clear voice said, "Frank, did you pick that up?"

This time another very faint voice could be heard. "Yeah – better answer them. Even if they are the enemy we're going to run out of air in a few hours anyway so what the hell."

"Hey!" said the first voice. "This is Brian O'Niel and I read ya loud and clear. We received a message that the town was under attack and then all contact was lost. What happened?"

Stricklen decided not to tell them that their home and families had been wiped out. That job would be left to the ship's psychologist. Instead, he replied, "We are still investigating. How many people are in your party?"

"Myself and three others. We're running short of air and supplies. How soon can you get us out-a-here."

"We should have a shuttle there to pick you up in under an hour," Stricklen replied. "If you have an emergency beacon, turn it on and we will home in on it."

"We have a beacon," came the reply. "As soon as I make my way back to the crawler I'll dig it out and turn it on. Captain," Brian said in a more serious tone. "Don't give me no political or psychological bull. The town is gone isn't it?"

Ken glanced up from his console and noted several of the bridge crew looking at him. *These are miners,* he thought. *They're a tough breed and, as men, they deserve an honest answer to an honest question.*

"Mr. O'Niel," Ken said. "As far as we know, you and your men are the only survivors. Do you have any information as to who attacked you?"

A long silence was eventually broken by Brian's subdued reply. "No – the only transmission we received told us that the town was under attack and that we should make ourselves scarce." After another moment of silence, "Thank you for being honest with us Captain."

"Welcome. Sit tight, a shuttle will be there as soon as possible. *Komodo Dragon* out."

The search of the remainder of the planet took just over 18 hours. Only the four initial survivors were found. The remaining 4,628 men, women, and children were listed as killed by the actions of an unknown enemy. The destruction had been so complete that no records or other means of identifying who may have attacked the outpost could be found. As the last probe was being brought aboard the *Dragon*, the ship prepared to leave.

"Preparations for departure are complete," the XO reported. "An HK has been programmed and is ready for launch."

The HK was a hunter-killer probe which Stricklen had decided to leave behind. This device would be placed into a passive orbit where it would wait and watch to see if the enemy made another appearance. If they did, it would report that fact and any other information it could gather concerning the attackers to the *Dragon*. HK's were specifically designed to remain undetected. They were invisible to most direct scanning devices and heavy shielding reduced their electromagnetic emanations to virtually undetectable levels. There was also the possibility that the attackers had left behind a similar probe. If needed, the HK could be switched to kill mode and attempt to destroy the enemy probe. The HK was armed with a ten megaton thermonuclear warhead for this purpose.

"Deploy the HK," Stricklen ordered. "Helm: set course for the location of probe one. Coms: inform sector command that we have recovered four survivors from Mintaka. Send them a copy of our planetary scans and tell them we will be investigating an apparent derelict prior to returning to Almaranus. Also, call all senior officers to the conference room."

Stricklen turned the bridge over to another officer and headed for the conference room. While the probes had been completing their search of Mintaka, he had been periodically reviewing the data from the derelict ship. The information disturbed him. Normally he would have left the investigation of such a discovery to a better equipped science and salvage ship, but the information returned from the probe had caused him to rethink this philosophy. He had restricted access to the probe's data to himself and Commander Scarboro.

On his way to the conference room, Ken used his wrist-com to call the ship's psychologist. "How are our guests holding up Tash?" he asked once the connection had been made.

"They're doing fine," replied the tiny voice from his earpiece. "It would be nice if we could find something for these men to do. They're not used to just sitting around and they need to feel useful. With your permission, I'll look into their backgrounds to see if we can't give them something to keep them busy on the way back."

Ken trusted Tasharra Ngur's judgment in this matter. She was, after all, the ship's psychologist. She was also a good friend of Ken's. The two had found each other to be good company ever since Tash had been transferred to the *Komodo Dragon* eight months ago.

"Permission granted. Thanks," Ken broke the link. Two minutes later Stricklen walked into the conference room.

After waiting another few minutes for his staff to assemble, Ken began the meeting. "As you are all well aware, prior to reaching Mintaka we discovered a gravitational anomaly. A probe was sent to investigate and the results are now available for our scrutiny. This information is a little unsettling and I have classified all information regarding the derelict. We are now en route to the alien ship to gather additional information and possibly to board it for inspection."

Ken typed a command on the keyboard at his chair. The lights dimmed and an enhanced view of the drifting spacecraft appeared above the conference table in full three dimensions. "Take a good look at it," Stricklen continued. "Something in its cargo bay is generating a gravitational field with a mass equivalence of over 30 billion metric tons. So far, none of the probe's scans can determine what is generating the field nor can it find the power source."

He paused for a moment to let that fact sink in. After an appropriate delay he hit them with the bombshell. "According to the data returned by the probe, this ship is over forty thousand years old."

Chapter 2

Silence filled the conference room. The impact of the Captain's last statement was something that could almost be felt. Finally, Skip Bucannon, the chief engineer said, "Forty thousand years? Our analysis must not be correct. Either that, or whatever is generating that grav-field is a recent addition. Do you have any idea what kind of power is required to generate a field of that strength?" The chief engineer was an unimposing figure. He stood only 162 centimeters tall and had a soft, round, clean-shaven face. Even though he was only forty-one, the top of his head was as smooth as a ball bearing. He always spoke quietly and was well respected by the entire ship. He probably knew more about the innards of the *Dragon's* engine room than the people who designed it.

Ken sat down and motioned to Doug Scarboro. The XO stood up and said, "I have been doing most of the detailed analysis and I assure you that the age of the ship as far as we can determine, is correct. The probe has scanned the ship from stem to stern and we have found no evidence to suggest that it is any younger. And yes, we know what the power requirements are. Using our current method of gravitational field generation, such a field would require a power source capable of delivering well over 100 terra-watts of power. A power plant capable of generating that kind of power, provided we could build one, would be enormous. It would also be creating a tremendous amount of EM radiation. No such leakage can be found. In fact, we can't locate a power source at all anywhere on the ship, only the evidence that such power is in use."

Doug started slowly pacing around the room as he continued. "The ship is constructed of more or less standard materials. The alloy used in the hull is very similar to what the Alliance used up until about 40 years ago. The area of damage which you see, appears to have been very recently made by an impact of some sort. This impact is what set the ship spinning. The damage is near the cargo area which is where we have pinpointed the energy leakage to be originating. This is also where the gravitational field is being emitted. Our scans have been unable to determine what is in the cargo bay. Something is blocking our sensors.

"It is our belief that some sort of shielded mechanism is responsible for the energy leakage and the gravitational field. We think part of the shielding was damaged during the impact. The bulk of the device and its power source are still shielded and thus a visual examination is needed to investigate further."

"Excuse me," interrupted the weapons officer. "Is that some sort of marking on the side of the ship? I can't recognize it."

"*Dragon*, display anterior section H-4 on the main screen and enhance," the XO commanded after looking where the officer had pointed. The ship's computer properly interpreted the command as being directed to itself and reacted accordingly. An enlarged close-up view of a section of the ship appeared on the large screen in the front of the conference room. The holographic image of the ship vanished to allow those on the far side of the table to see the screen. A faint symbol was discernible. Doug walked up to the screen and pointed. "This symbol has been compared against all known markings from all civilizations known to the Alliance. No match has been found. The ship is a true unknown."

"Where did it come from then?" someone asked.

"*Dragon*, display probable point of origin," Doug commanded. The ship's master computer created a holographic display over the conference table showing a star chart and a yellow cone. The cone's point coincided with the current location of the alien ship. The cone pointed out into unexplored space. "An attempt has been made to back-track the ship's course as it has drifted through space. Because of stellar drift and the unknown density of space along its entire path, a considerable margin of error is included in the resultant course as you can see from the size of the probability cone. Based upon this back-tracking we have found that the ship must have been in interstellar space when something happened and caused it to begin drifting. It has not passed within one light year of any star system as far back as we can plot its course with any degree of accuracy."

"Can this be some sort of trap?" This question was from Commander Mikial Kovalesky, the security officer.

"Possible, but even if it is, we are but one ship in the fleet. Setting a trap for a single ship does not make any sense. Besides, this would be a tremendous amount of trouble to go through to capture or destroy one or even several ships. The Captain and I both agree that the derelict warrants immediate attention and since we are the only Alliance ship in this area we are the ones who will be investigating this discovery."

"What other information do you have for us Doug," Stricklen asked.

"Not much I'm afraid. The ship is unique in that although it appears to be a large cargo carrier, it is also quite heavily armed. The weapons appear to be similar to ours and, if so, the weapons array would be comparable to those found on a medium destroyer. The energy leaking from the damaged section has a spectrum unlike anything on record so we can't use it to speculate what sort of power plant is in use. The ship has a high relativistic speed compared to other objects in this area of space. Finally, it is heavily armored, suggesting that it could have doubled as a troop carrier."

Doug finished and took his seat. Ken glanced around the room and said, "I want to put together a small boarding party to inspect the ship. Three teams each made up of two armed marines, an engineer, an electronics technician, and someone from medical. Our ETA is 2000 tomorrow—I want the names of the team members plus one back-up team on my desk by 1500. I also want a complete inventory made of what each team will take with them. All the equipment should be checked and ready before arrival. Finally, in the event we have to force entry, I want a demolition team to go along. You have your assignments, dismissed."

Tasharra intercepted Ken before he could exit the room. "I don't believe any of the crew are qualified to handle explosives. The miner's we rescued from Mintaka make a living by blowing holes in the earth. I think they would be more qualified to be on the demolition team than any of our regular crew members."

Stricklen thought about that for a moment and liked the idea. It would free up two of his own crew and it would give the miners a sense of responsibility. "I like it. I'll let the XO know of the assignments. Thanks Tash."

"Just doing my job. These men went through a horrific experience and so far seem to be dealing with it just fine. I want to make sure they feel as useful as possible. Thanks Captain."

* * * * *

Just to be on the safe side, Stricklen placed the ship at battle stations as it approached the drifting spacecraft. For the last two hours, the *Komodo Dragon* had been applying near maximum acceleration in order to match velocities with the derelict. Once in range, the more powerful sensors of the heavy-cruiser scanned the unknown craft. The results were much the same.

Two repair drones were deployed. These small multi-function robots attached themselves to the drifting ship and, using small thrusters, stopped the spinning motion and stabilized it. This allowed for a more direct approach by the shuttle. The Captain watched as it settled into position close to the now stable ship. The entry team exited and examined what appeared to be an airlock mechanism.

"There is no power to the door controls," reported an unknown voice. Grunting was heard followed by, "The manual operator is frozen – we'll have to cut the door open."

Two more suited figures approached and laid a strip of something around the hatch. After moving clear, a bright white flame surrounded the door. A small repair drone appeared and used a low power tractor beam to remove the section of the door that had just been cut out. The speed and efficiency of the operation impressed Stricklen. He was glad that he had followed Tash's advice and assigned the miners to the demolition team. The suited figures entered the airlock.

"Same situation at the inner door," the same voice reported. "Drilling a test hole for atmospheric analysis."

A few minutes went by – then, "Internal pressure is zero. The ship is at a vacuum. Demolition team, we'll need your services again." The miners exchanged places with the first group and another voice took up the commentary.

"Proceeding to cut the inner door."

The cutting procedure was repeated and finally the crew had access to the inside of the ship. The demolition team returned to the shuttle while the three boarding crews entered the ship. The Captain listened to the cross-talk between the search team members.

"No power, no lights, no sign of damage or struggle. No sign of the previous occupants either. Crew one: take forward. Crew two: check aft. Crew three: you're with me to the cargo bay. One marine first and one last. Try not to damage anything and touch as little as possible. Record everything. Let's move!"

Each team member had a miniature camera attached to their helmet. These cameras were sending their pictures back to the shuttle and from there to the *Dragon* where the images would be recorded. Each team also carried a small portable scanner and a tool kit.

The search progressed slowly throughout the ship. Nothing unusual or out of the ordinary was found. As far as the captain could tell, the team was searching an old Alliance ship which had simply been abandoned in space.

"This is team one," a voice said. "We have reached the control room. No bodies and no apparent usage of power. No damage evident. Looks like they just shut everything down and left."

"This is team two: We are passing through the middle of the ship. This appears to be the main engine room. Looks like a standard space-drive system. No damage evident so far."

"This looks like a fusion reactor," remarked someone. "Wait—I think—yes, that's what it is. I can identify most of the components. This is an auxiliary power reactor and that over there must be the main reactor."

"Is that what I think it is? Phil, is this the matrix coil?"

"Let me look... Let's see—main reactor, power core, conversion unit, main feeder, ... Yep, it sure looks like the matrix field emitter. Wait a minute... take a look at this... no, this over here. Found out why this ship is dead, looks like they overloaded and blew their primary matrix field coil. There is an area of warping and heat discoloration along the upper side of the coil alignment rig, most likely resulting from a major overload. This sort of damage would require a space-dock to repair."

"Copy team two. Team three has just found the cargo bay. There is a single large object inside. It looks like a large rectangular box about 15.5 meters high taking up most of the bay. I don't know how wide or long it is. We will investigate further."

"Team two, this is team one leader. We are working our way aft on the port side. Nothing to report so far."

"Team one copy. We just left engineering and are passing through various storage areas on the starboard side. Nothing to report."

"Base, team three leader: We have located an entrance into the structure. The door mechanism is powered and the indicators are lit. Request permission to attempt entry."

Stricklen pushed his com button and said, "Team three standby until the other teams complete their search. Team one and two: After completing your search, report to the cargo bay to provide backup to team three."

The rest of the ship was searched with nothing found. As far as could be determined, the ship had simply been abandoned and left drifting in space. With the single exception of the object within the cargo bay all equipment had been powered down. The two remaining search teams converged there.

"All team members present," reported the boarding party commander. "Attempting entry."

Stricklen had tapped into one of the video feeds from of the boarding party. The image was a sharp-edged contrast of blazing light and pitch-black darkness from the suit-lights. The camera which Stricklen had selected afforded a clear view of the person in front of the entrance. The door was barely visible. The person in front of the door extended his hand toward a faintly glowing button on the right side. He pushed it and a thin line of light appeared on the right edge. The door slowly slid to the left.

Stricklen leaned forward in his chair. Only a hazy white light could be seen coming from the now fully open doorway. "Oh my God!" exclaimed a voice, probably that of the individual in front of the door. Stricklen quickly switched through the video channels until he found the one he was looking for.

"Oh my God!" Ken repeated.

The monitor clearly showed the cause of their surprise. Although the view through the door appeared fuzzy and out-of-focus the interior was clearly visible. The inside of the structure was packed with operating, well-maintained equipment. To the right stood a massive machine of an unknown nature. Near the center of the room was a large horseshoe-shaped control console. To the left was a glowing, shifting, sparkling, ball at least ten meters in diameter. Stricklen had never heard of or seen anything like it before. The shifting patterns moving across the sphere's surface were almost hypnotic in nature. All around this sparkling ball were devices of a complexity Ken could only guess at.

Suddenly, the picture blanked out. "What's going on?" Ken snapped. "We've lost our picture."

Just as suddenly, the screen returned to normal. "You lost your picture when I stuck my head beyond the perimeter of the door sir," explained a voice Stricklen now identified as belonging to Corporal Franks, the marine in charge of the boarding party. "I received a loss of signal alarm from my suit diagnostics as soon as my head broke the plane of the doorway. I believe there is some sort of field in place that prevents signals from passing into or out of the structure. That explains why we have been unable to scan the interior of the cargo bay and it explains why the interior seems blurred. I've never seen or heard of a force field quite like this. Solid matter has no problem penetrating it and it's mostly transparent to visible light."

"Acknowledged," Stricklen replied. "Send a team in to scan the interior. They are not to touch anything. As soon as you are done, return to the ship. We are way over our heads on this one. This sort of discovery should be explored by people trained in these matters. We're turning this over to the experts."

Stricklen shut off the monitor and walked over to the communications station. "Send a priority message to sector command. Have the computer summarize what we have found and request instructions. Include the video from Corporal Franks' suit monitor. Send it encoded and send it priority one."

After making sure that the message would be sent, Stricklen retired to his stateroom. On the way there he kept asking himself the same question, *What is it? What have we found?*

Chapter 3

The derelict was located 26.5 light years from sector command. The FTL communications equipment aboard the *Komodo Dragon* could force a signal across that distance at a maximum speed of around 41,000c (usually expressed as 41Kc) Although the *Dragon* could send a signal at 48.4Kc, this speed was limited to a distance of about 8 light years. The power required to boost a signal to higher and higher speeds was tremendous and only a land-based transmitter or a very large spacecraft could send signals any great distance at the absolute maximum speed of 53.6Kc.

The priority-one signal that had been blasted through space required just over five hours to reach sector command. After a delay of about three hours, SecCom shot off their reply. It took almost four hours to make the return trip. Stricklen was eating in the ship's single mess hall when the message arrived. He had the ship's computer store it while he finished his meal.

In the privacy of his cabin, Stricklen ordered the computer to decode and present the message. Like all fleet communications – the message was in encrypted text. Ken ignored the complex prefix codes that identified the originator, the destination, and the routing codes and skipped to the main body of the message:

****
REMAIN ON-STATION UNTIL AUTHORIZED TO LEAVE BY THIS COMMAND. MASTER-DREADNOUGHT MOBIUS EN ROUTE WITH ATTENDANT SUB-FLEET TO PROVIDE AREA SECURITY – ETA 0300.5/02/22. SCIENCE VESSEL S. W. HAWKING EN ROUTE FROM ALMARANUS ETA 2100.5/01/22. FURTHER ENTRY INTO THE ALIEN SHIP IS FORBIDDEN UNTIL ARRIVAL OF SCIENCE VESSEL. ALL PREVIOUS ASSIGNMENTS AND ORDERS HEREBY CANCELED. ALL INFORMATION REGARDING THE ALIEN SHIP IS HEREBY CLASSIFIED AS LEVEL THREE SECRET. KOMODO DRAGON TO BE

TEMPORARILY ASSIGNED TO SUB-FLEET K140 (LEAD SHIP MOBIUS) UNTIL RELEASED BY THIS COMMAND. COMMANDING OFFICER OF KOMODO DRAGON TO COORDINATE ALL RESEARCH ACTIVITIES UPON ARRIVAL OF S. W. HAWKING. DETAILED ORDERS FOLLOW.

****

Ken had to read the message several times before he believed what it said. Once again the question popped into his head, *What the hell have we found?* After reading it and the accompanying detailed orders again, Ken convened a video conference of the senior staff and read it to them. Their response was pretty much the same as his.

The times and dates specified in the message indicated that the science ship would arrive first in about ten days. Until then, the Captain had no choice but to wait. He decided to use the time to give the crew a bit of a break. He ordered Commander Scarboro to give the crew 3 days of stand down. This meant that if a crew member was not on an assigned watch, he was basically free to do as he pleased. Stricklen was proud of his crew and he tried to make their lives aboard his ship as tolerable as possible.

Stricklen used this time to visit his new guests. He asked the ship's computer to locate them and found they were all in one of the two staterooms which had been assigned to them. A hardy "Come on in, the door's open!" followed his knock on the door.

The four miners were gathered around a single table with several piles of poker chips scattered about. The players glanced up to identify the new arrival. One of them placed his cards down and approached Stricklen with an outstretched hand.

Stricklen shook hands with the miner and introduced himself. "I'm Captain Stricklen. I'm sorry I haven't been able to see you until now but things have been a little busy around here recently. I want to thank the two of you who assisted in making an entry into the ship we discovered."

The man standing before him had a rough look about him. His skin was deeply creased and had a weathered look to it. His grip was firm and strong which agreed with the general condition of the rest of his muscular body. "I'm Brian. That's Frank. We blew the door on that ship. This here's Maz, and that's AJ," he said indicating each of the others as he made the introductions.

Ken had been surprised to learn that one of the survivors was a non-Human. Matlanaz (Maz according to O'Niel) was a Borillen. His eye stalks pointed directly at Ken. The other two were more or less normal enough looking Humans. The fact that they had worked in the mines most their life showed in their faces and strong hands.

"We can't thank you enough for picking us up off that rock skipper," Brian said as he pulled a chair out for Ken to sit in. "Any idea as to who hit us?"

Ken settled into the chair as he replied. "Not yet. We left a probe behind but so far it hasn't spotted anything unusual."

"Just as long as you get the bastards and make them pay," AJ piped up.

Ken talked with the miners for about twenty minutes updating them on the ship's change of course and learning a little about their lives as miners. He was surprised to learn that many of the miners routinely brought their entire families on expeditions. He did not realize it but many of the large mining companies provided teachers and other such support for the families of their miners. They had long ago learned that the miners would work harder and with fewer accidents if they had their families with them. In the end, Ken had a deeper understanding of them and the work they did. Eventually, he bid them farewell and left them to continue their interrupted card game.

* * * * *

About eight hours before the science ship was due to arrive, Stricklen's routine was interrupted by a report from the bridge.

"Captain, HK-1 reports identifying a possible alien probe," Doug reported. "It looks like it was in the system the whole time. The computer believes it is an HK similar to our own. It appears to be performing a scan of Mintaka. HK-1 is remaining passive but requests instructions. May I suggest that we order it to blow the bastard out of the sky."

"Suggestion noted," Stricklen replied more in jest than seriousness. "Confirm HK-1's original orders, it is to remain passive unless detected. I want as much information about this alien race as possible."

"Yes sir," Doug replied. "Too bad they didn't send a ship to investigate. We could at least have learned something about them that way. What kind of information can we get from a probe?"

"Not much," Ken admitted. "But if HK-1 remains hidden we stand a much better chance of learning more than if it was told to attack. This way is better.

Who knows, they may yet send a ship."

Several hours later, the science vessel *S. W. Hawking* arrived and, after a bit of maneuvering, settled into position near the alien ship. Prior to allowing them access, Stricklen had insisted upon meeting with the science team's leaders. The team leader had balked at the request saying that she needed to begin her research immediately. Ken would not back down, therefore, before the *Hawking's* engines had begun to cool, a small transfer shuttle made the short journey between the two ships.

Stricklen gave the team a few minutes to themselves in the conference room before making his entrance. He opened the door, took two steps, and froze. He found himself eye to eye with a creature the likes of which most Humans would have turned tail and run away from. The head was distinctly reptilian with two large deep black eyes spaced widely on either side. A bony ridge ran up the middle of the forehead and continued along the back. Two short arms jutted out from the chest area and the remainder of the large 3.5 meter long body was supported by four powerful stubby legs. The body was dark brown in color and covered with very fine, slightly iridescent scales. This was a Rouldian.

Although Ken had been briefed on the members comprising the science team, he had apparently forgotten that one of the most distinguished members was a female Rouldian named Falnath. Stricklen had never before met a Rouldian, although he had seen 3-D's of them in the past. He knew they were a highly developed race and, despite their appearance, very peaceful.

Stricklen watched in amazement as the Rouldian's head tilted slightly to one side and the corners of its mouth expanded in what apparently passed as a smile for this race. "I perceive you have never met one of my kind before," Falnath said through a translating vocoder which she wore around her thick neck. "Do not be embarrassed. Most Humans react the same way upon their first encounter with one of my species. I am Falnath, science team leader."

Stricklen quickly composed himself and replied, "Welcome to the *Komodo Dragon*. I am Captain Ken Stricklen. Please, you and your team make yourselves comfortable. My executive officer and security officer will be here shortly."

While they waited, Stricklen glanced at the three representatives. As his gaze passed over each, his mind conjured up a brief description of the individual. Falnath: Rouldian female; top expert in the entire Alliance on continuum physics. Stricklen wondered what she was doing on this expedition. T'Lorn Depna: non-sexual Omel; expert in xeno-biology. The

Omel were the medical magicians of the Alliance and were a very tall race. Their completely hairless bodies averaged over two meters in height. Their most distinguishing (and for most Humans, their most disturbing) feature was their nearly translucent skin. Travan McCallister: Human male; computer systems expert and electronics analyst. Ken's information had indicated that McCallister was strongly anti-military.

A few minutes later, Doug Scarboro and the security officer walked into the room together. After introducing them, Stricklen started the meeting. "I wanted to call this meeting in order to lay out some ground rules before any work is allowed to proceed on the alien ship. The *Komodo Dragon's* marine detachment will be providing security for the science team as they perform their work. I will expect the team to follow all orders given to them by the marines without question. On the other hand, the science team has complete control over all aspects of the research. This is to be a joint military/civilian operation and both groups must learn how to work together.

"All information regarding the alien ship has been classified. My security officer, Commander Kovalesky, will explain what security measures have been put into place to protect this information."

Commander Mikial Kovalesky was a powerfully built black man of Russian descent. He spoke in a deep, heavily accented voice. He remained very still as he spoke, only his head moved slightly to glance at each person in the room. "Information security will be maintained by control of communications. All transmissions must be routed through security prior to being coded. The *Hawking's* computer has been ordered to prevent release of any information concerning the derelict without proper Alliance approval."

"Physical security will be maintained by the *Komodo Dragon's* marine detachment. Your researchers are free to go wherever they desire as long as they are within sight of at least one marine guard. Anything removed from the alien ship will be under continuous guard until it has been returned. Are there any questions?"

Stricklen had been watching McCallister as Kovalesky talked. He appeared to be getting angry and upset at the security precautions that had been imposed. Stricklen was worried about a potential conflict before the research had even started. He decided to try to defuse McCallister's anger.

"I'm not sure why the Alliance has classified this project," he said spreading his hands flat on the table. "I want you to know that the marines are here only to provide security. This project is your area of expertise and we will stay out of your way while you work. If there are any problems with this arrangement I want to personally know about it."

Stricklen glanced at McCallister out of the corner of his eye and noticed that, although he was still unhappy, he appeared to have accepted the situation. Stricklen knew he would be trouble later on, but not right at the moment. Moving on he said, "I have assigned my executive officer, Commander Doug Scarboro, to coordinate any support which may be required of us. Doug?"

Doug stood up and faced the group. "The *Komodo Dragon* will provide whatever support you need to complete your research. If you find that you need anything, contact either myself or my alternate and we will see what we can do. We can provide things such as tools, computer time, shuttles, portable scanners, or whatever else you may need. If you find that you need something and we don't have it, we will try to either make it or get it here if it is something that is badly needed."

Doug returned to his seat and Stricklen stood up. "Before I allow your team to begin their work," he said. "I would like to know just what it is we have found. The Alliance would not send a small fleet just to protect an old relic. And, from what I've seen of the backgrounds of the scientists who have arrived on the *Hawking*, we have found something considerably more important than just an old cargo ship. Just what exactly is it that we have discovered?"

"We don't know," Falnath replied. "We know as much about this ship as you do. The Alliance military requested a science vessel to be sent to this area. The *S. W. Hawking* was the closest ship that could be freed."

"Why are you here," Stricklen directed his question toward Falnath.

The Rouldian looked intently at Stricklen for a moment before answering. "There are certain interesting properties of the energy leaking from the ship. My research activities on Almaranus were at such a point where I decided it would be convenient to investigate this phenomenon myself."

"Damned military thinks there's some sort of super-weapon on that ship," McCallister remarked. "They're going to want us to figure out how it ticks so they can use it."

"I do not agree with your assessment of the reasoning behind our being requested to come here," said Depna. "If this ship is indeed as old as we believe it is, then we would be exploring the lifestyle and technology of a civilization that traveled among the stars before our various cultures had progressed much beyond the use of stone tools."

"There is reason to believe that the object in the ship's cargo bay may be powered by a power source far more advanced than anything we are currently capable of building," Falnath added. "If so, then we could use the information gained from studying the object to advance our technology by a considerable degree."

"The military knows something they aren't telling us," McCallister said. "Why else would they have classified it so fast?"

"To be honest with you," replied Stricklen. "I initially classified the information when we first discovered the ship. I did so primarily because of its age. I don't know why the Alliance has decided to maintain this classification. I was shocked myself when the order to classify arrived. I intend on finding out the reasoning behind their decision. In the meantime, I have my orders."

Stricklen stood up and slowly began to walk toward the exit. As he walked, he said, "You may begin your study of the alien artifact as soon as you are ready. A marine detachment will be there shortly. I would like a status report twice daily. Thank you all for coming."

Stricklen waited until the scientists had departed before turning to his XO. "McCallister has a point you know. I'm beginning to wonder if he might be right."

Scarboro looked at his Captain with disbelief. "What? That the Alliance knows something they aren't sharing with the rest of us, or that bit about some kind of super-weapon? I find that a little hard to swallow."

"Tell me, do you know who Falnath is?" Stricklen asked.

"Other than having a close resemblance to a giant alligator, no—why?"

"I would classify her appearance as more like that of a dragon. Her being here raises more questions than answers and gives some credence to McCallister's statement about the Alliance knowing more than they're letting on. Falnath just so happens to be *the* top expert in continuum physics. I once read that she can juggle equations in continuum calculus as easily as I can add two plus two. Some people think that she actually understands the complete set of equations describing the underlying principle of our Kauffman stardrive."

Scarboro was thunderstruck. He knew that once Jay Kauffman, the father of the Human stardrive, had built the first crude faster-than-light engine, it had taken decades of work from hundreds of theorists and uncounted thousands of hours of super-computer time to develop the complex equations which describe how a modern stardrive works. In fact, a completely new branch of mathematics called continuum calculus had been created because the existing systems were unworkable. No Human, other than perhaps Kauffman himself, had ever understood even a fraction of the equations. He had just been within a few meters of someone whom he would have to describe as a super-genius.

"You're right," Doug said after a moment of reflection. "Why would they send her all the way out here to investigate a derelict ship unless they already knew what it might contain. It also explains the large amount of firepower they are sending our way. I'm worried now."

"Me too, Doug. To be honest with you, I think Falnath knows a lot more than she'd have us believe."

"How's that?"

"Somebody had to analyze the data we sent to Sector Command to determine what we may have found. I think Falnath just happened to be on Almaranus and they took advantage of her expertise and asked her opinion of what should be done. She probably took some of that data and plugged it into one of those ungodly equations she likes to play with and out popped a surprising answer. Now she's here, in person, to verify whatever it is that she thinks might be on that ship."

"Whatever it is, I'm sure I probably won't like it. Care to join me for a quick drink Captain?"

Stricklen considered his schedule for a moment then replied, "I think I will pass. I want to go over and personally take a look at this alien machine. Would you like to go with?"

"I think I'll stay here," Doug replied turning toward the door. "I need to make sure I'm available in case the science team needs some assistance. I guess that drink can wait a while longer."

Stricklen rode with a group of marines on one of the *Dragon's* small shuttles over to the derelict. An airlock had been installed, and the ship was being re-pressurized. Temporary lighting and heating had already been set up inside the ship along most of the major passageways but the temperature was not yet warm enough for an unsuited person. Ken found his way to the cargo bay, slowly approached the open doorway and stepped inside. It was even more spectacular in person. His attention was immediately drawn toward the sparkling ball of energy at one end of the chamber. It crackled slightly, sounding like the rustle of dry leaves on pavement. Threads of multicolored energy danced across its surface.

Ken forced his eyes away from the hypnotic effects of the unknown device and took in the rest of the room. The various machines and devices all appeared to be functional and in pristine condition. He would never have guessed that this equipment had been in operation for the last 40,000 years. It was if he had walked into some sort of high tech Alliance laboratory.

Stricklen slowly walked around the room trying to identify some of the alien equipment. He stopped at the control console and looked at the bewildering array of controls, indicators, lights, and buttons. Most of the controls consisted of touch sensitive computer interfaces, much like those found on his own ship. Although everything was labeled, the language was unknown and thus a complete mystery. He finally walked over and stood in front of the shifting ball of energy. His suit's external sensors did not even register the existence of the energy field and Ken wondered if something was wrong with the sensors.

A large figure approached and stood next to him. He turned to see who it was and discovered Falnath standing next to him. "Fascinating, isn't it?" she asked through her suit radio.

"Something must be wrong with my suit's sensors," Ken said turning his gaze back toward the shifting patterns of force. "This is obviously some sort of force field but it does not register on the sensors."

"Your sensors are fine. The energy field is very tightly structured and does not radiate any leakage. The visual effects are all that exist. As far as the suit's sensors are concerned there is nothing there."

"What is it?" Ken asked. His arm involuntarily started moving toward the surface of the sphere.

Falnath gently reached over and stopped him. "I would not attempt to touch it. We do not yet know what it is. As soon as our equipment arrives we will begin our analysis."

Falnath moved away to inspect the rest of the room leaving Stricklen to stare into the hypnotic patterns. Soon, several large pieces of scientific equipment arrived and Ken reluctantly decided that it was time to return to the ship. Taking one long last look around the chamber he exited and returned to the *Dragon*. Once there, he called Doug and told him he was ready for that drink. Stricklen had a distinct feeling that they were over their heads on this one.

Chapter 4

The *Mobius* and her compliment of ships did not arrive on-schedule. Stricklen was unaware of this fact since he was asleep in his stateroom at the time. He had left orders to be awakened when the fleet had arrived. He woke up to the sound of reveille and for a moment did not realize what had happened. It hit him as he was stepping into the shower. Cursing under his breath Stricklen called the bridge.

"We received a brief message that they had responded to a faint distress call from a heavy transport," the watch officer said. "It sounded as if they were under attack by unknown forces."

"Why was I not informed!" a now furious Stricklen yelled.

"I... Ah... I did not see any reason to sir," stammered the young officer. "The *Mobius* was responding and there was nothing that we could have done. I felt our primary duty was to remain on-station to provide security for the alien ship."

The man's logic was sound. Stricklen calmed himself, then said, "You were correct Lieutenant. If the *Mobius* arrives before I get to the bridge, please contact me via com-link."

Ken completed his morning routine without further interruption. After assuming control of the bridge he discovered that he had a message waiting for him from Doug. The scientists were going to present their first status report at 0900 and Scarboro wanted to know if this time was acceptable. Ken replied that it was.

At 0733, the *Mobius* arrived. It took the fleet until 0840 to match velocities and to position themselves in a protective shell around the alien ship. In all, sub-fleet K140 consisted of three medium cruisers, five destroyers, and one very impressive Tholtaran master-dreadnought. Ken had heard descriptions of Tholtaran warships but had never before seen one. The size of a Tholtaran warship was legendary.

The *Mobius* was roughly egg-shaped and had a maximum diameter of over twelve kilometers. Its surface bristled with weapon blisters. The Tholtarans had been instrumental in defeating the Human fleet during the brief Human-Alliance war which had occurred shortly after Humans had journeyed into space. There were still some bitter feeling between the two races even though the war had ended over 50 years ago. Stricklen's own grandfather had been lost in that war.

"Fleet Commander Trisk of the *Mobius* on com-three for you sir," said the communications watch.

Stricklen put aside his feelings as best he could, then made the connection. The leathery face of a Tholtaran appeared on his screen. "Fleet Commander Trisk, I am Captain Ken Stricklen. Were you successful in your rescue?"

"No," the gravely voice replied. "We arrived too late. All that remained of the transport was wreckage. We have established a security shield around your position. Although technically you are under my command, I have been ordered to provide assistance to you in whatever way possible. Therefore, you are considered under my command only in-so-far as fleet operations are concerned. The research effort is to remain under your control. Do you require any assistance from us at this time?"

It took a few moments for Stricklen to digest what Trisk had just said. Ken had expected to be relieved of responsibility for the research effort as soon as the *Mobius* had arrived. "No assistance is needed at this time," Stricklen replied. "The science team is about to present their first status report in my conference room. You are welcome to attend if you so desire."

"I will send a representative," Trisk replied after a moments consultation with another officer. "Are the Mintaka survivors ready for transport?"

The orders which Ken had received earlier had stated that a small courier ship would be taking the survivors back to Almaranus. As soon as the fleet had arrived Stricklen had sent word for them to get ready to leave. "They are ready. I will have them meet your shuttle at the docking port. I assume the courier is docked within your ship?"

"Yes. It will leave as soon as the survivors are aboard. *Mobius* out." The connection snapped and the monitor went dark.

Ken called the conference room and told the gathering crowd that he would be delayed a few minutes. He asked them to wait until he arrived before beginning. He then made his way to the docking port to await the arrival of the Tholtaran shuttle.

The four survivors rescued from Mintaka were there when Stricklen arrived. He exchanged pleasantries with them while they waited. Ken was still amazed as to how well they had handled the loss of so many of their close friends and loved ones. The ship's psychologist had explained that these people were used to death. She did say, though, that the miner's would most likely have a strong emotional reaction once they reached their respective home-worlds or at least the world they called home.

The shuttle arrived and discharged a single Tholtaran. The alien looked very much like a four and a half meter tall vulcanized version of a Human with large ears. Their leathery skin acted to protect them from the harsh ultra-violet light of their home-world's sun. Ken welcomed him aboard and then bid the survivors a final farewell. He watched until the docking portal had closed, then, turning to the Tholtaran representative he said, "The science team is waiting for us in the conference room. Please follow me."

The conference room was packed with 23 people when Ken arrived. The murmur of a dozen conversations slowly dropped off as Stricklen took his place at the head of the oval table. "Thank you for waiting," he began. "This is science advisor Bronack of the Tholtaran republic. I have asked him here as a courtesy to the Tholtaran fleet which will be providing the area security during our stay here. I will not delay you any longer—Falnath, please proceed."

The dragon-like body of the Rouldian scientist was positioned in an out of the way corner of the room. A computer keyboard had been placed in front of her. She entered commands and the room lights dimmed. A hologram of the derelict ship appeared in the center of the conference table. As Falnath spoke, the image constantly shifted apparently in response to verbal cues which she had instructed the computer to follow.

"For the last twelve hours we have subjected the derelict to an extensive series of tests. During this time we have learned a great deal. Some of the results have been amazing. I will start with the ship itself. Extensive testing has confirmed that the ship is roughly 44,600 years old. The margin for error is plus or minus 300 years. Multiple methods have yielded the same age and we are confident that this is an actual derelict and not something designed to appear as such.

"The general construction of the ship is roughly equivalent to the technological level of most Alliance spacecraft of about 40 years ago. We have not learned anything new from the ship itself but we have found several modifications which were made to the ship that are of a technological level superior to ours. These modifications were not easily found and would have been overlooked in any cursory examination of the ship. We are still looking into exactly what these modifications do.

"The object in the cargo bay is not of the same technological level as the ship but is far beyond even our abilities. Based upon the evidence, we believe that a technologically superior race was using the ship from an inferior race to transport the object. This would explain the modifications made to the ship and the presence of the object in the cargo bay. We have no meaningful explanation as to why an advanced race would use an inferior race's spacecraft as a cargo ship although several theories have been proposed.

"We have concentrated most of our efforts on the object in the cargo hold. As you are all aware, the ship was originally discovered when the *Komodo Dragon* detected a strange pulsating gravitational field. It is now known that a single device is the source of those gravitational waves. Until very recently, the entire object was shielded in such a way as to have prevented any detection even upon close examination of the ship. Recently, within the last forty-five days, a small asteroid, traveling at a high relative velocity apparently impacted the ship, penetrated the armor plate, and inflicted minor damage to the object in the cargo hold. Part of the shielding system was damaged along with an additional shielding system for a device which I will describe in a moment. This resulted in a leakage path for gravitational energy and, since the ship was slowly spinning, the *Komodo Dragon* detected this as a pulsating gravity field."

An overhead view of the object in the cargo bay appeared on the large display screen at the front of the room. The entrance was near the center of one side. Directly in front of the entrance was a control console. The right side of the object contained box-like equipment racks. The left end was taken up by the large glowing, shifting, ball and was surrounded by still more equipment. The entire back wall consisted of a single large machine. As Falnath spoke, the various areas she was referring to were highlighted.

"We have identified the equipment to the right of the chamber to be mostly monitoring devices. They are operating and, as far as we can tell, are functioning normally. The large box in the far corner is a computer of extremely advanced design. Most of its internal systems appear to be in some sort of low power standby state. At present, we do not believe we can fully activate it."

"The control console is of a very complex design and its purpose is still being researched. The object behind the console is a power reactor." Falnath lifted herself up until her head was nearly at ceiling level. She scanned the room slowly then continued. "Our instruments show that this reactor is currently generating a continuous power output of 120 terra-watts."

The reaction Falnath expected was instantaneous. "Impossible!" several people shouted at once. A babble of voices clashed and then subsided until a single quiet voice won out. The *Dragon's* chief engineer said, "That kind of a power plant would be tremendously huge and, assuming we could even build one, would consume enormous quantities of fuel each second. Where is it getting the fuel? How is it controlled? And most importantly what is demanding that much energy?"

"We have not completed our analysis of the reactor," Falnath continued. "However, we believe the ultimate source of power is based on matter/anti-matter reactions. At its current power output level the reactor is converting over 4.8 kilograms of mass to energy each hour. The fuel is being supplied by the two globular structures near one end of the reactor. These structures contain an extremely dense form of matter which is still being analyzed. Our readings are being hampered by some sort of shielding.

"The bulk of the power is being fed into the large device at the far left of the chamber. This is the device where we have focused virtually all of our research efforts and is generating a powerful gravitational field in the shape of a sphere. The field structure is very complex and we have detected other fields imbedded within the sphere itself. We have been able to determine that there is a null area of about seven meters in diameter within this sphere. The surrounding fields of energy consist of a complex mixture of gravitational fields and others, some of which closely resemble those generated by a stardrive."

"Stop!" Bronack said loud enough to cause everyone in the room to look in his direction. The Tholtaran got out of his seat, placed both arms on the table in front of him, and leaned as close as he could toward the hologram. The room was silent as he seemed to examine the contents of the chamber more closely. He turned to Falnath and said, "Stardrive fields cannot exist within an area of space permeated by gravitational fields. You are saying that this device is using a combination of gravitational fields and stardrive fields to perform its function? What you are saying is impossible. You also claim that this device is powered by a reactor of unimaginable power. You say that this power is derived from a matter/anti-matter reaction, yet it is common knowledge that anti-matter is too difficult to manufacture in even minute quantities to be a useful power source. Again what you are saying is impossible. Explain!"

Falnath looked at the Tholtaran. Stricklen could not decipher the Rouldian's expression. She reached out to her computer console and commanded the room's lights to full intensity before shifting her attention toward Bronack. A low hiss came from her throat before she replied. "I am presenting the facts as we have discovered them," the vocoder translated. Ken could barely make out her native language but he thought it sounded a little raspier than normal. "If you dispute the facts then I will be glad to discuss the matter with you at a later time. For now I wish to continue with this briefing."

"I agree with Falnath," Stricklen said. "Please return to your seat. You may meet with her after the meeting if you still have questions."

Bronack seemed to hesitate for a moment then stormed out of the room. "Typical Tholtaran reaction," an unidentified voice was heard to say. Stricklen informed security via his wrist-com so they could handle the situation. "Please continue," he said into the now silent room.

Falnath visibly calmed herself before continuing. "We have theorized that the combination of fields within the device has created a unique condition within the null region of the sphere. Tell me Captain, during your initial search of the ship did you find any evidence of the crew?"

Stricklen was caught off-guard by the question. "Um, no, we did not."

"Have you wondered where the crew might be?"

"We assumed they had left the ship after it was damaged. For some reason they never returned to tow it back to a space-dock."

"I submit to you," Falnath said in a slow, measured tone. "That the crew are still onboard the ship and have been for the last 45,000 years. There is only one theory that explains the existence of a hyper-gravity field in combination with stardrive-like control fields. It is my theory that the object you have discovered is nothing less than a time-stasis machine and that the crew are inside the null point of the sphere in a state of time-suspension."

As pandemonium broke out Stricklen's jaw hit the floor.

Stricklen sat stunned as everyone in the room tried to talk at once. So great was the noise that he almost did not hear his private com-link when it signaled an incoming message. "Captain, this is Commander Raferty on the bridge," the tiny hearing aid like device said. "The *Mobius* reports that one of its outlying sensor drones has picked up a very small object heading this way, possibly a probe. Drive wake signature is unknown. Distance – 0.69 lights. Speed – 1250c. A class 4 HK has been dispatched to intercept. Time to intercept 2.5 hours."

Stricklen reached down and clicked one of the buttons on his wrist-com thus telling the bridge that the message had been received. He then stood up and motioned for silence. It took almost five minutes before order was restored.

"Falnath, would you please explain your reasoning for this theory of yours?" Stricklen asked.

Falnath had remained passive during the entire episode. In response to Stricklen's question she said, "My reasoning is based mostly upon the research data which we have obtained. I am sure that nobody in this room understands continuum calculus so I am unable to present an accurate explanation. I will, however, try."

"It is common knowledge that a hypergravity field will affect time. In the presence of a hypergravity field, time will dramatically slow down. A gravitational field, however, also has other very undesirable effects which would normally render its use as a time stasis mechanism useless. The largest factor would be the tidal effects which would destroy any object near enough to have its time affected. The alien device uses a combination of hypergravity fields and space-warping fields that are very similar to our stardrive fields, only of a much higher level of complexity, to achieve a state of time-stasis within a null-point inside the sphere. The exact amount by which time has been slowed cannot be determined with our instruments."

"That might explain the device," Scarboro said. "But why do you believe the crew are inside the sphere? What was this thing doing on that ship in the first place? Whoever built the supposed stasis device must be very technologically advanced, more advanced than any member of the Alliance is now. The level of technology of the ship and that of the device are hundreds, if not thousands of years apart."

"We don't know for certain why the stasis device was on the ship," Falnath replied. "We do know that the reactor has enough fuel to enable it to run for at least an additional 8,000 years. I have a personal theory concerning the presence of the device on the ship and the crew being inside the stasis device.

"Consider this: Let us assume for a moment that my race is technologically superior to all other races in the Alliance. We are so far advanced that we are capable of doing what most other races would consider as the impossible. Despite our advanced level of technology we are non-aggressive and we try to live in harmony with the other races of the Alliance but we do not share our technology. How would Humans and the other members of the Alliance react in this case?"

Scarboro considered the question for a moment. "There would be many who would want to have your technology for themselves in order to give them a technological edge against their enemies. If you were unwilling to share it, your ships and people would be harassed or worse, attacked, in order to get the technology."

"A most accurate conclusion," Falnath replied shifting her considerable bulk out of the corner of the room to a position closer to the conference table. "The end result would be that our race would have no choice but to either flee the area or eliminate all other inferior life-forms in order for us to live in peace. Being as advanced as we are, the second alternative would be rejected. The first alternative is equally difficult because no matter where we tried to go the other races would pursue us. A better alternative would be to either hide our existence or flee in secret using the ships and technology of the inferior species around us. I believe that this is what happened to the builders of the stasis device."

"My belief is that the device was being transported to another location and something happened to damage the ship. If a distress signal had been sent, there would have been a good chance that a member of another race might respond and find the stasis device. It would make more sense for the crew to enter the stasis chamber and wait. When the ship did not arrive at its destination, another would be sent to investigate and thus a member of their own race would be performing the rescue. This, for reasons we can not determine, did not happen and the crew are still in stasis."

"Why would such a race need to transport a stasis machine anyway? What purpose would it serve?" Skip asked.

"I cannot answer your question," Falnath replied. "A stasis device would allow an individual who has been injured to be transported to a more advanced facility to receive care, or to store a sample of some short lived material while it is being moved to a research lab. There are many potential uses for such a device. This device, however, is capable of maintaining the stasis for thousands of years. If I were to make a guess I would say the device was meant to be used to place something or someone in stasis for many centuries. To what purpose I will not attempt to guess."

"Sounds like a plausible explanation to me," Scarboro said. "How do we go about verifying it? Do we know how to turn the thing off?"

"That is still being looked into. Simply interrupting the power could do it. There are other scenarios, however, which predict that interrupting the power could result in a catastrophic shutdown resulting in an explosion of quite titanic proportions. We are dealing with a technology which we do not even dimly understand yet. Eventually we will have to try something because as long as the device is operating we cannot move it to a better research facility."

"Huh?" Stricklen said. Then remembering he corrected himself. "Oh, I understand. The gravity field is preventing us from forming a stardrive field. That means we are stuck here until we figure out how to turn it off. That could be a problem because we might have some uninvited company soon."

"What do you mean?" Falnath asked, swinging her massive head in Ken's direction.

"We have picked up the drive wake of a small unidentified object, most likely an alien probe heading this way. My guess is that it has already informed whoever sent it that a large gathering of ships is just sitting out here."

"Great!" exclaimed Doug. Turning to Falnath he said, "If that probe is from our friends who attacked Mintaka you had better find a way to turn your time stasis machine off or we may just have to leave it here."

"You will not," said a strange authoritative voice. Stricklen looked around and, following the stares of the others in the room, located the speaker. He appeared to be a Lamaltan as he was enclosed within a bulky environment suit and had been standing along the back wall of the conference room. Lamaltans could not survive in an oxygen atmosphere but instead required a mixture of methane and ammonia at a temperature of several degrees below zero. They were one of the more bizarre life-forms making up the Alliance.

The figure stepped forward and, to the horror of the crowd, unsealed his suit. Poisonous, frigid gas did not, as everyone expected, pour into the crowd. Instead of a Lamaltan, a darkly metallic clad figure stepped out of the environment suit. He stood 173 centimeters tall and appeared to be completely encased within black armor. A special issue blaster was magnetically clamped to his left side. Dark, penetrating, cybernetic eyes seemed to stare into every corner of the room at once. Everyone recognized him as a peacekeeper. The peacekeepers were cyborgs invested with the authority to maintain the law throughout all planets of the Alliance. They were the equivalent of a galactic police force. This particular peacekeeper was either Human or a race closely resembling one. Ken was surprised since peacekeepers rarely traveled in secret.

"I am Sorbith, a Saulquin by birth," the peacekeeper said, stepping up to the head of the conference table and assuming command of the meeting. "This technology must remain in the hands of the Alliance. All efforts to protect it must be taken. Falnath, you are to concentrate your research efforts on finding a safe way of shutting down the stasis device. Captain, find a way of removing the device from the alien ship and placing it within your shuttle bay. This will allow your defense shield to protect it in the event of an attack. I choose your ship because the *Mobius* is not only an obvious target, but if needed, it will be used to provide for your escape."

The orders of a peacekeeper were to be obeyed without question and without delay. Falnath murmured an agreement and left the room. "This meeting is over," Stricklen said. "Doug, I want an emergency staff meeting in ten minutes. Sorbith, may I have a word with you in private?"

On the way to the Captain's quarters, Stricklen received a message via his private channel. "A second drive-wake has been detected. It has been identified as a Seeker-class scout belonging to a peacekeeper named Sorbith. The ship claims its owner is aboard."

Stricklen brought the bridge up-to-date on Sorbith's appearance and instructed them to inform Fleet Commander Trisk of the nature of the incoming ship. Once inside his stateroom he turned to Sorbith and said, "I would like an explanation as to why you were aboard the science ship posing as a researcher. Peacekeepers normally do not work undercover unless there is a very good reason for them to do so. I have had suspicions that the Alliance has been withholding information from us and your actions have strengthened that opinion. If this is true, then I want to lodge a formal protest. I cannot adequately protect something if I do not know what it is that I am protecting."

All peacekeepers had once been totally biological. After receiving extensive training and screening they underwent a series of operations which converted them into cyborgs. Their bodies were encased in an ultra-resilient black metallic armor. Their limbs and many of their internal organs were replaced or enhanced. They were endowed with phenomenal strength and abilities. Each peacekeeper was then assigned a Seeker class scout ship. These ships would be their home wherever they went. The capabilities of these ships and the peacekeepers was highly classified.

The peacekeepers had been created in order to extend Alliance law throughout all member planets by embodying the power to uphold the law into one easily recognizable law enforcement agency. The orders of a peacekeeper were to be obeyed without question and without delay by all members of the Alliance no matter what their species or position. Peacekeepers did not interfere or concern themselves with local politics or law, they had the power to enforce Alliance law and nothing more. The peacekeepers were allowed this power because they were continuously monitored by the computers aboard their ship. If a peacekeeper were to ever misuse his authority the ship could command that individual's cybernetic systems to shutdown.

"I was ordered to remain incognito unless the security of the alien device was in jeopardy," Sorbith said. "Your suspicions about withholding information is not only justified, but it is correct. Since your ship will be providing primary security for the device, I will provide you with the missing information. What I am about to tell you is to be considered classified – do you understand?"

Stricklen, still seething, sat down at his desk and replied, "I understand."

"Approximately 36 standard years ago an exploration team on a remote planet discovered the remains of a probe which had crashed on the planet's surface. The probe was taken to their ship and examined. The facilities aboard the exploration ship were limited and they were unable to learn much from it. The probe was eventually transferred to a research station near Almaranus where it was extensively analyzed. It was later determined that the probe had been constructed over 40,000 years ago."

"The crash had severely damaged the probe. We were lucky in that the planet where it crashed did not have an atmosphere. This prevented any further destruction of the probe's mechanism through corrosion or weathering. It was learned the probe was from a society far more advanced than any member of the Alliance or any species of which the Alliance was aware. Because of the extensive damage, very little could be learned about its operation. Two scientific advances resulted from the examination of its mechanism. One was the development of a superior stardrive and the other was the improvement in FTL communications speed and distance. Far more could have been learned if the probe had not been nearly destroyed on impact. We know the builders had a knowledge of continuum field dynamics that far surpasses our own."

"It was decided to classify this probe in the event that additional artifacts were discovered. When the *Komodo Dragon* reported finding an ancient ship, I was assigned to the science team in case your discovery was related to the probe. Because of the technological advances that will be possible from an examination of the alien device it must be protected at all cost. It also must remain the property of the Alliance and not allowed to become the sole property of any one member. For this reason, the peacekeepers have assumed ownership of the ship and its contents."

"That explains a lot," Stricklen replied after a moment to digest the facts. "Can you explain why Falnath, the top expert on continuum physics, just happens to be on the science team?"

"Falnath was on Almaranus attending a conference on applied continuum physics when your report arrived. We availed ourselves of the opportunity and asked her to review the data. She became very excited and demanded that she be placed in charge of the science team. We were unwilling to send such an important individual to a remote area of unexplored space until she explained her reasoning. She felt that the energy signature you had recorded indicated a new unique application of high energy field dynamics which, once analyzed, could allow us to improve upon our current stardrive technology. She convinced us she was the only person qualified who could perform the analysis, we agreed, and she became the team leader."

Stricklen sat in thought for several minutes after Sorbith had left. The existence of an ancient star-traveling civilization was still hard to believe. These people had been traveling among the stars and sending out probes to distant worlds before the Human race had discovered that the lights in the sky above them were anything more than just lights. What had become of these people? Where were they now?

Stricklen's thoughts were interrupted by his XO reminding him of the staff meeting. During the meeting, a plan was created for extracting the chamber from the derelict's cargo hold. Most of the *Dragon's* shuttles would be transferred to other ships in order to make room in the shuttle bay for the object. A needle beam would then be used to cut the cargo bay doors apart to allow the object to be extracted. It would then be towed to the shuttle bay and secured. The extraction operation was to begin as soon as the *Dragon's* hanger bay could be cleared and after the engineers determined the exact locations to make the cuts in the alien ship. Hopefully they would be ready to begin in about eight hours.

On his way to get some lunch, Stricklen received some disturbing news. "The alien probe has destroyed our HK," the voice on the other end of the com-link said. "Two destroyers have been dispatched to intercept. The probe has accelerated to 1560c and has begun evasive maneuvers. It is now at a distance of 0.33 lights and at its current speed will be within weapons range in less than two hours. *Mobius* has ordered the fleet to an alert status."

Stricklen ordered the *Komodo Dragon* to follow suit. He was not worried about the probe itself - it posed no threat and the destroyers would obliterate it. He did, however, recognize the tactic the probe was using. It was trying to get as close to the fleet as it could in order to gather as much information as possible before it was destroyed. To Ken's military mind it meant their uninvited guests would soon be arriving. Ken's lunch-time was filled with worry.

Chapter 5

The probe proved to be exceptionally difficult to catch. It was highly maneuverable and capable of bursts of speed beyond the abilities of the gravity mines which had been deployed to force the probe into normal space. Ships under faster-than-light drive were technically not in normal space but existed within a miniature universe of their own. In order to engage in combat or, such as in the case of the probe, to be attacked, the ship had to drop out of stardrive. The best way to force a ship to drop to normal was through the use of a gravity mine. This was a high-speed FTL capable drone which carried a short-lived but extremely powerful gravity field generator. The idea was to set the generator off close enough to the target so that the disruption of space caused an instability in the drive fields and the target was forced out of stardrive and back into normal space.

The alien probe made it to within two million kilometers of the *Dragon* before a gravity mine finally got close enough and forced the probe out of stardrive. Before the probe could move away from the area of warped space a Tholtaran destroyer had locked on and obliterated it. The probe, however, had sent back enough data for its makers to act upon.

Eight light years away, a group of warships had been making their way back home when the first report from the probe had arrived. The fleet had stopped as more information was obtained. Following the probe's destruction a meeting was held.

"You are certain of the identity of the ship?" the Master asked.

"Yes," replied the other keeping his eyes respectfully lowered "The description is ancient but has been faithfully preserved. The enemy are in possession of a ship of the ancients. The design matches within tolerance. We must act."

The last statement was almost provocative. Lower clans did not recommend actions to their superiors without specifically being asked. Given the gravity of the issue, however, the Master allowed the breach of etiquette to pass with only a look of disapproval. "Battlemaster, report on the strength of their fleet."

"One large dreadnought accompanied by nine ships of a class inferior to ours," the Battlemaster replied.

The Master considered this for a moment. His group consisted of five heavy warships; no match for the superior firepower available to the creatures. Reluctantly he came to a decision. "A message shall be sent to base explaining our situation. Additional ships will be required to reclaim what is ours. Until then, deploy probes to monitor the activities of these creatures and move the fleet closer. Inform me of any changes."

The meeting broke up. The message was sent. The fleet began to move and additional probes were launched.

* * * * *

"Here comes another one!" exclaimed Scarboro. He was on the bridge to observe the extraction of the stasis chamber from the alien ship which was about to begin. During the last three hours the Alliance fleet had intercepted and destroyed four of the annoying probes. This would be the fifth one.

Stricklen was worried. He had discussed their situation with Trisk at length and found the Tholtaran to be an arrogant fool. Ken pointed out that the probes had to be coming from an alien fleet which was very close, probably just beyond their detector range. He also believed that they were of the same race that had attacked Mintaka. He wanted to send out several probes of their own in order to locate the enemy ships. Trisk had disagreed, stating he needed his probes to maintain the defense perimeter. He felt his ship was powerful enough to ward off any attack and he refused to ask sector command for additional ships despite Stricklen's belief that the enemy must be waiting for reinforcements to arrive.

Stricklen approached Sorbith and was delighted to find the peacekeeper had already requested additional ships. Unfortunately, they would not arrive for several days. Trisk somehow found out that Stricklen had gone over his head and was furious. The fleet commander tried to remove Stricklen from command of his ship but backed down when Sorbith calmly informed him that if he tried, he would be stripped of rank and assigned to the galley of his own ship as a cook. Ken took the opportunity to launch three probes of his own on a search mission.

"Everyone is clear of the cargo bay," reported a voice. "We are ready to begin cutting."

A moment later an invisible beam of coherent energy leapt out from the side of the *Komodo Dragon* and struck the derelict's outer cargo bay doors.

Although the beam was invisible in the vacuum of space, its effect on the armor plating of the alien artifact was very visible. For a brief moment the armor plating resisted, but the powerful beam of energy won out and began cutting a long thin line across the cargo door. Three minutes later the beam cut off and the eerie bluish light of a tractor beam replaced it. Unlike the concentrated beam of pure energy that preceded it, this beam manipulated space and produced a visible track where it passed. An enormous section of plating was pulled from the side of the ship leaving a gaping hole into the cargo bay.

Several maintenance drones moved in and, using their own tractor beams, began the delicate operation of extracting the stasis chamber. As the chamber slowly cleared the newly cut entrance, a report came in saying that the fifth probe had been destroyed. Ken watched for a few minutes then put in a call to Travan McCallister who was the person in charge of figuring out how to shutdown the stasis device.

"Any progress to report?" Ken asked as soon as the connection had been established.

"Some," McCallister replied. Ken could see several computer screens with complex schematics on them in the background. "The main control systems are routed entirely through their computer. Because we stand little chance of gaining control of the computer, we have concentrated our efforts on the backup and emergency control systems. I believe we have identified at least one such system and several other circuits are being traced out now. We should have some idea about how the controls work within a few hours once we can get back to work."

"Excellent. Please let me know as soon as you learn anything." Stricklen cut the connection and went back to watching the transfer. The chamber had cleared the ship and was about one-third of the way to the *Dragon's* waiting hanger bay.

* * * * *

"The enemy is removing a large object from within the ship of the ancients," an underling reported.

The Master was seething inside. How dare these inferior creatures deface a ship of the ancients! He was also worried. The legends contained stories of the ancients having weapons of irresistible power. If such a weapon had survived and was aboard the ship the enemy had found, it would be unwise to let them examine it. He was forced to act.

"We cannot let them take what is ours. Bring all ships to battle readiness. Set course to the enemy fleet and engage at maximum. Bring me the person who has been instructed to learn the culture and language of these creatures," the Master ordered.

A few minutes later an individual stood in front of his superior. "How may this servant please his master?" he said.

"The creatures of the Alliance have found a ship which belongs to us and are removing something from within it," the Master said, giving the underling only the information required to perform his duty. "We have insufficient ships to effectively engage them in battle at this time. We need to delay their departure until the larger attack force arrives. You have been tasked with learning as much as possible about them. What is our best strategy for delaying them?"

The underling thought for a long moment before replying. A bad answer could end his assignment and his chance at achieving a higher status. "Their thought processes are alien to our own. My research into their culture has shown that we need only state they have found something which is ours and demand its immediate return. We should display force, but indicate no weapons would be fired if they return to us what is ours."

The Master considered this then replied, "I do not pretend to understand your suggestion, but it will be carried out. You will speak to these inferiors and convey to them the message you have indicated. You will be compensated for the dishonor of having to speak to them."

"I will do as commanded," the underling replied as he backed out of the room.

* * * * *

Stricklen was in the shower when the alarm klaxon sounded the call to battle stations. As fast as he could, he exited and headed for the bridge. Scarboro looked up from a display as Ken strode through the doorway and burst into laughter. Quickly controlling himself, Doug said, "Caught in the shower sir?" and motioned for Ken to examine the top of his head.

Stricklen brought his hand to his hair and encountered a soapy film. He had left the shower so fast he had forgotten to wash the soap out of his hair. Both angry and amused at himself, he took the recently vacated command chair and said, "Have someone bring me a towel. What is the situation?"

"*Mobius* reports incoming ships," Scarboro replied. "At least five coming in at 3.8Kc; distance now 0.76; ETA one hour forty-five minutes."

"Three point eight kay!" Stricklen exclaimed. "That's faster than anything we have by a considerable margin. Any logistics data yet?"

"No sir. Drive wakes are large but that could be due to their speed. Secondary field emissions and power signatures have not yielded anything yet."

"What is the status of the stasis chamber?" Ken asked as he took a towel from a crewman and began to run it through his hair.

"Secured in the shuttle bay. Last I heard, Sorbith was there watching McCallister try to figure it out. Request permission to take my post in CIC."

"Granted."

"Captain," the coms watch announced as Scarboro started to make his way off the bridge. "Sorbith on one and Trisk on two."

'Hold on a moment Doug, you might want to listen in on this."

Doug quickly reversed and retraced his steps. "Coms: Establish a split-screen multi-way on my main."

Following the Captain's orders, the communications watch created a three-way communications link between the parties. Sorbith's face appeared on the left of Ken's main screen while Trisk's appeared on the right. Stricklen quickly finished with his hair, smoothed it into place with his fingers as best he could then activated his side of the link and said, "A three-way has been established. What are your orders?" Ken directed his question at nobody in particular since he was not sure who would be giving the orders.

After a moments hesitation Trisk replied, "As soon as the chamber is secure within your ship you are to begin moving away from the approaching vessels as fast as possible."

Stricklen turned and nodded to his XO who left to issue the appropriate orders. Turning back to the monitor he said, "The chamber is already secure. We will be underway momentarily."

"Acknowledged, *Mobius* out," Trisk said and without warning his image ceased to exist. He was obviously still a little upset at Stricklen. Ken now sat facing Sorbith.

"I have some additional orders," Sorbith said. "It is obvious that you are unable to engage your stardrive until the chamber's gravity field has been shutdown. I am unsure as to whether McCallister will be able to determine how to do that before the incoming ships arrive. In order to allow you an avenue of escape I would like you to have a member of your engineering department in position to sever the power supply to the chamber at a moments notice. At the first sign of hostility I will order you to cut the power to the stasis chamber and head for Almaranus at max speed. Do not cut the cable unless I personally order it."

"I thought that an abrupt removal of power could result in a catastrophic reaction," Ken replied.

"That's correct. I know I'm asking a lot but, this device must not under any circumstances fall into the hands of a potential enemy to the Alliance. I would rather see the device destroyed than have it become the property of an enemy. If severing the power does not result in a catastrophic reaction then you will be able to engage your stardrive and make for Almaranus. Either way, the device remains out of enemy hands."

"Understood," Stricklen replied. "I'll have a man there within five minutes."

The communication link was terminated and Stricklen issued the orders he had been given. Slowly, the *Komodo Dragon* moved behind the shield of ships. Engineering reported that the intense gravity field from the chamber was making it difficult to establish and control even normal sub-light drive fields. These fields were similar to Kauffman stardrive fields but were much coarser and required far less power. But, because of the similarity with stardrive fields, the intense gravitational distortion was causing control problems.

It is interesting to note that the gravitation field from the stasis chamber had also caused some concerns during the movement of the device to the *Dragon*. Special precautions had to be taken as to where to place the object so as to minimize the effects of the gravitational field being emitted from the chamber. The situation was unique since the gravity field was unidirectional, almost as if they were dealing with an operating tractor beam which could not be shut down.

The incoming ships dropped out of stardrive a mere eight million kilometers from the *Dragon*. The two fleets stared at one another across empty space for several minutes.

Stricklen punched a button on his command console and said, "Tell me about our visitors Doug."

"I've never seen ships like those before," Doug remarked from combat control. "They mass about 120 kilotons. Power signatures indicate they're heavily armed. I would classify them as battleship class. Weapon systems and defensive capabilities are unknown at this time. They are too far away to get a visual."

The *Mobius* eventually reported that a reply to their communications attempts had been received. Instead of a language translation signal, which would be expected from a previously unencountered alien race, a standard communications channel had been activated. No video was present, so the *Dragon* listened in on the conversation between Trisk and the other ship.

"We are called Chroniech," said a difficult to understand voice. "You are in possession of a ship which belongs to us. We demand its return or we will open fire."

"You speak our language?" a surprised Trisk replied. After waiting a moment for a nonexistent reply he continued. "If you are referring to the cargo ship we have been examining then you are in error. We have determined that it has been drifting in space for many thousands of years, and therefore cannot logically be yours."

"The ship's configuration matches those built by our ancestors. It does not matter how old it is. We will not ask again – return it to us."

There followed a significant period of silence then Trisk said, "We are done examining the ship. You may take it if you wish."

"You have removed an object from the ship's cargo bay. Return the object to us."

"No, we have not completed our examination of it. The ship was found drifting in space and is therefore subject to become the property of anyone who happens to find it."

Another conversation then took place at the other end of the communications link. Two scratchy, rough voices were heard apparently speaking to each other. After a moment, a reply was heard, "I have been instructed to inform you that the Chroniech do not allow inferiors to disobey an order from us. Chroniech are superior to all other life. This has been a fact since our ancestors achieved sentience. It is written in our most ancient and sacred scrolls. Chroniech have been ordained to rule over all other species. Return to us what is ours or we will take it."

"It is not yours and therefore you will not have it!" Trisk replied. "Withdraw your request and we shall talk about opening relations with your people. Perhaps some sort of..."

"Enough!" the Chroniech shouted. "You creatures do not deserve the privilege of even speaking to a Chroniech. I have been dishonored in having been ordered to speak to you. You will return the object which you have taken – now!"

POWER STRUGGLE

"No," Trisk calmly said and waited as the silence grew.

* * * * *

Falnath pointed to the button which McCallister had indicated a moment before and said, "I believe you are correct. Depressing this button should initiate an emergency shutdown of the device. I especially like your reasoning behind the symbology depicted above the switch. I am not convinced, however, that the auxiliary system you mentioned is nothing to worry about. I still do not understand what it does."

McCallister had just finished showing Falnath the results of his analysis of the alien control system. He had reasoned that if the stasis device were meant to hold something in stasis for many thousands of years then one must assume that the language would change over such a large amount of time. An easily recognizable symbol would have to be present to indicate which button would initiate a shutdown. Such a symbol had been found and McCallister had targeted his analysis on the circuits connected to that switch. He had concluded the button in question would indeed begin the shutdown process. He had brought Falnath in so that his theory could be confirmed.

"I'm glad you agree with the first part," McCallister replied. "I do not pretend to understand the workings of this device. You are the expert here and if you agree with me then I believe we have found the correct button to push. I think the auxiliary systems I have traced to this switch are nothing more than additional backups. Why have a shutdown switch which would cause other problems?"

"You are perhaps correct. We should ask the Captain if he would like us to attempt a shutdown of the stasis device."

"Why? He specifically said this entire project was to be run by us. He gave us instructions to find a way to shutdown this thing ASAP. We've found a way and I believe we should go ahead and shut it down."

Falnath turned toward the chamber's door. As she walked she said, "Still, I think we should inform him..." Out of the corner of her eye she noticed a movement. Turning her head she saw McCallister reaching for the button. "What are you doing?" she shouted.

Before she could react, McCallister had placed his thumb on the button and applied a little downward pressure.

Chapter 6

"Sensors are picking up a stardrive matrix field forming around all Chroniech ships," a voice reported from CIC. "Request permission to go weapons active."

Stricklen knew that in order to begin fighting, the Chroniech ships would have to move in closer than eight million kilometers. Typical battle strategy would call for a short faster-than-light run to put them within striking distance of the Alliance fleet. The stardrive matrix fields were a sure indication the Chroniech fleet was about to do just that. As with all Alliance ships, the Chroniech stardrive required a matrix field to be established prior to engaging the main drive. This matrix field acted as a sort of conductor to guide the stronger and more complex stardrive fields as they formed. Alliance matrix fields required several seconds to become stable before the main drive fields could be powered.

"Permission granted, hold weapons until first shot detected."

By the time this order had been issued, the buildup time for the stardrive fields was completed and the Chroniech fleet had gone FTL. A few seconds later they appeared much closer to the Alliance fleet. As soon as the Chroniech ships were in normal space they opened fire.

A barrage of nuclear-tipped missiles leapt out from the attacking ships. Ultra-fast sensors detected the missiles almost the instant they were launched and fed this information to the combat computers. The computers calculated each missile's course, assessed its threat potential, assigned each of them a targeting sequence, and began a counter-attack. Powerful needle-beams lanced out from the Alliance warships to lick at the silvery defense screens of the incoming missiles.

The screens of the Chroniech missiles flared but, amazingly, held. The Alliance computers quickly digested the new data, analyzed the results of the first attack, and switched tactics. Now, instead of one beam per missile, five were used. Under this assault, the missile's defense screen flared white then blinked into failure. Bright actinic flashes indicated the destruction of each enemy missile. Soon space was filled with artificial stars as the missiles were intercepted and destroyed. But, since the Alliance had to use five beams per missile, some of them were bound to get through.

The missiles were not the only threat the Alliance had to contend with. Beams of hyper-accelerated particles and pure energy spat out from each Chroniech warship to strike the defense screens of the Alliance ships. The incredible power of the Chroniech weapons was dissipated in great blinding flares of raw energy. The Chroniech were a well-organized attacking force. Acting in unison, the five ships would direct a concentrated attack upon a chosen target all the while using secondary weapons and missiles to keep the other Alliance ships busy.

Stricklen watched the first few seconds of the battle before uttering a single comment. There was little he could actually do at this point since his ship was not directly in the line of fire. Even if he were at the forefront, most of the combat decisions were being made by the ship's weapons control computers. "They carry considerable more firepower than we do," Ken remarked to Doug over the open channel to Combat Information & Control (CIC).

"Logistics place their weapons at about 35% more capable than ours and their shielding is rated even better. They made a tactical error though in attacking since we still have them out-gunned," Doug replied.

Stricklen was about to make another comment when a computer screen flashed a warning and displayed a trouble-map. Simultaneously, several other stations around the bridge began to flash danger signs indicating something catastrophic had just occurred.

"Captain!" the woman sitting at the engineering station yelled out. Her hands flew over the console as she attempted to isolate and define the problem. "Indications of some sort of damage to the primary hanger bay area. Hull integrity has not been compromised. Power has been lost to several sections. A large area surrounding the hanger appears to have been damaged although no fires have been detected. There's no indication of an explosion or a weapons hit."

Before Stricklen could reply, another voice spoke up, "Gravitational interference has terminated. We are stardrive capable," said the helm.

Ken's mind put two and two together and came up with a conclusion. He turned to face Doug's image on one of his monitors and said, "They must have tried to shutdown the stasis field and something went wrong. Doug, send a damage control team to survey the damage."

Doug's reply was masked by another report. The face of Commander Kovalesky appeared on a monitor. Without preamble he said, "Captain, there is a force field surrounding the stasis chamber. It extends to a distance of about one meter from the chamber's outer wall and passes through several of the ship's bulkheads. Luckily, nobody was nearby when the field came on."

Stricklen took this new information and merged it with the other data he had received. He issued a rapid-fire string of orders. "Commander Scarboro: Cancel the damage control team. Commander Kovalesky: I want as many men as you can spare into the hanger bay – arm them. Coms: Inform Fleet Commander Trisk that we are FTL capable and are setting course for Almaranus at max. CIC: Drop a monitor probe – right now. Helm: Bring the stardrive on-line and engage for Almaranus at all possible speed."

A chorus of acknowledgments followed and the orders were carried out. Stricklen punched a button on his console and the ship-wide address system carried his next words. "All hands: Prepare for emergency transition to stardrive." Under normal circumstances, a ship's matrix field was allowed to build up slowly, taking around 20 seconds to reach full strength. The main stardrive fields were then ramped up to power over a three second period. These times could be shortened in an emergency but the effect was quite unsettling on the crew.

Seconds later, Stricklen felt the dizziness hit him and the room spun around for a moment as the ship made the transition to stardrive. Although the dizziness quickly passed, it left a bad headache as a reminder of what had just happened. As the *Komodo Dragon* raced toward Alliance space, the rest of the fleet fought for their lives. Through the eyes and sensors of the monitor probe Stricklen watched the battle as it progressed.

The Chroniech tactic appeared to be working to their advantage. Two Alliance ships had been destroyed and a third was being targeted without a single Chroniech ship having been touched. The enemy's screens were blazing with tortured energy but did not show any signs of weakness. The Tholtaran master dreadnought had not yet entered the battle as it had placed itself between the smaller ships and the *Komodo Dragon* in order to shield Stricklen's ship from any Chroniech weapons. Now that the *Dragon* was gone, the dreadnought was free to engage the enemy.

As soon as it was within range, the *Mobius* opened fire with devastating results. Five brilliant balls of coruscating, sparkling, spitting energy emerged from the side of the dreadnought along with hundreds of beams of pure destruction. The balls were actually a Human invention which the Tholtarans had improved upon. These balls of energy were from a weapon commonly known as a sledgehammer. The technical term was a particle-pumped soliton energy vortex. It was one of the most destructive weapons known to Alliance science.

The beams, which traveled at the speed of light, struck the defense shields of the Chroniech ships. The shields burst into a spectacular display of deflected raw power. The three closest enemy ships took the brunt of the attack. Under the incredible power of the dreadnought's weapons, the shields of the three ships weakened and began to leak enough energy to cause the armor plating to begin to glow in spots. The five glowing balls reached their targets a half second later. The balls broke and spilled torrents of energy into the now over-stressed shields. The result was a complete collapse and the instant destruction of all but one Chroniech ship.

The last ship attempted to run but it too was destroyed as the Alliance combat computers trained their weapons on the only remaining target. It joined its companions as it became an ever-expanding cloud of debris. The entire battle, from the first shot to the final destruction, had lasted barely five minutes.

Stricklen picked up on a communication between the *Mobius* and one of the Alliance cruisers. "*Tor-Al* this is *Mobius*, what is your status?"

As the link was completed, Stricklen looked into a scene of utter chaos. A Tholtaran officer could be seen floating near what appeared to be a control console. The artificial gravity was obviously not working. Behind him small flames erupted from several panels. Two other Tholtaran's were drifting near the floor with dark red blobs floating around them. The picture was unsteady and filled with static. The entire room had a hazy, smoky appearance. "We sustained a near hit from a missile," the officer said not really looking into the video pickup. His hands were busy working the controls on a console. "Stardrive damaged beyond repair. Main and most auxiliary reactors off-line. We have a runaway accumulator fault which I am... NO!" he said turning toward somebody out of the range of the visual pickup. "Do not cross-tie CM-eight with the main. It's not stable yet. I need you to bleed..."

The link snapped and Stricklen shifted his eyes to the visual feed from the probe. The stricken Tholtaran cruiser had a serious problem on their hands. An accumulator was a power storage device capable of absorbing tremendous amounts of energy which could then be delivered almost instantly upon demand. These devices provided the peaking power on all modern starships. The runaway condition which the officer had described told Stricklen that the accumulator was failing and could spontaneously discharge its entire complement of stored energy in a single burst. This would be the equivalent of setting off a small atomic bomb within the ship.

Ken could see the cruiser was drifting without power. It slowly spun end-for-end. An enormous gash was visible at one location on the aft section of the ship. Gaseous vapor and bits of debris were streaming out of the hole. Several areas of armor plate still glowed a soft orange indicating spots where the Chroniech had hit them with energy beams. As Ken watched, the entire back one-third of the ship seemed to expand. Cracks appeared in the hull and flames erupted from the gaps. A moment later, the entire ship exploded in a brief flash of light.

The final tally was three Alliance cruisers destroyed and two destroyers damaged verses five Chroniech warships destroyed. Sorbith ordered the *Mobius* to escort the *Dragon* back to Almaranus. What was left of the Alliance fleet would remain near the scene of the battle to conduct repairs and to salvage some of the Chroniech debris for later analysis.

Stricklen canceled battle stations and, after attending to a few items, turned over control of the bridge then made his way to the hanger bay. The first thing he noticed as he approached, was a marine in full combat armor standing guard near the doorway. As he entered the room, Stricklen saw the force field. It looked like a giant silver wall which reflected all light creating a strange lighting effect. Sorbith was standing with the *Dragon's* engineer and another individual whom he could not make out near one area of the force field.

The peacekeeper broke away and met Stricklen halfway. "So far we have been unable to analyze the force field," Sorbith said gesturing toward the silver wall. "It appears to be one hundred percent reflecting throughout the entire range of the electromagnetic spectrum. Our sensors are reflected back off the surface and we have not been able to penetrate its structure. I have ordered your engineering department to bring as much equipment as they need here to conduct a complete analysis of the field."

Stricklen looked all around the room taking in the size of the field. As he craned his neck to look at the upper portion of the force field he said, "Internal ship diagnostics show that the field passes through three of the ship's bulkheads. One on the deck below, one on the port side and the other just aft of the hanger. A minor power outage and loss of contact with some areas of the ship has resulted. Major systems are unaffected and we are currently on course for Almaranus at 2.8Kc. ETA – 6 days."

The silence that settled was interrupted by the chief engineer who had grown tired of being ignored and had walked over to where Stricklen and

Sorbith were talking. "This is incredible!" he exclaimed. "A perfectly reflecting force field has been a theoretical possibility, but it has been considered far too complex to even attempt to generate. Our own main defense shields aren't 100% reflective. Their technology must be light years ahead of ours."

At that moment, Commander Kovalesky approached and said, "Excuse me sir, the perimeter of the force field has been secured. There are sixteen marines in full combat armor on standby at the far end of the hanger bay. Do you have any further orders?"

"No Commander, well done," Stricklen replied. Turning back to Sorbith, he said, "What do we do now? Do we really know what this thing is? Are you sure we should take it all the way to Almaranus?"

Sorbith considered Stricklen's question. Almaranus was not only a strategically located planet, but it also possessed the largest spacecraft construction docks in the Alliance. The Alliance would suffer a great loss if the space-docks of Almaranus were damaged or, worse yet, destroyed. "You have a good point," he replied. "Divert to Masfuta. During the transit I would like your crew to make all possible attempts at cracking that force field."

Stricklen was only vaguely familiar with Masfuta. He seemed to recall it was nothing more than a barren rock in space near the border between the Tholtar republic and the Rouldian sphere. He contacted the bridge and ordered the course change. The new time of arrival was now only just under five days away. Stricklen then spoke to his chief engineer before retiring to his quarters.

In the privacy of his quarters, Ken pulled out an old-fashioned paper notebook and turned to the next blank page. He wrote:

5/14/22: First encounter with the Chroniech. They appear very aggressive and are a threat to the peace which the Alliance has finally achieved. Their ships are more advanced than ours. I fear the Alliance is in trouble and war is on the horizon. What is even more surprising is the Chroniech know our language. This tells me they have been monitoring our communications for some time. The stasis chamber (if that is what it really is) is now in the Dragon's hanger bay surrounded by an impenetrable force field. I am worried about the fate of the two scientists trapped inside. I have great concern about what this object is and what it contains. Why was it set adrift in space? What is in stasis? Are we about to unleash a force that can destroy us all?

Stricklen returned the diary to its place and poured himself a double rum. He felt as if the weight of the future of the Alliance had been thrust upon his shoulders.

Chapter 7

The first thing the researchers had noticed once an atmosphere had been established around the stasis chamber was the deep, low frequency, undulating sound which permeated the entire chamber. The instant McCallister felt a slight click from the button under his finger this sound shifted and became a little higher in frequency – not much, but enough to be noticed.

The second thing that changed was the appearance of the spherical shell of force. Instead of a steady, scintillating, glowing ball of energy, it now pulsed. Falnath had stopped dead in her tracks and was staring at the stasis field. A fine network of silvery, spiderweb-like filaments had formed across the surface. This network crawled like ghostly electrical sparks along the entire surface of the sphere. The pulsing sound increased until it was at almost the same rate as a resting Human heart.

As they watched, the intensity of the glow began to fade. The actual surface of the stasis field generator could be seen as if through a hazy tangled filamental web. The intensity of the sound began to drop and, at the same time, the web-work began to fade. Five minutes later, only the quiescent dull gray surface of the stasis device was visible. It was quiet and dark..

Falnath turned back toward the entrance and said, "I will inform the Captain the stasis field is shutdown. Do not touch anything else until I..." Falnath had reached the doorway. She stopped in mid-sentence as she looked out the entrance.

"What is it?" McCallister asked.

"We are surrounded by a force field," Falnath said. "We are trapped inside." She slowly turned around and stared at McCallister.

The Human took a step backward. He knew Rouldians were very peaceful, however, the look Falnath gave him caused his instincts to take over. An obviously upset dragon-like creature with a double row of sharp teeth and large black penetrating eyes was staring at him. A wave of primitive fear washed over McCallister. "I – I'm s–sorry!" he stammered his voice pitched higher than normal with fear. "We had no indication this chamber was equipped with a force field generator."

Falnath continued to stare for a moment then calmly said, "The emergency shutdown must also have activated a protective force field. Since we are, in effect, trapped, I suggest we use our time to scan the device now that the surrounding field is gone."

Without further explanation, Falnath walked over to the semi-portable scientific scanner and began operating its complex controls. McCallister recovered and looked around. "About two-thirds of the control console are now active," he remarked. "The stasis chamber appears to be shutdown and from the monitor near the computer, I'd say it is now active."

Falnath picked up a small device and walked over to the now dull-gray surface of the stasis machine. McCallister could hear her muttering to herself in her own language as she moved the device over the surface. Without stopping, she said, "Unbelievable! This entire surface appears to be a single, massive, micro-electronic fabrication. There are field generators, modulators, control circuits, and sensors all on a sub-micron level. Whoever built this, has created a device that has unbelievably fine control over the field structure in and around the sphere. This device is far more advanced than..."

Falnath was interrupted by a soft chime followed by a lilting voice in an unfamiliar language. McCallister almost jumped out of his skin. Falnath let out a short hiss and dropped the instrument she was holding. The chime and voice were repeated after a short delay.

"What the hell was that?" McCallister fairly yelled out.

Reaching down to retrieve the scanner Falnath replied, "Most likely an automated notification that the stasis device has been shutdown."

"Or a warning from some sort of security system."

Falnath ignored McCallister's last remark and resumed her methodical scanning. McCallister made a slow circuit of the room reporting on various changes. "Reactor output is now about 200 giga-watts; this bank of instruments is dead but the ones next to it are active; the computer appears to be fully powered."

A low thud was heard from the inside of the sphere. Falnath stopped her scanning and quickly backed away. McCallister retreated behind a rack of instruments and tried to hide. After about five seconds a second thump was heard followed by a series of loud clicks. A barely perceptible rectangular crack appeared in the surface.

As they watched, a rectangular section of the sphere sank into the device to a distance of about half a meter. Then, without a sound, it moved to one side revealing an entrance roughly two meters tall and one meter wide. A dim light illuminated the interior. A few seconds passed, then a shadow from the inside obscured the doorway.

"Za too lomara kyrra?" a soft voice spoke from within.

McCallister stood petrified, unable to move. He was sweating profusely and shaking with fear. Falnath, on the other hand, appeared to be more in control of herself. She slowly shifted her position so whatever or whoever was inside the chamber could see her.

As she did so, a soft moan was heard from within followed by a muffled conversation. Falnath waited quietly not saying anything or making any kind of motion.

Two minutes passed before the shadow reappeared. From inside the now inactive time-stasis device one of the occupants emerged. McCallister's eyes were round with a combination of fear and surprise. Falnath simply looked— her scientifically trained analytical mind taking in all the details without making any judgement. The creature before them was constructed along the same basic lines as virtually all member races of the Alliance. It stood on two legs and had the standard complement of two arms and one head with a pair of offset eyes in the front. All visible portions of the creature's body were covered with very fine, short, dense, polychromatic fur. The head was supported about 1.5 meters off the floor by a thick body which was partially covered by clothing. Two large, round eyes were set in the standard pattern above an almost invisible nose. The mouth was large and set almost flat. No ears were visible. The arms sported two elbows and were terminated by a hand with six digits.

As afraid as he was, McCallister could not help but think that the alien which now stood before them was the most beautiful creature he had ever seen. The alien's fur reflected light in a constantly shifting multi-colored pattern much like one of Earth's butterflies. The effect was not overwhelming and allowed the underlying primary color (which in this case was a very light brown) to be easily seen. Each subtle movement caused a new color pattern to flow across the alien's body.

The alien slowly exited the chamber and stood to one side. Another followed. Shortly there were five of them standing in the now crowded room. The occupants of the stasis chamber quietly stared at the two researchers. Falnath noted that each one had a slightly different coloration of fur thus allowing her to tell them apart. It was not possible to determine if they were male, female, or neither. After a period of time one of them stepped forward, gestured to the others and said, "Kyrra."

Falnath tapped herself on the chest and in her own language said something. The word "Rouldian" issued from her vocoder in the language which was standard throughout the Alliance. She then pointed to McCallister who was slowly regaining control and had left the protection of the instrument rack and said, "Human".

The Kyrra who had spoken, slowly walked over to Falnath and examined the vocoder which hung around her neck. Falnath removed the device and handed it to the other. He or she (gender at this point still could not be determined) turned the device over in its hands a few times and handed it back. Falnath put it back around her neck and made a connecting motion between herself and McCallister. The Kyrra seemed to understand and made a swaying motion with its head.

Falnath then pointed toward the doorway then to herself and then pantomimed with her hands someone walking in the direction of the door. The Kyrra looked confused for a moment and took a step toward the door. Falnath then placed her hands in front of herself and moved them toward her chest. She then pointed at the Kyrra again, placed her hands back in front of her, then separated them. The Kyrra thought about this for a moment then apparently realized that Falnath was trying to ask it to remove the force field. The Kyrra pointed toward the doorway and looked at the floor for a second. Apparently, this gesture meant no.

A conversation then took place between the five Kyrra. Falnath and McCallister were pointed to several times as they waited patiently. One of the five eventually broke free from the group and walked over to the computer. A quiet conversation then took place between the individual and the computer. McCallister noted that the language of the Kyrra had a very pleasant sound to it.

Another Kyrra took a seat at the control console and began manipulating switches and controls. A third began a survey of the stasis device paying particular attention to the area which had been damaged. The other two Kyrra remained still and continued to talk quietly between themselves.

"What do we do now?" McCallister asked approaching Falnath.

"We must wait. As soon as the force field is removed we will be able to begin the process of establishing meaningful communications. Neither you nor I are linguistics experts and trying to learn their language or teach them one of ours would be futile. I suggest you have a seat until the Kyrra, which is what I am assuming they call themselves, decide to release the force field."

"But what if they are hostile? They could decide to kill us and then take over the ship!"

"Be reasonable!" Falnath scolded. "If these people were hostile they would have emerged from the stasis chamber with weapons at the ready. Keep in mind that they are far more technologically advanced than we are which usually implies they are also sociologically more advanced. My opinion is that once these Kyrra begin to know us they will consider us a threat to their existence."

"Us? A threat to their existence? The technology their race possesses is so far beyond ours that their defensive and offensive capabilities must be staggering. How can we possibly be a threat to them?"

"I see no evidence of weapons or aggressive behavior," countered Falnath.

"This ship is armed to the teeth."

"This ship is also not theirs."

"We have not proven that assumption. Well, there's nothing we can do about it now. What's done is done and we will have to live with the consequences. Let's just hope that we haven't unleashed a power that can wipe us all out."

"We may have freed a power that can become an ally."

McCallister turned and sat down in the only seat available, the one in front of the portable scanner. Falnath positioned herself so she could observe as many of the Kyrra as possible and settled down to wait.

* * * * *

Stricklen had almost finished his rum when the intercom system chimed. He acknowledged the call by saying, "Stricklen."

The XO's face appeared on the monitor. "Communications has picked up a strange signal coming in on low-band," Doug said. "We have confirmed that it is coming from the hanger bay, most likely from the stasis chamber."

"That means the force-field has been altered to allow it to pass this signal. This implies there is now someone inside who understands the operation of the device. What sort of a signal is it?"

"It's very periodic. The computer believes it may be the beginnings of a language translation interchange. I think we should proceed along this assumption and allow the computer to attempt to establish a common translation."

"Understood, standby." The Captain broke the connection with the bridge then said, "*Dragon*, present analysis of the signal being received from the hanger bay."

The ship's semi-intelligent computer system instantly responded. "The data stream consists of a repeating sequence of binary data arranged in words of twelve bits each. There are thirteen words in each group and there are twelve such groups. By arranging the words to form a simple twelve by twelve matrix and using the first word of each group to indicate a binary representation of a number the data-stream forms a series of symbols which have a probability of 94.8% of representing the numbers of a base twelve numbering system beginning with zero. This data stream would therefore represent the beginning of an attempt at establishing a language translation between the originators of the data stream and ourselves."

Stricklen thought about this for a moment then said, "Display the symbols."

In response to the command, the monitor showed twelve symbols with their assumed meanings. The symbols stood for the numbers zero through eleven. Humans had a base ten number system with distinct symbols for the numbers zero through nine.

Stricklen looked at the symbols and asked, "Can you establish a language translation with these people if given the opportunity?"

"Yes. I have first-contact language generation programming available," replied the machine.

"Very well. Standby."

Stricklen reestablished contact with his XO. "Doug, I'm authorizing the computer to establish a link with the alien transmission. Go ahead and allow it."

"Understood, Doug out."

Stricklen then turned his attention back to the ship's computer. "*Dragon*, establish a communications link with the originators of this signal and initiate a language translation. Report your progress to me."

"Acknowledged. Opening return communications channel... Sending standard reply... Reply received... Initiating dialog... Based upon response times and message content the originator is most likely an automated system – increasing speed... Speed has been increased to the limit of this communications channel."

Stricklen followed this monologue with keen interest. He was witnessing the beginnings of a process that would eventually allow two species to communicate with each other. He thought there was nothing much more that could be done except to wait but that assumption was proven wrong a few seconds later when Doug called him back to report a new development.

"Sir, the frequency bandwidth of the signal has increased and the computer is requesting additional communications resources. Looks like they're trying to boost their communications rate."

"Go ahead and allow the computer to use as much bandwidth as necessary. The sooner we get this translation out of the way the faster we will find out who we're dealing with."

"Acknowledged." The link clicked closed.

In the early days of Human exploration, before space travel existed, when two species met that spoke different languages, many months would pass before the two could effectively speak to each other. Much time was required for one to learn and understand the other's language. As time progressed, computers eventually reached the point of complexity where the entire process could be automated. At the phenomenal speed at which modern computers operated, a complete language translation would only take a few hours.

The soft chime from the computer startled Stricklen. He had dozed off in his chair without realizing it. "A mutual language translation has been achieved," the machine reported. "Several vocoders are currently being programmed and will be available in twenty minutes."

Stricklen rubbed the sleep out of his eyes and said, "How long did it take? What time is it?"

"The current time is 2337. The translation process required two hours eighteen minutes, however, additional translation dialog is still taking place."

"Is there a non-machine entity that is willing to speak to us at this time?"

The computer's response had a noticeable delay. "Yes. Five individuals have been released from stasis and are available to speak to you."

"Five? How about our two researchers – are they all right?"

"Falnath and McCallister are both unharmed," the ship's computer replied.

"Good! Can you contact them?"

"No. Direct communications with the two researchers is being blocked. The Kyrra computer has informed me that communications will be established once the safety of the Kyrra has been assured."

"Kyrra? Is that what they call themselves?"

"Yes. Their race is known as the Kyrra."

They're going to love me for this, Stricklen thought. Standing up and stretching, he said, "*Dragon*: Staff meeting in thirty minutes."

Stricklen decided to wait until the staff meeting before gathering additional information. Before he left for the conference room he issued one more instruction, "Ask the Kyrra computer if it would please inform our researchers that we know they are fine and we are working toward getting them released. Also, tell the Kyrra that we will be speaking to them shortly."

The machine acknowledged the order as Stricklen left his stateroom. Part way down the hallway the computer informed him via his com-link that the message had been delivered. Stricklen walked into the still empty conference room, grabbed a cup of coffee from the dispenser on the wall, and took his seat at the head of the table. He activated a terminal and told the computer to tell him everything it knew about their new guests. Shortly thereafter the room began to fill up.

* * * * *

Falnath and McCallister watched the Kyrra as they worked at the various instruments within the stasis chamber. A lot of activity was occurring near the computer. All five of the Kyrra had gathered near the machine and two of them had placed some sort of helmet upon their heads.

"What do you think they are doing?" McCallister had asked after watching the unmoving Kyrra for about fifteen minutes.

"I'm not certain," Falnath replied. "Maybe I can find out."

The Rouldian walked over to where the Kyrra were standing and made a noise to attract their attention. One of them looked at Falnath. The scientist made several gestures which the Kyrra apparently understood. He (or she) approached one of the Kyrra which was wearing a helmet and they conversed for a second. The Kyrra who was wearing the helmet then removed it and handed the helmet to Falnath. She took the helmet and carefully looked it over.

"It appears to be some sort of virtual reality headpiece," she said. "It will not fit on my head. Would you care to try it?"

McCallister hesitated for a second before stepping forward. Falnath gestured again at the Kyrra who swayed its head in what McCallister now believed was their method of nodding yes. Falnath slowly placed the assembly on McCallister's head. The interior of the helmet adjusted itself until it fit snugly but comfortably. High-speed speech and images assaulted his senses. McCallister recognized some of the sounds to be words and phrases in the standard language of the Alliance. The images came so fast as to be almost a blur, however, the ones he could make out were those of everyday objects, celestial bodies, and other common scenes.

McCallister removed the helmet and handed it back to the Kyrra who placed it back on its own head. After a moment of recovery he said, "I think it's some kind of educator. The device is presenting them with images and words in both our language and in theirs, but I don't see how they could learn anything since it is coming at them at a very high rate."

"The Kyrra may process information differently than we do," Falnath theorized. "I, for example, can glance at most mathematical equations and understand them without effort. It is an ability which I have that many people lack. The Kyrra may be able to process information at a significantly higher rate than we. For all we know they may even possess an eidetic memory."

The two scientists engaged in small talk with each other while the two Kyrra remained under their educators, apparently learning to speak Alliance standard. The others had busied themselves with other tasks.

After about two hours one of the Kyrra suddenly removed its helmet and walked toward them.

"We return you to you kind soon," the Kyrra said in a halting voice.

With a deliberate effort at speaking slowly, Falnath replied, "I understand. May we speak with our people?"

The Kyrra seemed to consider this for a moment then replied, "Soon. Must learn first."

Falnath watched as the Kyrra returned to the computer and once again put the helmet on its head. There was nothing more that the two researchers could do but wait.

* * * * *

After everyone was in attendance, Stricklen began the meeting. He brought the attendees up-to-date as to what had been happening with the Kyrra and explained that a translation had been reached. He was hopeful they would soon be able to speak with the Kyrra themselves. Before allowing this though, Stricklen presented the group with a brief overview of what he knew about the Kyrra.

In response to a command, the computer displayed a three-dimensional image of a Kyrra to the assembly. A chorus of muffled comments briefly filled the room. A Human stood next to the image for comparison purposes.

"This is a Kyrra," Ken lectured. "Like most species, they are divided into males and females, however, the distinction is not made at birth. Each individual may choose to either act as a male or a female during their reproductive stages. The information received concerning this is very sketchy, however, it appears as if the Kyrra are exceptionally long lived and they reproduce very slowly. If an individual Kyrra chooses to become female, then she allows herself to be impregnated and will carry a single child. This individual will then remain female until the child no longer requires close care. During the vast portion of their lives an individual Kyrra is neither male nor female.

"The Kyrra are a unique species which evolved into a space-capable civilization many thousands of years ago. This particular group of Kyrra have been in stasis for a period of 44,881 standard years. The Kyrra have a recorded history which spans a period of roughly 33,000 years. They are unique in that their evolutionary path has been very different than all other intelligent species whom the Kyrra have ever come into contact with.

"According to the Kyrra, evolution is capable of taking two different paths in the formation of life. The most common is the survival-of-the-fittest or the aggressive evolutionary path. The second (of which the Kyrra are the only known intelligent example) is the cooperative evolutionary path. During the course of a cooperative evolution, a planetary ecosystem is established where virtually all life works in cooperation with each other. Competition between different species is almost non-existent.

"This evolutionary path has created a life-form and ecosystem which is completely alien to us. Many words and concepts which we take for granted do not exist in the Kyrra society. For example, the Kyrra, at one time, knew nothing of locks, keys, security systems, or other such devices. Through their observation of other species, the Kyrra have learned to understand these concepts to a limited extent.

"In general, the Kyrra are absolutely non-violent and do not pose a threat to Alliance security. On the other hand, because of their evolutionary background, they are ill-equipped to deal with other species and they have attempted to remain isolated. They would be unable to adapt to our society if they were to attempt to do so."

After this summary Stricklen said, "I have called this meeting now because the computer has established a language translation with the Kyrra. I have been informed that there are five Kyrra who have been released from stasis and they are willing to speak to us. Two of them have been learning our language almost as fast as the translation has been developed. I wanted the entire senior staff to be witness to this first-contact meeting between the Alliance and the Kyrra. Are there any questions before we begin?"

"What is the condition of Falnath and McCallister?" Commander Kovalesky, the security officer, asked.

"According to the Kyrra they are well. We have not yet been allowed to speak to them either directly or indirectly yet but, given what the computer has told us, I tend to believe them."

"Where did this information come from?" Scarboro asked. "I can't even begin to conceive of the sort of ecosystem that could develop from a cooperative evolutionary process. Sounds like something they made up to me."

Stricklen passed the question off to the ship's computer. "The information was obtained during the data interchange between myself and the Kyrra computer while a language translation was being developed. The information is highly consistent, however, there is a very remote possibility that the data was manipulated to present a false image of the Kyrra. I am unable to present any additional information to either confirm or disprove what has been learned."

"We will proceed for the time being with the thought in mind that the Kyrra could be as competitive in nature as we are," Stricklen said. "*Dragon*, open a channel to the Kyrra."

"Channel open," the machine replied and an image of the inside of the stasis chamber appeared on each staff member's private monitor. The five Kyrra were standing together as a group. Two of them removed the educators and handed them to two others who immediately placed them on their own heads. A small distance away the two research scientists waited.

Stricklen had thought long and hard about what his first words would be. He had run over several conversation scenarios in his mind while he had waited for the conference to begin. When the moment arrived, he promptly forgot everything he had thought he would say and instead said, "I am Captain Ken Stricklen of the Alliance heavy-cruiser *Komodo Dragon*. On behalf of the Galactic Alliance I would like to welcome you. Please be assured we wish you no harm."

One of the Kyrra who had just recently removed his educator stepped forward and said in clear, although slightly exaggerated speech, "I am Trel'mara. I assume the phrase 'Alliance heavy-cruiser *Komodo Dragon*' means we are aboard a spacecraft. Where are you taking us? What has become of our transport ship?"

Stricklen glanced at the others in the room. He knew they were all thinking the same thing. *These Kyrra don't beat around the bush.* Out loud he said, "Your transport ship was destroyed during a battle with a hostile race which has been attacking our outposts. You are being taken to a safe place on a planet within the Alliance. Tell me, why were you drifting in space?"

"Our ship experienced a drive system malfunction. We placed ourselves in stasis until help could arrive. From the length of time we have been in stasis it is apparent that help did not arrive as planned. May we see star-charts to determine our location?"

Stricklen thought about that for a moment then replied, "I shall have our computer transfer star-chart information to your computer. I see you are not using a vocoder but are speaking our language directly. How did you manage to learn it so fast?"

"The Kyrra are an old race. Many hundreds of years ago we evolved to the point where each of us has perfect memory recall. We crave knowledge and understanding. The ability to remember everything without error has enabled us to learn and understand more. Our computer taught us your language using methods by which learning is performed quickly." Trel'mara gestured towards the two who now wore the educators and continued. "These two are now learning your language through the use of a helmet which presents both visual and audible information to its wearer at a high rate of speed. What type of vessel are we aboard?"

"The *Komodo Dragon* is a warship. It was built to protect the Alliance against the aggressive acts of others. We understand that your people are non-aggressive, but I would like to know why a force-field has been set up around your stasis chamber."

"The force field was automatically established by the stasis control system during field shutdown as a precautionary measure in order to protect the environmental integrity of the chamber. I will drop the field if we will not be harmed."

"I assure you, we have no intentions of harming you," Stricklen said. "Please drop your force field and allow my researchers to leave. If you wish, you may remain in the stasis chamber and several of us will come there so we may continue this meeting in person."

Trel'mara consulted with the other Kyrra. "That is acceptable," he said after a moment. "We would like to meet with a limited number of your people. We will drop the force field and allow your researchers to leave." The other Kyrra who had been educated in the Alliance language started to walk over to the computer but stopped when Stricklen said, "Wait! Your force field represented a possible threat to us and I have posted armed marines around it's perimeter. Do not drop your field until I issue them orders to remain where they are."

Stricklen quickly sent orders via Commander Kovalesky to have the marine detachment remain at their posts and take to no action when the force field is dropped. Satisfied that his orders had been delivered, the Captain said, "Trel'mara, you may drop your force field now."

The Kyrra who had first started forward walked over and spoke to the computer. The force field vanished.

Stricklen adjourned the meeting after informing the ship's psychologist and the chief engineer that they would be accompanying him to the stasis chamber. Commander Kovalesky complained that he had not been invited but Stricklen stood his ground. Sorbith decided not to attend, stating that his non-biological appearance may affect the outcome of the meeting. Stricklen assumed Falnath would refuse to leave so he mentally included her as well.

A few minutes later, Ken stepped into the now inactive stasis chamber and introduced himself and the others to the five aliens. One of the Kyrra stepped forward and introduced itself as Trel'mara. As predicted, Falnath had elected to remain. To everyone's surprise, so did McCallister. Once the introductions had been completed, Ken suggested that the meeting be moved out into the hanger bay where there was more room. The Kyrra discussed this suggestion amongst themselves for a moment and then agreed that only the two who had been educated in the Alliance language would leave. The others would remain and continue their education. Ken ordered the marines to set up enough folding chairs to accommodate everyone and then had them clear the hanger bay. Once the marines had left, the group moved into the more spacious area and got down to business.

Stricklen and the others spent most of the rest of the night talking to the Kyrra. Two hours after the meeting first started two others, having completed their course in Alliance common speech, joined them. As they talked, Ken began to believe what the computer had said was true. He learned a great deal about them and they, in turn, learned a great deal about the Alliance. The Kyrra declined Ken's offer to assign them staterooms. At 0700 the now very tired but excited group broke up. Although he was very tired, Stricklen felt he needed to hold a high level conference to discuss the results of the meeting as soon as possible.

"Doug," Ken said into his wrist-com as soon as the XO had answered his call. "There is to be a senior staff meeting in the conference room in one hour. I want representatives of all senior staff to be present and representatives from the Tholtaran flagship as well. Most especially, I want Sorbith to be there. I'm going to go freshen up and I don't want to be bothered until then."

"Understood Sir! Scarboro out."

Stricklen forced his tired body to ignore the soft-looking bunk as he passed by it on the way to the shower. As the cool water seemed to wash away at least part of his tiredness, Stricklen started composing what he would say at the meeting. The story they had to tell was almost unbelievable.

Chapter 8

"Report," the council leader ordered.

"Attack force MK-114 has been destroyed," the Chroniech fleet commander reported. "Several ships of unknown type were detected but fled prior to our arrival. I have scanned what remains of the ship of the ancients and have found nothing. The pieces are being retrieved for closer examination. I await your orders."

The council leader did not hesitate. "Leave one ship to continue the retrieval. Locate and destroy the ships which were in the area prior to your arrival. When you have completed the task return to base."

"Orders received. The will of the council will be executed. I serve with honor," the commander intoned.

The instantaneous communications link closed and the council leader turned to the rest of the six Chroniech in the room. "The creatures calling themselves the Alliance have discovered an artifact of the ancients and have taken it. We all know the legends concerning the power possessed by the ancients. If the artifact that was taken is a weapon, then the enemy are now in possession of a vastly superior force and our plans for their extinction are in jeopardy. We must act now before they can learn to harness the power they have discovered. Is this agreed?"

All members of the council were of the same clan level and therefore could speak to each other as relative equals. The leader was recognized as such only because he was the head of his clan and his clan currently was in control of more territory than any of the others.

"Clan Tzalmlak agrees. I pledge all available ships and men toward this objective. The Alliance creatures must be eliminated to preserve Chroniech purity," one member said. The others echoed this pledge until a unanimous agreement had been reached.

The leader then said, "The council has reached agreement. All attack forces will be rescheduled immediately and additional forces added as they arrive. The extermination plan will be modified as needed. This ruling is effective immediately."

The council members then turned to the grisly task of laying out their plans for the extermination of the Alliance.

* * * * *

The conference room was packed with members of the senior staff and representatives from the science team. Stricklen looked around the room and was glad to see that both Sorbith and Fleet Commander Trist were in attendance. He stood up and motioned for silence. The dull roar of dozens of separate conversations died down until only the soft rustle of clothing could be heard. Even though Stricklen's shower had helped a little he still looked and felt fatigued.

"This meeting is being recorded," he began. "At its conclusion, the recording and all other information which we have obtained concerning the Kyrra will be transmitted to sector command. Much of what you are about to hear will surprise you; some of it will shock you; and some of it you may not even believe. I am also absolutely certain that many of you will not agree with some of the actions that I have taken. This is going to be a one-way meeting because I have been up all night and, quite frankly, I am dead tired. I will present the information that I have learned and the meeting will end. There are no exceptions to this. No questions will be allowed.

"Before I begin, I wish to inform everyone of a situation which has come to my attention within the last ten minutes. We recently received word that the ships which were left behind after the battle have been forced to leave earlier than expected. A larger group of ships was detected approaching and the group commander decided not to engage them in combat.

"The transmission also included a bit of information which is alarming from a logistics point of view. A recording device was retrieved from one of the Chroniech ships and some of the records were still intact. A playback of these recordings suggests the Chroniech may have a method of instantaneous communications across interstellar distances. If this is true, they have a tactical advantage over us which will be very difficult to surmount. At present, the communications device used to accomplish this has not been discovered among any of the recovered wreckage. I will provide additional information as it becomes available.

"As you have all heard, about an hour ago I concluded a long meeting with the Kyrra. A total of five have been released from stasis and are now our guests. They are: Trel'mara, who is a communications engineer; El'Narra and Nordlatak who are both biologists; Norgoola, a field dynamics expert and also the pilot of the cargo ship; and Tee'Chea, a construction engineer. Most of our talk centered around the history of both our cultures. Theirs is a very interesting history.

"Thousands of years ago, the Kyrra race had achieved a level of technology which allowed them to begin the exploration of space. After discovering faster-than-light drive, the Kyrra began to explore the surrounding star systems. Eventually, they found a planet which harbored life. They were very lucky that this life was not intelligent because what they found shocked them.

"Violence and aggressive behavior was something unknown and totally alien to the Kyrra. They had discovered a planet in which wild animals regularly fought with each other to the death. After a crew member was killed by one of these animals, the exploration team quickly left the surface. Over the years, the Kyrra managed to understand this aggressive behavior and, as they explored more and more planets, they learned this was the norm for all other life. The Kyrra reasoned that if this were the case for primitive life, then it might also be the same for more intelligent life. This worried them greatly. It was eventually decided they would not contact any other intelligent species for fear of their possible aggressive behavior.

"At first, the Kyrra remained content to stay within the confines of their own star system. It was feared that their risk of discovery by other space-capable cultures would be increased if they continued their explorations. Eventually, after nearly two hundred years, Kyrra technology reached a point where they could build probes which were virtually impossible to detect. They built a large number of automated probes which were then sent out to explore the surrounding star systems. As the technological sophistication and knowledge of the Kyrra grew, the probes became more and more advanced. Over the course of the next hundred years, several intelligent, space-faring races were discovered and observed from a distance. It soon became apparent to the Kyrra that a large number of space-capable cultures existed.

"Then, one day, a probe encountered an object which, until then, had somehow avoided detection. The Kyrra were shocked to discover that a small neutron star was approaching their star system and there was nothing they could do to avoid the destruction that would result by its passing. The Kyrra race had roughly two hundred years to survive.

"The resources of the entire Kyrra population were directed towards finding a way of saving their race. The Kyrra needed to find a new home. The probes which had been previously launched were reprogrammed to begin searching for this new home. This was a mistake which the Kyrra would eventually regret because this reprogramming caused the probes to purposefully search for areas of space which seemed to be devoid of existing space-capable cultures. This prevented the Kyrra from keeping track of the activities of the existing space-faring races which they had previously discovered.

"Colonizing a habitable planet was out of the question because of the aggressive nature of the life which would already exist on that world. The Kyrra realized their best hope would be to find a suitable uninhabited planet which they could terraform for their own use. They also realized that terraforming a new world would require hundreds of years and a method of sustaining their population while this was taking place was needed. Years of research finally resulted in the development of the time stasis device. The time stasis device offered a solution as to what to do with the population until a suitable home could be created.

"In addition to the thousands of probes that were now exploring all nearby space, it was decided that a group of exploration ships would be sent out as well to look for a possible new home world for the Kyrra. These manned ships would follow up on possible targets located by the probes. Until the new world could be made habitable, the vast majority of their people would be held in stasis. Because of the approaching neutron star, the population could not be placed in stasis anywhere within their own star system. A planetoid orbiting a nearby star in an otherwise featureless system was chosen to become the temporary resting place of the Kyrra people. To prevent detection from other space explorers, the time stasis devices were shielded and placed deep underground. The removal of the population began.

"Forty-three years before the neutron star was to pass through their system, an exploration ship from another race discovered the Kyrra home world. This was an event which the Kyrra had hoped would never happen. The initial contact with the explorers was peaceful. They claimed to be from a race which, like the Kyrra, desired only knowledge. However, before the ship had left, more ships arrived in the form of an invasion force. The Kyrra quickly discovered that the supposedly peaceful explorers were in fact a race of slavers.

"The Slavers invaded the Kyrra home world, destroying cities, manufacturing complexes and anything else they considered a threat to their domination. As the invasion began, the Kyrra reacted quickly and warned their exploration ships of the attack. Because of their nonviolent nature, the Kyrra did not have any weapons and could offer no resistance against the invaders.

"The Slavers quickly learned that Kyrra technology was vastly superior to their own. The Slavers, however, were unable to comprehend the Kyrra technology because for generations they had relied upon the technology and works of their slave races to provide them with advanced weapons and ships. The Slavers attempted to force the Kyrra to turn their technology into weapons. When the Kyrra refused, the Slavers began a period of torment. Hundreds of thousands of Kyrra died during the Slaver occupation. But the Kyrra learned quickly and the Slavers had problems of their own to worry about.

"The Slaver empire (which had encompassed an enormous volume of space) was quickly coming apart. Subject races had been rebelling against their masters for several years and a few of them had managed to actually force the Slavers off their worlds. The rebellions, coupled with internal strife among the various Slaver factions, was slowly ripping the vast empire apart. Soon, the number of Slavers on the Kyrra home world began to fall since the Kyrra were considered a 'passive' race and required little supervision to keep them in line. The Slavers needed manpower and weaponry in other areas of their empire.

"The Kyrra took advantage of the reduced number of Slavers. Over the course of many months, several groups built small portable force field generators. Using their advanced robotic assembly lines, the Kyrra eventually constructed thousands of these devices. After many months of planning and preparation, the Kyrra acted. On the choosen day, as many Kyrra as possible had gathered within the confines of their remaining cities. At a specified time, every force field generator was activated. Within each bubble of force there were Kyrra; sometimes as few as one or two; in others as many as several hundred. Those Kyrra who were not protected ran toward the nearest bubble.

"All Kyrra had been given a device that would allow them to pass through these force fields. Many hundreds were killed by the surprised Slavers as they ran for safety. After a specified period of time, another group of field generators were activated. These generators were far more powerful than the small ones protecting the Kyrra. They produced a force field that covered entire cities. But they were not normal fields of protective energy. After forming, they began to slowly contract, squeezing the air within them.

"As the pressure rose, the Slavers turned their efforts toward escape but nothing they tried allowed them to penetrate the Kyrra shield or slow its collapse. The Slavers eventually succumbed to the pressure and soon were all dead. The city-spanning force fields were then allowed to return to their original diameters. Although the Slavers had been killed, the collapsing fields of energy had also destroyed a significant portion of many cities.

"The entire Kyrra rebellion lasted less than an hour. Those Slavers who had managed to escape, found the Kyrra were now behind an impenetrable force field. Try as they might, no weapon they could apply would penetrate the city-spanning force domes. In their rage against the Kyrra, the Slavers lashed out and destroyed everything on the planet which was not protected. For a short time afterwards, the Slavers continued to test the strength of the Kyrra defenses. Eventually, the problems within the empire forced them to abandon their attacks and finally leave the Kyrra home world all together. The Slavers were pulling all their resources into defending their now shrinking empire. However, before the Slavers left, they decided that if they could not possess the superior technology of the Kyrra, then nobody would.

"The Kyrra watched, helpless to stop them, as the Slavers placed hundreds of fusion bombs around the protected cities. Each city was ringed with at least ten such devices. The rest of the planet was subjected to random bombing from 'dirty' nuclear weapons. Stunned, the Kyrra watched their world die around them as the radioactive fallout from the bombs filled the atmosphere with lethal radiation. The Slavers then detonated the bombs surrounding the protected cities.

"The destructive power produced by the release of a thousand megatons of nuclear weapons is something that cannot be imagined. Ninety eight protected Kyrra cities felt the full force of such destructive power. Seventeen of the cities were destroyed as their force fields collapsed. The rest experienced severe damage as the shock-wave of the explosions produced earthquake-like tremors. When it was all over, and the Slavers had left, the Kyrra evaluated the extent of the damage. Their non-stasis population had been reduced to a little over a quarter of a million, many of whom were injured and would probably die. There were about eleven million Kyrra in stasis deep within a planetoid orbiting a nearby star. The Kyrra home world had been rendered incapable of supporting life.

"After the Slavers had left, the remaining Kyrra repaired one of their long-range communications stations and recalled their exploration ships. While waiting for these ships to arrive, the Kyrra repaired a few of the ships which the Slavers had left behind. They were very lucky that several such ships had been within the confines of their city-wide force fields because stepping outside the protective energy wall would have meant certain death from radiation. Once these ships had been repaired, the Kyrra used them to again begin the transportation of their people to a place of safety. Time was now critical. The neutron star was due to arrive in just under 41 years and there were over a quarter of a million Kyrra still to be moved with only a handful of ships.

"The Kyrra also had another, more pressing problem. Because their world had become a radioactive wasteland, their source of food had been removed. Compatible plants from a nearby star system would have to be used until a hydroponics garden of sufficient capacity could be constructed. The Kyrra were also unable to build any more stasis devices which meant they would have to increase the capacity of the stasis chambers which had already been moved to the planetoid."

The ship the *Komodo Dragon* had discovered was one of the repaired Slaver ships. It was transporting one of the few stasis modules which had survived the Slaver invasion to the planetoid when the drive system malfunctioned. The Kyrra could not risk contacting their own people for fear the signal would be picked up by another race. They reasoned that if they did not arrive as scheduled, another ship would be sent out to search for them. Assuming this might take some time, the crew of the transport ship entered the stasis device. Help never arrived.

"Because of what has happened to them in the past," Stricklen continued, "the Kyrra are reluctant to reveal the exact location of the planetoid where their people were placed in stasis. They are also very cautious in talking about their technological abilities. I did find out some very interesting facts concerning their race.

"The Kyrra are exceptionally long lived. In our terms they have a normal life-span on the average of 380 years. Between 120 and 230 years of life, each Kyrra will produce an average of four children. This means that not only are they long lived but their population grows very slowly. This is probably due to the nature of their ecosystem.

"Another result of this slow growth, long life and lack of racial competition has been that Kyrra technology was very slow to start. The Kyrra claim to have a recorded history going back at least 33,000 years. Once they had achieved a certain level of technology their thirst for knowledge and understanding gave them the desire to improve, and their level of technological sophistication rapidly grew. The five Kyrra who are now our guests come from a civilization that over 45,000 years ago possessed a level of technology which is at least a hundred years more advanced than the best that the Alliance has to offer.

"They do not like to talk about what they can do, but in speaking with them I have learned a little about their abilities. For instance, the stasis field is powered by a matter/anti-matter reactor which uses super-heavy metallic hydrogen as a storage medium for both the reaction masses. This provides the reactor with enough mass to run at its full output of 380 terra-watts for over 50,000 years."

The silence, which had been total until now, was suddenly broken by gasps of disbelief and wonder. Stricklen motioned for silence before continuing. "The Kyrra were also capable of traveling at speeds beyond even our wildest dreams. They had very high speed communications across interstellar space. They understood and could manipulate matter on a sub-atomic scale. If their civilization has survived to this day, then the technology they now possess would appear to us to be nothing less than magical.

"All of their technology, however, did not prevent another race from nearly destroying them. They do not understand violence. It never occurred to them to build devices and weapons to protect themselves from aggressive species such as ours. We are extremely lucky that the Slavers were an ignorant race, because if they had ever realized what sort of technological wonders they were so blindly destroying we would most likely not exist today."

Stricklen stood up to emphasize his last point. "The Kyrra cannot exist in our society. They would remain isolated and would be subjected to endless questions about their advanced technology. The Kyrra's computer has examined the history of the member races of the Alliance and has reached a similar conclusion. Although we are not Slavers, all species which are currently members of the Alliance have had a history of aggressive behavior. It is their belief, and my fear as well, that their continued presence here will result in conflicts within the Alliance as one race after another attempts to gain the knowledge of the Kyrra technology in order to use it to their own advantage. The Kyrra will not allow this to happen and if I have a choice, neither will I."

Ken glanced at Sorbith and could not discern any clues as to how he was reacting to what had just been said. His cybernetic body was as still as a steel I-beam. Stricklen shifted his gaze to Trist and noted that the Tholtaran was close to interrupting him. Ken figured the only reason Trist had not broken his silence was he may be thinking that Stricklen had already discussed this issue with Sorbith and Trist did not want to anger the peacekeeper again. Placing his palms down on the table in front of him, Stricklen continued in a firm voice.

"The Kyrra have requested we provide them with a ship so they can return to their people. In exchange for this ship they will provide us with a set of mathematical equations which more accurately describes the field structure dynamics of the space-time continuum. In time, we will be able to use these new equations to construct faster stardrives and better communication systems. As a representative of the Alliance, I have tentatively agreed to their proposal pending final approval from the Alliance ruling council.

"Until that time, I am declaring the Kyrra guests of the Alliance under my protection and I am ordering all individuals to respect their privacy. Marine guards will enforce this privacy if required. This meeting is over."

Stricklen turned and quickly exited the room before anyone could recover from their shock. As the door was closing behind him he heard the stunned crowd break into an uproar. He did not care what they thought of him at the moment. He had made his decision and all he wanted to do now was sleep. He made it to his stateroom without being intercepted, set the door and intercom controls for privacy, and without bothering to remove his uniform, fell onto his bed and was instantly asleep.

Chapter 9

As soon as the Captain's meeting was over, Doug Scarboro personally checked the placement of the marine guards Stricklen had ordered and found the security arrangements for the Kyrra to be satisfactory. He then briefly checked with the Kyrra to see if they needed anything. Two of them expressed a desire to tour the ship. Doug assigned a marine escort to them and off they went. Scarboro then made his way to the bridge where he was scheduled to begin his watch.

Doug had barely assumed the watch when Sorbith stormed into the room. "Where is the Captain?" he demanded.

"The Captain is asleep in his stateroom," Doug replied keeping his temper under control. "He has been awake for over 24 hours and I do not recommend waking him. Can I help you?"

The cyborg stared at the *Dragon's* XO for a moment before saying in a much calmer voice, "Do you know of any reason why Captain Stricklen has agreed to furnish the Kyrra with a ship? Did he discuss this decision with you?"

"No he did not," Doug replied. "The Captain came to this decision by himself without any input from me. If he were to have asked me though, I believe I would have agreed with him. The Kyrra should not be forced to live in our society against their will. Doing so would be the equivalent of imprisoning them. They may be technologically our superiors but they are under no obligation to share that technology with us."

Sorbith seemed to consider this argument for a moment before replying. "You may be right, but, the Captain had no right to make such a promise to the Kyrra without first clearing it with me. As soon as he wakes I would like to speak with him." After receiving a nod of acknowledgment from Doug, Sorbith turned and departed. The crew of the bridge let out a collective sigh of relief as the doors slid shut behind him.

A moment later, Trist barged onto the bridge and also demanded to see the captain. Doug's response to his request was slightly different. "The Captain has left orders that he is not to be disturbed. I would recommend returning to your ship and I will…"

"We will just see about that!" Trist angrily interrupted and turned to leave.

"I would not attempt to interrupt the Captain's sleep," Scarboro calmly but firmly said. "The marine guarding his door has orders to arrest anyone who attempts to enter his cabin and seeing that this is his ship the Captain's orders will have precedence over anyone else including yourself – Sir."

Trist swung around and angrily glared at Scarboro for several seconds. Doug simply stared back with a questioning look on his face. Finally, Trist turned and angrily exited the bridge muttering a string of Tholtaran curses as he left. Doug smiled at his departing back.

A question had been bothering Doug since the meeting. Ken had mentioned something which he was not familiar with and the question still nagged at him. He decided to rectify his lack of knowledge. "*Dragon* – briefly explain to me what super-heavy metallic hydrogen is."

"Metallic hydrogen is an artificially created form of hydrogen which exists in a metallic state at low temperatures. This material is superconducting and is used throughout the Alliance in applications where low temperature superconductors are required. The material is very costly to produce. The reference to super-heavy most likely refers to the super-heavy form hydrogen."

Doug already knew that much. The computer had not really answered his question. "Explain to me what a super-heavy form of matter is," Doug commanded.

"As you are aware, the more protons and neutrons an atom has the more unstable the element becomes until a point is reached where the atom is so unstable, no additional nucleons can be added because the atom will spontaneously disintegrate. There is a theory which indicates that if an atom could somehow be constructed with a very large number of protons and neutrons a point would be reached where the atom would once again become stable. This has been referred to as the island of stability. Such matter would be extremely dense and, because of the arrangement of the nucleus and electron cloud, may possess physical properties similar to normal matter. It is believed the periodic table of the elements could be repeated, at least in part, by this form of super-heavy matter. To date no theory exists as to how such matter could be created."

"It appears as if the Kyrra have mastered that bit of theory," Doug muttered under his breath. After digesting what he had just learned, Doug turned his attention toward his roll as officer of the watch.

Two and a half hours after Stricklen had retired, the *Mobius* contacted the

Dragon. "We have received a report from the *Rotara-Ahr*." The *Rotara-Ahr*, Doug recalled, was the lead ship of the group which had been left behind to continue salvage operations at the scene of the battle with the Chroniech. "They have picked up a large group of ships in pursuit. Estimated intercept was about two hours. The message was sent about an hour ago."

"How many ships and what type?"

"At least fifteen. Their message stated that the exact types could not be determined accurately but the drive wakes suggest at least two of the ships are battleship class or above. They are out-gunned and there is nothing we can do to help."

Scarboro considered waking the Captain but decided against it; there truly was nothing they could do. A moment later, the bridge door slid open and a marine stepped inside. "Permission to tour the bridge with two guests?" he asked.

Doug granted permission and watched as the two Kyrra entered. Their presence created a small stir of excitement which quickly subsided when the XO displayed a look of displeasure. The marine gave the two Kyrra a brief tour of the bridge, momentarily stopping at each control and monitoring station.

After making a complete circuit of the bridge, the Kyrra approached Scarboro. Doug thought he recognized Trel'mara. One of them asked, "We would like to see the ships which attacked you and destroyed our transport."

Doug replied by saying, "*Dragon*! Display a visual of the Chroniech ships on my monitor."

In response to his command, one of the monitors on the command console came to life and a Chroniech battle-cruiser appeared. The picture had been taken from a distance by one of the other ships during the battle. The two Kyrra looked closely at the warship and conversed between themselves. One of them asked, "There appears to be a marking on the side of the ship. Can you enlarge the image?"

Scarboro looked closely and saw what might be some type of external identification. During the heat of the battle such details had been missed. Doug requested the computer to enlarge and enhance the section of the ship where the marking appeared. The computer replied, "The symbol appears on another ship which was recorded during the battle. A better enhancement can be obtained using that image. Shall I use the better image?"

"Use the best image available," Doug replied. The computer displayed a highly magnified view of one of the Chroniech ships. A blurred symbol appeared on the screen which resolved itself into a clear image in less than a second as the computer enhanced the picture. Doug stared at the symbol for a second then exclaimed, "I'll be damned! Why didn't anyone notice this earlier? *Dragon*, compare the symbol now displayed to the one on the derelict ship."

The screen split and the faint image of the derelict ship's markings appeared on the screen. "Although not identical," the computer said. "The two markings appear similar. There is a very high probability that the two symbols originated from the same race."

"SON–OF–A–BITCH!" Doug remarked in a slow even cadence. Forcing his eyes off the two symbols, he looked at the now frightened Kyrra. "The Chroniech are the descendants of the Slavers," he said in a measured tone.

Both Kyrra were obviously very upset. One of them said, "It appears as if the Slaver empire has recovered from their downfall. Your Alliance is in grave danger."

"Sir," the communications watch began.

Doug, still shaken by the recent discovery, slowly turned toward the communications station. "Yes?"

"The *Mobius* has forwarded a second message from the *Rotara-Ahr*. They have initiated a Lansing escape maneuver. We will be making contact with a support fleet in about 28 hours. The *Mobius* and most of the fleet will then depart in order to attempt a rescue. We have been ordered to continue on to Masfuta with the *General Patton*."

It took Doug's overloaded mind a few moments to make sense of the details of the message. The ships they were to make contact with must be the reinforcements Sorbith had called for. A Lansing escape maneuver was a last ditch effort to save some of the crew. Doug could picture the running Tholtaran fleet in his mind. They would have begun wild course changes, weaving in and out of each other's flight path in a complex pattern. At random intervals an escape pod would be ejected. Eventually, the ships would continue, unmanned, until the Chroniech caught up with them. The ship's computers would then do their best to engage the Chroniech ships in combat.

The Lansing maneuver was named after a British Captain who had managed to save most of his crew using this technique. The reasoning was that the escape pods would be spread across such an enormous volume of space and were so difficult to locate, that the Chroniech would not bother to take the time to find and destroy them all. The *Mobius* would be able to easily find the pods because a special signal would be broadcast causing the escape pods to begin transmitting a homing signal.

Scarboro returned his attention to the Kyrra. "Tell me what you know about the Chroniech."

"In our time," the Kyrra began. "The Slavers were the most aggressive species we had discovered. Little is known of their social structure. There were reports of Slavers fighting with other Slavers, sometimes resulting in death. They seemed to find pleasure in causing pain to others, including members of their own race. This behavior is beyond our ability to comprehend.

"We also noticed that some of them appeared to command more authority than others. We observed some Slavers falling to the ground in the presence of these more superior individuals, while others simply lowered their head or did nothing at all. I observed one individual who did not notice when one of these superior Slavers entered a room. That individual was severely punished. I have also been told that two of these superior Slavers were observed to engage in combat with each other for unknown reasons."

"From your description, I would say the Chroniech had a clan-based social structure. If they are actually descendants of the Slavers of your time, then their empire must have fallen to the point where their society existed on a very primitive level. Since they claimed your ship belonged to them, I would say that at least some memory of their past still exists in the form of legend."

"That seems reasonable," the Kyrra replied. "We have noted that Slavers seem not to understand a good portion of the technology they were using. They relied upon their slave races to build and maintain their ships and weapons. The Slavers appeared more concerned with themselves and maintaining their control."

The Kyrra left the bridge and continued their tour of the ship. Scarboro again considered waking his Captain and again decided there was no need to do so. He did, however, contact Sorbith and explain to him what they had discovered. The Peacekeeper was also surprised that nobody else had noticed the similarity. The remainder of Doug's watch went smoothly. He was eventually relieved by the Operations officer. After being relieved, Doug stopped by the Captain's cabin. The privacy indicator was still set and the marine guard indicated that the Captain was apparently still asleep. Doug left a message for Stricklen to contact him as soon as he was awake.

Three hours later, the Captain found Scarboro in the engineering section watching several mechanics as they disassembled one of the ship's auxiliary fusion reactors. Stricklen looked refreshed and was in a much better mood. "I kind of figured I would find you down here," the Captain remarked. "Still want to be an engineer I see."

"I think I would enjoy it more than pushing paper all day," Scarboro replied. "You look much better sir."

"I feel much better. You left a message for me to contact you as soon as I was able—what's up?"

Scarboro brought Stricklen up-to-date on the latest developments including Sorbith's demand to see him. When he had finished, Stricklen said, "I'm glad you let me sleep. I'm not too sure how I would have reacted to all this news while I was still tired. When is the *General Patton* due to arrive?"

"We should be within detector range in another 17 hours. As soon as we have a confirmed detector lock on the *General Patton* the *Mobius* will depart. We are still about three days out from Masfuta. Care to join me for a cup of coffee in the mess?"

"Sounds good, but we had better invite Sorbith. By the way, I want to start thinking about how we are going to provide adequate security for our Kyrra guests once we arrive. I'm sure there will be a large number of dignitaries wanting to impress them with their desire to learn. You and I both know what they will really want is to get their hands on some of the Kyrra technology."

The two friends headed off toward the mess hall as they continued their discussion. They did not even make it out of the engineering section before Stricklen's com-link demanded his attention. "Stricklen," he replied.

"Commander Tacket sir. Communications has just received a message which I think you need to view right away. It's from the Hess."

Scarboro could not hear the message from the bridge but he did hear Stricklen's startled response. "The Hess! Are you sure this is not some sort of hoax? The Hess don't send messages to Alliance ships, in fact they don't send messages to anyone."

"The authenticity of the message has been confirmed. It arrived under captain's seal."

"Very well, I'll take it in my cabin, Stricklen out."

Ken turned to his XO and said, "The Hess have sent us a message, can you believe this! We are carrying five guests who are forty-five thousand years old. We have been attacked by an alien race which is almost as old as our guests. And now, the mysterious Hess, who never seem to want to talk to anyone, have sent us a message. I'm waiting for God himself to appear to deliver the punch line because this sure seems like one enormous joke to me."

Scarboro had a confused look on his face. "Who are the Hess?" he asked.

Stricklen stopped dead in his tracks and turned to stare at his XO. "You mean to tell me you have never heard of the Hess?"

"I have no idea who they are."

"Let's swing by the mess and get that coffee then head for my cabin. I'll explain on the way. I want us both to hear that message," Stricklen replied. As they walked, he told Doug about a mysterious race known as the Hess.

Toward the end of the Human-Alliance war, a damaged Omel warship took refuge in a star system where they felt nobody would attempt to pursue them. The system consisted of three planets in orbit about a magnetar powered pulsar. The beams of gamma radiation emitted by the pulsar were angled about thirty-five degrees off the plane of the planetary orbits placing the planets close to but not inside the path of the beam. Entering a pulsar's complex gravitational and electromagnetic field pose a significant challenge to the navigational capabilities of starships. The magnetar's extreme magnetic field made navigation all that harder. Luckily, the navigational skills of the ship's helm were up to the task and they managed to establish an orbit around the outer planet without incidence. Once safely hidden, the ship's crew could shutdown their reactors and began their repairs.

As they were conducting repairs, one of the crew pointed the ship's instruments toward the second planet. He was shocked when he discovered possible signs of life. A series of large structures were spotted on the planet's surface. The civilization must have been ancient, since the star would have destroyed all life in the system when it went nova and became a pulsar. The Captain decided to send a probe over for a quick look.

Before the probe had made much progress toward the second planet a voice in perfect Omel hailed them. The signal was traced to the second planet. It warned them not to approach the planet or retaliatory action would be taken. Not knowing what sort of new culture they had discovered, and because of the degraded condition of his ship, the Captain ordered the probe to return.

The Omel Captain explained that their ship was in need of repairs and asked permission to remain in orbit around the third planet until those repairs could be completed. The inhabitants of the planet responded and identified themselves as the Hess. They allowed the Omel ship to remain in orbit long enough for them to complete their repairs. No further contact with the Hess was established until several years later when they contacted the Alliance. During the interim, several expeditions had been sent to the planet in an attempt to establish contact but all were turned back either by a very powerful repulsor beam or in one instance a weapon of irresistible force.

After multiple failed attempts at contact, some even from privately funded groups, the Hess contacted the Alliance. The Hess wanted to be left alone and asked the Alliance to station a ship near their system to keep others away. In return, the Hess offered their knowledge of mathematics. The Alliance agreed and they soon discovered the Hess were unbelievably well versed in mathematics. Nothing else is known about them. No Hess has ever been seen and virtually nothing about them is known. It is believed they are silicon based life forms, but it is only a theory. Contact with the Hess has always been sporadic and on their terms.

As soon as they entered his stateroom, Stricklen performed the necessary security actions to have the message decoded and displayed. As with all Hess messages, this one was text only. The two stared at it in disbelief.

****

STRONGLY REQUEST THAT KOMODO DRAGON IMMEDIATELY DIVERT TO SHAULAR. PERMISSION GRANTED FOR PLANETARY LANDING OF KYRRA AND NO MORE THAN TWO ALLIANCE REPRESENTATIVES.

****

The message was short, to the point, and completely unexplainable. After more than a minute of silence, Stricklen reached over and pushed the button which connected him to the bridge. "I need to see Sorbith in my cabin—now," he said.

"Doug, I had better see Sorbith alone. I'm sure he's going to have some interesting things to say to me when he gets here."

'I understand. I hope you're still the Captain after he's done talking."

Sorbith arrived a few minutes after Scarboro had departed, read the message once, turned to Stricklen, and said, "Alter course to Shaular immediately. I will contact the *Mobius* and have them continue with the rescue operation as planned. Have your helm compute a new rendezvous ETA and intercept course for the *General Patton* and relay the new course information to them."

Stricklen was dumbfounded. "Are you sure we want to do that? I know it's not supposed to be possible, but what if the message is faked? This kind of a request from the Hess simply does not make any sense."

"It is impossible to fake this message. Each originator encrypts their message with a unique algorithm and code. It can only be decoded if the decryption key for that specific originator is used. This ensures not only the security of the message but also validates the origin. The keys and the encryption methods were developed by the most capable minds of the Alliance and the algorithm has been checked by the Hess. Knowing the request is genuine, do you understand its significance?"

"Are you referring to the fact that, until now, the Hess home world has been strictly off-limits or that even though we have had contact with the Hess for over forty years we still have never seen one? Yes, I understand the significance of their request which is why I must question it. Why are the Hess so interested in the Kyrra that they would be willing to break their long standing isolation in order to meet them? Not only that, but the question must be raised as to how the Hess even know about the Kyrra."

"I cannot answer your questions," Sorbith said. "The only way we are going to know the answer is to honor their request. I have the authority to order the course change. Please carry out my instructions."

Stricklen ordered the course change and, after the navigator plotted the course, was surprised to find they were more than three weeks away from the Hess home world. He had forgotten just how far away their planet was from their current location. Ken turned his attention back to Sorbith after the order had been given and asked, "I had a message that you wanted to see me?"

"Yes. Why did you take it upon yourself to offer the services of a starship to the Kyrra so they could return home?"

Stricklen had known the decision he made was a controversial one. He needed to be very careful how he answered this question since the peacekeeper had the authority to remove him from command if he felt he had overstepped his authority. Ken had, however, thought through his response well in advance. "During the initial contact meeting with the Kyrra I learned they have a deep seated fear of other cultures. In my opinion, they are so afraid of us that the only thing on their mind is how to avoid any contact with us. Because they need our help to find their way home they had no choice but to ask us for our help. As the senior first contact representative present I decided it would be best to offer them a ship in order to give them some hope of returning home. When such a ship is provided, they may feel obligated to offer us some of their technology in return."

Sorbith considered the explanation for a moment then said, "Your reasoning seems sound, however, in the future you will check with higher authority before making any similar offers. Starships are not something we simply give away."

Sorbith turned and walked out of the cabin. After breathing a sigh of relief, Ken called Scarboro and asked him to meet him in the mess hall. "I see you still have your rank," Doug said as Ken sat down with his cup of coffee and breakfast.

"Very funny," Ken replied. "So what's your opinion on this message from the Hess?"

"Since I am not familiar with the mysterious Hess, I'm afraid I won't be of much help," Doug replied.

Try as they might, neither Ken nor Doug could figure out why the Hess would want to see the Kyrra. If they were so interested in speaking with them, why didn't the Hess simply grant permission to orbit their planet? Ken and Doug mutually decided to have a talk with the Kyrra.

On the way to the hanger bay, Stricklen contacted his most capable helmsman and informed her they would be entering the Hess system. Stricklen advised her that the approach would be tricky and dangerous because of the presence of the pulsar and ordered her to begin running simulations in order to come up with the best possible approach vector. Ken then told Doug that he wanted their best crew to be on watch during the approach.

The Kyrra were inside their now non-operational stasis chamber. They had refused several offers for other living quarters, and instead preferred to remain inside the chamber. Falnath was, as usual, working at the scientific scanner in the control section of the stasis device. She was so involved in her work she seemed oblivious of the visitors. Doug and Ken announced their presence to the Kyrra and were invited into the structure. This was the first time Doug had actually been inside the stasis chamber.

The inside of the chamber was a sphere approximately seven meters in diameter. The stasis chamber was divided into three sections. The upper two meters consisted mostly of storage compartments which the Kyrra said were filled with food and other items. The central area was just under three meters in height and contained sixteen small, cramped, hammock-like bunks and a tiny private area which served as a bathroom. The lower two meters contained a power source and the air and water recycling equipment. In effect, the stasis chamber was a small, very cramped, self contained environment.

Doug wondered why such an elaborate life support system was needed inside a time stasis machine. The Kyrra explained that the device did not stop time, only slowed it down by a huge factor. Trel'mara and the others had been in stasis for 44,881 years, yet according to them only fourteen days had passed. This meant the stasis chamber could slow time by a factor of about 1.7 million. Doug also learned that the occupants of the stasis chamber were completely isolated from the outside with no way to turn the field off once it had been turned on.

After the brief tour, Ken told the Kyrra about the message from the Hess. The Kyrra replied that they had no idea who the Hess were, so Ken also told them all he knew about the mysterious race. "Although their behavior seems strange," El'Narra said. "It does suggest the Hess may also be a very advanced race similar to my own people who do not desire contact with other races. Our probes had not made it to this area of space when we entered stasis. There is a chance the Hess are aware of my race and they are simply offering their help in returning us to our people."

"Do you really believe your people are still in existence?" Scarboro asked.

"Yes, the Slaver empire was disintegrating and we had re-established control over our planet. The other races of the Slaver empire were more interested in fighting with the Slavers and were paying us no attention. Most of our people had been placed into stasis and no decision as to the location of our new home had been made. I have no doubt, however, that my people are thriving on their new world."

"How will you find them?" Stricklen asked. "It sounds to me as if they will go to extraordinary measures in order to prevent themselves from being found. Do you have any idea at all as to where they might be located?"

"No we do not. We have discussed this problem among ourselves at great length and we believe we can eventually regain contact with our people. To increase the chances of a successful mission, we have completed the specifications for the ship which we will need. Your ship's computer has the information. Has your government made a decision concerning our request?"

"No word has been received. You must realize that decisions like the one you are asking will not be made quickly. I do not expect an answer for at least another several more days. I will instruct our computer to forward the specifications to the council. As soon as an answer is received I will let you know. Can you at least give us an idea as to the general area of space you will be searching? It will help us in ensuring that a ship capable of making the journey is provided."

"We will have our computer forward the information to your system."

The two officers continued their discussion with the Kyrra for another twenty minutes. They emerged from the cramped living quarters without having had any of their questions answered. Outside the stasis chamber Scarboro made a suggestion. "I recommend we drop to normal as soon as we are within decent two-way communications range and contact the Hess to get them to answer our questions. I don't know about you, but this just doesn't feel right."

Stricklen thought about it for a minute then said, "Sounds like a good idea. I'll bounce it off Sorbith and see what he says. Lord knows I don't want the wrath of a peacekeeper to come raining down on me for making another wrong decision."

The two friends parted company. Ken made his way to the bridge so he could perform his duties as Captain of the *Dragon*, while Doug remained behind. Scarboro approached Falnath who still had not noticed his presence. After watching her for a few minutes he said, "May I have a word with you?"

Falnath made a few more adjustments on the controls then turned toward the Human. "I am very busy. If you think it is important then I will take the time to speak with you."

"I was only wondering if you had made any progress at all at figuring out any of the Kyrra technology," Doug said.

"Very little," she replied. "The basic operation of the power reactor is solvable but the question as to how they managed to produce the fuel is something the Kyrra will have to give us. The ability to create so much anti-matter in such a stable form is far beyond our capability. Even the existence of super-heavy elements has been only a theoretical possibility. The Kyrra have not only managed to create anti-matter but have created it in a form that we cannot duplicate even in normal matter. I have, instead, concentrated upon the time-stasis device since this is where my expertise lies. The technology involved is extraordinarily complex. It will require a great deal of time before we understand how the device works."

"Will we ever be able to build one?"

"Not for many years. Their technology is too far advanced."

Scarboro was confused. "What do you mean? Once you know how it works all we have to do is to apply the same methods and we can construct a similar device."

The scientist turned her large penetrating eyes toward him. "I do not think you understand," she said as if beginning a lecture to a small child. "Let us assume that you were transported back to the past as it existed two hundred years ago. A scientist from that era asks you about the workings of a stardrive. You just happen to have with you the complete technical plans for the stardrive and you willingly give them to this scientist. He takes the plans to his government and presents the plans to them announcing that they can now go to the stars. Is he correct?"

Doug thought about the question for a moment, then said, "I don't think so. The manufacturing abilities of the time would be incapable of building the components. The technological and engineering abilities would not yet exist. An entire industry would have to be created before a single part could begin to be built. I think I see your point."

"You now see that receiving advanced technology from another race is not as easy as you might think. Unless you already have the abilities to use the knowledge, the information is practically useless. That is the case with the technology of the Kyrra. We know the outer sphere of the stasis chamber consists of a single, integrated, precisely machined equivalent of a giant microchip. We can duplicate most of the circuitry on a small scale, but we do not have the technological abilities to duplicate the actual device. We may understand it, but we can't build it."

Scarboro understood now. On a smaller scale, he knew, down to the last detail, how a fusion reactor worked, yet he could never construct one with his own hands because he did not possess the mechanical knowledge and abilities. He thanked Falnath and left her to her work.

Sorbith listened to Ken's suggestion about dropping out of stardrive a good distance from Shaular and couldn't find any reason to reject it. The *Komodo Dragon* eventually made contact with the Human dreadnought *General Patton* and the two ships continued on to the Hess home world.

Ken took the time to ask the computer to display the target area provided by the Kyrra where they believed their people to be located. He was shocked to discover that it was over 3000 light years away and involved travelling through suspected Chroniech space. This changed everything! Instead of a simple spacecraft outfitted for a short journey, they would need a large, very powerful warship supplied and equipped for a year long journey. Stricklen put in a call to Sorbith and told him about what he had just discovered. Sorbith said he would look into it, and disconnected.

Shortly after making the course change, a torrent of messages had begun arriving. As soon as the officials who had been waiting for the arrival of the

Kyrra discovered that the *Dragon* had made yet another change in destination they started filing complaints. Stricklen told the communications watch to forward all such messages to Sorbith; after all, he was the one who had ordered the course change. Eventually a message arrived from Masfuta. It was a personal message directed to the Captain from the base commander and it read:

****
WE ARE CATCHING HELL FOR YOUR DECISION TO MAKE THE COURSE CHANGE TO SHAULAR. EVERY DIGNITARY WITHIN A FIFTEEN LIGHT YEAR RADIUS WHO COULD COMMANDEER A SHIP IS HERE. I UNDERSTAND THE DECISION WAS NOT YOURS BUT IF ANYTHING HAPPENS TO THE KYRRA, I WILL HOLD YOU PERSONALLY RESPONSIBLE. AS SOON AS YOU CAN, GET YOUR ASS BACK HERE! CAPTAIN WILLIAM ROSEWOOD (BASE COMMANDER)
****

Stricklen chuckled when he read the message. He and Captain Rosewood had served on the same ship years ago as junior officers and they had remained good friends ever since. He had no idea that his old friend had become the base commander at Masfuta. Ken had assumed William was still in command of a ship somewhere.

Three other important messages arrived while the *Dragon* was en route to Shaular. The first was from the *Mobius* saying they had recovered most of the escape pods. The Chroniech had caught up with and destroyed the Alliance ships. They hadn't bothered to search very long for the escape pods and all but two had been recovered.

The second message was from sector command. This message indicated that an increase in Chroniech activity near the outer border of the Alliance had been detected. Two military bases and an agricultural research center had been attacked along with several ships. Sector command had issued a general alert and was requesting that fleet command send reinforcements.

The last message was from the Alliance grand council. They had agreed to provide the Kyrra with a ship and all supplies necessary for the trip. Ken doubted they knew where the Kyrra intended on going. He made a mental note to discuss this with them as soon as he could.

* * * * *

The ships dropped out of stardrive about a light-year from their destination. The course they had taken had brought them in above the plane of the radiation field emitted from the pulsar. Since the beam was highly directional, the *Dragon* and her escort were quite safe.

"Logistics, give me a scan of the system. Concentrate on the second planet and put the results on the main screen," Stricklen ordered.

The main navigational display changed to a computer simulation of the Hess star system. A single, tiny star was shown surrounded by three planets. There was a noticeably large distance between the pulsar and the first planet. When the star had gone supernova it had not only transformed the original star into a pulsar but had also apparently destroyed any planets which had existed in close orbits. Stricklen knew the pulsar did not shine like a normal star. The pulsar which now ruled the star system was a tiny sphere no larger than a small planet. Instead of shining, this star now radiated its energy in the forms of two incredibly intense beams of radio frequency radiation as it spun on its axis at a rate of over 3 times a second.

Various planetary data was displayed on the screen, remained for a moment, and then faded away as the focus was shifted to Shaular. Stricklen emitted a low whistle as the planet's data appeared. "What do you make of that electromagnetic signature?" Stricklen asked Sorbith who was on the bridge.

"Far too complex to be natural," Sorbith replied. "The field was not there when the Omel first discovered the Hess but appeared immediately thereafter. The field structure and power output are unique in all of explored space. All attempts at trying to determine the source have failed. No analysis of the field dynamics has yielded any sort of intelligence or pattern. The origin and purpose of the field remains a mystery."

"Kim, do we have a safe approach vector?" Stricklen asked his top helmsman.

The helmsman turned from her own computer display and said, "Yes sir. The planet is outside the pulsar's beam and I have computed an approach which will keep us clear of it."

"Captain, incoming audio message from the Hess," the communications station reported.

"Let's hear it," Stricklen ordered.

"You have been identified as the Alliance heavy-cruiser *Komodo Dragon*," a monotonous voice said. "Permission has already been granted for a planetary approach and landing. A beacon has been activated on the surface for you to home in on. Once on the surface, a force field will protect your shuttle from the pulsar's radiation. The *Komodo Dragon* is to remain in orbit using the mass of our world as a shield against the pulsar. The dreadnought *General Patton* and the scoutship *Tri-Star* must remain at the previously agreed upon distance of one million standard kilometers. Proceed on course."

"This is Captain Ken Stricklen of the *Komodo Dragon*," Stricklen said. "Before proceeding, we would like to know why the Hess have broken their long standing policy of isolation in order to see the Kyrra? Never before have the Hess allowed an Alliance ship to approach their home world. This change of policy has given us concern for the safety of the Kyrra. If you could send a representative to us we would feel more comfortable about proceeding with a planetary landing. I also must inform you that we will be making planet-fall with the *Tri-Star* instead of a shuttle since the shuttle does not have a defense shield."

Stricklen paused for a moment then asked, "*Dragon*, What is the communications delay at this distance?"

The computer's response was instantaneous. "One way travel time for the message is 1 minute, 4.316 seconds."

"Then we have about three minutes before they reply," Ken said to nobody in particular.

After about three minutes, the reply was received. "It is impossible for the Hess to leave the surface of this planet. The Hess is very ancient. It is believed the Hess may have had contact with the Kyrra at some time in the past. This can only be determined by close examination of the Kyrra. The Hess is peaceful, and has never engaged in harmful activities in the past. Permission for planetary landing of the Alliance scout ship *Tri-Star* is granted. The *Komodo Dragon* is allowed to assume a parking orbit. We again request you proceed on course."

Sorbith looked directly at the Captain, he had a bewildered look on his face. Even though his body was cybernetic, he still had a face that could show emotions. "That message came back far too fast. Just a moment and I'll have my ship run a check."

The peacekeeper stood silent for about ten seconds. Stricklen knew he was using the biolink to speak to his ship. The biolink, as Stricklen understood it, was an implanted bioelectrical interface between the peacekeeper's brain and his ship allowing the two to communicate by thought alone. "I thought so!" he finally said. "Our message required 64.316 seconds to travel from us to the Hess. Their reply, which was on a higher speed carrier, required 58.0704 seconds to make the return trip. Total travel time was therefore 122.3864 seconds. We received their reply 122.4784 seconds after we sent our message. This is a difference of only 92 milliseconds."

It took Stricklen a moment to realize what the problem was. The message they had just listened to (even though it had been compressed for transmission) required about 30 seconds to play-back. This meant the Hess would have required the same amount of time to record the message. Stricklen's own message also would have required several seconds to listen to. "Are they a lot closer to us than we think?" Stricklen asked.

"No. Our instruments show the source to be the Hess home world which is currently roughly 0.987 light-years distant. There is only one explanation — the Hess are either silicon based or operate like some sort of large living computer. They process information far faster than we can. In fact, the only way the Hess could have replied so quickly is if they have the ability to directly understand a compressed message and to reply using the same technique. Either the Hess are a very extraordinary race, or we are dealing with a very intelligent computer and not the Hess."

Stricklen listened to this explanation and then pushed the transmit button to send his reply. "An analysis of your response has brought up a question concerning your race. We wish to have this one question answered before we proceed. Are the Hess a silicon based life form or am I speaking to a machine?"

Stricklen calmly waited for the message to make the round trip. "The Hess is much like your AI computers. The Hess, however, is sentient. Please continue your approach."

Stricklen looked at Sorbith and shrugged his shoulders. "I'm not too sure if that answered the question, but it adds more evidence to the fact that the Hess are silicon based. I've read science fiction stories about such creatures, but I never thought one could actually exist. Do we believe their explanation and proceed or turn around?"

"We proceed. We have already learned one piece of information about the Hess that nobody else has discovered, probably because the Hess have never talked to anyone. There's no telling how much more we will learn after we land."

"Helm, proceed on course for Shaular," Stricklen ordered. Then, to

Sorbith, "Speaking of the landing, have you decided who else will be going? The Hess specified only two Alliance representatives."

"Yes, in addition to myself, I think Falnath would make a good choice. She has a scientific mind second to none and having her there as an observer would increase our chances of getting the most out of this trip."

"I agree. You and Falnath. I'll let her know."

Stricklen turned his attention to the main navigational display as the *Dragon* slowly made its way toward the Hess home world. In a few hours, the Alliance would get their first ever look at a Hess.

Chapter 10

"*Dragon*, this is *Tri-Star*: All passengers are aboard. We are breaking orbit and beginning our decent," Sorbith reported. He then turned his attention to the control console and manually took control of his ship. Falnath was observing from the doorway while the Kyrra were patiently waiting in the ship's only stateroom.

Seeker class scoutships were not designed as passenger ships. They were designed solely to provide support and living quarters for the peacekeeper to whom they were assigned. The Seeker class of ships were unique in many ways. The ship's computer was the most advanced system in existence and was considered a semi-sentient entity. The ship was also equipped with a stealth capability which could render it virtually invisible under certain conditions. This stealth capability made the Seeker class the most expensive single-person ship ever built.

The control room was built for one person and was very compact. Since Sorbith was occupying the only available space, Falnath was forced to observe from the doorway. One of the many monitors displayed an exterior view. Falnath watched the image of the *Komodo Dragon* shrink in size as they began their departure. The scene spun until the planet below was visible. As she watched the surface grew closer.

"What is the surface of the planet like?" she asked.

"No atmosphere. Surface temperature about minus 320. Electromagnetic field readings are all over the place. The orbit brings it to just within the outer edges of the pulsar's radiation beam once every 447 days. All-in-all I would not recommend this place a vacation spot."

"Incoming message from the *Komodo Dragon*," the ship's computer said. Although it was speaking in Sorbith's native tongue Falnath's vocoder was translating it for her.

"On speaker," Sorbith ordered.

"Sorbith – The *Patton* has just informed me they have picked up the drive wakes of several ships coming this way," Ken's voice said. "Estimated arrival is about four hours. IFF returns the ID codes of seven LA class destroyers. No answer to our hail at this time."

"Interesting," Sorbith replied. "Those are very old ships. What are they doing here and who's operating them? Have the *General Patton* intercept. Send them a message from me. Tell them they are to alter course immediately. This system is restricted and they are in violation of that restriction. If they do not turn around, have the *General Patton* take whatever action is required to prevent them from assuming orbit."

"Message received and understood. *Dragon* out."

The surface of the planet was now close enough for some of the details to be seen. The planet appeared completely dead and lifeless. The ancient supernova had stripped this world of any atmosphere it may have once had and laid to waste to the entire surface. Why anyone would want to remain here was beyond Sorbith's understanding.

"Auto control signals detected," the computer announced.

"Allow auto control," Sorbith ordered and took his hands off the controls.

After a few minutes a large structure appeared on the viewer. Falnath tried to fit more of herself into the already crowded control room. "That looks like a communications array," she remarked.

Sorbith glanced at several readouts then replied, "If it is, then it is the largest planetary based array I have ever seen. Computer, estimate the size of the object on the main viewer."

"The structure is approximately 33 kilometers in length and 29 kilometers in width."

Sorbith shook his head in amazement. "It sure looks like an FTL array, but I've never heard of one that large before. I don't see any other structures."

"Perhaps they are underground to protect them from the pulsar's radiation," Falnath said.

"We'll soon find out – that is our destination," Sorbith said. He then pushed a button and said, "Trel'mara, do you recognize the structure on your monitor?"

The Kyrra had been watching the descent from a monitor in their room. The face of one of them appeared on a small screen to Sorbith's left. "It is similar to a deep space communications array which we had built to maintain contact with our probes. But an equivalent communications system built by another species would involve similar design decisions and would result in a structure that would appear similar to ours. Further details of the construction is needed before a conclusion concerning the structure's origin can be reached."

"Thank you. Let me know if you spot anything of interest."

The rest of the descent was made very quickly and without incident. The *Tri-Star* was brought to a smooth landing several kilometers from the communications array. Once they were on the ground, the ship's computer reported that a powerful force-field had enclosed the area surrounding the ship and a breathable atmosphere was forming outside. As soon as the atmosphere had stabilized, the Hess spoke to them again.

"Please exit your ship. A Hess unit will meet you outside to provide guidance."

Sorbith informed the Kyrra and they met at the ship's hatchway. Once everyone had arrived, Sorbith bypassed the interlocks and opened both airlock doors. A small, featureless, metallic device was waiting for them outside the ship. It stood about 1.5 meters tall and appeared to float a few centimeters above the ground. As soon as the hatch opened it curtly said, "Follow," and immediately started moving away at a slow walking pace.

Falnath mentioned to Sorbith that the voice was identical to the one they had heard from the planet while they were in orbit. The machine led them to a small building. Inside was a large elevator. The group piled into the spacious cabin and it began to descend. After a moment it stopped and the door opened to expose a long underground corridor which seemed to extend into the distance as far as the eye could see.

They walked a short way and turned into a bare, unfurnished room. Four other identical machines waited within. As soon as the last person had entered, the door silently slid shut. One of the machines approached the Kyrra and said something in a language Sorbith's computer could not translate. Tee'Chea's reaction was one of utter astonishment. He looked excitedly at his fellows and quickly replied in the same or a similar untranslatable language. A rapid-fire conversation followed.

After about a minute, Sorbith could stand no more. "What is going on here?" He said in a loud voice. "What language are you speaking? Where are the Hess? Explain!"

The nearest machine moved closer to Sorbith and said, "To answer your second question. They are speaking a local Kyrran dialect. The Kyrra, like Saulquin and Humans, speak a common language but they also speak several local languages. The answer to your first question is the Hess is verifying the identity of the Kyrra. Finally, your third question should have been stated as 'Where is the Hess?'. The Hess refers to the conglomerate of data gathering devices which exist on this world. The Hess is not a living creature nor is it a collection of individuals. It is a data collection and transmission unit constructed by the Kyrra 41,326 of your years ago."

Falnath emitted a sharp hiss of surprise and her tail began twitching nervously. Sorbith was stunned into silence. After recovering, Falnath said, "The Hess, then, is nothing more than a probe built by the Kyrra. I'm assuming then that you have contacted the Kyrra and they are now on their way here. When will their ship arrive?"

"This Hess has been unable to contact the Kyrra for the last 41,173 years. When it was learned that an operating Kyrra stasis chamber had been discovered, this Hess hoped the Kyrra within would be able to provide guidance as to how to contact the creators. It is now known the Kyrra you have freed from stasis do not possess this knowledge. However, this Hess has an obligation to protect these Kyrra from harm at all cost."

"You don't know where the Kyrra are?" Sorbith asked. "What have you been doing for the past forty-thousand years?"

"When the Kyrra did not respond with an acknowledgment to a routine data transmission this Hess performed fifty re-transmissions and verified all communications equipment was functioning properly. This unit then took action to search for and attempt to contact other Hess units. Since no information concerning additional Hess units had been provided, a detailed search using wide-beam FTL inquiries was commenced. After searching for eight years, contact was established with another Hess unit. It was learned the other Hess unit had also lost contact with the Kyrra."

"It was decided to continue the search for additional Hess units. After 97 years the search was completed to the limit of the range of all the communications equipment involved. Seventeen other Hess units had been contacted. Eleven have since self-destructed as those units considered themselves without purpose. Two Hess units were discovered by other races and those units also elected to destroy themselves. Another unit was destroyed when the star it was in orbit about went nova. The remaining three Hess are now beyond our communications range. Contact was lost with these units when the Hess providing the communications link ceased to exist."

One of the Kyrra approached and said, "The Hess has asked me to request your assistance in locating its creators. Without a purpose, the Hess believes it should not remain in operation. It has remained functional because there has always been a chance the Kyrra would eventually regain contact with them. This Hess has also found purpose in that it has assisted the Alliance in various ways. Since the goal of the Hess is the same as ours, we see no reason why this request should not be honored. Will you assist?"

Sorbith's thoughts raced through his mind. After a short delay, he said, "We have already agreed to provide you with a ship, but that was before we knew just how far away you planned on going. Based upon the coordinates you provided to us and the suspected area of space controlled by the Chroniech, we believe you will be travelling through Chroniech space and given their latest hostile activities I do not think you would survive for long. I am beginning to believe it would be to our mutual benefit if, instead of just giving you a ship, we take you there ourselves. Before I can decide on this though, I need to know the precise location of where we will begin our search."

The room immediately darkened and a star map hologram was projected into the unoccupied corner of the room. The voice of a Hess remote explained, "The green pulsing dot is our current location. The red line terminating at the red dot indicates the most direct route. The distance is roughly 3158 light years."

Sorbith was stunned. "Even at maximum drive, it would take our fastest ship over a year to make the trip. You are asking the Alliance to invest a considerable amount of equipment and funds into this search. Now that I know the facts, I can tell you the council will most likely modify their original agreement, especially now with the Chroniech making war on the Alliance."

"Understood," the machine replied as the room returned to normal illumination. "In exchange for your assistance, the Alliance will be provided with the technical details required to construct a communications device capable of transmitting a signal at three million cee over a distance of 300 light years. You will also be provided with the technical specifications for a stardrive which is capable of sustained speeds in excess of 4,000c and a more complete mathematical description of the space-time continuum."

Sorbith tried very hard to maintain his composure. The Hess were offering to nearly triple the distance that a signal could be sent, increase its speed of transmission by several orders of magnitude, and to boost their maximum FTL speed to unheard of levels. "That is an offer I think the Alliance can not refuse," he replied in a somewhat shaky voice. "I will have my ship transmit the offer to central command with a request that the Alliance council convene an emergency meeting to decide the issue. The only problem remaining, will be the logistics of outfitting a ship for such an extended voyage."

"There is a way to shorten the voyage," the machine said. "Although the transport ship which brought the Hess components here was cannibalized for its parts, the stardrive remains operational. With the appropriate modifications, the stardrive can be installed within an Alliance ship. If properly aligned and powered, the ship should be able to reach speeds of at least 11,000c and possibly higher."

"Eleven thousand!" Falnath exclaimed. "Such a speed of travel is unbelievable." Turning to Sorbith she continued, "You cannot let this opportunity pass. You must insist that the council accept. If the council will not, I'm sure one of the member races would jump at the opportunity to obtain this level of technology."

Before Sorbith could reply, the Hess said, "The stardrive would only be installed for use in the search ship. Precautions will be taken to ensure that it is not used for any other purpose."

"Agreed," Sorbith said. "I believe the council will ac..." He stopped in mid-sentence and was silent for a moment. Falnath did not interrupt for she knew the peacekeeper was receiving a message from his ship important enough for the ship's computer to interrupt the conversation. After a moment Sorbith said, "I have just been informed that the *General Patton* has engaged the incoming ships. They claim to be from a group calling themselves The Army of Humanity and they are demanding that the stasis chamber and the Kyrra be turned over to them. A battle is in progress."

"I was afraid of this," Falnath said.

"What do you mean?" Sorbith asked, turning a curious ear toward the Rouldian.

"The opportunity for advancing ones technological superiority by several decades is too tempting to pass up for those species who still possess a warlike nature. I had thought the Tholtarans would have been the first to attack us but it seems as if the Humans have gotten here first. We must return the Kyrra to their own people or the Alliance will face another internal war as those hungry for power try to gain control of the Kyrra technology."

"Order your battleship to disengage and move to within 100,000 kilometers of this planet," the Hess said. "Your ships will be under this unit's protection. The Kyrra and the stasis device are to remain here until the search ship is ready."

Without hesitation Sorbith gave the order to his ship which then relayed it to the *General Patton*. After a moment he said, "The *General Patton* has broken off its attack and is moving this way. It has been damaged but is still able to maneuver. Two of the destroyers have been eliminated and a third damaged. The rest are in pursuit. The *Komodo Dragon* is breaking orbit and moving to assist the *Patton*. I have ordered my ship to send for additional reinforcements in case there is further trouble."

Throughout all this the Kyrra had been silent. Trel'mara appeared shaken. Nordlatak moved closer to Trel'mara to provide comfort. Looking up he said, "Our presence has caused death and violence among your people. We cannot remain in your society without causing further disruption, please, take us to our own people."

"I understand," Sorbith said. "But we don't have any idea what happened to your people. Can the Hess give us the history of the Kyrra from the time you left? Perhaps we can better figure out where they are now."

The Hess could and they did.

Following the Slaver departure, the Kyrra civilization had been on the brink of extinction. The food supplies in the remaining cities would, if properly rationed, last about four weeks. Even after increasing the capacity of the stasis chambers to uncomfortable and dangerous levels, there was insufficient capacity to put the remaining population into stasis. Virtually no industrial capacity existed, which forced the Kyrra to use what was already available.

A planet with primitive life had been discovered which could provide a sufficient food source to sustain the Kyrra population. Several thousand Kyrra were moved to this world to construct and operate an enormous farm. Much of the harvesting and processing had to be done by hand. The completed food products were then loaded into the few ships at their disposal, again by hand, and shipped to the home world. This temporarily solved the food problem.

The second problem lay in getting the remainder of their population to safety. The Kyrra had no choice but to move them to the planet which now supplied their food. Lacking modern construction equipment, they were forced into building crude, low technology shelters for themselves. The planet's indigenous life was hostile, at least as far as the Kyrra were concerned, so they built walled towns. The planet was soon dotted by thousands of such towns, each one supported and fed by the farms and wild plant life surrounding them. Most of the Kyrra population lived in such primitive conditions. The important point though was they were alive.

With their main problems solved, the Kyrra turned toward the long-range goal of finding themselves a new home. Their probes and exploration ships had been searching the heavens for many years and had not found a suitable planet. The Kyrra's industrial capabilities had been reduced to zero. They needed a place to rebuild that ability. Near the food planet there existed a star system which had never quite formed. The entire system consisted of small metal-rich rocks orbiting a tiny dim star who's fusion furnace burned too slow to generate any light. The Kyrra decided to use this readily available source of raw material to construct a space station. The space station would then become their manufacturing center.

Work began on the space station but problems soon cropped up. Without a sufficient industrial base to support them, the starships, especially the ones salvaged from the Slavers, began to fail due to lack of repair parts. Since the Kyrra were starting over from scratch, even the carefully planned out work on the space station was becoming harder. Items which were readily available to an industrialized society were difficult or impossible to obtain. The Kyrra re-evaluated their plan and made a very hard decision.

The work on the space station was abandoned and the Kyrra turned all their abilities toward establishing themselves on the farm planet. Soon, only two of the original exploration ships remained operational. Thirty five years before the neutron star entered their home system all Kyrra had been either placed in stasis or moved to the farm world. The original Kyrra home world had been abandoned and the Kyrra were effectively trapped on a world they looked upon as hostile. Starting from ground zero, they began to slowly rebuild their society. Even though the knowledge was there, it still took a terrible amount of time, mostly because the Kyrra were working with a limited population.

Over the course of 1200 years the Kyrra slowly regained most of what they had lost. They took great pains to limit the damage that was done to the planet since the Kyrra considered themselves 'guests' on their temporary home. As soon as they had the ability to repair their old starships, the Kyrra once again resumed their interrupted construction of the space habitat. Their ultimate goal was to get themselves off the planet which had held them prisoner for so long.

It took the Kyrra 33 years to complete the first space manufacturing complex. The station housed six hundred and was soon working at full capacity. Because of its modular construction, increasing its size was relatively easy. The result, once a certain point had been reached, was the geometric increase in their industrial capabilities.

Soon, construction began on additional space habitats and starships. These habitats were self sustaining and could house tens of thousands of Kyrra. Two thousand nine hundred and eighty years after the Slavers had left, the entire Kyrra population was out of stasis, off planet, and living in 1056 space habitats in orbit about a star that did not shine. A suitable lifeless planet had been found and selected as the new future home of the Kyrra and its terraforming had begun.

Up until this point, the Kyrra had been more concerned with their own survival than with anything else. It was noted, almost in passing, that no other starships had been detected. After their survival as a species had been assured, the Kyrra began to wonder what had become of the Slavers and the races they had dominated. They built a fleet of space probes and sent them to investigate. The Kyrra were shocked at what they found.

Each planet which had once harbored life was now a radioactive wasteland. Four planets were still populated and were relatively undamaged, however, the planet's inhabitants were at war with one another and had been for so long that only primitive weapons were now in use. No trace of any surviving Slaver's were found. None of the cultures which had possessed space travel before the break-up of the Slaver empire still operated starships. It was as if all civilized cultures had either been destroyed or had been pushed back to a primitive level of existence.

Over the next 400 years, the Kyrra probes continued their outward search until all systems within a 1000 light-year radius had been explored. The Kyrra discovered several FTL capable civilizations and carefully avoided all contact with them. Because of their experience with the Slavers, the Kyrra had made it a common practice to shield themselves as thoroughly as possible. Their communications were scrambled and utilized a technology which rendered the signals virtually impossible to detect.

The terraforming project was well underway by this time and according to the time-table established by the Kyrra, their new home world would be completed in about 55,000 years. The Kyrra turned their energies toward science and the further exploration of the universe. Over the next 115 years the Kyrra probes searched farther and farther out into the unknown. An area of space 2500 light years in radius had been completely explored and mapped. The Kyrra wanted to look further.

The Hess exploration probe was designed and built. These probes were sent out to a specific area of space and instructed to locate a secure planet upon which to base themselves. The Hess were purposefully designed such that if discovered, they would self-destruct so the location of the Kyrra habitats would remain unknown. Each Hess could build and launch probes of its own and would send back its findings periodically through a system of relay stations. The Hess which had established itself near the Alliance had been built 3555 years after the Slavers had left, which meant it was an early model.

Throughout all this time, the Kyrra had remained undetected, even though many space-capable races had been discovered and observed including the remnants of the Slavers. The Slavers had established themselves in a remote system far from the Kyrra. After finding them and assessing their technological capabilities, the Kyrra forgot about them. Kyrra technology had reached such a level that they could shield their probes and ships from the sensors of other races.

Forty-one thousand one hundred and seventy three years ago the Kyrra stopped responding to the Hess transmissions. No explanation was received. As far as the Hess was concerned, its creators had vanished and now they had the opportunity to find out what has become of them.

The Hess finished its story by adding, "A more comfortable room has been constructed for you. We will move to this room so further discussion concerning this unit's proposal can be conducted."

The Hess robots led the group into a well furnished room. There was even a seat specifically designed for the comfort of a Rouldian. Falnath settled into it with a great sigh of relief stating in the process she was getting very tired of standing. The five Kyrra excitedly talked among themselves when they discovered the Hess had provided them with beverages and snacks with which they were familiar. Falnath and Sorbith also found refreshments and snacks available from their own cultures.

After everyone was finally seated the Hess presented its detailed proposal. The discussion continued for several hours.

* * * * *

"The *General Patton* reports another ship has been destroyed," the XO said. The battle with the Army of Humanity was being closely monitored by the *Komodo Dragon*. "That leaves four."

"Current status of the *GP*?" Stricklen asked.

"Considerable damage, battle capability down almost 40 percent," Doug replied after consulting a screen-full of information. "Shields are being strained by continuous weapons fire from the remaining destroyers. Some shield leakage is present. The helm is rolling the ship to minimize the damage they're taking but this is also reducing their ability to target their own weapons."

"I did not think LA class destroyers were that good?" Ken remarked. "That class of ship was designed and built back during the war."

"Apparently the Army of Humanity has done some major upgrading. Who the hell are these people anyway?"

"I believe they are a militant group of Humans who are still fighting the war of fifty years ago," Stricklen replied. "I've heard several reports over the years of them attacking other races but I did not know they were in possession of any old battleships. What really surprises me is they weren't smart enough to disable the IFF transponders. What is our time to intercept with the *Patton*?"

Doug consulted a monitor and replied, "About fifteen minutes assuming we don't begin decelerating. We have a considerable delta-V between us and if we don't slow down we will be within weapons range for less than two minutes.

"How long before they are within the 100,000 kilometer limit specified by the Hess?"

"About forty-five minutes at their present rate of acceleration."

Stricklen considered all his options and made a tactical decision. "Commander Scarboro, prep the ship for emergency acceleration maneuvers."

"Aye Sir!" Doug responded and then sprung into action. He knew what the Captain was planning. Because of the velocity differences between themselves and the enemy ships, they would pass each other at a high rate of speed. This did not give them much time to engage the enemy. The *Komodo Dragon* could apply significantly more thrust than normal, but the excess acceleration could not be compensated by the internally generated artificial gravity field. In order to increase the amount of time they would be in weapons range, Stricklen had decided to utilize more than normal maximum thrust to slow the ship quicker.

Scarboro turned to his console and said, "*Dragon*: initiate emergency thrust protocol."

Instantly, an alarm began sounding throughout the ship to alert the crew. They scrambled to stow all loose items in preparation for the acceleration which would be felt inside the ship. The ship's computer also made several thousand internal adjustments to protect the integrity of the ship. Maintenance robots quickly moved to their posts to act as additional structural supports for critical components.

While Doug was tending to preparing the bulk of the ship, Stricklen got up from his command chair and walked over to his helmsman. "I want a trajectory plotted to give us as much weapons engagement time as possible. Can you bring up a chart showing the engagement time verses intercept time assuming we utilize 120% over-thrust?"

"Yes sir." The helmsman busied himself at his computer console for thirty seconds and a graph appeared on the screen. If the *Komodo Dragon* started decelerating too late, they would intercept the *General Patton* sooner but would fly past the enemy ships so fast they would not have much time to engage them. If they began deceleration too soon, they would be within weapons range of the enemy ships for a longer period of time but they would also arrive later—possibly too late.

Stricklen consulted the graph, analyzed the tactical situation, combined the knowledge of what he currently knew with the capabilities of all the ships involved and came to a decision. "Begin 120% over-thrust deceleration at intercept minus four point five minutes. Give the crew a two minute warning and then a fifteen second countdown. While we are within range you are to maintain an optimum weapons orientation no matter how much return fire we take."

The Helm acknowledged the Captain's orders and Stricklen stepped over to his weapon's officer. "Mr. Gavin, the moment we are within range I want you to throw everything you can at the lead ship. Once its been put out of commission, start on the next ship."

Stricklen returned to his command chair and said, "*Dragon*: Over-thrust is authorized. Captain's code omega-nine-seven-three-sigma-four-seven."

"Over-thrust authorization code accepted," the ship's computer replied.

Soon, an attention tone sounded and the helm announced, "Attention! One hundred twenty percent over-thrust in two minutes. All hands make final preparations. Fifteen second countdown to commence."

Throughout the entire ship, last minute checks were made to ensure everything was prepared for a high-G maneuver. When the time came, the helm calmly gave the crew a fifteen second countdown and then pressed a button on his console. For a brief moment, nothing could be felt but within seconds the crew started to feel their weight increasing as more and more thrust was applied. The ship started to creak and groan and a small vibration could be felt. Within fifteen seconds the ship was at 120% of its maximum compensatable thrust and each crew member felt as if they weighed nearly twice their normal weight.

Just over four minutes crept by, then the weapons officer announced,

"Weapons range! Commencing attack on the lead ship."

The *Komodo Dragon* was at the extreme range of its long-range weapons. These were the beam weapons and they reached out to touch the shields of the ship closest to the ailing *General Patton*. As they raced closer, the power impacting on the enemy shields ramped up. As soon as the *Dragon* was within range, it let loose with a volley of sledgehammers and the enemy shield collapsed. The weapons officer had timed the firing of the four energy vortexes perfectly. The first two had been fired about a second before the second volley. The first group had weakened and then breached the shield allowing the second two to pass through and impact directly on the armor plating of the destroyer.

All warships are armored to provide some protection in battle against weapons fire when the ship's defense shield starts to weaken and allows some of the energy from the weapons to leak through. The armor, however, was never meant to withstand a direct assault, especially from a weapon like a sledgehammer. Although less powerful than the Tholtaran's version, the *Dragon's* sledgehammers still packed a huge amount of power into each bolt. The armor tried to resist but within a few milliseconds it had melted and much of the weapon's energy was dissipated inside the hapless destroyer. The *Dragon's* weapons officer directed a single nuclear-tipped missile toward the doomed ship and turned his attention toward the next target.

While the sledgehammers were recharging, the *Komodo Dragon* concentrated all available beam weapons and a few missiles at the next destroyer. Unlike the first target, this one's shields had not been under constant assault from the *General Patton*. Also, unlike the ship which was now an expanding cloud of lightly glowing gas, this one, along with one more, decided to fight back. Because of the attack vector which the helm had chosen, only two of the enemy ships were able to get a clean shot at the *Dragon*.

Several powerful beam weapons impacted the *Dragon's* defense shield and were harmlessly reflected back into space. This defense, however, did not come without a price. The shield's defensive capabilities were weakened with each drain placed on it. Eventually, the shield would begin to loose its reflective ability and start to leak. This was where the armor came into play. But, if the shield leaked too much energy, the armor would be overwhelmed and damage would be sustained.

The helm had been carefully watching his board and announced, "We will be out of weapon's range in two minutes."

POWER STRUGGLE

Stricklen checked his master board and noted the shields were beginning to show signs of weakening. Several spots on the *Dragon's* hull were beginning to indicate a rising temperature. If the Army of Humanity didn't have anything left to throw at them they would come out of this with barely a scratch.

The entire battle had lasted for just over three minutes so far. The weapons officer quickly checked the status of the sledgehammers, made some mental calculations then quickly programmed a series of instructions into his console. Abruptly, one of the *Dragon's* beam weapons ceased fire. Stricklen made note of this but did nothing, he had the utmost trust in the capabilities of his weapons officer. By shutting down one of the weapons, the excess power could be redirected toward charging the sledgehammers. "Give me a sixty second count," he calmly directed the helm.

For a long minute the warships battled each other with beam weapons alone. Either the destroyers did not have any missiles available, or they were saving them for later. The helm started to count down from sixty. He only managed to reach a count of forty-nine when the weapons officer depressed a button on his console and activated the firing sequence which he had previously set up. A series of closely spaced missiles left their launch tubes, directed at specific points on the enemy ship's shield.

The destroyer chose that moment to spring their own surprise. "Inbound missiles!" the weapons officer announced. "I count at least fifty. They're all unpowered and shielded." At this range, all missiles used conventional drives. Faster than light missiles took too long to form a stable drive matrix and could be easily destroyed. The missiles being used against the *Dragon* were of a vastly different type. These missiles had no propulsion system, but they did carry a short-lived defense shield. The missiles were launched electromagnetically and were quite hard to detect.

"Helm: Cut acceleration and…"

"Captain!" Gavin interrupted. "Hold for just a moment please!"

"Belay that last order helm."

Although several of the *Dragon's* missiles were intercepted and destroyed most made it to the target. As the first missile exploded all four sledgehammers fired. The crackling balls of concentrated energy passed several missiles and struck the weakened enemy shield. For a moment, the shield resisted this titanic onslaught but it was severely weakened. The first missile then struck and detonated with the power of fusing atoms. The second and third missiles found no resistance as the destroyer's shield was now gone.

They impacted on bare armor and the resulting nuclear explosion completely annihilated the ship.

As soon as the sledgehammers had fired, the weapons officer yelled, "Evade!"

The Captain seconded this request, making it an order and the helm cut the acceleration to zero and applied all possible thrust to changing the ship's orientation and direction. The internal gravity field fluctuated wildly as these maneuvers were performed and the Captain felt his equilibrium being challenged. Several indicators glared red on Stricklen's master board indicating they had sustained some damage due to these extreme maneuvers. A moment later the missiles which had made it past the *Dragon's* defenses struck.

The computer brains aboard the enemy missiles detected the change in the target's approach vector and recomputed when to explode. Although they did not directly impact the *Dragon's* shield, they detonated quite close. The *Dragon*, however, was extraordinarily lucky. With the destruction of another enemy ship, the beams from that ship had ceased and the drain on the shield had dropped. Forty-two fifty-megaton nuclear missiles detonating within thirty kilometers of the ship, however, were too much for the shield and it failed. The distance from the explosions saved them as well as their high speed which quickly carried them away from the center of the blast. The damage control board showed considerable damage but they had survived and they still had propulsion.

As the *Komodo Dragon* passed out of weapons range, it left two destroyed ships in its wake. "Helm: Plot us a course back to Shaular. Make sure we stay clear of any unfriendlies. Doug: Take a census of the damage and report back to me in five minutes. Lieutenant Gavin: Hell of a job with the weapons! Good work!"

A few minutes later, Scarboro presented his findings. "Most of the damage is restricted to the starboard side of the ship. We have three hull breaches, all aft of frame 220 located here, here and here," he continued, using a flexible schematic of the ship which he had lain out on top of a console. "Two dead and eight injured. Damage has been restricted to non-critical exterior compartments such as berthing and perishable storage. Missile tube six is out of commission. Sledgehammer three's confinement generator was knocked out of alignment. All other weapon systems are unaffected. The high acceleration evasive maneuver caused a water transfer pump at frame thirty deck four to break loose and damaged several other minor internal systems."

"Not bad Doug," Stricklen remarked. Turning to his weapons officer he said, "Gavin, tell me about those missiles that hit us. How did they manage to get so many off at once?"

"I believe that the Army of Humanity has modified their old destroyers pretty heavily. They appear to have installed a large number of magnetically launched missile tubes giving them the capability of simultaneously firing off a volley of fifty missiles. Each missile is not only shielded but they appear to have been partially cloaked. The shields did not activate until they were quite close which is why we did not pick them up sooner. Their major weakness is that they are unpowered. Had they been powered, we would not be sitting here."

"An interesting weapon system. We should pass this on to the Alliance to see if it can't be enhanced," Doug remarked.

The *Komodo Dragon,* using significantly lower thrust, slowly made a long U-turn back towards the Hess home world. While they worked on getting back to the planet, the *General Patton* continued on its previous course. Eventually, they passed the line the Hess had drawn in space.

"Some sort of weapons fire from the planet!" announced the tactical officer from CIC.

"Can we get a visual?" Stricklen asked.

"Yes sir, coming up on the main screen."

A second later, a highly magnified view of the destroyers appeared on the main screen. Ken and Doug saw two pencil-thin beams of green light striking the shields of the attacking destroyers. This amazed the two seasoned officers since such beams of energy should not have been visible in the vacuum of space. At first, the beams had no effect and simply bounced off the reflective defense screens. As they watched, the beams seemed to shift and run through the entire spectrum of colors within a matter of seconds, finally settling on a sort of dull blue-gray. Both beams then thickened and pulsed. The result was dramatic.

The destroyers suddenly began moving in wildly insane directions. After a couple of seconds of dashing about, the ship's engines shutdown and they began drifting in space. The *Dragon* picked up an all-channel wide-band broadcast: "This is the Hess to the remaining destroyers which have attacked the Alliance dreadnought *General Patton.* Your ship's control and navigation systems have been rendered temporarily inoperative. A repulser beam will shortly push you away from this planet. When your systems return to normal, you will leave this star system never to return. If you attempt to return, your ships will be destroyed. This is the only warning you will receive."

True to their word, two repulser beams reached out and touched the destroyers. Within minutes they were hurtling away from the planet. One of the destroyers fired off a volley of missiles. Quick as lightning, a bright white energy beam lashed out and vaporized all thirty-seven missiles in the blink of an eye. Stricklen was impressed.

"Coms: Get me the Captain of the *GP*. I don't want to interrupt if he's busy so make that clear to them when you transmit," Stricklen ordered.

After a brief moment, the face of Captain Mulgany appeared on Stricklen's screen. As soon as he noticed the connection had been made Mulgany said, "Thanks for the assist Ken. We took a beating but we'll be OK. We've got several hull breaches and, at last count, 63 casualties. The power grid is intact and, with the ship compartmentalized, we're holding air. She'll need a month or two in space dock but at least we'll make it there under our own power."

Stricklen was relieved. Tension flowed out of him as he listened to the Captain's report. "I'm glad we were able to assist. We took some damage of our own but it was all pretty minor. We should be back in orbit in under an hour. If you need any assistance, just yell. Stricklen out."

"Your offer is appreciated but from the reports I'm getting, our damage control teams are handling the cleanup just fine. We may need some spare parts after we assess the damage. I'll let you know. Mulgany out."

"Any word from the surface?" Stricklen asked.

"We are still getting good data from the *Tri Star*," the communications watch reported. "Sorbith's onboard computer reports negotiations are still underway and it has transmitted a recording of what has transpired since their arrival.

Ken was anxious to see what had been going on down on the planet, but he wanted to do so in the privacy of his stateroom. "Very well, keep me informed. I'll be in my stateroom. Inform me when we've achieved orbit." Stricklen said.

Just as he reached his stateroom door, a voice from his earpiece said, "Captain to the bridge! Sensors have picked up additional incoming ships."

Cursing softly the whole way, Ken retraced his steps. "Report!" he barked as soon as he cleared the doorway.

The main viewer had switched to a tactical display and showed a large group of ships approaching. The tactical officer looked up from his console. He had a very worried look on his face. "We've identified at least thirteen incoming ships, one of which is so big it must be a juggernaught. The drive signatures are Tholtaran."

Stricklen paled when he heard the word juggernaught. These ships were simply too huge to comprehend. The Tholtaran's had built five of these invulnerable battleships. Each one was a massive weapons platform measuring nearly 20 kilometers in diameter. Most of the ship's functions were automated, which meant the vast majority of the internal space was used for machinery. During the Human-Alliance war only one juggernaught had ever been lost in battle, and only at a tremendous cost in lives and ships. As far as Stricklen was concerned, a juggernaught was virtually indestructible.

"Contact Sorbith immediately!" he ordered. "I don't want to hear any excuses for him not responding. I want to see his face on my monitor in 30 seconds."

Stricklen got the second best thing. Sorbith's voice rang out from the console, "What is it Captain? Your coms watch informed me it was a matter of life and death that I speak to you."

"That's putting it lightly," Stricklen replied. "We have picked up a large group of ships heading this way. One of them is a Tholtaran juggernaught. I suggest we conclude our negotiations at a later date so we can leave this area of space post-haste."

"A Tholtaran battle fleet?" Sorbith replied, his voice full of surprise and anger. "I hope like hell they can explain what they're doing here. I'll transmit a demand for an explanation personally. My ship informs me the communications delay will be about 15 minutes. I'll let you know what their reply is."

"Just in case they are up to no good do you want us to make preparations to leave?" Stricklen asked.

"Negative, standby," came the terse reply.

Stricklen could not understand what Sorbith was doing but, being a good officer, he waited. Looking up at the tactical display he noted the juggernaught would be within weapons range in just under 5 hours. Stricklen wanted to be long gone before then. His patience had almost run out when Sorbith finally replied, "Remain as you are Captain. The Hess assures me it can handle the threat. After what I've seen down here, I believe it."

"It?"

"You had better review what has taken place down here since we've arrived. Your computer should have the recording of our meeting with the Hess. I suggest you look at it. I should also congratulate you on your successful engagement against the Army of Humanity destroyers. Very good tactics. Sorbith out."

Stricklen stared off into the distance for fifteen seconds while he nervously tapped his fingers on the edge of his console. Taking a deep breath he announced, "Well, if that's the way he wants it, that's what we'll do. We are under the protection of the Hess, or so I am told. God help us!"

Without another word, Stricklen walked off the bridge and went straight to his stateroom where he immediately opened a fresh bottle of rum. Before taking his first drink he looked at the gold colored liquid and thought, *This job is going to turn me into an alcoholic. I should have followed my Dad's advice and become a lawyer.* And with that he tilted the bottle and took a long slow swallow.

Stricklen, however, was not an alcoholic and, despite what some might think, he was always very careful as to how much he drank. The ship's executive officer, who was also a good friend, understood completely. Years ago, Doug had thought Stricklen had an alcohol problem but, after getting to know his Captain, he learned otherwise. Doug understood Stricklen needed to feel as if he was always in control. Alcohol affected that feeling, which was precisely why Stricklen would never allow himself to become intoxicated. Ken simply enjoyed the taste of good rum and the warm sensation it created as it slid down his throat. It was his personal method of dealing with stress.

Ken was still in his stateroom when Sorbith called back. "The Tholtaran's are here to take the Kyrra and the stasis device back to their home planet for analysis," Sorbith announced. "Apparently, the Tholtaran high command has decided we are not handling the situation properly and they are going to take control of things. A strong concern was also expressed about the fact that a Human ship was carrying the device. The high command claims that without the Kyrra technology the Alliance will loose the war with the Chroniech. We have been given four hours to come to a decision."

"What was your reply?" Stricklen cautiously asked.

"You Humans have a good term—I told them to go stuff themselves. I have sent a message to sector command informing them of the situation. As for your orders, they have not changed. The Hess will provide protection. Negotiations are proceeding smoothly and I expect to return within a few more hours. Until then, sit tight."

Stricklen grudgingly agreed and ended the link. He then settled down to sip his rum and to contemplate his possible future. In his eyes, things had just gone from bad to worse. The self-inspection lasted less than a minute as Stricklen realized why he had come to his cabin in the first place. Putting aside the approaching danger, he instructed the ship's computer to play back the recordings from the *Tri Star*.

Thirty minutes later, Ken's concentration was interrupted by a report from the bridge. "We have achieved orbit," the bridge officer informed him.

"How are the repairs coming?"

"Sledgehammer three has been repaired. All hull breaches have been sealed and the affected compartments repressurized. All other repairs are proceeding as best as possible."

"Thank you. Have the bodies of our dead been recovered?"

"Only two sir. One was blown out into space. The two that were recovered have been placed in the morgue."

"Thank you, Stricklen out."

Stricklen paused to silently consider the lives that had been lost. This was not the first time he had lost some of his crew in battle and he was sure it would not be the last. The bodies would be held in the cold morgue until they could be delivered to their respective families. He would have to conduct a funeral service for the one who had been lost to deep space. He quickly checked in with Scarboro to make sure the damage control teams were not having any problems and then returned to his review of what had been taking place on the planet below.

Some Captains probably would have been out keeping a close eye on the repairs. Stricklen took a different approach. He knew the capabilities of his crew and he trusted that they would always do their best. He knew he did not have to oversee their every activity and the crew seemed to appreciate it.

Three hours later, Ken had finished watching the events of the first meeting between the Alliance and the Hess and he was pacing back and forth trying to figure a way out of their situation. The door chime announced that the XO was requesting permission to enter and Ken ordered the door to open. "What is it Doug?" Stricklen inquired.

"The Tholtaran ships have taken up a position just outside the system. We monitored a communications between them and the destroyers which attacked the *General Patton* earlier. Apparently the much reduced Army of Humanity offered to join with the Tholtaran fleet in order to obtain the 'secrets of the Kyrra' as they put it."

"And their reply?"

"The Tholtaran commander quite frankly told the Army of Humanity to leave or be destroyed. They left ten minutes ago when two heavy assault cruisers broke formation and headed toward them."

Stricklen sat down heavily in a chair and motioned for his XO to join him. Ken held a glass containing a tiny amount of gold rum in front of him and swirled it around. After a moment he said, "I'm not going to be the focal point of another war. And that's exactly what's going to happen if we can't think of a way to stop it."

"How do you figure?" Doug asked reaching for a glass.

Stricklen poured a small amount of rum into Doug's glass as he said, "We have a Tholtaran battle fleet waiting to jump us as soon as we leave the protection of Hess space. Sorbith has already called for Alliance reinforcements and the Army of Humanity will no doubt be back with more ships – if they have them. What will happen when the Alliance ships get here? Some of them will undoubtedly be Human, some Tholtaran, and others crewed by who knows which species. Will they remain with the Alliance fleet or will they side with one of the others or will they try to take the device for themselves? How many other races are going to try to make a grab for Kyrra technology? I'm telling you, this is going to tear the Alliance apart before it's over."

Doug sipped his rum before replying. "You're right, of course. And right now, a divided Alliance is the last thing we need with the Chroniech on the warpath. Have you reviewed the happenings from below?"

"Yes. This entire situation is just too much to believe. Technology so advanced it makes ours look almost primitive by comparison; ancient civilizations that existed before we even learned how to make fire; and now the Chroniech. Tell me Doug, why do you think they started attacking the Alliance like they have?"

"I would guess their expanding empire finally ran into ours. You heard what they said. To them, we are nothing more than a disease which needs to be eradicated."

"I think their recent attacks indicate that there's something more than our just being in their way," Ken said. "They were attacking outposts and now all of a sudden they have launched an all-out offensive. Have you seen the latest from central command?"

"I have not had the time to review the reports. I figured it would just show more of the same."

Stricklen turned around and activated his computer console. *"Dragon,* display tactical summary of recent Chroniech activity." A star map appeared on the screen. The information was displayed as various shapes and color codes which, to a practiced eye, quickly showed what was happening. "Do you see what they are doing?"

Doug scanned the display for several seconds. He let out a long whistle as he settled back in his seat. Still staring at the screen he said, "They're working their way into the heart of the Alliance, destroying everything in their path. Looks like they pick an area, attack the military bases first beginning with the largest, and then systematically destroy everything else. They're making a beeline toward the heart of the Alliance and we don't seem to be putting up much of a resistance. Aren't we fighting back?"

Stricklen turned the monitor off as he replied. "The Alliance has been at peace for over fifty years. We are mobilizing as fast as possible but it seems the Chroniech have us outgunned for the moment. Incidents like this Tholtaran fleet sitting out there aren't helping us either. Those ships should be protecting the Alliance, not threatening us."

"The Chroniech seem to have an gigantic supply of ships at their disposal. Ships from all parts of the Alliance are on their way to the battle zone, but most are still weeks away. The enemy can coordinate their attacks with uncanny accuracy, probably because they can talk to their central command almost as easily as you and I are talking right now, while we have to rely on a communications system that is slow in comparison. Their ships are faster than ours with better weapons and more capable shields. Unless something breaks in our favor—such as assistance from the Kyrra or the Hess—the Alliance is finished. Look at the map. At their current rate of progress, the Chroniech will be at Almaranus within two months."

Angry, Doug stood up and set his glass down with a loud thunk causing a small amount of rum to splash unnoticed onto the table top. "I will not accept that! I don't care how old the Chroniech are. We will fight them with everything we have and we will win whether or not the Kyrra help us."

"My original question," Stricklen said, ignoring Doug's anger, "was why are the Chroniech attacking us in such an all out manner? They've known about us for a long time, long enough to learn our language, and they did not attack us with such force until just recently. Why?"

Still angry, Doug picked up his glass of rum and finished it off. Rolling the empty glass between his hands he said, "I don't know. I suspect you have a theory though."

"It's just a theory, but it makes perfect sense to me," Stricklen began marking off each point by grasping a finger of his left hand with his right. "The Chroniech have known us long enough to learn our language. Why we have not detected them until now is another mystery. They are also descendants of the Slavers. We know from the Kyrra that the Slaver empire collapsed and the Slavers became a hunted species. The first time the Chroniech ever contacted us was when we discovered the old Slaver transport. When we refused to give them the stasis chamber they attacked and they have continued to attack ever since."

Doug had turned to face his Captain. A look of understanding appeared on his face. Interrupting Stricklen, Doug continued the thought process. "That's right! The Chroniech mentioned that the ship belonged to them. In other words, they remember their past of forty thousand years ago. You think, they think, we have obtained some sort of weapon from their past glory and we will use it to destroy them. They are trying to wipe us out before we can figure out how to use it!"

"Exactly!" Stricklen almost shouted. Pouring his XO another small drink he continued. "The Chroniech have obviously passed down from generation to generation the story of their past and how they were once a mighty and feared people. The story probably goes on to tell how the inferior races rose up to destroy them. Today, instead of enslaving other races, the Chroniech simply wipe them out. Their entire culture must be infused with stories of revenge and hatred. If that's true, then there can never be peace with them, they will fight until one of us is eliminated."

"I'm not too sure I like the sound of that," Doug said sitting back down. At that moment the intercom chimed for attention.

Stricklen pushed a button and said, "Stricklen, what is it?"

"This is the communications watch on the bridge sir," a voice replied. "Sorbith is on his way back. He has ordered a meeting of all senior officers from both the *Dragon* and the *General Patton* in the *GP's* conference room in one hour."

Ken looked quizzically at Doug who simply shrugged his shoulders. "Very well," he replied. "The senior staff will shuttle over to the *Patton* as soon as possible. Have the duty crew prepare a shuttle for immediate departure and inform the rest of the senior staff."

Ken terminated the link then turned to Doug and said, "Well, let's go see if the peacekeeper has found a way out of this mess."

Chapter 11

The air in the *General Patton* was a little stale and Stricklen could identify the smell of overheated metal and burnt insulation. The route they took to the conference room showed little damage but Ken knew there were sections of the ship which were still at a vacuum. Sorbith was already in the conference room speaking to Captain Mulgany. Stricklen approached and shook hands with the Captain. "How are the repairs coming?" he asked.

Mulgany was a small man, standing only 163 centimeters. His features were almost boyish and anyone meeting him for the first time found it hard to believe he was the Captain of a warship. Behind the boyish face and blond colored hair, however, lay a finely trained, highly respected Alliance officer. Returning the shake with a firm grip Mulgany replied, "Very well. We'll have her patched up in no time. Those old LA class ships have had some serious enhancements done on them. If they had been original we wouldn't have received a scratch."

"That opens up a whole series of questions," Ken said.

"Excuse me!" Sorbith interrupted in a voice loud enough for everyone to hear. "I would like to get this meeting started—everyone please take a seat."

After a few seconds of shuffling, the crowd was soon seated around the conference table. "I have some late-breaking news," Sorbith began. "On the way up from the surface, I received a transmission from Almaranus. In anticipation of the Council's approval of the Hess/Kyrra request they are outfitting a military transport with sufficient supplies and spare parts for an extended duration voyage. This ship will leave Almaranus tomorrow evening and should arrive here in about four weeks."

"I have also just received word that the Tholtaran fleet has begun moving toward us. Sector command and the Grand Council have both been appraised of their actions. By the authority invested in me as a peacekeeper I have declared the actions of the Tholtaran's to be against the wishes of the Alliance and, as of ten minutes ago, the Tholtaran's are considered to be in violation of their treaty with the Alliance. All Alliance governments have been informed of this action and have been ordered to immediately remove all Tholtaran citizens from sensitive areas and positions throughout the

Alliance. I have declined to impose any actions against the Tholtaran government at this time, as I feel this is a matter best performed by the Alliance Grand Council. I have also informed the commander of the Tholtaran battle fleet that if he approaches the Hess home world without authorization, it will be considered an act of war against the Hess and appropriate retaliatory action will be taken."

Stricklen and Doug looked at each other with concern in their eyes. Their worst fears had just become reality. Stricklen had this sinking feeling that the Alliance was not going to be destroyed by the Chroniech, but would self destruct from within because of the overwhelming desire of some races to possess more power than their neighbors. Silence fell about the room.

Sorbith continued. "I have been in discussion with the Hess and the Kyrra for the past several hours and an agreement has been reached. The implementation of this agreement will commence as soon as this meeting adjourns. The purpose of this meeting will be to hammer out the details of how we are going to accomplish what we need to do."

Sorbith walked over to a wall-sized display and activated it. As he talked, a list of items appeared on the display to highlight what he had to say. "The Hess have agreed to the following: They will provide us with the technical plans for a communications system which will allow us to send transmissions over a distance of 300 light years at a speed of three million cee. They will also provide us with the technical plans for an enhanced stardrive with a top speed of about 4,000c. Since the central field emitters of a stardrive are very similar to those used to generate a ship's defense screen, these plans will also allow us to produce a more effective screen.

"The final item to be provided to us required a considerable amount of effort on my part. As you have learned from your brief sheets, the Hess is actually a sophisticated probe. Its original core programming should have prevented it from ever contacting us. The Hess has somehow managed to override this programming. It will not say just exactly how it is managed to do this. Part of this programming prevents the Hess from divulging any of its advanced technology to any race other than the Kyrra. After I learned that the route which we must take to reach the suspected location of the Kyrra took us through Chroniech space, I insisted the Hess provide us with a means of defense. Such a question would normally have resulted in the Hess wiping its memory and initiating a self destruct. Because the core programming has been bypassed, this did not happen, but the Hess still resisted.

"After explaining to them that the safety of the Kyrra would depend upon our ability to defend ourselves, it agreed. Apparently, it will give the information for a new weapon system to the Kyrra who will then give it to us to build. This strange arrangement has satisfied some sort of internal coding which the Hess has been unable to fully bypass. I have not yet seen the specifications for this weapon but the Hess assures me it is far beyond anything we currently possess.

"I want to stress that just because the Hess is giving us this technology does not mean we will have an instant advantage over the Chroniech. It will take us time to develop the abilities and expertise to build one of these new devices. The communications device alone will require a considerable enhancement in our ability to produce super-fine control fields and super-ultra-high frequency resonators. It's going to be a race between our ability to use what the Hess will give us and the Chroniech's ability to wipe us out."

"What do they want in return," someone asked.

"It!" someone else corrected. "What does IT want?"

"We are to try to reunite the Kyrra with their people," Sorbith replied. "In order to do this, we will supply the Hess with a ship which it will then modify. The major portion of the modification will be the replacement of our stardrive with its own. The Hess stardrive, like ours, is an integrated package consisting of a power reactor and a closely coupled energy conversion system. Their drive system is unique in that it not only produces the stardrive fields, but it also generated the primary defense screen for their ship. When the Hess arrived here, the stardrive reactor became the main power reactor for the entire facility.

"Since we will be taking the Hess' primary power source, a replacement will be needed. The Alliance does not possess a reactor of sufficient power to be used as a replacement. The only other power source available was the reactor for the stasis chamber. This reactor will be modified slightly and it will become the new main power reactor for the Hess. The only item required at this point in time is a ship."

Sorbith had been slowly making his way toward Stricklen. He stopped in front of the Captain and looked at him for a moment before continuing. "Captain Stricklen, by the authority vested in me as a peacekeeper I hereby confiscate your ship."

Stricklen's mouth flopped open but the shock of that statement was so severe he was at a complete loss of words. Before he could say anything Sorbith continued, "I would have preferred to use the *General Patton*, but she has been too severely damaged. In order to increase our chance of survival on this trip we will need a warship. The troop transport which Almaranus is sending does not carry enough fire-power for this mission. I also want to get underway with as little delay as possible so I have been forced to commandeer your ship.

"A good portion of your crew will be transferred to the *GP* in order to make room for the spare parts and supplies which will be transferred from the transport when it arrives. Several of the *Dragon's* weapon pods will be removed and replaced with Hess weaponry. The stardrive will be replaced with the Hess stardrive. Since its stardrive requires more detailed information concerning the state of the space-time field around the ship, the navigational system of the *Komodo Dragon* will also be enhanced and upgraded by the Hess. Your main computer will be re-programmed to allow it to properly control the new system."

Ken found his voice and asked the obvious question, "Who will be taking my place as Captain?"

"Nobody. You will remain in command of the *Dragon*. I am simply confiscating the ship and all its contents, including the crew."

Inside, Stricklen was relieved. But he still had many concerns, "And who is going to do all this? How long will it take?"

Returning to his seat, Sorbith replied, "The Hess is building a small army of robots which will perform the work under the supervision of the Hess central processor. We never realized it, but the Hess has a complete manufacturing complex buried beneath the planetary surface. It actually mines metals from the planet's mantel. This complex was used to build the probes which the Hess sent out to scan all surrounding space. Now it is being used to modify your ship. Think of it Captain – by the time the Hess is through with the *Komodo Dragon* it will be the most powerful and the fastest ship in the Alliance."

"How long?" Ken repeated.

"Baring any unforeseen problems, the Hess claims that it can make the modifications to your ship in under twenty days. Work will begin in about fifteen hours, which is when the null-gravity work zone will be completed on the planet's surface. Construction is already underway. As soon as it is ready, the *Dragon* will make planetfall."

A planetary landing? With a heavy-cruiser? Ken's thoughts raced. The *Komodo Dragon* had been built in space and massed over 215 thousand tons. She had never been designed to rest on a planetary surface. Structurally, the *Dragon* could probably take it, especially since it was designed to take a considerable amount of acceleration stress, but the ship had no landing pads and was not configured to support itself within a gravitational field. Stricklen feared the landing would result in considerable damage. He said as much to Sorbith.

"Ken," Sorbith replied in a soothing voice. "I know you are concerned, but the Hess knows what it is doing. The descent will be under its control and it has assured me the landing can be made safely. They are building a special null-gravity dock which has been specifically designed to hold your ship. Trust them."

"Now," Sorbith continued, dismissing Stricklen's unconvinced look. "We need to get down to business. The Hess has been standing by for our signal. Through a link which will be established with the *Patton's* main computer, the Hess will present its plans to modify the *Dragon*. We will work with them to ensure their plans will not impact any of the ship's functions. We will also determine what the new crew compliment will be."

Not long afterwards, the Hess had established a link and through that link presented its plans to the group using the conference room's main monitor and holographic projector. Soon, Stricklen forgot his concerns as he concentrated on the task at hand.

When the meeting was finally over, Stricklen had a good feel for what the Hess would be doing to his ship. The good thing was he would remain in command. As he started his walk back to the shuttle bay, his forward thinking mind began reviewing what he would need to do in order to allow his ship to make a planetary landing. Scarboro walked with him in silence, apparently considering the same thing. Captain Mulgany suddenly appeared around a corner seemingly in a big hurry. Slightly out of breath, he paused long enough to speak to the two officers. "The juggernaught is about to cross the line beyond which the Hess have promised to take action. You're more than welcome to observe from the bridge."

Without waiting for a reply, the Captain continued on his way at a pace just short of a run. Stricklen quickly followed with Doug tagging along.

A computer enhanced visual of the approaching juggernaught was displayed on the main screen when the trio burst through the door of the bridge. An officer was seated in the command chair. Upon seeing his Captain, he relinquished the chair and said, "The juggernaught has stopped just short of the line. The image on the main viewer is being transmitted from a probe currently located about 120 kilometers from the ship. No actions have been taken by either side."

"Range and status?"

"One hundred and ten thousand kilometers with all weapon systems fully powered," the officer replied.

"What a monster!" Doug remarked. Seen by itself, the juggernaught's size could not be determined because there was no frame of reference. Doug's comment was made when a Tholtaran assault cruiser drifted into view. The assault cruiser measured roughly 975 meters in length. Compared against the backdrop of the juggernaught, it looked like a small, fat stick.

"Picking up another drive-wake," someone reported. "Very small, distance zero point seven lights, traveling at high speed, possibly a probe. Wake signature analysis in progress."

Eight brilliant points of light appeared on the surface of the juggernaught. "They're charging sledgehammers!" the weapon's officer reported. Stricklen knew the sledgehammers of the juggernaught were hundreds of times more powerful than those carried aboard the *Komodo Dragon*.

Being the type of weapon which it was, the sledgehammer required a few moments to build to full charge. Each vortex was held in the grip of powerful magnetic fields as it was charged with energetic particles. After receiving a full charge, the vortex would be launched toward its doomed target at nearly one-quarter the speed of light. Running the numbers quickly through his head, Stricklen realized the bolt from the weapon would take almost four seconds to reach their position.

"Drive wake analysis of the incoming is complete," CIC reported. "The signature is consistent with a Chroniech reconnaissance probe."

"That's all we need right now," Captain Mulgany remarked.

For six long seconds the sledgehammers built up power. Each point of light appeared brighter than a welder's arc. Then, as one, the weapons were fired. Stricklen watched them approach as if in slow motion. Each glowing ball seemed to crackle and spit excess energy into space as it flew toward them. Suddenly, all eight points of light stopped moving. Held in space, the solitons which made up the sledgehammer's energy containment bottle slowly lost their integrity and the deadly balls of energy simply snuffed themselves out in brilliant flashes of light.

The juggernaught responded with a volley of hundreds of missiles and at least twenty energy weapons. The energy cannons of the juggernaught were more powerful than many planetary based weapons. Each one was backed by the full output of a five gigawatt fusion reactor. Even at the extreme range they were, the juggernaught's energy cannons could inflict serious damage on all but the largest Alliance warship.

Stricklen watched in amazement as the power of those weapons was harmlessly deflected thirty kilometers from their position. The missiles, which had been traveling at low FTL velocities, had already struck that impenetrable shield and detonated in silent points of light. Apparently infuriated with their inability to inflict damage, the entire Tholtaran battle fleet accelerated forward with all available weapons blazing away.

The Hess had promised to take appropriate retaliatory action. They did. Brighter than a thousand suns, a brilliant beam of light reached out and struck the defense shield of the juggernaught. Amazingly, the shield held off the attack. The power contained within that single beam must have been titanic because the shield was flaming with deflected energy. As Ken watched, the glaring rod of energy seemed to briefly pulse and the shield failed allowing the deadly beam to strike the unprotected skin of the juggernaught. Like a surgeon with a laser scalpel, the Hess carved out huge chunks of the once indestructible ship. After an incredible, heart stopping 45 seconds, the beam finally winked into nothingness.

Stricklen could not believe his eyes. The juggernaught had been neatly carved into three pieces. The rest of the Tholtaran battle fleet quickly retreated. The bridge was absolutely silent. Doug looked down to find he had been gripping the arm of the chair in front of him so hard his fingers were white. Relaxing his grip, he looked at Ken. Stricklen looked back and let out blast of air which he had been holding. "I'm glad they're on our side," somebody muttered under their breath. So complete was the silence that it was heard throughout the bridge as if it had been shouted.

The communications watch noticed something on his panel and turned to investigate. After a moment he reported, "Message from the Hess. They have contacted the Tholtaran fleet and informed them that one ship will be allowed to return to recover any survivors."

"Captain," someone at another console began.

Instinctively, Stricklen turned around and was about to reply when he remembered he was not on the *Komodo Dragon* and the statement had been meant for Captain Mulgany. The *General Patton's* Captain looked at Stricklen and let out a knowing chuckle. Turning to the person who had asked for attention he replied, "Yes Mr. Tong?"

"Two items sir. First, the Chroniech probe has veered away and is exiting our sensor range. Second, CIC has analyzed the weapon which the Hess used and has reported it was traveling at FTL speeds. CIC estimates it to be about two hundred cee."

Mulgany's jaw flopped open then snapped shut. What Mr. Tong had just stated was an absolute, beyond a shadow of a doubt, impossibility. Beam weapons had a propagation velocity of exactly one cee – no more, and no less. The mere possibility of a superluminal energy weapon would send physicists screaming for their computers. Mulgany recovered enough to ask, "Are they certain?"

"Yes sir. Several independent sensors have verified the fact. They are attempting to perform an analysis of the weapon's beam structure at this time."

Stricklen wanted to get back to the privacy of his own ship so he could think about what he had just witnessed. He motioned for the still stunned Scarboro to follow him. After saying their good-bye's to Mulgany, the two officers left the bridge. On their way to the shuttle bay Doug said, "I hope we're going to get one of those as part of our upgrade."

Stricklen looked at his XO for a moment then replied, "I hope not. I don't want to be responsible for that kind of destructive power."

In silence, the two officers boarded their shuttle. As soon as they were settled, the hatches were closed and the shuttle returned to the *Komodo Dragon*. The entire return trip was made in silence. Each person privately contemplated what they had just witnessed. Stricklen's thoughts were more toward the future. *If the Hess, which was built thousands of years ago, possess weapons of such power, what kind of technology do the Kyrra have today? How will they react when a primitive, aggressive race tries to return one of their own?*

Chapter 12

In light of the Hess' ability to protect them, Sorbith contacted sector command and canceled all reinforcements—the ships were badly needed elsewhere. The expected approval of the Hess/Kyrra proposal arrived from the Grand Council. The transmission gave Sorbith full authority to negotiate on behalf of the Alliance. The Tholtaran fleet left the area after retrieving the survivors of the now destroyed juggernaught. That once mighty ship was slowly being pulled into the gravitational field of the pulsar where it would eventually fall to its total destruction.

Upon arriving back at the *Dragon*, Stricklen ordered his personnel officer to go through the ship's roster and arrange the transfer of all but a skeleton crew to the *General Patton*. After approving the transfer orders, Stricklen retired to his stateroom where he caught up on some missed sleep. While he slept, the crew complement of the *Komodo Dragon* was cut in half.

Stricklen awoke feeling refreshed and in a surprisingly good mood. He was on the bridge when the Hess signaled it was ready for the *Dragon* to begin its decent.

"*Dragon*," Stricklen said. "Access command stack omega-four and execute."

"Command stack requires voice authorization," the machine replied.

"Omega-four password is: We must all be crazy," Stricklen replied with a grin on his face.

"Voice authentication of command stack omega-four verified. Executing... All navigational interlocks and warnings bypassed... All automatic defense systems deactivated... All weapons placed in safe storage mode... External sensors retracted and configured for space dock... Commencing main fusion reactor shutdown... Initiating shutdown of unnecessary auxiliary fusion reactors... All preparations for land-based dock complete. Command stack omega-four execution complete."

The command stack which Stricklen had activated was one he had previously prepared and contained a series of instructions which caused the computer to place the ship's systems in the proper configuration for a planetary landing. If this had not been done, the computer would have automatically attempted to override the navigational controls to prevent the ship from getting too close to the planet. With the ship in the proper configuration, Stricklen told the Hess to begin.

A very slight shudder was felt throughout the heavy-cruiser. "We've been seized by a tractor beam," the tactical officer reported.

"Analysis?" Stricklen calmly asked.

After working the controls on his console for a moment, the tactical officer replied, "The primary beam is a very finely structured, torsionally balanced, TR beam. It is encased within an open-ended force-field with an unknown matrix structure."

The descent to the surface took forty-five minutes. When the Hess released them, the *Komodo Dragon* rested lightly on the surface of the Hess planet in a special dock designed to safely support it. As soon as the ship had settled to a stop, a force field had been erected. Within a few minutes, the heavy-cruiser was surrounded by a breathable atmosphere for the first time in its twelve year history. Stricklen ordered the main hanger bay door interlocks to be bypassed and the ship was opened to the atmosphere. Moments later, an army of small robots descended upon them.

The Hess wasted no time in beginning the alterations and repairs to the *Komodo Dragon*. As soon as the robots had started their work, the Hess lived up to its side of the agreement and transmitted the data which had been promised to the Alliance central information system. Within hours, technicians from all parts of the Alliance were pouring over the technical specifications for devices which they had only dreamed of. One glaring exception were the Tholtaran's, who had been banned from receiving all sensitive information.

A few hours after making planetfall, Stricklen toured his ship with his chief engineer at his side. Everywhere they went, the Hess robots were there doing something. Part of the interior of the ship was being rearranged to make room for food and spare parts storage. The navigational system was undergoing a complete retrofit. Weapons were being removed in preparation for replacement by more advanced designs. But, by far, the greatest changes were taking place in engineering. Stricklen was thunderstruck by what he saw when he entered the *Dragon's* engine room.

The engine room was located at the very center of the ship. In the exact center of the engine room stood the massive, highly complex device known as the Kauffman stardrive. The stardrive was the heart of every starship. The power requirements of the Kauffman stardrive were supplied by a dedicated fusion reactor. The main reactor and the stardrive field generator were so closely linked that the two were inseparable.

The *Dragon's* engine room was crowded with no fewer than forty of the fast moving, never stopping Hess robots. What appeared to the eye to be a confusion of work was actually a closely choreographed, highly efficient, operation, scheduled and carried out with mathematical precision. The stardrive itself was a massive device weighing over 175 tons and measuring almost 10 meters in diameter. Stricklen wondered out loud how it was going to be removed.

"Believe it or not, the ship is actually designed to allow for a complete swap out of its stardrive," Skip replied. "It's something rarely seen since the Kauffman stardrive is one of the most reliable pieces of equipment ever put together, but it can, and has, been done. The bulkheads of several decks above the drive are removed. The compartments along this path are either storerooms or other easily cleared compartments. In our case the drive will pass through machinery storage three, food storage eight, the main conference room, the mess hall, and finally the recreation room where it will reach the hanger bay. From there the drive can be easily moved off the ship."

Stricklen continued to watch the robots as they dashed around performing their tasks. "The Hess claims the modifications will be complete in twelve days. How long would it take an Alliance space-yard working around-the-clock to perform the same modifications?"

"I would guess that it would take a minimum of five weeks to perform the grunt work and another two days to properly tune the stardrive to match the ship's gravimetric signature. I don't see how the Hess could do it any faster."

As he watched, it soon became apparent how the Hess could complete the job in the time specified. The robots were not only much faster and nimbler than people, but they could work in close proximity to each other without interference, always had the right tools with them, and were much stronger. The robots also worked without any breaks or hesitation between tasks. Ken watched as several robots stood within a few centimeters of each other working so fast their movements were almost a blur. One of the robots, apparently finished with its task, moved over to another location a few meters away and immediately starting disassembling a piece of equipment. Shaking his head in amazement, Ken decided to take a walk around the rest of the ship.

Stricklen finished his tour and headed for the bridge. Several robots were at work under the close scrutiny of a single marine guard. Since the ship was in a stand-down condition, the normal bridge watches had all been secured.

Over the next several days Stricklen made daily tours of the ship. He watched the slow but steady transformation of his ship from a heavy-cruiser to a heavily armed, top-of-the-line, high-speed, extended-duration, spacecraft. With the Hess doing all the work there was very little for him to actually do. To pass the time, Ken tried to keep abreast of the growing problem with the Tholtarans and the Chroniech. The Grand Council had decided to punish the Tholtaran republic by excluding them from all Alliance planets, activities, and assistance. In order to be re-admitted to the Alliance, the Tholtaran's would have to agree to the same restrictions which had been placed on Humans immediately following the Human-Alliance war.

For ten years following the war, all Human ships (both civilian and military) were required to carry an Alliance representative as part of the crew. Implanted within each representative was a miniature transmitter which was keyed to the representative's unique biological makeup. The Omel, supreme masters of biological knowledge, had designed and implanted the transmitters. This transmitter sent a continuous, encoded signal to a small device located in a tamper-proof enclosure. If the device stopped receiving the signal for a short period of time it would deactivate the ship's stardrive by permanently damaging the main reactor.

The Tholtaran's, probably because of their intense dislike of Humans, believed the conditions to be far too harsh and demanded that the Grand Council reconsider. Tension between the Alliance and the Tholtarans and especially between Humans and Tholtarans was running very high. There had already been several instances of Tholtaran ships interfering with the movement of Human ships. The coordinated Earth government had lodged an official protest with the Grand Council and warned that if the harassment did not cease, they would consider providing military escorts for all Human ships passing near Tholtaran space even if it meant reducing the number of Human ships taking part in the defense of the Alliance against the Chroniech.

The Chroniech push into Alliance space had been slowed due to the arrival of large numbers of ships from the interior of the Alliance. Star systems located in possible Chroniech attack areas were either being evacuated or reinforced with the additional ships. The Alliance was also constructing planetary defense systems where possible. It did not take long, however, for the Chroniech to change their strategy. Instead of attacking the same area, the Chroniech would look for weakly defended systems. When one was found, the system was attacked.

Stricklen learned of another Chroniech tactic which for some unknown reason made him very uneasy. It had recently been discovered that the Chroniech probes, which had been spotted all over the area, were dropping some sort of passive monitoring devices whenever they passed a star system. These devices were virtually impossible to detect. There was no telling how many had been planted within Alliance space.

The Chroniech still had a tactical advantage in that their ships were faster than those of the Alliance and they had a virtually instantaneous communications system. Stricklen asked the Hess about the Chroniech's apparent ability to send signals across vast distances with almost no delay. According to the Hess, the Chroniech were most likely using some sort of interdimensional communications system. Such a method of communication was beyond the ability of the Hess. This surprised Ken because it meant that in at least one area, the Chroniech were technologically superior to the Kyrra.

The Alliance was working feverishly at building the new Hess FTL transceivers, but several technological hurdles needed to be overcome first. The best time estimate for being able to build a production model version of the new transceiver was three months. Similar problems faced the development of the faster stardrives – delivery of the first new drive was at least six months away.

There was one ray of hope however. The advanced weapon system which the Hess had provided to the Alliance appeared to be fairly straight-forward to build. A prototype would soon be available for testing and shortly thereafter the weapon could go into large-scale production. Stricklen requested and received the technical specifications for this new weapon system. He was both impressed and scared at what he learned.

The new weapon relied upon a property of matter which Alliance scientists still could not explain. Using a complex, oscillating field which, structurally, was very similar to a stardrive matrix field, the weapon somehow converted normal matter directly into anti-matter. This conversion occurred only during certain phases of the field's cycle, which meant that if the field was applied to a beam of particles, it would convert that beam into a series of packets of alternating matter and anti-matter. When this beam struck a target, the packets would mix and the matter and anti-matter would annihilate each other releasing a huge amount of energy. The device could be added as a retrofit to all standard continuous-beam particle cannons. The addition of the retrofit would increase the destructive potential of the cannon by many orders of magnitude.

Stricklen asked the Hess to provide him with a basic description of the types of weapons which were being installed on the *Dragon*. In addition to the shield penetrator which he had seen used on the Army of Humanity ships, Stricklen discovered that the *Dragon* would be armed with two of the matter/anti-matter particle beam cannons. His new weapons were not retrofits, but were complete units built by the Hess. These cannons were so powerful, Ken realized, that they would allow him to take on anything short of a juggernaught if he so desired. Carrying so much destructive power was an unsettling thought.

Six days after beginning the modifications to the *Dragon*, the Kyrra made a completely unexpected proposal. Stricklen and Sorbith were discussing the growing Chroniech problem over a cup of coffee in the ship's mess when one of the Kyrra approached them. "May I intrude?" he asked.

Sorbith offered the Kyrran a chair and replied, "You are not intruding Norgoola. Please, join us. Can I offer you a blue-petal fizz?" The drink, Stricklen recalled, was a favorite of the Kyrra. The ship's dietitian had learned how to create it using the various juices available from the *Dragon's* food stocks.

Norgoola accepted the chair but declined the drink. After seating himself he said, "We have been monitoring the growing problems which the Alliance has been experiencing. We have noticed a trend which, if not halted, will result in the complete breakup of the Alliance and therefore its eventual destruction by the Chroniech. We feel this situation was caused by our presence and we have decided to make an offer which hopefully will correct the problem."

Sorbith leaned back in his chair and gave the Kyrra a long hard look. The chair creaked dangerously under his more than normal weight. It never ceased to amaze Ken how natural the movements of a peacekeeper's cybernetic limbs appeared even though they were much heavier and hundreds of times stronger than natural ones. "I'm not too sure I understand what you mean," Sorbith replied.

"The facts are as follows," Norgoola said. "Despite your efforts, the Chroniech continue to advance. Because of the recent confrontation with the Tholtaran's here, they have withdrawn their support in the defense effort and instead have concentrated their forces around their own star systems. This has decreased the effectiveness of your ability to defend the Alliance. There are growing tensions between the Human and Tholtaran cultures which, if not resolved, will eventually result in open conflict between the two races. This will seriously degrade the defense effort and will actually assist the

POWER STRUGGLE

Chroniech in the destruction of the Alliance.

"Finally, it should be noted that your scientists will require a considerable amount of time to understand the principles of the devices for which we provided technical information. This means the Alliance will remain at a tactical disadvantage with respect to the Chroniech for many months. We have discussed these problems and would like to propose a solution."

Sorbith appeared neutral during all this. Without moving he said, "What is your proposal?"

"The Hess have several hundred probes in storage on this planet. It also has almost three thousand probes currently stationed in various locations throughout the Alliance and beyond. Each of these probes is equipped with a transceiver which is more capable than the type for which you were provided the technical specifications. These transceivers can be removed and installed in Alliance ships thus allowing them to communicate with the network of probes. Once properly positioned, these probes can form a communications network linking all areas of the Alliance."

Stricklen could not believe his ears! Unable to hold back his thoughts he blurted out. "You're telling me that the Hess has had a high-speed communications network in existence all this time and you did not think to let us know about it? Why are you so reluctant to help us? What do you want in return for the use of this communications net?"

Stricklen had more to say but he was silenced by Sorbith. "Captain! The Kyrra are not obligated to discuss with us the reasons behind their actions. They are making us an offer which I cannot refuse. Whatever they want in return, we will give them." Facing Norgoola, Sorbith asked, "What must we do?"

"The Tholtar are to be readmitted to the Alliance with no repercussions for their past actions provided they offer a formal apology to both the Hess and the Humans."

Stricklen was infuriated. "An apology!" he shouted standing up so fast his chair fell over. "You can't dictate policy to us. Once the Tholtar get their hands..."

"Silence!" Sorbith commanded in a menacing voice. He slowly stood up and faced Stricklen. "The Alliance is in mortal danger and you are going to allow it to break apart because of racial intolerance? I represent the Alliance in this matter and I alone will make the decisions. I understand your concern but, at the moment, the welfare of the Alliance is paramount."

Sorbith stood glaring at the Captain. Stricklen chewed on his inner lip for a moment then reached back to retrieve his chair. Sitting down and making a visible effort to calm himself, he said, "My apologies. I have personal reasons for distrusting the Tholtar. I'm afraid I let them override my judgment."

"The Kyrra would like to offer one more item," Norgoola continued in a somewhat shaky voice. "The manufacturing facilities of this planet are capable of producing a number of the particle beam retro-fit units each day. Provided you agree to the terms, we will begin supplying these units. This will give the Alliance a better chance at defeating the Chroniech."

"The Alliance agrees to your proposal," Sorbith said without hesitation. "As long as the Tholtar also agree. I shall send a message to their government immediately."

After Norgoola had left, Ken tried to apologize to Sorbith again. "I understand your feelings," Sorbith interrupted. "Humans and Tholtar have much to work out. But for now, we must learn to work together. Consider this matter closed."

"Thank you sir," a much relieved Stricklen replied. "By the way, how do you tell the Kyrra apart? I couldn't help noticing that you addressed Norgoola by his name without a moment's hesitation."

Sorbith smiled and let out a chuckle. "I can't. They all look alike to me. My ship, however, can tell them apart," he said pointing to his cybernetic eyes. "I have standing instructions with it to keep me informed as to which Kyrra is whom."

"Clever," Stricklen said. "That link you have with your ship sure has its advantages."

"True – I have full access to the entire Alliance data-net. It becomes second... Hold on!"

Sorbith seemed to be listening to an inner voice. After a moment he said, "Sensors have picked up a high-speed probe entering the system. The drive-wake is Chroniech in composition. As soon as the probe is within weapons range, the Hess will destroy it. Needless to say, our presence here is no longer a secret."

"The other probe must have sent back enough information for the Chroniech to decide to launch an attack here. This one probably means a Chroniech attack force will be here within a matter of days. I hope we're ..." Stricklen paused as if remembering something important. After a second his eyes grew wide and he uttered a very un-officer-like explicative. Looking intensely at Sorbith Stricklen explained. "I recently read a report about Chroniech probes dropping monitor drones as they passed a system. Just before the juggernaught opened fire, we picked up a Chroniech probe but it did not enter the system, it only passed through. I'll bet we have been under surveillance ever since and this new probe is a prelude to an attack. They're trying to get a better idea as to our defensive capabilities."

"Why would they even bother with us?" Sorbith asked. "Because of the pulsar, this system is a very hostile place to base an attack force. Besides, the Chroniech will not bother to send a force this far into Alliance space just to destroy a few ships."

Stricklen stood up as he replied, "They're not interested in just a few ships. If they recognized the *Komodo Dragon*, they'll be here—and they'll be here in force."

On that note Stricklen turned and strode out of the mess hall leaving a slightly confused Sorbith to ponder why Ken had said what he had. Stricklen went straight to the cabin of Lieutenant Trueblood, the ship's psychologist. Ken sought her out not only because he had a lot on his mind, but also because the two had become very close friends over the last few months. She was happy that Ken wanted to speak with her.

Ken told her what was on his mind, his concerns for the Alliance, and about what had just happened in the mess hall. After patiently listening Tasha said, "Your concerns are valid Ken. You have a deep desire to protect the Alliance and to see it become more than it is. I think what is really bothering you though, is your deep distrust for the Tholtarans. This is also natural, considering what your family has gone through. On one hand you know Humans and Tholtarans must work together in peace. On the other hand you distrust them to the point that at times it affects your judgment. Internally, you are divided – much like the Alliance is now and it upsets you."

"You're right. You're also very perceptive. So tell me, what do I do about it?" Ken asked.

Tasha moved from her seat across from the Captain and sat next to him on the same bunk. She reached over and took his hand and said, "In time you will learn to deal with your feelings for the Tholtarans. This latest situation with them has only caused a minor setback by making you angry thus bringing out some of your bad feelings. I am sure that as long as you understand why you have such feelings, you will eventually be able to put them aside. Coming to me is a good sign."

Stricklen returned her grip. Their friendship was a close one and the rest of the evening was spent talking about more interesting things. They ate dinner together in the mess hall. After dinner, Ken bid her farewell and, feeling much better, retired to his stateroom and took out his diary. He opened it to the next available page and hesitated, pen poised in mid-air. A confusion of thoughts were running about in his head. Taking a deep breath he started with the loudest of them and began to write.

Just returned from having dinner with Tasha. As a ship's psychologist she is tops – as a woman she is exceptionally beautiful! I must admit that I find her company very pleasant. I should be careful though since I am her commanding officer. But still, there are possibilities there.

Another Chroniech probe appeared today. I am sure it is a sign of a Chroniech attack. They will try to retrieve the stasis chamber from us and they will undoubtedly attack ASAP with as many ships as they can muster. I only hope the Hess defense system is adequate, even though we are removing their main reactor and replacing it with another. From what I have seen of their abilities, even the Chroniech will be turned back.

I have mixed emotions about the upcoming journey to take the Kyrra home. Even at 11Kc, it will take us about three months to make the trip. According to the Hess, most of this journey will be through Chroniech space. What will we find when we get there? Will we get there? If the Kyrra are gone, what then? If they are still there, how will we be received? What will happen to the Alliance in our absence? Can we defeat the Chroniech? Will I have a home to return to?

I am very glad of one thing. I am glad I am not married. Most of the crew who remain aboard the Dragon were picked because they were not married. I did this because, for many reasons, I feel this is going to be a one-way trip. I hope I'm wrong.

Chapter 13

Departure day! For weeks, the Hess had been working furiously to finish the modifications to the *Komodo Dragon*. The last bulkhead had been welded back in place days ago and the final preparations were being made. The transport had arrived and tons of extra supplies were being transferred to the *Dragon*. Most of the post installation checks had been completed and things were finally beginning to wrap up.

The Chroniech had been strangely quiet, no new attacks within twenty-five light years of the Hess had been reported. There was a very good reason for this. Suspecting a pending attack, the Hess had sent out several probes to search the surrounding space and, after days of searching, one of them had located a large Chroniech fleet gathering just over two light years away. The probe, however, had amazingly been detected and destroyed. Prior to its destruction, the probe had managed to identify at least one planetary assault platform and picked up indications of nearly a hundred other ships.

Stricklen was on the bridge as the ship was preparing for its long journey. Some of his fears had been put aside by recent developments. The Tholtaran government had accepted the Hess proposal and their ships were back at work protecting the Alliance. Several Alliance ships had already been outfitted with the Hess transceivers and the high-speed communications network was working perfectly. And, Alliance ships were starting to be equipped with the advanced weaponry of the Kyrra.

"Fusion reactor three is lit and stable," engineering reported. "Commencing startup of reactor six."

"Acknowledged," Stricklen replied. "What is the status of the drive system?"

"Zero-power alignments are almost complete. Zero-emission standby alignments will begin immediately thereafter. The drive should be available for low power operation in about three hours."

Amazing, Ken thought. *It would have taken a small team of Alliance engineers all day to do what the Hess will accomplish in a few short hours.*

"Bridge - CIC," a voice announced over the com. "Multiple drive-wakes detected. Distance zero point eight one cee; speed three point seven kay cee;

approach vector 136 by 28 galactic. Wake signature is Chroniech."

Stricklen felt a surge of adrenaline course through his body as he listened to the report. "Composition and ETA," he queried.

"At least 138 ships. Three planetary assault platforms, seventeen dreadnoughts, and 118 lesser support craft. ETA, three hours twenty minutes assuming standard Chroniech gravimetrically forced deceleration."

"Good Lord!" Ken exclaimed. The Chroniech usually used only one of the massive planetary assault platforms when they attacked a fortified planet. Never had two been seen together, much less three. Planetary assault platforms were very much like Tholtaran juggernaughts in both size and function.

Stricklen reached out and activated the ship's address system. After the attention tone had sounded he spoke to the crew. "This is the Captain. Sensors have picked up a large Chroniech attack force heading this way. In the event the Hess is unable to protect us, I want this ship ready to lift in two hours. Don't worry about putting things where they belong, just get all the supplies onboard. If you can do something faster, even if it's not quite perfect, then do it. The second we are able, this ship lifts. I know you can do it – let's move!"

The already hectic activity throughout the ship became even more so. Supplies and stores were put wherever they would fit to be sorted and correctly stored later. The Hess told the engineer that it would accept a marginal alignment of the drive system which could be fine tuned later. The risks, it explained, would be minimal.

Stricklen received word that Sorbith had ordered the *General Patton* to prepare to return to Almaranus at max speed. "I'll be leaving in a few minutes myself," Sorbith said in the same communication. "I want to wish you and your crew luck on your journey. Tell Falnath she had better live up to her promise to return – the Alliance can't afford to lose a great mind like hers. We'll keep in touch via the Hess as long as possible. Sorbith out."

Sorbith was unable to go with them because his ship was not fast enough and was too big to fit inside the *Dragon's* hanger bay. If he was out of contact with his ship for too long, his cybernetics would automatically power down as a safety precaution. Falnath had demanded that she be allowed to go, sighting the fact that she was the best qualified person in the entire Alliance to understand Kyrra technology. Stricklen had feared she would go as far as to stow away on his ship if he had not officially granted her permission to go.

Confident of their invulnerability, the Chroniech ignored all warnings and entered the Hess system. As they approached, the three planetary assault platforms fell into a triangular formation. Doug Scarboro, who was in combat control, signaled for Stricklen's attention. Once the connection had been made he said, "Something isn't right about the Chroniech attack vector. Take a look at your tactical and their projected course."

Stricklen switched one of his screens to a tactical view and looked at the display for a moment. "I agree. If they continue on their present course they will remain out of weapons range. What the hell are they up to?"

"I don't know," Doug replied running his hand through his red hair. "As soon as we figure it out though I'll let you know." The screen darkened as Scarboro ended the link.

An hour and thirty-five minutes before the Chroniech's closest approach, the Hess informed Ken that all alignments had been completed and the *Dragon* was declared marginally spaceworthy. The final drive system adjustments would have to be done after the ship reached orbit. Stricklen ordered everyone aboard and all non-crew to leave. Ten minutes later the *Komodo Dragon* was once again on its way back into its element. As soon as the ship was in orbit, the Hess began the low-power alignment of the stardrive. Ken put the ship at battle stations and waited.

Painfully, slowly, the minutes crept by. Stricklen paced the floor of the control room, his attention alternating between the tactical display showing the position of the approaching Chroniech fleet and the propulsion system status board. He knew that the drive system must be properly aligned or the *Komodo Dragon* could tear itself apart when they attempted to use it. Until the alignment was complete, all he could do was wait. It was going to be very close.

"Chroniech are dropping to normal," CIC reported. "Their weapon systems are active."

"We're not going to make it," someone said just loud enough to be heard.

"What are they doing?" Stricklen muttered to no one in particular. The approaching fleet was shown in three-dimensional detail within the large tactical viewer. The various consoles on the bridge were laid out in the shape of a large parabola with the Captain's chair located at the apex. This chair was raised slightly higher so the Captain could have a clear view of all the consoles. The tactical viewer was placed inside this parabolic arrangement of consoles thus affording each and every bridge officer a view of the tactical situation.

The tactical viewer was a large globe capable of rendering images in full three dimensions. Special colors and codes were used to indicate velocities, distances, types of ships, etc. A trained bridge officer could interpret the various codes and colors at a glance. The computer was also programmed to make visible many of the things that were normally invisible, such as energy beams. Stricklen was paying very close attention to what was being displayed inside the viewer. Instead of the standard vee-shaped attack formation, the Chroniech were splitting their forces. As he watched, the assault platforms joined themselves together with a network of bluish energy beams. Each of the platforms emitted two beams – one to each of the other assault platforms. The rest of the ships began to drop back and appeared to be entering a holding position.

"Logistics, analysis of the Chroniech formation," Stricklen said.

Before logistics could reply, another voice said, "Bridge, this is engineering. The drive system is aligned. We are FTL capable but you're going to have to take it slow for awhile. The propulsion control computer will not allow you to exceed a one cee per second velocity change and will force you to halt at one hundred cee intervals for a few minutes so the final alignments can be completed."

Stricklen acknowledged the message from engineering. Before he could utter another word, the door to the bridge opened and the marine guard who was supposed to be preventing unauthorized entry was backpedaling into the room. He took about three steps before he completely lost his balance and fell with a loud thump onto the deck. He was quickly followed by an obviously enraged Falnath. She let out a loud hiss toward the marine which seemed to dare him to challenge her. The marine started to reach for his blaster but was stopped short by a command from Stricklen.

"Hold your weapon!" he yelled. "Falnath! You've got five seconds to explain yourself or I will order you to be put in the brig."

Falnath spoke so fast her vocoder lagged behind. Being a simple translator, it did not impart the urgency that Stricklen knew was in her voice. "You must tell the Hess to override its programming and open fire immediately. The Chroniech formation must be destroyed before they can position themselves in the beam of the pulsar."

"Why? You don't really think that..."

"There is no time to explain," Falnath interrupted. "Give me an open channel to the Hess and I will explain the situation to it." Without waiting for a reply she started to move toward the communications console.

Coming to a quick decision, Ken motioned for the communications watch to establish the connection. Falnath rushed over to the console and spoke rapidly. The Hess responded in Falnath's native language. The conversation lasted for about a minute and then abruptly ended. Falnath slowly turned toward the Captain and said, "We must leave orbit immediately. The Chroniech are about to destroy the Hess and there is nothing that we nor they can do to prevent it."

Stricklen was momentarily stunned into inactivity. The Hess destroyed? How? Then, realizing the source of the information he turned away from Falnath and said, "Helm, get us out of here as fast as possible. Set a coarse to put as much distance between us and the Chroniech. As soon as you can, set course for our destination." Turning back toward Falnath he said, "Explain."

Falnath had a dejected look about her. Her tail drooped and her head slowly swayed back and forth. She spoke quietly, the vocoder translating her words but, as before, not her tone. "I have been watching and analyzing the Chroniech's activities and I have determined the purpose of their formation and the Hess agrees with me as to its potential. The defense screens of the three assault platforms have been configured and tuned to form a gigantic, highly efficient lens. It is their intent to place this lens within the beam of the pulsar and to focus and concentrate the beam onto the planet. If they are successful, the Hess believes its defense shield will be penetrated and it will be destroyed. So far the Chroniech have remained outside of the Hess' weapons range."

"They're going to focus the pulsar beam onto the planet? That's preposterous!" Stricklen remarked. "The beam coming from that pulsar consists of more raw power than could be generated by thousands of planetary assault platforms. How the hell can you even think the Chroniech have the ability to control that much energy?"

"I will not waste my time trying to explain to you anything about hyperdimensional theory or how a small force can be used to control a much larger one. You must simply believe me when I tell you that the mathematics predict that what they are attempting is indeed possible." Falnath did not bother to wait for a reply. She turned and slowly made her way out of the control room. She muttered an apology to the marine as she passed. As the door closed behind her the communications watch said, "There goes our new high speed communications network."

Stricklen jerked himself back to the business at hand. He checked the displays and tactical readouts to verify that the *Dragon* was making its way out of the system. He then looked at the engineering readouts to make sure the propulsion system was functioning properly. If all went well, the ship would be able to engage the stardrive in a matter of minutes. After all the important items had been checked, Stricklen thought about the communications watch's comment. What he had said made perfect sense.

"Open a channel to the Hess!" he ordered.

Once the connection was established Stricklen said, "You have stated there is a strong possibility that the Chroniech will be able to destroy you. If they succeed, the Alliance will no longer have access to the communications network provided by your probes. Is there anything that can be done to prevent this?"

"The destruction of this unit is highly probable," the emotionless voice responded. "The probes are programmed to render themselves inoperative if approached by an unauthorized ship. The recognition codes for the probes and a procedure for preventing this self-destruction in the future is being uploaded to the Alliance network. The exact location and heading of each probe is also being uploaded. In addition to this, a method of accessing the network is being provided. In the event of this unit's destruction the network will remain active and under Alliance control."

"Is there anything we can do to help improve your chance of survival?"

"Negative. The Chroniech have technical knowledge concerning the manipulation of multidimensional space which this unit does not possess. They have obviously been monitoring the activities in this area for some time and they have devised a method by which our defenses can be circumvented. Your highest priority at this point in time is to return the Kyrra to their people."

"Captain," Scarboro said as his face appeared on a screen. "The Chroniech fleet is moving to intercept. I detect at least forty ships breaking formation. Until we get the stardrive aligned, we will not be able to outrun them. Assuming they steer a course that keeps them out of the range of the Hess weapons, they could intercept in as soon as forty minutes."

"Thanks Doug. Power up all weapons and drop a couple of probes to see what happens," Stricklen replied. Turning back to the Hess he said, "The Chroniech fleet is trying to cut us off. We will not get very far before they catch us. Let's just hope our new weapons can get us out of this, *Komodo Dragon* out."

The minutes ticked by as the *Komodo Dragon* slowly made its way out of the gravitational influence of the pulsar. The tactical viewer showed the Chroniech fleet taking a long looping course toward them. Ken strongly suspected they knew what sort of weapons were at the disposal of the Hess

POWER STRUGGLE

and they were maintaining a comfortable distance from them. The tactical viewer showed a continuous analysis of their progress. They were slowly closing the gap between themselves and the *Dragon*.

"I have an idea sir," someone said.

Stricklen turned around to see his communications watch looking at him. "Let's hear it Mr. Jurasinski."

"If I recall, the Hess stated they have several hundred probes in storage on the planet. Unless I'm mistaken, each one of those probes is powered by a small reactor which could be somehow made to detonate. In effect, the Hess have a small supply of missiles."

Stricklen was impressed. "Mr. Juransinski, I think you may have a career in battle tactics after this is over. Open a channel to the Hess."

As the channel was being opened, the *Dragon* made the change-over to FTL drive. Unlike the standard Kauffman stardrive which the Alliance used, there was no noticeable effects as the drive fields formed around the ship. "Channel open sir."

Stricklen quickly outlined the proposal to the Hess. "Only an aggressive species would think of using a probe as a weapon," the Hess replied. "In order to make the probe as small as possible and to enable them to travel for very long distances they are powered by matter/anti-matter reactors. Although there are numerous safeguards, a method of triggering an explosion is possible. Your suggestion will be implemented."

"The planetary assault platforms are in position," Scarboro announced from CIC. "A visual from our probe is available on com channel eight."

Stricklen switched the tactical viewer so they could all see what was happening. "Multiple launches detected from the surface," Doug announced. "Looks like at least 375 small high speed probes are heading this way. ETA three minutes."

"They must have used their entire inventory of probes," Stricklen commented.

The formation of assault platforms had entered the radiation beam of the pulsar. Although the intense radiation was invisible to the naked eye, it had an extraordinary effect on the defense screens of the three ships. Each of the powerful defense screens was ablaze with deflected energy. Stricklen was amazed the Chroniech shields could withstand that kind of punishment considering how close they were to the pulsar. Acting as a single structure, the formation altered their position slightly. A moment later, some sort of intense green energy field formed between the three ships. At first, nothing seemed to be happening but as Stricklen watched, something strange began to occur.

The pattern of deflected energy began to change. Streamers of excited particles began to flow across the defense shields toward the center of the three platforms. Stricklen entered a command into his console and finally understood what was happening. The sensors of the probe had detected a powerful force field coming from the assault platforms which was acting like a gigantic funnel. The radiation beam from the pulsar was being guided so that it passed through the center of the formation where other forces were at work.

In a process too complicated for him to understand, the Chroniech defense shields were acting like a giant lens. In effect, all the available power from a large portion of the pulsar's radiation beam was being concentrated and focused into a coherent beam of indescribable power. The Chroniech were apparently having some difficulty stabilizing the effect, since the beam never fully reached a highly focused pattern. It seemed to sputter and spray out into space almost as soon as it was formed. Stricklen watched as they worked to bring the beam into proper focus.

"Hess probes approaching Chroniech fleet," Doug announced. "Detecting massive weapons discharge...Picking up several large explosions...Chroniech fleet is now sub-light...More explosions...Drive wakes detected, they are in pursuit again. Looks like seven...no – make that eight ships still on an intercept course."

"Look!" someone shouted. The probe had turned its pickup toward Shaular. A large silvery dome of force had formed over the Hess installation. This was the defense shield of the Hess in its most protective mode. Something was beating against this shield with unbelievable force. Huge solar flare like discharges of deflected energy erupted from the shield's surface. The entire shield seemed to waver and ripple as it fought to protect the Hess. As suddenly as it began it ended. The Chroniech were unable to accurately direct their new weapon to a given target and thus the beam wavered about the surface of the planet. In its wake, a red hot ribbon of molten rock tens of kilometers wide and several deep marked its path. Bare rock met with the unleashed power of a dead star. It did not glow, or even boil, it literally exploded instantly into vapor. Wherever that finger of energy touched, destruction resulted.

Eventually, the wandering beam of incomprehensible power once again reached the Hess base. As before, enormous ribbons of energy cascaded off the defense shield. The silvery surface of the shield wavered and rippled and then promptly ceased to exist. With horror, the crew of the *Komodo Dragon* watched as the Chroniech allowed their awesome beam to pass over the Hess several times. On its third pass a massive explosion occurred. An enormous column of molten and solid rock was thrown into the sky – some of it achieving escape velocity. The entire planet shook with the force of the explosion. The containment field holding the anti-matter within the stasis chamber's power plant had been breached. The Hess were no more.

Stricklen waited until the pursuing Chroniech fleet was only a few minutes away before he issued his next order. "Helm, disengage stardrive and drop to normal. Weapons, bring all systems on-line and designate all incoming targets as hostile. Permission is granted to open fire as soon as they are within range. CIC, give me a tactical of the incoming ships."

Stricklen had decided to stand and fight when and where he choose and not the Chroniech. The planetary assault platforms were not an immediate threat since they were so far down the pulsar's gravity-well that it would take them many minutes before they could try to engage their own stardrives. The tactical display which appeared on the bridge's main viewscreen showed him what they were up against.

Eight Chroniech warships had survived the Hess attack. Five of them were heavy cruisers and the other three were battleship class. If he had been in command of the old *Komodo Dragon* Stricklen would have tried to run. But the *Komodo Dragon* which he now commanded was protected by the advanced weapons technology of an ancient civilization. Kyrra designed and Hess built, these weapons provided the *Dragon* with unparalleled destructive power and Stricklen had no qualms about using them against the Chroniech. After hearing what the Hess had said earlier about Chroniech technology he fervently hoped his new weapons would be adequate.

"Chroniech ships dropping to normal," a voice from CIC reported. "Sledgehammers are charging. All other weapon systems are on-line and locked. Sensors show the Chroniech weapons are powered."

Confident of their ability to destroy a single Alliance warship, the Chroniech advanced. They soon discovered their intended pray was no ordinary Alliance ship. It had been previously learned that the Chroniech weapon's had a range of about 115,000 kilometers. At a distance of 130,000 kilometers the *Komodo Dragon* opened fire. Two brilliant white beams of energy stabbed out from the Hess weapons. Two Chroniech battleships found themselves in a loosing battle for their own existence.

The defense screens of the two enemy ships flared into brilliant denial, throwing enormous bolts of dissipated energy back into space. Try as they might, the shields were no match for the Kyrra weapons. Within a few seconds, they began to leak and soon portions of the hulls they protected began to glow. After a few more seconds, the shields collapsed entirely and two Chroniech ships were no longer a threat.

The remaining ships were now within their own weapons range but held their fire. Instead of pressing the attack, they began to slow and veer off. The *Dragon's* weapons officer, however, continued to evaluate the situation. The now fully charged sledgehammer's were assigned a single target and they joined the battle along with every non-Kyrra weapon the *Dragon* had to offer. At the same time two new targets had been assigned to the Kyrra weapons. In no time at all, three more Chroniech ships became lifeless hulks.

The remaining enemy ships engaged their stardrives and retreated. After watching them for a moment, Stricklen said, "Stand down from battle stations. Helm, resume our original heading; maximum possible speed." He then activated the ship-wide address system and said, "Congratulations on a job well done! The Chroniech have retreated after suffering heavy losses. We have a very long journey ahead of us. I would like all hands to help in stowing our supplies. Once that is complete, you are free to take it easy as long as you are not on watch. I am canceling the rest of the normal workday routine for today. There will be a senior staff meeting in the main conference room at 0800 tomorrow morning to discuss the ship's routine for the remainder of the journey. The results of this meeting will be put out at department level meetings as soon as possible tomorrow. That is all."

Stricklen then contacted his chief engineer. Skip's image appeared on the monitor and, judging from the background, he was in his favorite spot – the primary engineering control center. As soon as he noticed the connection had been made, Skip looked directly into the monitor and said, "What can I do for you skipper?"

Stricklen saw the obvious joy on his engineer's face and knew he was in heaven. Watching an alien stardrive take your ship to previously unheard of speeds would excite any engineer. Stricklen smiled and asked, "How long before we will be at maximum speed?"

"With the acceleration we're allowed and the required pauses for the dynamic tuning to be done, I would say about six hours," Skip replied. Stricklen noticed that his eyes kept glancing off to either side.

"Is everything OK down there?"

POWER STRUGGLE

"Oh yes! Kyrra technology is amazing. This stardrive practically aligns itself. You should come down here and have a look."

"Thank you but I think I will pass this time. Let me know if you experience any problems." Stricklen then called up a tactical display showing their present course. He entered some information into the console and observed the results. Satisfied with what he saw, he shut down the viewscreen and stood up. After stretching with the appropriate accompanying verbal utterances (along with a few cracks and pops) he announced. "I'm going to get something to eat and then I'll be in my stateroom.

As he made his way to the mess hall Stricklen thought about the future. By the time the *Komodo Dragon* reached the Chroniech border she would be traveling far beyond their ability to intercept. They should be able to simply get out of the way of any ship attempting to intercept them. They were finally on their way! In a few months, if their luck held out, he would soon be face to face with a member of a civilization which has been in existence since his own's early stone age. The thought was a little frightening.

Chapter 14

The council chamber was deathly quiet. The leader stood before the council with his claws fully extended indicating he was exceptionally angry and would kill anyone or anything that crossed him. The air was tense as the rest of the Chroniech ruling body waited for their leader to speak. "You have all seen the reports," he began in a slow low voice. "The creatures calling themselves the Alliance have been able to use some of the technology of the ancients. Even as we speak, one of their ships is on a direct course into our space. It is believed that this ship will attempt to penetrate our defenses and attack our planets. These creatures must be eliminated. I am ordering all available ships, including all reserve units, to be used in the effort to rid the galaxy of this Alliance. Is this council in agreement with this?"

The leader's gaze paused on each of the eleven council members, noting as each one signified his agreement. After an unusually long hesitation, the leader continued. "The Alliance warship which is entering our space must be stopped. Its combat capabilities have been greatly enhanced and its speed is far beyond anything we can achieve. Are there any recommendations as to how to destroy this ship?"

For a Chroniech, especially a leader, this was a dangerous statement. One of the other council members could decide this was a sign of weakness and challenge him. After a carefully calculated silence one of the attendee's said, "I believe I have a solution. It will require a number of ships to implement."

The leader evaluated the response and who it had come from then said, "The council will hear your plan." Relieved that his response had been accepted, the councilman presented his proposal.

* * * * *

Stricklen stood before his assembled senior staff. "We have embarked upon an unusual voyage," he began. "We are traveling farther than anyone else in the Alliance has ever dreamt of going. We are using alien technologies which have allowed us to travel faster than any Alliance ship has ever gone. The journey will last for months and our chances of success are questionable.

POWER STRUGGLE

Needless to say, we are in a unique situation. Because of the duration of this mission and the reduced size of our crew, I have decided to drastically change how we do business on this ship.

"Military protocol will be relaxed. This does not mean discipline will not be kept. Dress codes, watch rotation, routine maintenance schedules, and all other military functions will have to be modified. This will allow the crew to find their own methods of reducing boredom in order to hopefully keep the tension low. I am charging all department heads with developing a set of guidelines which will achieve this goal. Are there any questions at this point?"

After waiting for a brief moment, Stricklen continued. "We will be traveling through Alliance space for another ten days. After that, we will be in Chroniech space. As you all know, we have not set our course directly for the target system. If the Kyrra are indeed still there, I believe they would be rather upset at us if we were to point out their location to the Chroniech. My intentions are to remain on this course (which does not intersect with any star system for at least 5000 light years) until we have cleared Chroniech space. According to the latest information provided by the Hess the Chroniech empire extends for roughly 2100 light years in the direction we are traveling. Once we are clear of the Chroniech, we will set our course for the target system. In order to traverse Chroniech space with as little loss of time as possible I plan to avoid any contact with them. Minor course corrections will be made as required to accomplish this.

"Finally, because of the duration of this trip, I must insist that all personnel be told to conserve supplies as best as possible. There are no Alliance ports for us to pull into to restock. Any questions?"

Once again, there were none. "If you have any questions please get in touch with me. I will be on the bridge for the rest of the day. Thank you, meeting adjourned."

On the way out of the room Scarboro noticed there was a new bounce in Stricklen's step as he made his way to the bridge. "You look to be in a very chipper mood this morning Captain!" he called out as he hurried to catch up.

"Now that we are finally on our way I feel pretty good," Stricklen replied. "Even the fact that we will be traveling through Chroniech space doesn't bother me because I know with this ship we can simply avoid any conflict. Nothing can catch us!"

"I sort of hate to pass up the opportunity to use this ship's firepower on our way through," Doug said. Catching Stricklen's alarmed look he quickly continued, "Don't worry Ken, I won't try to avenge the Alliance while I'm on watch."

The two officers walked together in silence for a few moments. "How are things between you and Tash?" Doug asked without warning.

Ken stopped in his tracks and looked at his executive officer not knowing what to say. "You're not in a better mood just because we are on our way," Doug explained. "The whole ship knows that you and Tash have become close friends." Seeing the shocked look on his Captain's face Doug said, "Don't worry sir. No man is an island and you are no different. You and Tasha make a good couple and the crew is happy for you both."

"But I'm her commanding officer. We are just good friends!" Stricklen said in shock.

Smiling, Doug said, "There's no need to worry, your reputation as a good captain has not been harmed. In fact, I think this relationship may well enhance your status with the rest of the crew."

"The rumors must be flying," Stricklen remarked as he started back down the passageway.

"There have been a few but everyone realizes they are only rumors." Suddenly, becoming concerned the Captain might be considering ending his relationship with Tasha Doug said, "Ken, don't let rumors and such affect the relationship you have established with Tasha. I think it's great. If any of the crew feels differently, then I will have a heart to heart talk with them. It would not only be unfair to you, but to Tash as well."

"You will do no such thing," Stricklen replied, an idea popping into his head . "If the crew wants to talk about me, then let them, as long as they continue to work together as a crew. Besides, having something to talk about will help keep their minds occupied during the trip. Nothing like a good rumor about the Captain to liven things up."

The next few of days passed without incident. The crew of the *Dragon* began to settle into the routine of a long, extended voyage. The alien stardrive appeared to be functioning perfectly as the heavy-cruiser blasted through space at 11,121 times the speed of light.

The *Dragon* had its first encounter with Chroniech ships eight days into their voyage. "Chroniech ships detected!" the report came from CIC.

"Tactical," Stricklen automatically ordered. The tactical viewer shifted to a computer generated plot of the situation. A large fleet of Chroniech warships stood squarely in their path. They were spread out over a large volume of space forming a net meant to trap them. Stricklen looked at the display for a minute then said, "Helm: alter course to 264 mark 11. That should steer us clear of the fleet."

The course correction was fairly significant but it kept them going in the same general direction. Once the helm had entered the new settings into the ship's controls the tactical viewer shifted to show their new projected course. They would pass within half a million kilometers of the nearest Chroniech ship even if that ship altered its own course to attempt an intercept. Two hours later, the enemy fleet was behind them and out of sensor range.

* * * * *

"The cowards refuse to engage us!" the frustrated Chroniech hissed. "We have attempted to intercept the Alliance ship on two occasions and each time they have altered course to avoid us."

As angry as the Chroniech leader was, he could not find fault in the deployment of their forces which had been ordered by the commander making the report. No punishment was therefore warranted. "Where is the ship heading?"

"We do not know. Their course does not intercept any star system for hundreds of light years. Each time they make a course correction, their destination seems to change."

The Chroniech leader had risen to his current position because of his ruthless and often brilliant combat strategies. He considered the situation for several minutes, the rest of the council waiting in patient silence. "Show me a star chart of the area of space where the Alliance ship is now located," he ordered. A moment later, a holographic image of the space currently occupied by the *Komodo Dragon* appeared.

"Expand to double," he ordered and the display shifted. "Indicate current position and type of all warships." Again the display changed to show hundreds of tiny colored dots. The leader's gaze moved about the image. "Perhaps we can use their cowardice to our own advantage," he stated and then proceeded to lay out a plan.

* * * * *

Over the course of the next fifteen days, the *Dragon* encountered ten more Chroniech fleets attempting to intercept them. Each time, they made a minor course correction to avoid contact with the enemy. "Chroniech ships detected!" the report came from CIC for the eleventh time. The tactical viewer automatically shifted to encompass the new threat. Stricklen was about to order the standard avoidance course correction but paused for a moment to consider the situation again. "*Dragon*," he said, addressing the ship's computer. "Display a summary of all course corrections over the past two days."

In response to his command, the tactical viewer shifted again to show a larger section of their course. All of their past course corrections could clearly be seen indicating where the *Komodo Dragon* had altered course to avoid conflict with Chroniech ships. Stricklen stared at the display for a moment then said, "Using the past course corrections as a guide and the assumed course correction which would be required to avoid contact with the Chroniech ships now approaching, develop an estimated travel path for the next five days."

A bluish cone indicating their possible course appeared on the screen. A yellow cone formed around the blue one indicating an area of lower probability. "Identify any pulsars within the projected course cones." Two blinking red lights appeared with an identification code next to each one. Stricklen slowly stood up and looked intently at the display. One of the red lights was near the center of the blue cone.

Sitting back down heavily in his command chair, Stricklen smiled slightly and said in a low voice, "Nice try, but I'm smarter than that." Then, in a much louder voice, "Battle stations! Helm, maintain present course. Minor course corrections are allowed but only if required to avoid a collision. XO to the bridge."

A moment later Doug Scarboro appeared on the bridge. He was dressed in shorts and sweating heavily. "I was working out in the gym," he explained. "What's going on?"

Stricklen pointed to the tactical display and asked, "See anything that bothers you?"

Doug scanned the image for a couple of seconds then let out a whistle. "Tricky son-of-a-bitches aren't they? What are you going to do?"

"We are going to stay on our present course. If they manage to drop us out of stardrive we'll just deal with them and be on our way. I'm tired of messing around with these people. As soon as we've passed this group we'll start making minor course changes twice a shift to keep them on their toes."

"Just keep us clear of any pulsars," Doug said. "The only ships we really need to be afraid of are the planetary assault ships. We should be able to detect them long before they are a threat unless they happen to anticipate our course accurately enough to position one in our path with its stardrive shutdown. Even then, we might still have a chance. What is our ETA to this group?"

"*Dragon*, display current tactical." The display changed to one more suitable to their short term situation. "ETA about eight minutes. I doubt they've anticipated this move since we have always avoided contact in the past. Our next encounter might very well be different."

The minutes ticked by as the *Dragon* closed on the Chroniech ships. Zero hour arrived and the Alliance ship simply went through the loose formation. With the enemy ships behind them, Stricklen canceled battle stations and the crew returned to their normal routine.

For three more weeks the *Komodo Dragon* sped through Chroniech space without incident and without encountering any additional Chroniech ships. One day, the chief engineer asked to see the Captain. Stricklen, who was enjoying the luxury of reading a book, invited him up to his stateroom. "Captain, we have a problem," Skip said after being admitted into the Captain's cabin. "The stardrive is showing some strange readings. I've run all the diagnostics the Hess loaded into our computer but I still can't pin down what's wrong."

"Explain what you mean by 'strange readings,' " Stricklen asked. Then, before he could reply, Stricklen said, "Wait, let's get Norgoola here to listen to this." He had the bridge track down Norgoola and request that he come to the Captain's cabin. A few minutes later he arrived.

"I understand you are familiar with the operation of your people's stardrive?" Stricklen asked after Norgoola had found himself a seat.

"My primary area of expertise is in field dynamics, but I also know a considerable amount of information concerning the inner workings of our standard stardrives," Norgoola said. "Is there a problem with the one provided by the Hess?"

Stricklen motioned for the engineer to proceed. "I think there is," he began, "I've started getting some strange readings from the matrix field flux shaping system. Specifically, there is a zero point zero one three percent variance in the harmonic feedback loop compared with the desired flux tilting from the dynamic compensator module. At first I thought..."

The rest of the conversation was complete and utter gibberish to Stricklen. He made a pretense of listening, but for the most part, his mind was elsewhere. At one point in the complex technical discussion, the engineer used the Captain's computer terminal to display several graphs and a portion of the technical schematics for a section of the stardrive control system. After ten minutes of highly technical conversation, Stricklen finally heard something he could understand and he did not like what he had just heard.

"You have to take the stardrive off-line? Can you put the reason in simple terms for me," he asked.

"Very simply," the engineer responded. "The drive stabilization system is experiencing a harmonic feedback which will only get worse. Eventually, the drive will shut itself down as certain parameters exceed their threshold values. We estimate this will happen in about twelve hours unless something is done to correct the problem."

"What is causing it?"

"We are not absolutely positive, but we believe it is a malfunctioning field sensor within the drive generator itself. It could also be a loose field emitter coil. We won't know for sure until the drive is opened and we can get access to the internals."

"How long?"

"About eight or nine hours. Norgoola and I should have everything set up to get to work in about four or five hours."

"You do realize that by taking the stardrive out of service you are also leaving us without any sort of defensive shielding."

"I realize that Captain. But, there is nothing I can do about it."

After thinking about the situation for a moment Stricklen replied, "Very well. Get everything you need staged. I don't want to be dead in space and vulnerable for any longer than we have to. Let me know as soon as you are ready."

After Norgoola and the engineer had left, Stricklen called Scarboro and told him the bad news. "I figured things were going too well," Doug replied. "Let's just hope the Chroniech aren't close enough to cause us any problems."

Stricklen then made his way to the bridge. Once there, he ordered the navigator to alter course to take them as far away from all nearby star systems as possible. As soon as the word came that the technicians were ready, Stricklen sounded battle stations. Within minutes the *Komodo Dragon* was ready for the worst. Ken then made an announcement to the crew. "This is the Captain. Our stardrive has experienced a failure which will force us to take it off-line. This will leave us without propulsion and without a defense shield. All hands will remain at battle stations until the repairs are complete. To minimize the possibility of detection by Chroniech vessels I will be setting condition dog zebra throughout the ship. We want to become as indistinguishable as possible from any other piece of floating space debris. All hands set condition dog zebra and report completion to the bridge."

The dog zebra setting was a holdover from the old navy method of designating the compartmentalization of a ship. Dog zebra indicated that the ship was to become as electromagnetically invisible as possible. All active scanners and communications arrays were secured. Half of the ship's fusion reactors were powered down to standby. Internal equipment that generated any sort of energy that could be radiated into space was shutdown.

Ken gave the order to drop to normal and shutdown the stardrive. The tension level seemed to rise as soon as the characteristic dull thrumming of the stardrive had faded. A few minutes later, all sections had reported that condition dog zebra had been set.

Stricklen nervously paced the control room for almost two hours. Finally, he decided to go have a first-hand look at the work. The first thing he saw as he neared the massive stardrive was Norgoola half buried in the internals of the drive unit. An access panel had been removed and several pieces of equipment lay off to one side waiting to be reinstalled. A portable diagnostics console was positioned near the access panel and several cables snaked from it into the interior of the drive. Not wanting to impede their progress Stricklen was content to just watch.

Norgoola extracted himself from the access panel and handed a technician a small device stating its name. The technician carefully labeled it and put it with the others. Over the next forty minutes several more devices of varying size were removed, labeled, and stored. Finally, Norgoola motioned for a technician to turn on the diagnostics console. Stricklen moved in a little closer to see what was happening. The screen of the console showed a complex series of waveforms and what appeared to be mathematical symbols.

"We have determined that one of the field emitter monitor modules has partially failed," Norgoola explained. "The analyzer will determine which one. Once the failed module has been identified, it will be replaced."

Several minutes passed. The analyzer's display shifted and a schematic of the stardrive's internals appeared with a component marked in red. Skip looked at the results, grabbed a small tool and stuck his half his body into the access port. He squirmed around for a couple minutes and then emerged with a very small black object in his hand. Norgoola handed him a new one and he dove once more back into the internals of the drive unit. A couple of minutes later, Skip pulled himself out and straightened his back with a loud grunt.

Norgoola adjusted some settings on the analyzer and once again the display showed that it was working. "The analyzer will verify that the new unit is working properly and determine what adjustments, if any, are required," Norgoola explained walking over to the Captain. "Several remote manipulators have been attached to the phase transducers and modulator control emitters. These manipulators will allow the analyzer to automatically make the required adjustments. Because there are five separate interdependent adjustments to make, the process will require a fair amount of time. The analyzer must determine what effect each adjustment has had on the other parameters in order to keep the entire drive in alignment."

"I can't make any sense of these readings," Ken said motioning to the display. "Just how much of an adjustment are we talking about?"

"This stardrive is an order of magnitude more complex than your best drive system. The field coil alignments must be absolutely precise to an accuracy of at least two angstroms. The frequencies and phase relationship of the field emitters must be controllable to within one part in four trillion. Each time one parameter is adjusted it affects the alignment of the other four."

"I think I understand," Ken replied. "I'm surprised that we even have the spare parts necessary to repair the drive. Did the Hess provide us with spare parts for everything?"

"It is my understanding," Skip answered, "that the Hess gave us a full compliment of spare parts for all of the equipment which they installed. Even though the reliability of their equipment is much higher than ours it is also much much older. Having these spares on hand was a good precaution."

They stood in silence for a few moments watching the numbers dance on the face of the analyzer readout. "You must be very anxious to get back to your own people and away from us primitives," Stricklen said to Norgoola.

Ken still had a hard time reading Kyrra facial expressions, but he thought he noticed a look of surprise on Norgoola's face. "You are mistaken," Norgoola said after a moments reflection. "We have learned much about your people since our release from stasis. I have come to respect your race although there are many aspects about you I still do not understand. You live in a hostile environment, yet the Alliance is proof that peace between vastly different cultures can be obtained. Your race is not primitive. It is only not as advanced as ours."

Motioning toward the disassembled stardrive, Norgoola continued, "This stardrive is far more advanced than any I have ever seen before. It was built by my people long after I had entered stasis. I understand it only because it is based on principles which I am very familiar with. My people have been learning and advancing for thousands of years while I and the others with me have remained in stasis. We are glad we are returning to our own people, but we are also apprehensive because we may not understand them when we are reunited. We feel very much alone."

Stricklen looked at the Kyrra with a new sense of understanding. These five individuals were from a people far more advanced than his own yet, because they had been in stasis, the tables had been turned on them and their own people were now far more advanced than they were before they had entered stasis. They did not fit in with anyone and were truly alone. Stricklen suddenly felt very sorry for them.

Ken returned to the bridge where he impatiently waited for the word that the stardrive had been repaired. As each minute went by, he kept thinking that the next would bring the bad news that a Chroniech attack force was vectoring in. Despite his fears, the sensitive instruments of the *Komodo Dragon* showed that space remained clear of enemy ships. Eventually, the chief engineer reported that all repairs had been completed and the stardrive was again operational.

With a loud sigh of relief Stricklen ordered, "Helm: engage stardrive and resume course. Stand-down from battle stations. Secure from condition dog zebra."

Ken could not believe their luck. They had been dead in space for eight hours and not one Chroniech ship had come within detector range. He turned the watch over to a junior officer and went to his stateroom to relax for the evening.

About an hour later, Stricklen decided he wanted a snack and headed for the mess hall. As he stepped out of his stateroom he felt a sickening lurch. His vision blurred for a split second and a wave of dizziness swept over him. Ken tried to reach out and hold onto the bulkhead for support but instead he fell forward. On the way down, his head impacted the edge of a cabinet and he started to black out. As he struggled to regain consciousness he thought he heard the alarm klaxon sounding the call to battle stations. Something had caused them to suddenly drop out of stardrive very quickly.

Someone pulled Stricklen to his feet and shouted his name. Ken was barely aware of a voice in his head – it was the bridge trying to contact him through his earpiece. A face floated into his blurred tunnel vision and again shouted his name. The thick fog surrounding Ken's brain slowly lifted and he recognized the face as that of the ship's supply clerk. Shaking his head, Stricklen finally managed to clear his vision and his mind. "What happened?" he dumbly asked.

"I don't know sir. We dropped out of stardrive and went to battle stations. The bridge has been trying to get your attention for the last couple of minutes. You're bleeding, let me take you to sick bay."

Stricklen pressed his hand against his head where it hurt the most. When he pulled it away and looked at it, he saw that it was covered in blood. The entire right side of his head behind his ear was sticky. Wiping his hand on his pants he firmly said, "No! I'm fine now, thanks." Stricklen shrugged off the last bit of disorientation and took off at a run toward the bridge.

The marine guard must have heard him coming because he was holding the door open for him as he rounded the corner. Stricklen burst onto the bridge amidst utter chaos. "Out!" he commanded the junior officer who was occupying his chair. The officer looked up and seeing who it was immediately exited the command chair. He started to say something about the Captain's injury but was waved off.

Stricklen's gaze quickly swept the entire control room while he was in the process of sitting down. His fingers flew over the command keys bringing up several screens of ship status. A gravity mine had somehow been placed in their path. Its intense gravitational field had caused them to drop out of stardrive. The gravity mine had already been destroyed but the damage had been done. Stricklen knew it would take engineering a few minutes to get the stardrive stable enough to once again use. Until then, they were vulnerable—and everybody knew that where there were gravity mines, there were warships.

"Multiple drive wakes detected!" came the expected report. "Nearest contact will arrive in just over one minute. Signature is Chroniech."

Stricklen quickly figured out what had happened. The Chroniech had apparently known that they had dropped out of stardrive and expected them to eventually resume their course. Instead of attacking directly (which would have been disastrous for the *Dragon* since she had been without a defense shield during the repairs) the Chroniech had decided to lay a trap along their course. They had done so at a distance beyond their ability to detect the drive wakes of the ships laying the trap. Stricklen had been caught off-guard and he was not pleased with himself.

The tactical display showed at least eight incoming ships. The descriptors next to the enemy ships showed that they would be dealing with some pretty powerful warcraft. The first ship, a heavy cruiser, dropped out of stardrive dangerously close to them and immediately opened fire. The Kyrra-powered defense shield easily deflected the energy beams and was not seriously challenged.

The *Komodo Dragon*, however, did not remain silent. Two beams of energy leapt out from the *Dragon's* guns and struck the Chroniech's defense screen. The screen briefly deflected the attack but was no match for the Hess-built weapons. The enemy ship was soon speared clear through and exploded in a blinding flash.

Two more warships dropped out of stardrive and engaged. One of these was a huge battleship of a type which had not yet been seen by the Alliance. As the *Dragon* targeted the smaller vessel three more ships appeared and added their firepower to that of the other two. Once again, the two particle beam cannons opened fire and a second Chroniech ship was soon reduced to junk.

"Looks like they're trying to englobe us," Doug reported from CIC. Ken's tactical display showed the Chroniech ships moving in a random pattern around his ship. As he tried to make sense of what they were doing a third ship was destroyed and two more appeared. As the new arrivals added their firepower to that of the others the *Dragon's* defense screen began to show signs of being heavily loaded.

"Sledgehammers are charged – targeting the largest ship with all weapons – target locked – firing!"

Four bright balls of sparkling energy sped through space and struck the battleship's defense screen. At the same time, the *Dragon's* entire arsenal of projected energy weapons struck at the same location. The result was completely unexpected. The enemy defense screen wavered and fought in vain to prevent the destructive beams from passing through. The energy of the sledgehammers were expended in breaking down the battleship's screen but the rest of the weapons made it through and touched bare metal. Instead of punching a hole in the ship, an enormous cloud of vapor was blasted into space.

At first, Ken did not know what had happened. Then realization dawned on him. "The battleship is encased in some sort of ablative coating," Ken told the XO. "It boils away and dissipates the energy from our weapons. We'll have to burn our way through it."

"We have another problem sir," the XO responded. "We have detected hundreds of very small objects being dumped into space by the attackers. We just ran a detailed scan of one of these objects. They're fusion bombs and we're surrounded by them."

"Helm! Maximum drive – get us away from this area!" he ordered.

The *Komodo Dragon* had barely begun to move when all of the surrounding fusion bombs detonated. Several panels showed red warning lights and Stricklen's command console lit up with warning indicators. Their defense shield, as powerful as it was, had been partially breached. Ken listened to the damage reports as they flooded in.

"Fusion reactor one and four are off-line—Hull breach on deck six amidships—Sledgehammer three damaged—High radiation warning on all decks forward of frame 58—Communications array damaged—sub-light engine off-line."

Theirs had not been the only ship damaged, however. As soon as the sensors had recovered from the overload, Stricklen saw that three of the Chroniech ships had been destroyed by their own bombs. Unaffected by all this activity, the *Dragon's* combat computer targeted the remaining ships and opened fire. The smaller ship ceased to exist with a single shot. All available weapons were then turned on the battleship. For two minutes the two ships battled it out. The superior firepower of the *Komodo Dragon* eventually resulted in the destruction of the last remaining enemy ship.

Stricklen quickly assessed their situation. Punching a button on his console he said, "CIC this is the Captain, are there any more incoming?"

After a second's delay the response came back. "Yes sir. Picking up at least nine more drive wakes from multiple vectors. First contact in three minutes."

Stricklen pressed another button and said, "Engineering, I need the stardrive back on-line in under two minutes or we're dead."

"Working on it sir!" a winded voice responded. "Give us another thirty seconds to reset the matrix field generator and clear up some power grid problems."

Confident in his engineering staff, Stricklen did not bother them when the thirty seconds went by with no word. At the forty second mark, the helm reported that the stardrive was available. Stricklen glanced at the tactical display, choose a course which would take them away from all incoming ships, and ordered the *Komodo Dragon* to exit the area at maximum speed. Within seconds, the *Dragon* was accelerating away from the Chroniech ships and out of danger.

POWER STRUGGLE

It took three days to complete all the repairs they were capable of making while underway. Part of the ship remained at a vacuum because of a massive rupture in the *Dragon's* armor plating which was beyond the ability of the crew to repair. Luckily, nothing vital had been seriously damaged. Unfortunately, four of the crew had been killed and six others injured as a result of their encounter. Stricklen had immediately taken steps to prevent a re-occurrence of what had happened. He ordered the helm to change their course by at least five degrees in a random direction every three hours as long as their general heading was in the right direction.

For the next month and a half the *Komodo Dragon* zigzagged its way through Chroniech space. On only six occasions did the crew pick up the drive-wakes of Chroniech ships. Small course corrections allowed them to avoid contact. The newly aligned stardrive functioned flawlessly during the entire trip. Eventually, Stricklen was satisfied they had finally left Chroniech space far enough behind them and gave the order to set course for their actual destination.

Their first target was the planet which the Kyrra had been terraforming. Stricklen felt that since the terraforming project would still be going on, the Kyrra would be there to monitor its progress. This planet was the best place to begin their search and had the highest probability of allowing them to make contact with the Kyrra.

Chapter 15

"Entering the target system," the helm announced.

"Full scan," Ken ordered. After a few seconds, the tactical viewer began to display some information about the star system they were now entering. A total of seven planets had been located, all in a pretty much standard orbital configuration. From the information obtained from the Hess, the Kyrra had been terraforming the third planet. The star appeared to be a very stable main sequence star near the middle of its expected life.

"Let's see the third planet," Stricklen said after looking at the data on the rest of the system for awhile.

The viewscreen shifted and displayed the image of a small world. From this distance, it appeared much like a bluish ball with small white dots at two ends. "We are still too far away to get any detailed readings at this time," the science station officer announced.

Several hours later, the *Komodo Dragon* was in a tight orbit around the planet. Several probes had been cruising through the atmosphere and others had been taking soil samples. "The planet has obviously been terraformed," Sharan Carter, the ship's science officer addressed the small group. "There are shallow impact craters where water-bearing asteroids or comets have impacted. This has resulted in the formation of several large bodies of water. However, it appears as if they abandoned the project at least a thousand years ago. The atmosphere consists of a combination of nitrogen, carbon dioxide, methane and oxygen, but it is not yet capable of supporting unprotected Human-like life. There are several varieties of microbes which have been slowly converting the atmosphere into what we currently see. These microbes could never have originated here and must have been part of the terraforming process. There are no higher life forms."

"Why do you think this project has been abandoned?" Scarboro asked. "It looks like the atmosphere is coming along just fine."

"At this point in the terraforming process," El'Narra, one of the Kyrra biologists said. "Plant life should have been introduced into the ecological structure. This would have sped up the atmospheric conversion and would have laid the groundwork for the introduction of more advanced life at a later date. As it sits now, the planet will stabilize in another four or five thousand years but no life higher than a microbe will exist. For some reason, my people have abandoned this terraforming project."

"Any clues as to where they may have gone? Did they leave any monitoring stations behind?" Ken asked.

"No to both questions," Sharan replied. "We can see the results of their work but there is no evidence as to who started this process or where they are now."

"That's strike one," Stricklen said with finality. "Where to next?"

"I would suggest the storage planetoid," Norgoola finally said. "I have been there several times and therefore I am familiar with it. There should be some indication as to what happened to our people in the planetoid's monitoring system."

After glancing around the room and seeing approving nods Stricklen announced, "It's settled then. We will set course for the stasis storage planetoid."

As the meeting broke up and the attendees filed out of the room Stricklen took one last look at the aborted terraforming project. *This could have been their new home,* he thought. *Why did the Kyrra abandon it?* Shaking his head, Stricklen left the conference room and headed for the bridge to give the helm their new destination.

*****

It took the *Komodo Dragon* twelve days to make the trip from their first stop to the next target system. Norgoola was on the bridge as they made their approach.

"In my time," he explained to the assembled team, "the planetoid orbited at a distance of roughly 330 million kilometers and had an orbit that was tilted about seventy degrees off the planetary plane. Your computer has the exact dimensions and characteristics of the planetoid so you should be able to locate it."

"You heard him," Scarboro said. "I want all detectors scanning the most probable area of space for a planetoid matching the pattern of our target. Because we are talking about such a large volume of space, this could take several days. The ship has been put into an orbit which will allow us to scan the entire probable target area in four days. As soon as the target is located, feed the coordinates to the helm."

Stricklen watched the progress of the scanning for a moment and then walked over to Norgoola. "It's been a long time since you've seen this sun," he remarked.

"Actually no," Norgoola replied without turning from the viewport. "Subjectively, I was in this system only a few months ago, but that is only because I have been in stasis. It is different this time, because we do not know where the planetoid is located. When I was piloting the transfer ship, the exact location of the planetoid was known at all times and I would simply set the autonavigator to take me there."

"Do you think we will find any clues as to where your people are?"

Norgoola lowered his gaze from the stars briefly. Lifting his head back up and once again looking back out into space he said, "I can only hope. There is always the possibility that something may have been left behind. My people are the only ones to know of the existence of this planetoid. It is conceivable that a message or a clue may have been purposefully left behind so that any Kyrra who did not go with the main group could find their way to wherever my people have gone. There is also the possibility that some information may be retrieved from the planetoid's monitoring system."

Stricklen then did something he had not done in the many weeks of being in close proximity to the Kyrra. He reached out and placed a reassuring hand on Norgoola's shoulder. The alien's fur felt soft and very fine under his touch. At first Ken feared he may have broken a racial taboo but Norgoola slowly turned around and returned the gesture. It was much harder for him, since he was considerably shorter than the Captain. "Thank you Ken. My people and I cannot thank you enough for what you are doing for us."

Stricklen thought he saw tears in the alien's eyes as he turned and walked away. Ken looked out at the vastness of space and discovered that he did not even know if the Kyrra could cry. "How little we know of them," he muttered under his breath. "We have lived and worked with them for several months and we still know next to nothing about them. Will we understand their people when we finally meet?"

It took two days to locate the planetoid. After a couple hours of maneuvering, the *Komodo Dragon* was alongside it. "It's an exact match with the one in the computer," Scarboro said. "But our readings indicate that it is nothing more than an ordinary chunk of rock. I can't detect any kind of an opening nor any tunnels; in fact, I can't find anything out of the ordinary at all about it. Are you sure it's the right one?"

"Norgoola has looked at the topological scans and assures me that this is the storage planetoid," Stricklen answered.

One of the *Dragon's* three shuttlecraft was prepared while a crew was assigned. In addition to the five Kyrra, the Captain had chosen himself, the chief engineer, six marines, and (of course) Falnath to lead the initial exploration team. When he stepped into the shuttle, Stricklen was surprised to see Norgoola at the controls. "He was there when I arrived," the chief engineer, whom Stricklen had assumed would pilot the craft, explained as soon as he saw the Captain. "He claims he can pilot the shuttle and won't budge from the controls."

Norgoola cocked his head to one side and, while still running through the initial instrument setup, said, "I have read all of your piloting manuals and operation guides for this ship. I have also practiced in your simulator. I was the pilot of the Slaver ship in which you discovered us and I know the exact location of the entrance to the tunnel system, therefore, I should pilot the shuttle."

Taking a seat next to one of the other Kyrra Stricklen said, "I can't argue with that, proceed with departure."

Skip Bucannon looked as if he was about to say something but thought better of it. Instead he sat down heavily in the copilot's chair, crossed his arms on his chest, and closely watched every move which Norgoola made. After making several more adjustments Norgoola announced in a quiet voice, "Beginning departure."

The shuttle gracefully lifted off the hanger-bay floor and slowly left the protection of the *Komodo Dragon*. Five minutes of flight brought them to within a few hundred meters of the planetoid's surface. Norgoola circled the 155 kilometer bulk of the miniature planet until he spotted a landmark he had been searching for. Because the planetoid was so far out in deep space there was not enough light to illuminate the surface. Norgoola was relying on a computer enhanced topological surface scan which was displayed on his console's center screen.

Bringing the shuttle to a halt Norgoola said, "The double impact crater below us is a landmark indicating the location of the tunnel entrance. The entrance is located in the exact center of the inner crater."

As had been previously agreed, an open communications link had been established between the shuttle and the *Dragon*. Scarboro, who had heard Norgoola's comment, said, "We still are unable to verify that there is an entrance there. Sensors show only undisturbed rock."

"As it was intended to," Norgoola explained as he manipulated the shuttle's controls. Several powerful lights burst into action illuminating the bleak landscape below. Two impact craters, one inside the other, were now visible. The surface of the planetoid was very rough and jagged. "The doorway was created by removing a large piece of the surface with a force field. This separated the rock at the molecular level. Observe."

A repulser beam was activated and directed at the center of the inner crater. Nothing happened until Norgoola pulsed the beam sending a slight shudder throughout the shuttle. As they watched an enormous circle formed in the crater's smooth bottom. A slug of rock almost 20 meters in diameter slowly sank into the interior of the planetoid. "Oh my God!" the chief engineer explained. "Just how thick is that door?"

"It is just over thirty meters thick which is sufficient to block any scans of the interior. It rides on a series of glide rails attached to the walls. The entrance was sized to allow one of our ships to enter," Norgoola explained keeping his eye on the repulser's instrumentation. When one of the indicators started to climb he shut off the beam and announced, "The entryway is clear. I'm starting into the planetoid."

Slowly, the shuttle moved inside the enormous tunnel entrance. All available external lights had been switched on. The tunnel walls were as smooth as glass except for where the doorway's glide rails had been installed. The tunnel opened into a gigantic cavern. There was a large landing area to the left with numerous smaller tunnels leading off into the interior. With barely a jar, Norgoola set the shuttle down on the smooth landing area. He then reached out and activated the tractor beam at a low power to hold the shuttle in place.

The exploration party sealed their suits and exited the shuttle. Stricklen was overwhelmed at the enormity of the cavern. It seemed to extend forever. Norgoola took the lead and led the group toward one of the tunnels. Because the planetoid had almost no gravity they used the thrusters on their spacesuits to fly through the ancient tunnel. "These tunnels extend into the interior of the planetoid," Norgoola began a running commentary. "Side tunnels branch off from these main tunnels at regular intervals. The chambers which housed the stasis machines are located off these side tunnels. Each chamber holds about twenty stasis machines."

Just before they entered the first of the tunnels Norgoola turned into a small alcove. The group stared at the featureless walls for a moment. "This was where the monitoring system was housed," he said. "It appears as if none of the equipment has been left behind. We will have to search the storage chambers."

During the next hour the group visited a dozen of the holding chambers. All they found was rock. Not one piece of physical evidence other than the tunnels themselves existed to show who had constructed the labyrinth. The Kyrra were silent as they made their way back to the shuttle. While they prepared for departure, Stricklen told Scarboro to make up several crew assignments so round-the-clock surveys could be performed. He wanted the entire tunnel system scanned and examined for anything useful.

It took them six days to survey the entire vast network of tunnels. The result of their intense labors was a detailed map of the planetoid's tunnel system but not a shred of anything belonging to the Kyrra. Not even a tiny piece of forgotten garbage had been found. The entire planetoid had been swept clean of all evidence. Reluctantly, the last shuttle closed the massive door and returned to the *Komodo Dragon*. As soon as the shuttle had been secured, Stricklen gave the order for them to proceed on to their next destination – the last known location of the Kyrra space habitats.

According to the Hess, the Kyrra's last known location was in the star system which they had used to obtain all the raw material for the construction of their space habitats. This system would be very difficult to find since it did not have a normal star as its central sun. The system's star had never quite become large enough to sustain a constant fusion reaction. It was a brown dwarf but of such a small size that it could barely be classified as a star. It did not shine and thus would be very difficult to locate.

Using the Hess star-charts, the *Komodo Dragon* traveled to the approximate location of this dark system. After eighteen hours of flight, the heavy-cruiser was once again drifting free in space with all sensors wide open. The ship's astrogator was hoping they were now close enough to pick up the invisible star's x-ray radiation or even its infra-red signature. Even though the Hess knew where the star system was once located, stellar drift had caused its position to shift.

The star was eventually located via its radio emissions. Its location was fixed and the *Dragon* made a short three hour trip to get there. Stricklen ordered a detailed scan of the entire system and went to his stateroom. Ken barely heard the door close behind him as he stood in the middle of his small stateroom his hands jammed deep in his pockets. He stood almost perfectly still staring at a spot about eight centimeters in front of his shoes deep in thought.

Ken finally heard the door chime as it rang for the third time. "Enter," he reluctantly said. As the door slid open his attitude changed. Ken recognized the Kyrra who stood at the doorway as Trel'mara. "May I enter?" the Kyrra asked.

Indicating a seat Ken said, "Certainly, what can I do for you?"

"I do not believe that we will find any evidence of my people in this system," Trel'mara said without preamble. "I have come to the conclusion that my people do not wish to be found and therefore we will not find them."

Ken had been thinking along those same lines himself and he said so. "What has led you to this conclusion?" he asked.

"From the condition of the stasis repository planetoid," Trel'mara replied as he carefully sat down. "My people went to a great deal of trouble to remove all indications of their existence. Even the internal lighting systems and other expendable equipment were removed. Since the location of the planetoid was a secret and the main entrance was undisturbed I can find no reason for their doing this other than the desire to eliminate any possible chance of their existence being discovered. I have been monitoring the progress of the current search. We should have found evidence of massive mining operations by now, yet, no evidence of any activities in this system have been found. It seems as if all traces of our existence have been erased."

"If you're asking me to abandon the search, my answer is no."

"That is not why I have come here. I wish to discuss the future of my people in your society. We have avoided this issue because we have always felt that my people would be found. Now, because of what we have seen so far, we believe our quest will fail and we will be forced to return to the Alliance with you. Have you given any consideration to this alternative?"

Stricklen looked at the alien with a sense of deep respect. Here was an individual who had suddenly found himself among primitives. While the possibility of returning to his own people had existed he had a future to look forward to. Now that future had been drastically altered and he was looking at the possibility of spending the rest of his long life among a far less advanced, aggressively inclined species. "I can't say I've thought much about it," he answered as truthfully as he could. "No matter where you go you will not find complete peace."

"We would like you to give this matter some consideration. We ourselves have begun looking at possibilities. There is one more request which we would like to make at this time."

"And that is?"

"If our search here proves fruitless, we would like to visit our home system. We realize that this was not part of the original plan but if we are going to spend the rest of our lives among a people other than our own we would like to look upon our home sun one last time."

Stricklen stood up, walked over to where the Kyrra was sitting, and crouched down next to him. "When I was twelve years old, my parents took me on a trip to a recently discovered world named Valknor. They were part of a geological survey team, and they felt I was old enough to finally see what they did for a living. Apparently, they were getting tired of my constant questions each time they returned from exploring an alien world. The highest intelligent life on the planet was a species of social creatures that lived in very crude shelters. They were friendly, but the Alliance has strict rules against disturbing indigenous life and we therefore avoided them when possible.

"We had just boarded the flitter after spending several hours taking survey data and were stowing the gear when a magnificent animal appeared at the edge of the woods. I grabbed my video recorder and told my parents I would be right back. As I stepped out of the flitter, the animal moved behind a hill and I went after it, determined to capture it on video. I was following a shallow dip between two hills in order to get to the clearing I knew existed in the distance and where I felt the animal had gone to graze. I did not see what happened but I heard the flitter make a strange noise and then it exploded. Both of my parents were killed instantly.

"After two days had gone by I began to think I would have to spend the rest of my life with the primitive Valknorians. I knew they would except me, but I also knew they would not treat me as one of their own. I was rescued four days later."

"I remember, very vividly, thinking to myself that I would never again feel the light of my home star upon my skin. To this day, the sight of my own star shining in space brings back the memories of that lonely, helpless feeling I had when I thought I would be trapped on an alien world. Your request is not unusual and, although it will take us out of our way, it will be granted."

Trel'mara stood up and placed one of his hands on Ken's shoulder. "I understand," he said. "And now I know that you understand what we are feeling. Thank you Ken Stricklen for telling me your story. We shall talk later." Ken was still crouching down as the door slid shut behind the Kyrra.

The *Komodo Dragon* searched the black star's planetary system for six days before concluding that no evidence of the Kyrra could be found. Ken called a meeting to discuss their plans. After going over the lack of evidence so far, he opened up the table for comments.

"I see no other choice than to go back home," Doug Scarboro said. "Their are no more star systems to search and even if there were, I think we would find the same thing, namely nothing."

"What about the farming planet?" Commander Stiles asked. "The Kyrra lived there for many years – long enough for them to build cities."

"We considered it for a short time but decided that because of the proliferation of plant life, all evidence of any previous occupancy by the Kyrra would have long been erased. We have been told the Kyrra were very careful not to damage much of the planet. We will find nothing there. And, since we have found nothing so far, I can only assume that the Kyrra do not wish to be found. We should return home."

A chorus of agreements filled the room. Stricklen was acutely aware that his crew was eager to return home. Inwardly, Stricklen agreed with the majority. He was quickly becoming convinced that no amount of searching would reveal the whereabouts of the Kyrra if they still existed. After several others echoed the same feeling, Ken finally said, "Then it is agreed, we shall return home. I have, however, promised the Kyrra that we would travel to their home system for a brief visit. Once we have done this, we will return home by the fastest possible route."

"Going to the Kyrra home system will take us another week," the chief engineer noted. "That's a two week round trip from here. We know for a fact that nothing survived the passage of the neutron star through the system so why are we going there?"

Stricklen felt a twinge of anger well up inside him but he quickly quelled it. In a level voice he replied, "Because I gave them my word that before we abandoned the search for their people I would allow them to look at their home star with their own eyes. Does anyone else have any other comments to make before I adjourn the meeting?"

Falnath, whom Ken had seen very little of during the entire trip, stirred in her corner and said, "I do." As all eyes turned toward her, she fixed her own sights on the Kyrra representative who had attended the meeting. "Did your people have a method of signaling distress in the event of a problem with one of your ships?"

Trel'mara hesitated for a moment. He had not expected a question to be directed at him. "If you are referring to a distress signal similar to your own, yes we do or, rather, did. Like yours, it uses a pulsed spherical superluminal wavefront much like a ship's drive wake only it is harmonically encoded with the ship's location."

Most faster-than-light communications were carried out using a signal which was beamed toward the receiver. This provided a lot of power in a small area and allowed the signal to travel for great distances before it dissipated. A distress signal used a spherical signal much like the old-style radio waves. However, because of the shape of the signal, the range was very limited. The advantage of such a distress signal was it broadcast in all directions instead of being beamed to a single recipient.

Falnath turned toward the Captain and said, "I would like to modify our own distress beacon to emit a Kyrra-style distress signal and to send it once every ten minutes."

"To what purpose?" Ken asked.

"It is possible that the Kyrra still monitor this area of space," Falnath replied. "They may not wish to be found, but if they detect a distress signal from one of their own, they may be curious enough to investigate its source. We have nothing to lose."

"Other than attracting the attention of every other spacecraft in this part of the galaxy," Scarboro scathingly replied. "If we start transmitting a distress signal we will have every alien ship in the sector vectoring in on us, some of them may not be very friendly."

"You are mistaken," Trel'mara spoke up, surprising everyone in the room. "Even in my time, we wished to avoid contact with other races. We therefore developed a distress signal which would remain undetected by anyone who was not specifically monitoring for it. Your own sensors would register the signal as a random noise spike. Only a Kyrra receiver will be able to receive and decode the message."

"Then why are you here?" Falnath asked.

"I do not understand your question," replied Trel'mara.

"You just stated that you had a distress signal which could only be picked up by the Kyrra. Yet, you placed yourselves into stasis because you claimed you could not risk sending out a distress signal which would be picked up by another race. The two statements are inconsistent with each other."

All eyes turned toward the group of Kyrra. "Our ships and transmitters were destroyed during the Slaver invasion. Slaver stardrives did not incorporate any means of sending out a distress signal. We did not have the time nor the resources to modify the Slaver transmitters to produce our special distress signal. The modifications would have taken far too much time and effort. The Hess stardrive was built by my people and therefore it might already possess all of the necessary capabilities to generate a proper distress signal."

"I am satisfied with that," Stricklen said. "Try making the modifications to one of our own FTL transmitters first. I don't want to do anything which may affect the stardrive unless we have to. We will be setting course for the Kyrra home system. Meeting adjourned."

It was quickly discovered that the existing FTL transmitter aboard the *Komodo Dragon* could not be modified to produce the desired signal. Trel'mara then proposed that the stardrive be used instead. Stricklen, chief engineer Bucannon, Trel'mara, and Falnath had gathered together around a table in the mess hall to discuss their options over lunch.

"Why can't we modify our transmitter?" Stricklen asked as soon as he was brought up to date.

Trel'mara held a stalk of celery in one hand as he talked. "The frequency required is far beyond the abilities of your transmitter. The field complexities involved and the harmonic signal encrypting are also not possible with your transmitter. The stardrive powering this ship was built by my people and as such is capable of generating the desired signal."

Stricklen finished a bite of his own meal then said, "Won't that interfere with its operation? I don't want to have to take the drive off-line to make these changes."

Falnath, who had restricted herself to a large drink because her normal eating habits would have caused the others at the table to quickly loose their appetites, replied. "The stardrive we are now using has several unique features which our own drives do not possess. Kyrra stardrives were meant to double as FTL transmitters. The emitters are similar and the power available to a stardrive is many times that available to a standard transmitter. All we need to do is to connect the control circuits to an appropriate interface in order to activate the distress signal feature of the drive. We will need to build an interface that can convert our location coordinates into the coordinate system used by the Kyrra. The drive will not have to be taken off-line but when we are ready to begin transmitting we will have to make a minor adjustment to our velocity in order to match certain field dynamics to allow the signal to be propagated."

"How long?"

The chief engineer paused in his efforts to slice a piece of steak. "I've glanced at the plans of the proposed interface and interconnection diagrams. I would estimate about twelve hours to assemble it, an hour or two to make the connections, and another four to align the interface. We should be able to start transmitting in a couple of days. I don't see the need to work this one around the clock."

"I agree," Stricklen answered. "Just let me know when you are ready." The rest of the evening's conversation turned to unofficial matters.

Two days later, Stricklen received word that the transmitter was ready. A minor speed adjustment was made (barely noticeable) and the first signal was transmitted. From that point on, the signal automatically repeated itself every ten minutes. As the days wore on, Stricklen quickly forgot all about the signal. Before they knew it, the light of the birthplace of the Kyrra shown on their screens.

All five Kyrra were on the bridge as the *Dragon* entered the star system. Following standard procedure, a full scan was initiated. The more advanced Kyrra designed stardrive allowed the heavy-cruiser to penetrate deeper into the star's gravity-well than an Alliance stardrive would have. After an hour, Ken ordered the ship to make the shift to the sub-light drive.

"What a mess!" the logistics watch announced after looking at the preliminary results of the system scan.

"Be more specific Mr. Stillman," Ken said in a warning tone.

"Sorry sir. What I meant was, this system's planetary population has become completely unstable. The system originally consisted of eleven planets, all in a standard orbital plane. There are now only eight planets remaining and their orbits are highly elliptical and skewed off the normal orbital ecliptic. I'll put it on the main."

The crewman entered a command into his console and the main viewscreen shifted to show a representation of the planetary system. Thin lines representing the projected orbits of the remaining planets appeared. Ken had never seen another star system like it. Each of the eight planets had highly elliptical orbits. Instead of being all in a common orbital plane, the planets had orbits which tilted crazily to one side or the other.

"Picking up several large asteroid fields in various orbital planes," Stillman continued. "The two planets in sensor range show massive meteor impact damage. Long-term orbital dynamic calculations predict that the inner two planets will eventually collide with each other within another three thousand years and the outer planet will be ejected from the system altogether."

"You were right the first time," Stricklen remarked. "This system is a mess." Turning to the cluster of Kyrra guests he said, "I'm sorry, perhaps we should not have brought you here."

Norgoola answered for the group. "This eventuality was predicted and is an unchangeable act of nature. Seeing it only confirms in our hearts that our home is no more and my people have either become extinct or have moved on to a better place. We thank you for allowing us to see our home one last time. We have no further need to remain here."

Stricklen watched as the Kyrra filed out of the bridge and the door slid shut behind them. *Poor devils,* he thought. Taking a deep breath to still the feelings inside him, Stricklen turned toward the helm and said, "Set a direct course for the Alliance, maximum possible speed. It's time to go home."

As the helmsman turned to his console to carry out the command the entire mass of the ship shuddered. Alarms instantly started sounding and several indicators glowed an angry red. "Report!" Stricklen ordered.

"We've been seized by a tractor beam," the helm announced. "Routing emergency power to propulsion system."

"Battle stations! Weapons: Give me a fix on the source."

Over the clamor of the alarms, people passing information to each other, and the other noises of a warship preparing itself for battle, Ken heard the reply, "Direction zero four three point eight tack one niner five point two; distance unknown; no targets identified."

Ken quickly put the coordinates into perspective and was shocked. The tractor beam was coming from the direction of the star! One by one the various alarms were silenced, but the danger still existed. A tactical plot appeared on the main screen showing the unseen tractor beam as it tugged at the ship. A secondary screen showed the ship's vital stats.

"Shear away," Stricklen ordered. "CIC I need a target!"

The navigator punched a few keys on his console and announced, "I'm at maximum emergency power now sir. No effect. The tractor is cutting right through our defense shield and we can't break free. We're being pulled toward the sun. Velocity is now twenty-thousand KPS and increasing. Distance – 105 million kilometers."

Stricklen's hands flew over his command console. A rapid succession of screens flashed before him. With a practiced eye he gathered the important information from each of them and assembled a picture of what was happening. A tractor beam of enormous power had reached out and grabbed them. The source of the beam was as yet unknown but was located in the direction of the star. Sensors could not analyze the beam's field structure and therefore could not provide any information as to how to break free. Even with the ship's engines at full power they had not had any appreciable affect on the beam's ability to drag them toward the sun.

"*Dragon*, Shutdown override on all reactors. Authorization omega theta one seven sigma four. Helm, Take the engines to 130%. Watch the internal temperature and back it off if it approaches 620 degrees. Engineering, Monitor all reactors and advise the helm if any are approaching any ultimate red-zones. CIC, do we have a target?" Ken spat out the series of orders.

"No target identified," Doug's voice came from the speaker. "We've scanned all the way to the sun's corona without finding anything. The beam itself appears to be emanating from within the star."

"Damn it, that's not possible!" Stricklen angrily shot back. "Launch a probe straight down that beam and send me a data feed."

Moments later, a probe was launched in the direction of the tractor beam's origin. The probe rode inside the beam at it raced away from the ship. Stricklen watched the data feed from the probe as it sped away.

"Sir, engine core temperature at 600 degrees and rising," the helm reported a few minutes later. "We seem to be having no effect on the tractor beam. Our velocity has remained steady at 60,000 KPS."

"Very well, back off to 115% and hold there. Engineering: How are the reactors holding up?"

"Doing good," Skip reported. "We have a balanced load so all the reactors are sharing the burden. We can handle this for as long as necessary."

Fifteen agonizing minutes went by as the *Komodo Dragon* fought a loosing battle with the tractor beam. Ken continued to watch the data feed from the probe. Soon the temperature of the probe's outer plating began to rise. Another minute passed and the temperature had risen to dangerous levels. After a few more seconds the probe stopped transmitting. "Probe destroyed by exposure to the sun's corona," Doug announced. "No target identified."

Stricklen sat back in his seat and stared disbelievingly at the now blank screen which moments before had carried the probe's data feed. What he had just witnessed was impossible. The only conclusion which could be drawn was that the source of the tractor beam was inside the photosphere of the star itself. No ship of whatever power known to Alliance science could survive at that distance from a star's fusion blaze. "How far into the star's photosphere can you scan," Stricklen asked Doug.

"Approximately three hundred kilometers. Ken – you don't think there is a ship inside there do you?"

"What else can it be? Tractor beams just do not appear out of nowhere and they sure as hell aren't natural."

The crew had exhausted their options. Stricklen looked around the bridge and noticed the lack of activity. They were waiting for him to come to some sort of decision. After thinking for a moment he reached out and touched a stud on his console. After the attention tone sounded, Ken made an announcement to his crew. "In case everyone has not been informed I would like to bring the crew up-to-date. We have been seized by a tractor beam which apparently originates from within the star. Nothing we have done has affected its ability to continue to pull us in. Since the ability to navigate a ship within the photosphere of a star is beyond our science I can only come to one conclusion; we have made contact with a species which possesses a technology far in advance of anything we have ever encountered.

"Very shortly I am going to order our propulsion system to be shutdown and that we take no further action. There are two possible outcomes to this action. The first is that whoever is controlling the tractor beam is not intent on our destruction and we will be safely transported to wherever they are taking us. The second possibility is that we will be destroyed. Either way there is nothing we can do at the moment. I will keep you informed as the situation changes. Trel'mara please report to the bridge immediately."

Stricklen then ordered the helm to shutdown the drive. After hesitating for a moment he reluctantly complied. Turning back to the Captain he said, "Velocity now steady at 35-thousand KPS. ETA to outer coronosphere: 31 minutes."

The marine guard admitted Trel'mara to the bridge. "How can I help you Captain?" he asked as he approached the command console.

"I am betting your people are responsible for the tractor beam. I can think of no other species that could even come close to developing the level of technology required to park a ship within the photosphere of a star. If they are your people, you might be able to establish a dialog with them. Would you like to try?"

Stricklen had seen very little emotion from the Kyrra in their many weeks together. Trel'mara's eyes widened, he became very fidgety, and his breath quickened. In a voice quivering with excitement he replied, "Yes! If those are my people then I should be able to establish contact."

Stricklen accompanied the now obviously excited Kyrra to the communications station. The operator manipulated several switches and then indicated he could proceed. Speaking in his own language Trel'mara sent a greeting.

POWER STRUGGLE

No reply. "Add visual and a translation for our benefit," Stricklen said.

The communications watch made the necessary adjustments and Trel'mara repeated his message. This time the computer translated his words. "I am Trel'mara. Pilot of stasis cargo transport 138 which last departed from Ky on..." here, the computer repeated Trel'mara's words since it could not translate their calendar into the Alliance dating system. "I have been in stasis until now. If any Kyrra receives this transmission please respond."

Trel'mara repeated the message twice more. Each time the enthusiam in his voice diminished. Halfway through his forth message an audio only reply was received. The computer translated it as, "Trel'mara, what is your current vroocha and where did you dirmolo?" The machine then added, "Automatic message translation detected at message source." This told Ken that whoever had sent the message had used a computer to translate it into the Kyrra language.

Stricklen had not understood the question and he understood the answer even less. "I am strush. Dirmolo took place in Varesh as my birthplace was Pioto."

Trel'mara saw the confused look on Ken's face and explained. "This question could only have been answered by one of my own kind. Vroocha is a reference to my current reproductive status, what you would call male and female. Unlike your species we can choose our sex. Strush is non-reproductive which in your terms would mean that I am currently sexless. I was born in the city of Pioto. Dirmolo refers to a period of time when a young adult leaves its birthplace to wander. Other communities except these wandering individuals and allow them to experience various occupations. When dirmolo is over, the individual has found an occupation which suits its mentality and will begin studying the area of interest. Some people choose multiple occupations. It is a time where one searches within oneself to find not only what talents are there but also what pleases them. I completed my dirmolo within the city of Varesh."

"We're getting a visual feed," the communicator announced.

On the screen, the furry face of a Kyrra appeared. Stricklen's heart pounded, for he was now looking at an individual who's race commanded technologies beyond his wildest dreams. "We welcome you home Trel'mara. The records of those times are incomplete and we have only the barest of information concerning you and your cargo ship. Our language has changed in the time since you have been gone and we are using a translator to speak to you. Are there others with you?"

Trel'mara, his voice trembling with excitement and joy, listed the other four members of his group and gave a very brief explanation as to how they came to be in stasis and what had happened since their discovery by the Alliance. "The Alliance agreed to try to return us to our people," he concluded. "A Hess stardrive was installed in this ship and after a long journey we have returned home. I will provide a more complete report when we arrive."

Indicating Ken, Trel'mara said, "This is Captain Ken Stricklen. He is responsible for bringing us here. We owe him a great thanks."

"Captain Ken Stricklen, our deepest thanks for returning our people to us. Leave your propulsion system in its current state and we shall bring your ship to a safe dock. We will talk further when you arrive. In order to facilitate any further exchanges, have your computer initiate a language translation request using any communications method you desire. Our computer will respond." Without waiting for an answer the communication link closed.

Trel'mara turned and started to rush out of the room. On his way he said, "I must inform the others—WE ARE HOME!" And the happiest creature Ken had every seen skipped out of the control room, past a startled guard, and down the passageway.

Ken looked at his communications watch and said, "I did not even get a chance to ask him why we were being pulled into a star. I hope they know what they are doing!"

Stricklen returned to his command chair and informed the crew as to the latest developments. After canceling battle stations and ordering the computer to begin a language translation, he devoted his attention to watching his ship as it drew closer to the sun. Suddenly, the light of the approaching star was cut off and the external monitor showing the outside view went black. "We've been surrounded by some sort of force field," Doug explained from CIC. "We'll try to get an analysis of its field structure."

At least they're not going to let us burn up, Ken thought. A few minutes later, Doug appeared at his side. "I was very tempted to fire a missile down that tractor beam," Stricklen said. "As advanced as these people are, I doubt it would have done any damage but it certainly would not have been very diplomatic."

"I'll second that," Doug replied. "Their technology is so far beyond ours that we can't even get a preliminary reading on the internal field structure of the force field surrounding us. Our sensors show that something is there but we cannot penetrate it in order to analyze it. I can't begin to imagine the scale of energy needed to shield us from the star. All I can say is that we had better not piss these people off."

Chapter 16

External sensors were useless as the ship continued its plunge into the star. Stricklen could feel the tension of his crew as they realized they were actually within the photosphere of a sun. Barely 100 meters from the hull of their ship was a seething inferno of fusion energy which, if the protection of the surrounding force field was lost, would incinerate them in the blink of an eye. Stricklen did not feel very safe and he found himself silently praying.

After what seemed like a very long time, the external monitor sprung to life. It showed what appeared to be the interior of a more-or-less normal hanger bay. What made it noteworthy was that the hanger bay was capable of accepting the entire bulk of the heavy-cruiser with room to spare. Stricklen realized that the hanger must be huge and the ship which contained it had to be unbelievably gigantic. Once again, the scale of Kyrra technology shocked him.

"Incoming transmission," the coms watch announced.

"Translate and put it on the main screen," Stricklen ordered.

"Captain Ken Stricklen," the Kyrra said as soon as the link had been established. "Your ship is now safely berthed. Please shutdown all of your non-essential systems. A vehicle will arrive shortly at your forward port airlock to transport you to a place where we can speak. Your ship is being held in a null-gravity field but is surrounded by a compatible atmosphere. A normal gravity field exists at a distance of 50 meters from your ship. I am looking forward to meeting you in person."

With the usual Kyrra abruptness the image blinked out as the link closed. Stricklen ordered the ship to be placed in a standby condition and called for the Kyrra to assemble in the main cargo bay. He told Doug he would be going alone and left the bridge.

The excited group of Kyrra were waiting for him as he entered the cargo bay. Each of them had to grasp Ken's shoulders and thank him for helping them find their way back to their people. The Kyrra reminded him so much of large polychromatic bunny rabbits that his heart warmed to their thanks. Deep down, he knew exactly how they felt. He found himself having to fight back tears of joy.

After the emotional outpouring, Ken led the way to the airlock. Once the atmosphere on the outside of the ship was verified to be breathable he ordered the airlock's interlocks to be overridden so that both doors could be opened at the same time. As the second door opened, a slight breeze of cool air rushed in. Instead of the stale smell of another ship, Ken thought he smelled the fresh air of a planet's surface.

Since the *Komodo Dragon* had never been expected to land on a planetary surface, there were no ground-level entrances. The airlock the Kyrra had specified to use as an exit was located nearly 30 meters above the floor of the hanger. Trel'mara stepped to the edge of the open airlock and looked down for a moment then turned around and looked at Ken. The Captain stepped up to the edge and took in a deep refreshing breath. He then looked around for a moment. Just as he was about to turn back around he saw a vehicle approach from the aft section of the ship. The transport smoothly and silently floated up to the airlock and dropped a section of its side down to form a ramp. It then slide sideways until the ramp just touched the edge of the airlock floor.

There was no place for a driver to sit and no form of locomotion could be seen. Ken stepped up the ramp and settled into a seat that was much too small for his Human frame. He was surprised, however when the seat shifted beneath him and expanded to accommodate his larger size. It was very comfortable. As the last passenger settled into the seats the ramp silently closed and the vehicle started off on its own.

As the transport moved away from the *Komodo Dragon*, Stricklen was able to see more of the interior of the Kyrra ship. The scale of the hanger was even larger than Stricklen had imagined looking at it through the eye of the external monitor. The *Komodo Dragon* stretched for 1300 meters from stem to stern. It sat in the center of the hanger with at least another 200 meters to spare at either end. Ken looked up and guessed that the ceiling rose over 500 meters above him but such distances were hard to guess.

Ken looked back at his ship. It was suspended several meters above the floor of the hanger. He could just make out some sort of device attached to the hanger's ceiling and an identical device located beneath the his ship. He reasoned the devices must be some sort of gravity field generators, probably very similar to those used aboard the *Komodo Dragon* to generate the artificial gravity field.

As they approached the wall of the hanger, Ken could see several Kyrra waiting for them. A few meters away from the group, the transport slowed to a stop and the travelers exited. Without hesitation, the five long-lost Kyrra walked over to the waiting group and for a long time Ken was ignored as they talked and hugged each other. Ken noticed that each of the new Kyrra had a small device hanging from their neck, probably their version of a language translator. After the reunion had died down, Trel'mara and another Kyrra approached Ken. "This is Norpock," Trel'mara made the introduction. "He will be speaking with you. The device around his neck is a translator much like your own. We are being taken to another location but I assure you we will see you again. I cannot thank you enough for what you have done Captain."

As Trel'mara walked away, Norpock said through his translator, "Please follow me." Obediently, Stricklen followed the Kyrra through a small door, down a short hallway and finally into a large, well furnished conference room. Norpock indicated that he should sit, and Ken settled into the chair. Like the chair on the transport, this one quickly adjusted to his human dimensions. Before he could think of anything to say, a door at the other end of the room opened and six more Kyrra filed into the room. Without saying a word, the new arrivals took their seats at the table.

After everyone was seated Norpock said, "These people are the central advisory council. Yours is the first alien ship to have contact with our race in over forty thousand years. Although you have done us a great service in returning our people to us, your presence has started a debate within our population. We have remained isolated by our own choice and your arrival here endangers this isolation."

Ken suddenly had a bad feeling about this. "If you are so intent on maintaining this isolation, why did you contact us? We were making preparations to return home when your tractor beam hooked us."

An older, gray-furred Kyrra answered. "We detected your ship as it entered this area of space several weeks ago. Our curiosity was immediately aroused when we detected the unique drive wake created by your Kyrra-built stardrive. We watched as you explored the planet which we had started to terraform, the old planetoid which housed the stasis machines and the dark star system. We were very curious as to how you came about this knowledge. We concluded that you had discovered a deactivated Hess observatory and had somehow extracted the information from its databanks. When you began transmitting an old Kyrra distress signal we became even more curious since the signal you were using had not been used in centuries.

"Eventually, you made your way here, to our home system. We still had not come to any conclusion as to how you knew about us. Curiosity finally won out and the decision was made to bring you here. We were very surprised when Trel'mara sent his message."

Ken leaned forward and placed both hands flat on the table. "And now you are trying to decide if you will allow us to leave, correct?"

The older Kyrra, whom Ken had decided was the spokesperson for the group, replied, "No decisions have been made concerning this problem. Forcing you to remain here would be no different than if you had refused to return our people to us thus forcing them to live in your society. Since this issue concerns you, I will ensure that you be kept informed as to the progress of the debate."

"What do you mean by debate? Does not this council govern the Kyrra?"

"Not directly. Major issues involving the entire population are debated and then voted upon by all Kyrra. This council makes decisions which require quick actions. We also make decisions regarding other issues for which this council has been granted authority. We don't actually govern but we do perform many of the functions of a governing body."

A very light furred Kyrra then said, "Your journey has been a long one and the quarters on your ship are cramped. We are preparing accommodations for your entire crew so they may rest. Several guides will be available to answer any questions and to bestow our hospitality upon you. You are free to go wherever you wish. We have also noticed that your ship has been damaged. It will be repaired while you are here."

"There is no need to trouble yourselves," Ken replied. "The *Dragon* carries a crew of over 300 and although this ship is the largest craft I have ever seen, there is no need to make room for us. We will stay on our ship until we arrive at your home world."

The Kyrra looked at each other for a moment then began making the small yipping noises Ken had learned was their equivalent of laughter. Norpock put his hand on Ken's shoulder and explained. "I am sorry, but you do not understand. This is our home. You are inside a sphere having a diameter of over 3,000 kilometers. All Kyrra live here."

Stricklen was stunned into silence. An artificial world 3,000 kilometers in diameter imbedded in the photosphere of a star! Ken could not even begin to imagine the level of technology required to accomplish this feat. His emotions ran wild as he tried to put it all into perspective. At first he was awed by the Kyrra and the powers they possessed. Awe gave way to fear as he imagined how helpless they would be against such power. Fear was finally pushed aside by respect as he fitted what he knew of Kyrra mentality into the picture. Eventually, Ken found his voice. "I would like to learn more of this place. How was it built? How do you protect it from being destroyed? Why have you remained isolated for all these years?"

Norpock rose and said, "All of your questions will be answered in time. For now, please accept our hospitality. The transport will return you to your ship. As soon as your accommodations are ready, we will contact you. Please consider yourselves as our guests."

Stricklen was led back to the waiting transport which then returned him to the *Komodo Dragon*. Once aboard, he informed the crew of what had transpired. He then had Scarboro make up a minimum watch rotation for the ship. After listening to his Captain's orders Doug said, "Are you sure you want to let the crew leave the ship? What if the Kyrra aren't as benevolent as we have been led to believe? We will be leaving ourselves wide open."

"Doug, if the Kyrra wanted to harm us they could have done so at any time. These people control technologies which, to us, are nothing less than magic. If they can hold back the fusion fires of a star, then there would be nothing we could do to stop them from doing anything they wanted to us. They have extended their hand in thanks and I have accepted. Now go pack your things and get ready—we're both going to be on that first transport."

Six hours later, several transports larger than the one Ken had previously used, arrived. A message from the Kyrra informed him that the crew would be transported in five groups of up to 50 in each group. The message also requested that Falnath join the first group. Special quarters had been prepared for her larger bulk. Ken had the computer randomly select 45 of his crew and had them muster outside the ship where he joined them.

After being loaded, the transport began its journey. They passed through a large metal door which opened only long enough for them to pass through. After traveling through a short, well-lit tunnel, they passed through another metal door. On the other side lay an almost unbelievable sight. Stricklen could not believe his eyes.

The transport had exited the tunnel not at ground level, but at a height of several hundred meters. Below them lay a vast expanse of forest. Quickly turning around, Ken saw the metal wall which they had just passed through and gasped. The wall extended as far as his eye could see in either direction and appeared to rise many kilometers above his head. Looking up, he was shocked to see what appeared to be light wispy clouds and a warm sun in the sky. If it were not for the receding wall behind them, he would have sworn that they had just been transported to a warm, comfortable planet.

The transport moved without a sound. Ken noticed that although the passenger compartment was open, the wind was not whipping in their face despite the fact they were now traveling at a very high rate of speed. Some sort of force field that could block the wind yet remain transparent must have been erected. As he watched, Ken saw several small villages pass beneath them. Birds (or at least animals capable of flight) could be seen flying over the tree tops. The trees themselves were tall and fully leafed. A small city soon became visible and the transport headed directly for it.

Before reaching the city, however, they slowed and dropped lower in altitude. A series of small, cottage-type buildings arranged in three concentric circles could be seen in a clearing. The transport dropped into a clear area at the center of the cottages and settled into the grass. A single Kyrra approached and said through a translator, "Welcome. These dwellings have been prepared for you. Each one will accommodate up to four people. There are fifteen dwellings in this area and everyone except Falnath may choose to occupy any one of them. A special dwelling has been prepared for Falnath which will better suit her needs. These accommodations are yours for as long as you will remain with us. Your guides will be arriving shortly. Until then, please do not leave this area. Falnath, please follow me."

Stricklen walked toward the nearest of the cottages followed closely by his XO. "Mind if I room with you?" Doug asked.

"Not at all!" Stricklen replied. The inside of the cottage consisted of a large central room with several smaller rooms accessible from it. One of these appeared to be for preparing meals. Another had a table and several well-cushioned chairs in it. There was a sun-room which could be quickly converted into an open porch. Stricklen found an alcove with four sets of stairs leading into an underground portion of the cottage. Each stairway led into a private room where Ken found a large, comfortable bed, a properly equipped bathroom, and storage for his personal belongings. A small study could be accessed from the room. In the study was what appeared to be a computer or a communications terminal.

After making a quick tour of the room he had chosen, Stricklen returned to the central living space and discovered a small Kyrra waiting for them. "I am Silstras, and I will be your guide," he said in greeting. Ken noticed that Silstras spoke to them without a translator.

"I am Ken Stricklen. Doug Scarboro is apparently still inspecting his room. How is it that you know our language?"

"I was taught your language by one of our teaching machines. We are able to..."

"That's right! I forgot," Ken interrupted. "No need to explain further. The Kyrra we recovered from stasis used a similar device to learn our language only it took a lot longer."

"We have advanced," Silstras said matter-of-factly. "We have learned that your species requires sleep and have therefore provided you with suitable sleeping arrangements. Are the accommodations adequate?"

"They most certainly are!" Doug exclaimed as he entered the room. "This sure beats sleeping on my cot on the ship!"

"What did you mean by 'your species requires sleep'?" Ken asked. "Don't Kyrra sleep?"

"No. Fifteen thousand years ago it was discovered that a change was taking place within our people. We had apparently advanced in biological complexity to the point where sleep was needed less and less. Over a period of several thousand years this change eventually resulted in our people no longer requiring sleep. Our brains have developed the capacity to process and sort the information as it is received and therefore sleep is no longer needed. We rest our bodies, but unconscious sleeping is no longer possible or necessary for us."

"Good Lord!" Doug exclaimed. "Imagine the amount of additional work that could be done if we did not have to sleep."

"It would give a whole new meaning to working overtime," Stricklen remarked.

"It has improved our efficiency," Silstras replied. "It also resulted in many changes to our society. Some of the changes were not easy."

"Have you taken a close look at how this building was constructed?" Doug asked Ken.

"No," he replied with a matter-of-fact, I don't really care, sort of voice. "Looks like a regular cottage to me."

"The corners are rounded; there are few, if any, seams; and, unless I miss my guess, they were apparently all built within the last several hours."

Ken's eye's widened as he glanced around the room to confirm what he had just been told. "Amazing! How do you do it?" he asked.

"The building is constructed from a fast setting plastic which can be quickly formed into virtually any desirable shape. The material is easy to work with and is our primary construction material for simple structures. We have machines which can build one of any number of structures in a matter of hours. I am not sure how they work but if you wish to know I can find out for you."

"Not at the moment," Stricklen replied. "I'm sure we will have plenty of time."

Silstras explained some of the appliances included in the cottage. The data terminal in each person's room was programmed to respond to spoken commands much like the computers of the Alliance. By simply making a request, the terminal could provide the answer to virtually any question or function as a communications device. A similar terminal was located in the kitchen area. Silstras demonstrated its operation by asking Ken to provide the device with a food item. After thinking for a moment Ken said, "How about a piece of apple pie?"

"Assembling components," a voice replied. After two minutes the same voice said, "Apple pie equivalent is ready, please remove from processor."

Silstras opened a door and removed what appeared to be an apple pie. Stricklen's eye's popped out of his head and his jaw dropped. Doug reached out and broke off a chunk of the crust. After examining it closely, he popped it into his mouth. "It's not like any apple pie that I've ever tasted but it's not bad."

Stricklen picked up a fork and tried a bite. His eyes squinted as he chewed. "You're right. It might look like apple pie but it sure doesn't taste like it. But I like it. How is it done?"

"We have received a large database of information from your ship's computer concerning the foods you eat," Silstras explained. "This database gives us basic information concerning your food but does not give us the molecular structure of the item. We have extrapolated the information to create food items using our own foods which should hopefully please your tastes. The pie you have just eaten is probably based on the molecular structure of a fruit which we call chinfla."

"But how did you make the pie?" Doug asked.

"We are able to manipulate matter on a molecular scale within certain limits. There is a supply of the basic food elements stored within the food preparation machine. The bulk of this device is located beneath the cottage. The proper elements are combined and manipulated to create the requested food item. As we learn your tastes we can provide you with actual fruit and food items which you can prepare although you are more than welcome to continue to use the food dispenser."

"I'll be damned!" Doug exclaimed. "Artificial food from thin air!"

"Not quite correct," Silstras replied. "The elements of the food are actual fruits and other organically grown items. The original fruit has been converted into an easily manipulated form which is also compactly stored. We normally prefer unprocessed foods, however, this form of nutrition is both convenient and fast. It will serve you until we learn your tastes."

"On my world," Doug said, holding up the pie for emphasis. "This would be called fast food."

After being shown how to work the bathroom fixtures and other items in the cottage Silstras then offered to take the two Humans on a tour of the city. "I would like that very much," Ken replied. A moment later a small egg-shaped craft landed lightly near the cottage. Stricklen did not recall seeing Silstras call for the taxi. When he mentioned this to Silstras the Kyrra replied, "Each of us has a small device implanted within us which allows us to communicate with any nearby data terminal. I simply told the terminal we needed a small conveyance and it responded."

As they boarded the egg, Doug asked, "I hope you don't mind my asking, but: how old are you?"

"In your measurement system, I am 37 years old. In our society I am considered a youngster. I have not yet chosen my occupation."

Silstras slowly cruised through the streets of the city, if one could call them that. The egg floated without a sound and easily maneuvered between the widely spaced buildings. The city was unlike any the two had ever seen. No structure over eight stories tall existed and all the buildings were surrounded by parks and vegetation. The typical concrete landscape of a normal Human city was not present. There were no roads, as all travel was accomplished by floating eggs. There did not seem to be very many people about and Stricklen asked about their absence.

"Throughout history, our population has grown very slowly. We have become accustomed to open spaces and uncrowded conditions. We have no lack of space within the worldship to build new cities or additional housing. All of our manufacturing complexes are located in the industrial areas which are on the levels below us. There are large portions of the worldship which remain unoccupied or unused."

"You seem to have created a paradise," Ken remarked.

Silstras showed Ken and Doug as much of the city as he could from the air. The city appeared clean and well organized with a large number of parks and open spaces located throughout. Silstras then took them to a large air purification plant which drew in enormous amounts of air to be purified. This plant was responsible for a steady breeze which blew across the entire area. On their way back to the cottage Ken remarked, "It's easy to forget that you are living inside an artificial world which is itself inside a star. Don't you ever worry that your shields will fail and your entire race will become extinct?"

"No. It is impossible for the shielding system to fail. There are hundreds of backups and thousands of safeguards in place. This structure has existed within the photosphere of our home star for tens of thousands of years and it will remain here for tens of thousands of years in the future. Do not concern yourself with it, you are safe."

After a full evening of exploration, the two travelers returned to their cottage. Doug tried to order a steak from the kitchen but instead received a bland tasting plant substitute. The Kyrra, he remembered, did not eat the flesh of other animals. Ken used his data terminal to contact the ship. After ensuring himself that all was secure, he stretched out on his bed. He had intended to lay down only long enough to relax but before he knew it he was fast asleep. He dreamt of his sailboat on a calm ocean, only this time, he was not alone.

* * * * *

After almost nine hours of sleep, Stricklen woke up, used the bathroom and shower facilities, and changed into a clean uniform. He checked in with the ship and was surprised to learn that the repairs to the damaged hull were almost complete. He then started up the stairs. Halfway to the top he stopped and sniffed the air, the unforgettable smell of bacon and eggs filled his nostrils. As he entered the large central room, Ken saw Doug sitting in a chair with a plate of bacon and eggs in his lap.

Doug looked up and through a mouthful of food said, "Well hello there sleepy-head! Get some breakfast and have a seat because I have got a story to tell you."

Stricklen could not believe his senses. "Is that real or does it just smell like it?"

"While you slept, I did some research using the data terminal," Doug replied sitting his plate down. "I got tired of drinking coffee that tasted like warm root beer so I asked the machine if it would be able to reproduce our food if it had samples. When it said yes I told it to send someone to the ship to collect as many samples as they could carry back to their lab for analysis. I then called the ship and told them to expect company. Later on, I found out that instead of a person, a machine had arrived and asked to see the food storage area. One of the guards escorted it to the food stores and, following its directions, pointed to each item and named it. The machine took a small sample from each item and then left. After a couple of hours I was told that the food duplicates were ready. Now when I order bacon and eggs I get bacon and eggs."

Stricklen walked into the kitchen and ordered a steak and egg breakfast with fresh coffee. Five minutes later, he walked back into the room carrying his meal and happily chewing on a perfect steak. "I could get to like it here," he said between bites. "How long did I sleep anyway?"

"Oh, about eight and a half hours," Doug replied. "If I remember right, you had been up for a long time. I, on the other hand, had just woke up since I had taken the late watch. I was still wide awake when you zonked out. Do you know that the sun, or whatever the hell that thing is that looks like a sun, never sets here? They don't have a night!"

"They don't need a night because they don't sleep," Stricklen said. "What's this story you said you have to tell me?"

Doug scraped the last bit of egg off his plate with a piece of toast and popped it into his mouth before continuing. "Like I said, I did some research using the data terminal and I found some very interesting information. I asked it to give me a brief history of the Kyrra starting with the time period just after the Hess were created and launched. I learned a lot more about them than I really wanted, but I let the machine ramble on. Let me condense it as much as possible for you."

The Kyrra had spread themselves over many star systems. The space habitats in which they lived were capable of interstellar flight and the Kyrra used them as giant spaceships to explore the galaxy. If an interesting cosmological event was occurring somewhere, then one or more habitats would be there to conduct research. It was decided that this kind of existence was preferable to settling back down on a single world. The terraforming project was abandoned and the Kyrra considered all of space as their home. They were very careful about not making contact with other cultures; although the Slavers themselves had become a dim memory, what they had done had caused the Kyrra to become isolationist in the extreme.

The Kyrra did not bother trying to follow the activities of all the various races which they had discovered. Instead, they directed the energies of the Hess toward reporting on cosmic events and maintaining the map of the galaxy up-to-date. The Kyrra themselves delved deeper and deeper into the mysteries of the underlying structure of the universe. Unknown to them, the Slavers had rebuilt their empire and were slowly expanding in all directions.

POWER STRUGGLE

The Slavers had changed how they dealt with other cultures. Instead of stealing their technology without learning it and then relying upon their slaves to maintain a technology which they themselves did not understand, the Slavers had become scientists and researchers. Now, when a race was subjugated, the Slavers learned all there was to know about the other culture's technology and incorporated it into their own. In this way they no longer relied upon the knowledge of their slaves to maintain their ships and weapons. Subjugated cultures became forced laborers in mines and factories.

Eventually, a Slaver scout entered a star system where several Kyrra habitats were located. Under normal circumstances the Kyrra would have left the system long before they were discovered but two factors prevented this. The star they were observing was being consumed by a black hole and the resulting radiation had interfered with the Kyrra's long range sensors. The other factor was that the Slaver scout had been partially cloaked. The scout detected the Kyrra and reported this to its base. An enormous attack force was assembled. The Slavers attacked the first Kyrra habitat without issuing a warning or making any attempt at communication of any sort. Even though the Kyrra had detected the approaching ships, the habitats were caught off-guard and were unable to out run the Slaver battle fleet. Before the Kyrra could respond, the habitat was destroyed and fifty eight thousand Kyrra were lost.

After an easy first victory, the Slavers then set their sites on the next habitat. The Kyrra had presumed themselves to be safe and had never considered the possibility of being attacked. The habitats were unarmed and were easy prey to the Slavers. On that day, three habitats were destroyed, ending the lives of over 160,000 Kyrra. The Slavers returned to their base triumphant in their victory. The Kyrra responded in a completely unexpected way – they decided to retaliate.

Of course, the Kyrra did not think of their actions in terms of retaliation. Such emotions were unknown to them. The records were searched and the atrocities of the Slavers were once again brought into present memory. The Kyrra decided, quite calmly and logically, that a species which attacked other races without provocation or cause, did not have the right to exist. They determined that the loss of the entire Slaver race would be beneficial to the galaxy as a whole as it would prevent the loss of even more lives. Once the issue had been decided, the Kyrra looked for a way to implement it. Within a very short time they found one.

The Kyrra designed and built a number of automated ships which were programmed to seek out and destroy Slaver planets. The unique drive-wake signature of the Slaver's stardrive was programmed as the determining characteristic of a Slaver planet. The planet-killers were programmed to follow a Slaver ship until it reached a planet. Once a Slaver world had been discovered, the ship would settle into orbit and begin seeding the atmosphere with antimatter. The radiation released from the matter/antimatter annihilation would sterilize the planet. Each ship was also equipped with a titanic energy cannon which would be used to remove any Slaver installations protected by an energy screen.

Powered by the vast energy of matter/antimatter annihilation, the planet-killers were unstoppable. If any Slaver ships attempted to attack a planet-killer, they were fired upon and destroyed. Once the planet-killer had found a Slaver planet, then any Slaver ships which were within range were also destroyed.

With a determination to protect themselves and other races, the Kyrra quickly built a small fleet of these planet-killers and sent them off toward Slaver space. Unknown to the Kyrra, their mad decision to wipe out an entire race had caused them to overlook a tiny flaw in their logic. To their horror, the Kyrra watched as the planet-killers not only sterilized Slaver worlds, but also targeted the worlds of non-Slaver's. Wherever a Slaver ship was found to be destined, whether it be a warship returning to its base, or a scoutship reconnoitering a possible planet for attack, the planet-killers struck. Innocent cultures that had never know spaceflight were indiscriminately obliterated.

After realizing their error, the Kyrra rushed to stop their own creations. The only way to do so, was to send someone to each of the planet-killers and reprogram the ship to destroy itself. After many long weeks, and the loss of even more Kyrra lives, all of the planet-killers had been destroyed. In the end, not only had all the Slaver worlds been wiped clean of life, but so had the worlds of 17 other intelligent races.

The entire Kyrra race was stunned at the enormity of what they had done. They had been directly responsible for the destruction of all life on over a hundred worlds and the extinction of 17 advanced life forms. For many days, the whole population was in a state of catatonic shock and virtually all activity ground to a halt. As time passed, the Kyrra recovered and carefully considered their next action. They decided to isolate themselves from all contact with any other cultures including severing all contact with their Hess probes. Exploration was abandoned as the habitats gathered in the dark-star system. Safe from detection for the time being, the Kyrra began the construction of a single colossal habitat which would become the home of all Kyrra.

Their original plans called for them to leave the galaxy altogether but, before the new structure had been completed, a scientific discovery was made which allowed them to park their new world safely within the photosphere of a star. The Kyrra decided to return to their home system. After almost 115 years of continuos construction, the world ship was ready. The old habitats had been dismantled and used to build their new home. All evidence of their existence was wiped out and the world ship was moved to its present position within the photosphere of their original home star where it has remained ever since.

Ken had finished his breakfast while listening to the history of the Kyrra. He sat in stunned silence for many minutes after Doug had finished. The enormity of what the Kyrra had done was hard to grasp. Something Doug had said started to nag at Ken's thoughts. Doug was returning with another cup of coffee when the question solidified. "Doug, you mentioned that this artificial world of theirs was built in the dark-star system, right?"

"Yes," Doug replied with a smirking smile on his face. The tone of his voice indicated that he knew Ken had discovered the implications of what he had been told.

Ken's eyes grew wide as he completed the thought. "In other words, this world-sized habitat of theirs is capable of interstellar flight!"

"You've got it," Doug replied taking a large gulp of his coffee.

Before he could utter another word, a knock sounded at the door. Stricklen and Doug shot questioning looks at each other. "Come in!" Ken shouted.

The door opened and a familiar Kyrra entered the room. "I hope you are enjoying your stay," he said as he walked through the doorway.

Stricklen, who had finally developed an ability to recognize an individual Kyrra, replied, "Trel'mara! Your people are amazing. Have you and your fellow time traveler's been well received?"

Trel'mara settled into a chair as he replied, "There have been changes, but that is to be expected considering how long we have been gone. We have been treated well and soon we shall be able to support our people as we should. There is a matter of importance I need to discuss with you."

Always jumps right to the point, Ken thought. Aloud he said, "I take it your leaders have reached a decision concerning whether or not to allow us to leave and they have asked you to convey their decision to us."

"Very perceptive," Trel'mara replied. "The council has decided to allow you to return. Although you would be comfortable here, you would not be happy. Preventing your departure would be equivalent to sentencing you to prison. We Kyrra have no prisons or jails and we would not want your crew to think of our world as one. You are free to depart any time you wish."

Stricklen was glad he would not have to try to force their departure. He was certain that if the Kyrra had decided to keep them here there would have been nothing he could have done to prevent it. "The council could have conveyed the message themselves but instead they sent you. That tells me you have another message from them – correct?"

"Once again, you are very perceptive. Although you may leave at any time, I have been asked to request that you remain with us for a few days longer. There is another matter which must be decided by the population and it involves you and your Alliance. When you return, our existence will become known. Many of us believe that there are those in your society who will try to contact us for the purpose of obtaining advanced technology which will eventually be used to construct weapons. We will of course not allow this. Eventually, your people may decide to attempt to take the information from us by force, even though it would be an impossible undertaking."

"That sounds like us," Doug said. Ken shot him a warning glare and he shut up.

"What do you need from us?" Stricklen asked.

"Our people have remained isolated from the galaxy for the last forty thousand years. They have become accustomed to this isolation and are reluctant to rejoin the galactic community. I believe my people are afraid and have become mildly phobic."

Stricklen was puzzled. "I am not aware of having asked your people for help, although the thought has crossed my mind. I had assumed that if the Kyrra wanted to help the Alliance, such help would have been given freely. Asking for it would not make it happen."

"You personally have not asked, but others in your crew have." Seeing Ken's reaction Trel'mara continued, "Do not be harsh with your crew, they are only trying to ensure the continued survival of the Alliance. After having lived with your people, I agree with their request – we should help."

"I'm not too sure what you could do at this point. Our resources are stretched as it is and trying to develop the industry to support the construction of advanced weapons would mean cutting back on current production. Short of the Kyrra taking an active roll in our war with the Chroniech, I truthfully do not know how you can help."

"There is a small group of us that believe the Kyrra should no longer remain isolated. These people believe we can help other cultures and we should no longer hide ourselves. The council will allow the population to debate this issue and a decision will be made in the near future. In order to make a proper decision, we need as much information as possible concerning the Alliance and its various cultures. I have been tasked with asking your permission to place the historical records of the Alliance as they are recorded in your computer into our databanks so the population can make an informed decision."

"You may be shocked at what you find," Stricklen replied. "But, I see no reason why I should not grant your request. If your people decide to open relations with us you will eventually learn all there is to know about us anyway. It is better that you know our history before coming to any decisions. You may transfer the Alliance historical records to your system."

"There is one other request," Trel'mara continued. "You and your crew are here and are thus representatives of the Alliance. We would like each of you to record a message to our people."

"What sort of message?" Doug asked.

"The questions to be considered are; What would be the result of our establishing relations with the Alliance? Why should we? How would your people react? What would you expect from us? How would it benefit all cultures involved? But, you and your crew may record any message you desire, or none at all. Before the population can make a decision, we must have as many facts and as much information as possible. Will you record a message? Will you ask each member of your crew to record one?"

"I'm not going to make it an order, but I will recommend that if anyone so desires, they should record a message. Bear in mind that we are not diplomats, we are members of the Alliance military."

Trel'mara stood up and in a very Human gesture offered his hand. Stricklen grasped it and the two shook. "Thank you, Ken," Trel'mara said. "Please have your crew record their messages as soon as possible. I believe the council will ask for a vote in four days. As soon as the decision has been made, I will speak with you again. Until then, enjoy our world."

Ken used the facilities provided by the Kyrra to send the message to his entire crew informing them of the decision to allow them to leave and the request for a recorded message. He contacted the ship and instructed the computer to release all historical files to the Kyrra. He then decided to take a solitary walk in order to clear his mind and to consider what he would say in his own personal message.

As he passed one of the cottages on his way to the woods, the door opened and a very exuberant Falnath stepped out. She shouted a greeting in her own language and approached. It was more than obvious to Ken that Falnath had been having a glorious time. "I hope we are not going to be leaving any time soon," she said. "There is so much to learn here! Have you seen their physics lab yet? The Kyrra have developed the most unbelievable..." Seeing the look on Stricklen's face, Falnath paused. "What is wrong Captain?"

Stricklen chuckled and through his smile replied, "It's just that I have never seen you act like this before. You are usually one of the most series, intellectual individuals I have ever met and here you are practically hyperactive. I take it you are enjoying your stay?"

"Very much! I have toured the most fantastic research laboratory imaginable. I have seen with my own eyes a power plant which could power my entire world with energy to spare. I have seen technological wonders that Alliance science hasn't even begun to dream of. I could spend several lifetimes learning their science."

"Sounds to me you would be so caught up in your studies that you would forget to publish any of it."

Falnath seemed taken back by the remark. She cocked her massive head to one side then said, "I would at that. I will have to be more thoughtful—thank you, Captain." Without another word she was gone.

Ken looked after her for a moment then resumed his walk. He reached the edge of the woods and without a second thought kept going. The trees were widely spaced and the ground relatively clear of vines and the normal tangle of plants. Soon, the cottages were out of sight. Through his knowledge of the Kyrra, Ken knew the woods harbored no dangerous animals. The Kyrra ecosystem did not include biting insects, poisonous snakes, or dangerous creatures. Ken could walk all day and not fear for his safety. He continued into the woods deep in thought.

A low rumbling sound caused him to pause and listen. He had no idea how much time had passed since he had started his walk. The noise he had heard sounded like distant thunder. Ken knew it was impossible since he was not actually on a planet, although the illusion was virtually perfect. Deciding he had walked far enough, he turned around and started back toward his cottage. Although there were no trails or markers of any sort he felt he could easily find his way back, he had always had a good sense of direction.

After a few minutes of walking, Ken once again heard the rumbling noise.

POWER STRUGGLE

This time he was certain it sounded like thunder, and it was getting closer. Activating his wrist-com he called the ship. "*Komodo Dragon* computer system responding," the small voice answered. "How can I help you Captain?"

Ken explained where he was and what he was hearing. After a brief delay the computer replied, "The Kyrra have informed me that a shower has been scheduled to take place shortly. The thunder is artificially generated and acts as a warning to those who might be outside. The shower will begin in about ten minutes. Do you wish to have transportation sent to your location?"

Artificial thunder, and rainstorms for an artificial world – it made sense, Ken thought. "No, I'll tough it out," he replied. It had been a long time since he had taken a walk in the rain. Sure enough, ten minutes later the rain started. It was warm and came down in a gentle shower. The trees were too widely spaced to provide much cover and soon he was soaked from head to toe. Ken, however, was enjoying himself. The shower ended about an hour after it had started, leaving the air clean and refreshed. Ken felt the same way.

Fifteen minutes later, still soaked and grinning from ear to ear, Stricklen walked out of the woods. He had made it back to the cottages and had come out of the woods very close to where he had entered. He made his way back to his own cottage and discovered that Doug had left on his own adventure. After drying off and putting on a dry set of clothing he sat down in front of the data terminal and told it that he would like to record a message for the Kyrra people. When the terminal said it was ready Ken started to speak.

"My name is Ken Stricklen," he began, feeling a little uneasy. This message, he knew, would be viewed by millions of Kyrra and could very well change how they would vote. "I am the commanding officer of the *Komodo Dragon*. I am sure you are all familiar with the chain of events which have brought me before you here in this technological wonder which is your home. I just finished taking a walk in the rain, which is a luxury I have not enjoyed in many months. I must admit that I find this world of yours to be addictive, but I will be leaving soon and returning to my own world, provided it is not under the control of the Chroniech or as you might know them, the Slavers.

"When we left Alliance space, we were at war with a hostile race known as the Chroniech. You call them Slavers and I know your race has had contact with them several times in your past. I am aware of your history concerning this race and of the actions which you took many thousands of years ago. An artificial life form created by the Kyrra known as the Hess has provided us with a slight technological advantage in our struggle against the Chroniech but, I am not certain that this technology will be sufficient to prevent them from accomplishing their objective of exterminating all other species. I feel compelled to return home so I can either live or die among my own people.

"Until just recently, it has always remained a mystery as to why the Chroniech have attacked us as they have. Before the discovery of your ancient cargo ship, the Chroniech had attacked only remote outposts. After the discovery, they seemed to begin an all-out assault on the Alliance. I believe the Chroniech have remembered enough of their past in the form of legends to have recognized the markings on the cargo ship as one of their own ancient ships. I believe the Chroniech initiated their invasion in such force because they thought the Alliance was about to acquire advanced technology.

"I personally do not believe that any race, no matter how evil it may be, deserves to be completely destroyed. I do know, however, that the Chroniech need to be stopped. The support provided to us by the Hess was a step in the right direction. The Kyrra, with your far more advanced technology, could possibly provide a solution to allow the Alliance to stop them. I know that violent and aggressive behavior is hard for you to understand, but it is a way of life for the rest of the universe.

"Your race has a decision to make. Should you remain isolated and hidden, ignoring the fact that other races and cultures exist or; should you establish contact with other cultures and risk exposure to behaviors which you do not understand. I would suggest you use your technological knowledge and abilities toward the betterment of all life regardless of species or culture. The Kyrra are the most technologically advanced race which we have ever encountered. You control forces and energies we can only dream about. Because of this, you are immune to direct attack. You can either use this ability and become a guide to the less advanced cultures such as my own, or you can retreat into your own world and ignore the fact that my race may soon become extinct.

"You have an opportunity to atone for the error your race made thousands of years ago which resulted in the extinction of a number of advanced cultures. With your help, the Chroniech can be stopped. With your guidance, our own violent behavior can be turned to more productive uses. The Kyrra hold the key to the future of the galaxy. The decision you are about to make will determine the future of hundreds of other races. Consider it carefully. Thank you."

Ken leaned back in his chair and took a deep breath, held it, then slowly let it out. He hoped his message was not too harsh for the gentle Kyrra. After

POWER STRUGGLE

sitting for a moment longer, he got up and headed toward the kitchen. On the way, he wondered if the food replicator knew how to reproduce a good strong rum. There was only one way to find out.

Chapter 17

Stricklen had decided to take advantage of the unique opportunity presented to him. He had spent the last couple of days inspecting the exterior of the *Komodo Dragon* without the use of a spacesuit. It was a rare Captain indeed who could say he had had the opportunity to walk on the hull of his own ship in street clothes. Because the *Dragon* was being held in a null-G field, Ken could jump to any position on the ship's hull without mechanical assistance. The *Dragon's* own artificial gravity generators were located centrally, down the axis of the ship. Ken had ordered the generators to be set to a lower field strength which created a very light gravity field along the exterior of his ship. This allowed him the luxury of being able to jump long distances along the hull of the *Dragon*. Two days after he had recorded his message to the Kyrra, a visitor arrived during one such inspection.

Stricklen was staring down the barrel of the massive sledgehammer weapon when a voice said, "May I speak with you for a moment Ken?"

Turning around, Ken was surprised to see Trel'mara standing only a few meters below him. "Certainly!" Ken replied. "What brings you here?"

"I have been watching the progress of our people's debate concerning whether or not we should abandon our policy of isolationism. I thought you should know that your message to my people has carried a great deal of weight. Falnath's also generated a large interest. The population will vote in six of your hours. If what I have been hearing is any indication of how the majority feels, then I believe the population will vote to rejoin the galactic community."

"That is good news. I'm glad my message helped." Jumping down to Trel'mara's level Ken continued. "But you did not come all this way just to tell me that. Why are you really here?"

"In going over the historical information which you provided, I have discovered a cultural custom of yours which we have neglected. I have asked the council for permission to correct this oversight, with your concurrence of course."

Ken had no idea what Trel'mara was talking about so he asked him. "I have found that your society customarily honors those individuals who have performed great deeds with various types of public displays of appreciation. Since all Kyrra put forth their best effort towards the betterment of the entire population, such activities are unknown to us. Your parades and ceremonies mystified us because we could not see the purpose in such activities. After a good deal of discussion and consultation we have concluded that these activities arise from the competitive nature of your species. Being publicly gratified is a method of showing your competitors that you have won at least one part of the competition. Does this not sound correct?"

Stricklen had never thought of parades and award ceremonies in such terms. But, the more he thought about it, the more sense it made. After a few moments in silent thought he replied, "I think you are right. I've never looked at an award ceremony quite like that but, I think you hit the nail on the head. So what are you going to ask your council's permission to do? Certainly you are not going to have a parade in our honor?"

"No, nothing quite so dramatic. I would like to host a banquet for your entire crew at the largest entertainment center we have available. It will be my way of personally thanking you for returning me to my people."

"I think the crew would appreciate the gesture," Stricklen replied. "Just let me know when and where and I'll pass the word on. How have things been going with your re-introduction back into your society?"

Trel'mara hesitated for a moment, apparently considering how he should answer the question. "Before placing ourselves in stasis I was a communications engineer. My skills and knowledge served my people well and I was happy. All of my knowledge and skills are no longer useful to me or my people. I have been learning, but even with our advanced learning techniques, the information will take a fair amount of time to acquire. The skills associated with that knowledge must then be learned.

"There are other problems we have learned to deal with," Trel'mara continued. "As you know, my people no longer require sleep. I, and the others that were in stasis with me, do require sleep. This initially created problems since my people have not had to deal with such lost time in many centuries. Eventually, they learned to accept our needs, but we feel inadequate and hampered by this biological requirement. It has caused some concern for us."

"Where are the other members of your group?"

"They have decided to take up residence in other areas of the world ship. Norgoola, for instance has established living quarters near the center since that is where most of the activities associated with his field of expertise take place. Each of us wishes to be close to the centers of knowledge for the areas in which we are trained."

Stricklen had the feeling that something was bothering Trel'mara. He walked over to the Kyrra and placed a hand on his shoulder. "You feel as if you are a burden on your people, don't you?"

For a moment, Stricklen thought Trel'mara was going to cry. After a period of silence, he walked over to a support strut and sat down, or rather floated down because of the low-grav field. Looking at Ken, Trel'mara replied, "We Kyrra are a very social race. Each of us strives to become a productive member of our society. Humans obtain deep personal satisfaction when they have out-competed all others to the point they feel that they are number one. Kyrra, on the other hand, obtain a similar satisfaction in the knowledge that we have helped our society. No awards are given. One is simply recognized as an expert in one field or another. If another becomes more knowledgeable in the same field, there is no sense of loss because each of us is doing the best we can.

"When a Kyrra can no longer provide a useful service in the area of chosen expertise, then the individual will change to a different occupation. Many of our elderly become clerks, child caregivers, or teachers. We must all work toward the improvement of our society. When an injury or other such circumstance prevents one of us from being a useful member of society, that individual quickly becomes extremely depressed. It is not uncommon that such an individual suffers an early death. Recently, I have been feeling as if I will not be able to become a useful member of our society, not just because of my lack of skills and knowledge, but because the Kyrra culture has undergone such a dramatic change since before I went into stasis."

Stricklen was taken aback by what he had just heard. For a long time he did nothing other than sit close to his friend. He did not understand the Kyrra culture and his mind drew a complete blank as to what to say. Suddenly, Trel'mara's last statement replayed itself and Ken asked, "What do you mean your culture has changed? How? In what way?"

"The people of my era were explorers. We desired to see all there was to see and learn all there was to learn about the universe. Our thirst for knowledge was unquenchable. It was what motivated my people to reach for the stars. The people I see today are satisfied with exploring the microcosm within the world ship. They have focused inward instead of outward. I believe the Kyrra thirst for knowledge is beginning to decrease and my race will eventually reach a point where we will be satisfied with the knowledge we have. I foresee a time when the Kyrra will stagnate. We have lost the drive that has provided us with the technological knowledge which we now possess. It is quite possible that your arrival here will change this, but I don't know for sure."

An idea had popped into Ken's head as Trel'mara talked. "I believe I know how you can become one of the most productive members of your society," Ken said. Seeing he had gotten Trel'mara's attention, he continued. "If your people decide to establish a relationship with the Alliance, a spokesperson will be needed. This person must be intimately familiar with how to properly deal with the Alliance. I believe you would be the best choice for such a spokesperson."

Trel'mara was silent for several moments and stared at the ship's plating, apparently deep in thought. When he looked up, Ken could see that his spirits were lifting. "For the moment, I agree with you. A change in one's chosen occupation should not, however, be taken lightly and I will give it the proper consideration. The banquet will be held at 1800 hours your time two days from now. Transports will begin arriving at your quarters at 1700. Thank you Ken, thank you very much."

Ken watched as Trel'mara turned and executed a perfectly calculated jump which caused him to sail through the air in a wide arc. As the Kyrra disappeared behind the bulk of the ship's cargo hatch, Ken mentally patted himself on the back. He knew Trel'mara would make an excellent representative for the Kyrra. After glancing at his wrist-piece he decided to end the inspection and headed for the nearest maintenance airlock. He had some personal business to attend to within the ship.

A few minutes later, he was seated in the deserted mess hall with Tasha and two cups of hot coffee. "You seem to be in a good mood," Tasha said testing her coffee.

"I think I just saved the life of a very good friend of mine," Ken replied and related what had transpired between himself and Trel'mara. "I just hope he was right concerning the vote," he concluded.

"These Kyrra are going to be quite a psychological research project if they do join up with us," Tasha said. "Their society is unique, no Alliance culture even comes close to their sociological behaviorisms."

Ken was in no mood to talk psychological shop, but he did have one important question that needed answering. "How is the crew holding up?"

Tasha knew exactly what Ken wanted by this question. "Despite having such a good time since arriving here, I have detected an underlying sense of concern for the situation back home. The crew is cut-off from all information concerning their homes and many are getting anxious to begin the return trip. This situation is, of course, more pronounced with those who have families. I have also noted that we now have a few more couples to deal with since arriving. The release in tension has allowed several people to find a compatible person to share their time with."

Stricklen reached out and held Tasha's hand. "Then I don't feel obligated as the Captain of this boat from refraining from taking advantage of a certain person whom I like to share my time with."

"As the ship's psychologist I am officially encouraging such activity," she replied squeezing Ken's hand for emphasis.

The relationship between the two officers had been growing throughout the entire mission. As Ken looked into Tasha's eyes, he realized that their friendship for each other had crossed over into something deeper and more personal. Seemingly on their own accord, Ken's hands reached up and gently placed themselves on either side of Tasha's face. They both leaned forward and lightly kissed. After looking at each other for a moment Ken leaned back and smiled. "Do you like rum?" he asked.

Tasha placed her chin in her hands and her elbows on the table as she replied. "As a matter of fact, yes I do. Now where do you suppose we can find a bottle of rum on a warship over 3000 light years from home?"

Ignoring the last of his coffee, Ken stood up and offered his hand. "I think I might know exactly where to find one, after all, being the Captain does have certain advantages" Tasha took the offering and followed Ken to his stateroom. Soon afterwards the privacy lock snicked tight.

Hours later, Ken happily strode onto the *Dragon's* bridge. After taking his usual seat, Ken said, "*Dragon*, what is the status of the Kyrra vote concerning whether they should establish relationships with the Alliance?"

"Eighty-eight percent of the population has voted so far with seventy-eight percent of the votes going toward establishing official contact with the Alliance," the machine replied. "It is now mathematically impossible for the vote to be turned."

Ken was very pleased. It appeared as if the Kyrra would be joining the Alliance. Ken only hoped there would be an Alliance to join by the time they got back. With that bit of good news, Stricklen turned his attention to taking care of some of the other routine items he had been neglecting since their arrival. As Captain of the *Komodo Dragon* he still had responsibilities and duties to perform.

Stricklen spent the next two days aboard the cruiser making sure the ship would be ready to leave as soon as possible after the banquet. He heard no complaints from any of the crew members when he called them back to the ship to begin the extensive checklist required to prepare the ship for an extended voyage. When it was time to leave for the banquet, the *Komodo Dragon* was once again ready for the vacuum of space. Ken allowed everyone who wanted to to leave for the banquet. In light of the Kyrra mentality he had decided not to even bother posting a marine guard. The ship's computer would inform him of any problems. For the first time in its long history the *Komodo Dragon* was empty of all crew.

Ken, with Tasha at his side, was one of the last to arrive at the entertainment center. The building reminded him of one of Earth's famous domed football stadiums. There was a large central area where the activities took place and room for thousands of people to sit and view the entertainment (whatever type of entertainment the Kyrra provided themselves with Ken did not yet know). Roughly one-quarter of the playing field (as Ken decided to call it) had been converted into a large banquet area with long rows of tables filled with food and other rows of tables for eating. Trel'mara approached them as the couple neared the banquet area.

"Thank you for coming Ken," he said extending his hand in the Human gesture of greeting. "As is your custom, I have reserved a seat for you at the head of the first table."

Ken was overjoyed to find the rest of the Kyrra he had released from stasis were present at the table. He exchanged warm greetings with all of them and said, "Thank you for all this! I'm sure the crew appreciates it."

Laid out in front of them was a large assortment of different foods. After ensuring that his guests of honor had been seated, Trel'mara excused himself. Stricklen eyed the vast expanse of food and selected a white fruit about five centimeters in diameter with small yellow dots covering its surface. Upon cutting it in half, Ken discovered the inside to be pinkish in color, much like a grapefruit. He bit into it and his mouth was flooded with a rich, delicious, sweet tasting liquid. The fruit itself practically melted on his tongue.

In between bites, Ken talked with the friends he had not seen in so long. All had pretty much settled back into their society and were now performing useful duties. El'Narra and Nordlatak, the two biologists, had become lab technicians until their knowledge and skill level increased. Tee'Chea, the construction engineer, was working in an automated factory as a control room monitor. Norgoola had found a position as a research assistant in the high energy field dynamics lab. All-in-all Ken was glad to see that his old friends had been reintegrated into their society.

A loud gong sounded and the din of conversation quickly turned to silence. In the unoccupied area of the playing field, a figure many times larger than life materialized. Trel'mara pretended to survey the crowd then announced, "The Kyrra welcome all crew members of the *Komodo Dragon*." Ken was surprised that Trel'mara was delivering his speech in Alliance Standard.

"Although my people do not normally recognize others at a gathering such as this, I felt that doing so in accordance with your customs would be an appropriate way to show our appreciation for what you have done. Since I am one of the five people who have benefited the most from your decision to return us to our home, I have decided that it would be best if I organized this affair.

"In my time, before I and my crew were forced to enter stasis, our race believed that a peaceful relationship between ourselves and any other civilization would not be possible. The differences between us and all other races are so numerous as to present an insurmountable obstacle to a mutually beneficial and peaceful relationship. Although the various cultures which make up the Alliance are all species which have a violent and competitive past, they have managed to forge a society where they can all live in relative peace among themselves. I, and my fellow Kyrra who were in stasis with me, have been honored to have lived among these people. They have taught us that other races can exhibit very Kyrra-like behavior.

"I would like to conclude by introducing Norpock, speaker for our council."

The image shimmered for a moment and Trel'mara was replaced by Norpock. "Greetings from the council. As you know our population has been asked to decide if we should establish formal relations with the Alliance. The voting has concluded and the population has decided in favor of this proposal."

Ken quickly glanced around after hearing this remark and noted that his crew seemed to be breathing a collective sigh of relief. "During the debate preceding the vote," Norpock continued, "the council discussed what actions it would take if the vote was for the establishment of formal relations. With the conclusion of the vote, these actions are being implemented. Preparations are now being made for our departure. I am also happy to announce that Trel'mara has been named as the liaison between our people and the Alliance. The council has also concluded that the Chroniech must be stopped. We will not, however, repeat the mistakes which were made many thousands of years ago. Another way must be found. This problem will be discussed in the very near future. Finally, I have been told that some of our best entertainers have asked to display their abilities for our guests. Please, enjoy what they have to offer."

Stricklen was surprised to hear that the Kyrra would be leaving. He wondered how fast their ships were compared to his own. He was about to reach for an as-yet untried fruit when a familiar voice called out to him. Ken looked around and spotted Doug working his way toward him with a slender brunet in tow. Ken recognized the woman as a fusion reactor specialist whom Doug had mentioned a couple of times in the past.

"For such a dull race these Kyrra sure know how to throw a banquet!" Doug yelled over the din. "Too bad they don't serve alcohol."

"Agreed," Stricklen replied. "I haven't seen you for a couple of days. What have you been up to?" Seeing the look that passed quickly between the XO and his partner Stricklen quickly added, "Never mind, as long as you've been enjoying yourself. We have a long trip ahead of us."

Doug introduced the brunet as Cheryl Snidler. "Good evening Captain," she replied in a timid voice.

"This is a social occasion," Ken replied trying to ease her tension. It was obvious to him that she was slightly worried about her relationship with the ship's executive officer. "Please call me Ken. We are a long way from home and I'm certainly not going to be a stickler for rules this far out. This is Tasha, although you probably already know her." In order to break the ice even further Ken leaned over and gave Tasha a quick kiss.

That seemed to ease Cheryl's tension. From that point on, the foursome talked and enjoyed themselves for the rest of the evening. Trel'mara joined then toward the end of the evening. The entertainment consisted of various dancers, musicians, and acrobats. All in all it was a memorable evening. Ken especially enjoyed the Kyrra music. It was very much like jazz but with a bit of classical thrown in. He asked Trel'mara if he could obtain some recordings. "I will see to it that you receive a large collection," Trel'mara replied.

On the way back to the cottage, Ken asked Trel'mara, who had decided to ride with them, what he thought was an innocent question. "How many Kyrra will be returning to the Alliance with us or are you taking one of your own ships?"

Trel'mara gave Stricklen a funny look for a moment then started laughing.

After a moment he replied, "I believe you have misinterpreted what our council leader said earlier. When he stated that preparations were being made for our departure he did not mean that a select few would be going. He meant that the world ship would travel to the Alliance. All Kyrra will be going."

Doug, who had been watching the scenery as it passed below the transport snapped his head around and said, "Huh? What do you mean you're all going?"

Ken was thunderstruck. The entire Kyrra population was moving? This monstrous spaceship, the size of a small planet, would be making the months long journey to Alliance space? Just how would the Grand Council react when their sensors picked up a planet traveling at faster-than-light speeds heading into Alliance space? Panic? Just what capabilities did this mobile world of the Kyrra possess? Ken decided he needed answers.

"I would like to meet with your council of advisors," Ken replied. "There are things we must discuss before the Kyrra move this world ship into Alliance space."

"One moment Ken, I will find out if the council can meet with you," Trel'mara replied. He then turned to the transport's communications center. After a few moments he turned back to his guest and said, "The council can see you now if that is your wish."

Stricklen glanced at the other passengers and seeing the look of approval in their eyes replied, "That would be fine."

Trel'mara silently turned to the transport's automated guidance system and changed their destination. After a moment he said, "We will arrive at the council chamber in about ten minutes."

Stricklen's earpiece buzzed for his attention. Not wanting to answer aloud, he clicked his teeth together in the silent code which informed the caller that he was ready to receive the message but he would be unable to respond.

"This is the *Komodo Dragon*," the voice said. "Sensors have detected a massive change in the configuration of the force fields surrounding the Kyrra worldship. I thought this information important enough to contact you."

Ken glanced at Doug and said both to Doug and the ship's computer, "The world ship is preparing to leave. Looks like we're getting underway sooner than expected."

Minutes later, the group stood in front of the Kyrra advisory council. "The council has gathered at your request," Norpock said. "How may we help you?"

"You have decided to move the world ship into Alliance space," Stricklen began. "Before we arrive, there are many things which must be discussed with the Alliance. I am not empowered to make the high level decisions that must be made. You cannot simply waltz into Alliance space and announce you want to take up residency!"

"Do not be alarmed Ken Stricklen," the council leader replied. "The world ship will stop outside your space so the appropriate negotiations can take place. We have reviewed your history and your customs concerning events such as this, and we will follow all appropriate protocols so that the Kyrra and the Alliance can achieve a relationship which is beneficial to all parties involved."

"I'm glad to hear you have thought all this out," Doug said. "Where do you plan on making your approach to Alliance space and when will we get there?"

Norpock muttered something in his native tongue and the lights dimmed. A star map appeared in the center of the table. After studying it for a few moments Ken recognized it as a map of the area near Almaranus. A bright blue line appeared in the map terminating just outside of Alliance space near Almaranus. "We have chosen Almaranus as our first point of contact," Norpock continued. "This planet was chosen because it serves as your sector command for this area of space and it is relatively close to the Alliance border. We shall stop at a distance of one hundred light years where we shall initiate contact. We estimate arrival in twenty eight of your days."

"Twenty eight days!" Doug fairly yelled out. "How the hell fast does this thing go anyway?"

"Wait," Doug said before the Kyrra could reply. "Are we underway already?"

"The world ship stardrive was activated a few minutes before your arrival. This ship can travel at a maximum speed of 46,128c, however, because of energy consumption and other concerns we normally limit our speed to 32,300c."

"What about the Chroniech?" Tasha asked.

"We can detect the Chroniech ships long before they can detect us. Minor course corrections will be made to avoid contact with them. Even if we are intercepted, their ships are incapable of penetrating our defenses. The Chroniech do not pose a threat to us."

"If I remember right," Ken said. "The world ship masses about as much as a small moon. Is it wise to bring it close to a planet? I would think its gravitational field would cause perturbations in the orbits of any other nearby object."

"The world ship's gravitational footprint is neutralized through the use of cancellation fields. If we had not done so, the presence of the world ship within the photosphere of our sun would have caused instabilities and would eventually have resulted in the destruction of the star. The world ship can safely orbit a planet without causing any disturbances whatsoever."

"I am assuming that the world ship is controlled from a central location," Stricklen said. When the Kyrra nodded his head in agreement he continued. "Would it be possible for me to see this control room?"

"Of course," the council leader replied. "All areas of the world ship are accessible to anyone. When would you like to see the central operations room?"

"Right now I would like to get back to my cottage and go to sleep," Ken replied. "It has been a long day for all of us. How about if I make arrangements to see it tomorrow?"

"We shall await your call."

Stricklen lead his group back to the transport which took them back to their cottages. Ken and Doug walked their dates back to their respective cottages and bid them good night. Back in their own cottage, Doug talked to Ken as he was pouring himself a small glass of rum. "Something about the Kyrra does not quite ring true."

After taking a sip of his rum, Stricklen replied, "What are you talking about Doug? I think these people have been more than honest about their intentions with us."

"It's kind of hard to describe but I'll give it a try. The Kyrra are an advanced race, so advanced that parts of their technology appears as magic to me. For the past forty thousand years they have been comfortably hiding inside a star. We arrive on the scene and now suddenly they decide to move themselves, lock stock and barrel, three thousand light years through a known hostile area in order to establish relations with a group of races who are, by comparison, primitive and aggressive. Sounds fishy to me."

"Now that you mention it, it does sound sort of odd. I wonder if they have another reason for going to the Alliance. A reason they are not sharing with us."

"I don't know," Doug said getting up and stretching. "But I'm going to try and find out before we get to Alliance space. I've about had it for the evening Ken. I'm calling it a day and turning in. Good night."

"Good night Doug." Ken sat alone with his rum milling over what he and

Doug had just discussed. The more he thought about it, the more questions he had. A light knock at the door startled him out of his thoughts. When he opened it he found Tasha and Cheryl standing outside.

"We are so excited about going home that neither of us could sleep," Tasha explained.

Ken invited the two women in. "I was just relaxing. Doug has already gone to bed, but I'm sure he would not mind a visitor. First stairwell on the right."

After Cheryl had departed, Ken and Tasha settled into the couch together. "I'm glad we're finally going home," she said.

"Me too. I like the Kyrra, but I think I prefer the company of Humans better."

After a few more minutes of silence, Tasha quietly asked, "Do you think they're doing OK back home?"

Holding her closer, Ken replied, "I don't know. But now that the Kyrra have decided to join forces with us we cannot lose. I don't know what kind of weapons the Kyrra possess, but I am certain the Chroniech will be quickly defeated."

The couple chatted for a few more minutes and then retired to Ken's room.

Chapter 18

The central operations room was a vast compartment filled with rows and rows of consoles. "Each major facility within the world ship has a small automated monitoring station associated with it," their guide said. "If several such facilities are nearby, they will share a single station. The world ship is divided into wedge-shaped sections with each section possessing both a primary and a backup section monitoring station. These sector monitoring stations transmit summarized data to this operations room where the overall health and functionality of the world ship is monitored."

Ken was impressed at the size of the central operations room. By his estimate there must have been at least 200 consoles. What amazed him even more, was how quiet the room was. "Where do you control the world ship's stardrive?"

"This way please," the guide replied and started forward. "World ship navigation is controlled from a separate area."

They followed an upper walkway until they came to a set of large doors. The first thing Ken noticed as they entered the navigations center was the holographic star map which hung in the center of the room. The room was circular and had two concentric rings of consoles running around it. The center of the room held the three meter diameter star map. His years of experience guided his eyes as he scanned the various displays. He recognized those responsible for monitoring the vast amounts of power being demanded by the world ship's stardrive and the all important helm. Something, however, was missing.

"There is no captain's chair!" he remarked.

"Correct. Unlike your society, we do not have a structured hierarchy of ranked individuals. All are equal."

"But who calls the shots when things don't go as planned?" Doug asked.

"There are several people who share responsibility for decisions affecting this aspect of the world ship. For example, if an unexpected course correction is needed the helm will make the appropriate change."

"And what happens if you are attacked by a strong hostile fleet of ships?" Ken asked.

The Kyrra gave him an odd look then replied, "The world ship has both offensive and defensive weapons. If the need arises they will be used. One individual is in charge of the defense systems."

"But how are things coordinated with nobody in charge?" Ken asked.

"We talk among ourselves," the guide responded matter of factly. "If the situation requires us to defend ourselves then the person at the weapons console is guiding the others. It depends upon the situation."

"May I ask what type of weapon systems the world ship is armed with?" Doug asked.

"We have a compliment of defense shields plus a wide range of offensive weapons. When our ancestors constructed the world ship they designed it to be able to protect us from any conceivable situation. Of course, we have made some significant upgrades since that time. The world ship is continuously updated as our technology improves."

"This ship must be capable of awesome levels of destruction," Stricklen remarked.

"Captain, your race and ours are very different. You tend to continually think about who is more powerful or who could be a threat to you. We think in terms of how we can benefit our society. The weapons of the world ship have never been fired except during testing. They were installed only because we felt they may be required to protect us. Ever since their installation, the weapons have been maintained by machines and we have mostly forgotten they even exist."

"Sorry," Ken replied. "I keep forgetting the Kyrra are a different breed altogether."

"Is it possible to see the stardrive?" Doug asked.

"Unlike your ships, the stardrive of the world ship is built into the hull of the entire ship. Have you examined the construction of the time stasis chamber?"

"I have listened to and read the reports from the teams of scientists performing the analysis."

"If you recall, the outer shell of the chamber consisted of a very large number of emitters, sensors, and field modulators. These devices work in concert to create the stasis field. The stardrive of the world ship works much the same way. The hull of the world ship consists of billions of small interconnected devices which work together under a distributed control system to produce the stardrive field. Power is supplied via several thousand matter/anti-matter reactors."

"Incredible! Kyrra technology is so incredibly far advanced when compared to ours that we must seem like children in comparison," said Doug.

"Not at all," the guide replied in a surprised voice. "Our race has advanced to our current level of technology due to many factors. The fact that your culture has advanced to its current stage of evolution shows that you have overcome your specie's tendency toward self destruction. We do not consider ourselves any better nor any worse than you. We are simply two widely different cultures which have followed different paths of evolution—nothing more."

After the tour, Ken asked if he could remain in the control room to watch how the Kyrra worked. Over the next several days, he learned that the Kyrra system was actually very efficient. Four days after their departure, a Chroniech ship was detected. Ken was amazed at how smoothly the ship's operators handled the information. In order to listen to the Kyrra, Ken had taken to wearing his translator whenever he was in the control room.

"I have detected a ship," one of the operators calmly announced followed by a string of numbers. Ken looked at the large star map showing their progress and noted that a red dot had appeared. "Scanning for identification."

After a brief moment the same operator said, "Ship has been identified as a Chroniech warship, recommend course change."

The helm made a minor adjustment and said, "Course correction initiated."

The efficiency and smoothness of the entire sequence of events amazed Ken. These Kyrra operated a ship with no central authority and yet seemed to do it with the utmost of efficiency.

One day, after having explored the inner workings of one of the world ship's many automated factories, Ken found Tasha and Doug sitting next to each other on the porch of the cottage. As his taxi (as he liked to call them) touched down, he felt a twinge of jealousy rise up within him. It passed just as quickly as it had come when Cheryl exited the cottage carrying several glasses. Upon seeing Ken, she waved and went back inside. As Stricklen approached the cottage, she reappeared and handed him a glass of lemonade. "Thank you," Ken said.

"Don't mention it, sir – or is it Ken right now," Cheryl replied.

Stricklen noticed that her uneasiness around him had gradually turned to one of comfortable tolerance. "Ken will do," he replied. He sat down next to Tasha and kissed her hello. "So how have you folks occupied your day?"

"We were given a tour of one of the hospitals," Tasha replied. "But that did not take very long, so we spent the greater part of the evening just sitting together and talking. To be honest, I'm getting tired of going on tours."

"I'll second that thought," Doug exclaimed. "Kyrra technology is great but I'm getting a little tired of continually seeing how far advanced they are compared to us. It will be nice to get home."

"Believe it or not, I tend to agree with you," Ken replied. "It's not that the Kyrra are not good hosts but, let's face it, I miss my home world."

"Let's just hope we have a home to return to," Doug said.

"That's beginning to worry me too," replied Ken.

"You're not the only ones with this same feeling," Tasha interjected. "Ever since we have started home I have noticed that a good portion of the crew I have met share the same thoughts. Now that we are actually on our way, people are beginning to think about what they may find when we return."

Standing up and taking Cheryl's hand, Doug turned to the Captain and said, "Speaking of returning home—before we get there, Cheryl and I have an official request to make."

Ken had an idea what the request might be so he stood up and faced his two friends. "As the commanding officer of the *Komodo Dragon* we would like you to marry us," Doug asked in his most official sounding voice.

"I would be honored of course. When would you like this event to take place? Would you prefer a private or a public ceremony?"

"As soon as you can and private if you please," Cheryl replied. "I would like to have Tasha and one other friend there plus whoever Doug would like to invite."

"I don't see why we could not schedule the event for tomorrow or even tonight if you wish," Stricklen replied. "All I need is a time and a place. Think about it and let me know."

Doug reached out and extended his hand. "Thank you, Ken. We will let you know as soon as we agree upon the details."

Ken grasped his XO's hand and firmly shook it. The two women embraced each other. "Congratulations, Doug. I'm sure you two will be happy."

Doug and Cheryl then made a hasty exit to discuss their upcoming wedding. As soon as they were out of earshot, Tasha turned to Ken and said, "I'm glad you agreed to marry them, they were worried you would deny their request since they are both officers on the same ship."

Ken sat down and pulled Tasha beside him. As she nestled on his shoulder he said, "Why shouldn't I? They are two people very much in love. Captains have been performing marriages for hundreds of years and I don't see why I should not. Now the question remains as to who is going to perform our wedding."

Tasha sat bolt upright and stared wide-eyed at her lover. Her mouth moved a few times but no words came out. "You don't think I would let my executive officer do something I myself would not do, now do you? What do you say, Tash? Will you marry me?"

Unable to speak, Tasha reached out and embraced Ken. After a moment she whispered, "Yes. Oh yes, I will marry you. I love you." A short time later, the happy couple retired to Ken's room.

* * * * *

The next day, Ken did a little research and discovered there were no rules prohibiting him from performing his own wedding. Therefore, once Doug and Cheryl agreed, it was decided that the wedding would be a double one. Two days later, among a select few of their closest friends, Tasha Trueblood became the wife of Ken Stricklen and Cheryl Snidler became Mrs. Cheryl Scarboro.

After the brief ceremony, Doug approached Ken and asked, "What are your plans after we get back to the Alliance? Now that you and Tash are married are you going to try to get assigned to the same ship?"

"What do you mean? We are already on the same ship?"

"Oh come now," Doug chided. "You don't expect to still be commanding the *Dragon* after this, do you? Fleet command will award you with a promotion to admiral after they see what you've brought home."

"To be honest, I really have not thought about it," Ken admitted. "There is another more pleasant option. I could retire."

"Retire! You are nuts! You would go crazy unless you had a command chair to sit in. Listen Ken, you are one of the best captains I have ever served under. Retirement would not suit you."

Tasha passed nearby and Ken reached out and grabbed her. Pulling her close he said, "But I will be the Captain of a ship. I plan on settling down on Earth at my parent's old home on the lake. My dad's sailboat is still there and it is mine now. I plan on spending many quiet hours on the lake with my wife."

"As long as you are happy," Doug replied.

"And what about you?"

"Well, I was sort of hoping that when you made admiral I could count on you keeping Cheryl and myself at least in the same sector of the Alliance. But, since you'll be retiring I guess I'll have to look into other alternatives. I hear fleet command is supposed to be looking into keeping married couples in duty rosters where they at least have some time to see each other."

"If I have any pull because of this mission, I'll try to make sure that you and Cheryl get assigned to some nice ground-based job together."

Later that evening, Ken wrote in his diary:

Got married today. So did Doug Scarboro. I am happy and I hope Tasha is too. The crew's tension level seems to be rising the closer we get to home. I think this is because we do not know what we will find once we get there. Have the Chroniech beaten us? Are our families still OK? How will the Alliance react to the Kyrra? Will the Kyrra actually help the Alliance? Too many questions and not enough answers. My new wife waits for me as I write this. I won't keep her waiting.

* * * * *

Ken received word that the world ship would soon be within communications range of the Alliance. As previously agreed, he was transported to the world ship's central operations room. Trel'mara, who had been appointed as the official Kyrra liaison to the Alliance, was already there. Upon seeing Ken, he said, "We are now 450 light years from the Alliance border. Sensors have picked up a number of Chroniech ships which have changed course to intercept. We plan on stopping at a distance of 100 light years and then establish contact with Almaranus. Is this acceptable?"

"Sounds good to me. Why so far out though?"

"We did not want to alarm them by coming too close to their border without announcing our good intentions. Since we have been gone, the Alliance may have established an early warning net which would detect our approach."

"Excellent thinking!" Ken exclaimed. He was truly surprised since such thinking was unusual for the Kyrra. "Which communications method will we try first, the Hess network?"

"Yes. At 100 light years the signal will require only 18 minutes to make the trip."

"Eighteen minutes – I still don't know why the Hess could not duplicate the Chroniech communications speed. We have evidence that shows they could communicate over vast distances virtually instantaneously."

"The Chroniech may have some knowledge of hyperdimensional physics. There are certain applications of such technology which would result in an instantaneous communications system across enormous distances. The Kyrra of the past, and thus the Hess, knew little of hyperdimensional physics."

"What about the Chroniech?" Ken asked, not wanting to delve into a subject he knew nothing of. "If we stop won't they eventually intercept and attack?"

"Yes. At present, there are roughly thirteen Chroniech ships of various capabilities vectoring in on our position. There are numerous probes in this area of space which are acting as a detector web. We will allow the Chroniech to attack and expend whatever energies they desire upon our defense screen. They will be ignored."

Ken was shocked until he remembered the size of the world ship and that it could fend off the energies of a star. Compared to those energies, the weapons of even the most powerful Chroniech ship were puny indeed. "Why not show them what they are up against and blow them to dust?" Ken asked.

"We will not engage in the wholesale destruction of ships," Trel'mara said matter-of-factly. "The council is developing a plan for dealing with the Chroniech once we reach your space, but now is not the time. They do not pose a threat to us and we shall therefore ignore them."

"They're not going to like that very much," Ken replied. The humor of his statement, however, did not register with Trel'mara.

In hardly any time at all, the world ship reached the designated distance and dropped out of stardrive. "Drive system disengaged," an operator announced. "Defense screen stable; nearest Chroniech ship: zero point six nine light years; ETA 1.9 hours," someone else said. Finally, "Communications channel ready to record."

Stricklen stood in front of the video pickup and said, "Almaranus defense control, this is Ken Stricklen of the *Komodo Dragon*. I am currently at a position about one-hundred light years from the Alliance border. I would like to report that my mission was a success and I am returning with the Kyrra. As soon as I receive confirmation that this transmission is being received I shall transmit a complete transcript of all that has happened during my mission. I request that this message be passed immediately to the sector commander. Once you have evaluated the transcript, I would like permission to enter the Almaranus control zone. Captain Stricklen aboard the Kyrra world ship standing by."

"Message encoded, compressed, and transmitted," a voice reported. Ken and Trel'mara began their wait.

Nearly an hour went by before a reply was received. Ken was beginning to wonder if the message had been picked up when the communications operator announced that an incoming message had been received. A non-Human Admiral whom Ken did not recognize appeared on the monitor.

"I am Admiral Singth in charge of the Almaranus defense zone. Your message has been received, Captain Stricklen. Congratulations on your mission. However, I am afraid you are too late. We have been under Chroniech attack now for the last six days. Our outer defense perimeter has been breached. We believe that Almaranus will be under direct attack within one day. It is unsafe for you to enter the system. I will grant permission for you and the Kyrra to enter Alliance space. If you will transmit your transcript, I will ensure that it is forwarded to Tollbeck which is where I suggest you set your course. The Tollbeck system is currently well defended and free from Chroniech at this time. Admiral Singth out."

"Good Lord!" Ken exclaimed. "What the hell has been happening since we left? Trel'mara, are the Kyrra willing to stop the Chroniech from attacking a populated Alliance planet?"

Trel'mara turned to a communications console and spoke for a brief moment with someone. Turning around he said, "Yes. The council has authorized the world ship to take action against the Chroniech to prevent them from attacking Almaranus."

"Good! Then proceed on course to Almaranus at best possible speed. We have a planet to save."

Without any arguments, the world ship leapt ahead. "Stardrive engaged at maximum speed. Estimate arrival at Almaranus in nineteen hours."

Stricklen then sent another message to the Admiral. "Almaranus control this is Stricklen. We are proceeding to your assistance at maximum possible speed. ETA nineteen hours. After you review the transcript of our activities I think you will agree that we can help. I recommend pulling in all your defenses as close to Almaranus as possible until we arrive. If you can hang on until then the Kyrra will deal with the Chroniech."

After the unavoidable time delay a reply was received. "Great Maker Captain! If the Kyrra weapons are half as good as you believe then we will have no problems. Permission granted to enter Almaranus space and engage the enemy. Our ships will be warned of your approach. I will be sending a complete tactical report as soon as possible. Almaranus sector control out."

Ken called Doug and brought him up-to-date on the situation. Doug said he would inform the crew. Half an hour later, he showed up in the central operations center. "What's their status?" he asked as soon as he had found Ken who was sitting at a control console.

"The Kyrra computer has learned how to interpret the situation report after talking to the *Dragon* about it. They have set up a spare console for my use," Ken replied indicating the console in front of him. Several screens were active and were displaying the familiar tactical data used by the Alliance.

"I'll summarize it for you. The Chroniech currently have a fleet of about 200 ships near Almaranus. Several of them are used to intercept any reinforcements trying to arrive thus preventing them from ever reaching the planet. The rest, including three planetary assault ships, have been attacking the Almaranus defense grid for the last week. Apparently, the Chroniech are aware of the importance of Almaranus since they have continued to attack despite loosing an estimated 210 ships. I'm glad we built the Almaranus defense system with room to spare."

"Three planetary assault ships? How can their defenses stand up against such firepower?"

"Because of its military importance, Almaranus is the most heavily defended planetary system in the Alliance. There are, or rather were, four complete shells of automated defense stations completely englobing the system. Many of the larger asteroids and every planet and moon contained weapon systems and robot attack ships. I believe there used to be a total of over 24,000 automated defense stations within the Almaranus system. It has not been easy for the Chroniech, but they are winning."

Doug's eye had been scanning the other consoles while Stricklen talked. After a moment he said, "That's about to change."

* * * * *

"We are within sensor range," one of the operators calmly announced. Ken had been dozing at his console but quickly came awake when he heard the announcement. Ken scanned his various screens which now showed live data. He was appalled at what he saw. The once mighty Almaranus defense perimeter had been pushed to within one million kilometers of the heavily defended planet. The three planetary assault craft were relentlessly pounding away at the defenses trying to punch their way through. They were dangerously close.

As the two Alliance officers watched, four of the powerful defense stations fell almost as one and suddenly there was a clear, unobstructed path to the planet. "Oh no!" Doug muttered. The surrounding defenders moved to close the gap but the damage had already been done. The planetary assault ships were now moving at top speed toward Almaranus and its precious space-construction yards.

"How much longer until we are within weapons range?" Ken asked.

"Ten minutes twenty seconds," one of the Kyrra replied.

"They should have spotted us by now," Doug announced.

Ken's military mind was working at high speed trying to come up with a solution. Fifteen precious seconds went by before an idea popped into his head. "Trel'mara, can your computer translate your language into that of the old Slavers?"

Trel'mara forwarded the question to the network and replied, "Yes, the translation algorithm has not been used for thousands of years but it is still available."

"Excellent! Here's my idea. The Chroniech may still remember your race, whether it be part of their actual history or legend does not matter. What does matter is that we get their attention long enough for us to get within weapons range. Talk to them Trel'mara."

"It may work. I will try," Trel'mara replied. He then turned and requested that communications set up to broadcast a broad-band signal in three languages: Kyrra, Alliance standard, and old Chroniech. As soon as he received word that the channel was open, Trel'mara stepped in front of the active video pickup so his image would be transmitted and said, "Attention Chroniech warships. The Alliance has requested our assistance in ending this conflict between the you and the Alliance. Our ship should now be visible on your sensors. You will note that it is considerably larger than any of your own. You should also be aware that it is correspondingly more powerful. All Chroniech warships will immediately cease their hostile actions and return to their own space or they shall be disabled."

"Chroniech planetary assault ship will be within firing range of the nearest space yard in two minutes," Doug announced. "My screen shows that all weapon systems are active."

Thirty seconds crept by. Ken turned to Trel'mara and said, "Try again. They may not have under..."

Ken literally jumped in his seat when the reply came blaring out of the speaker. "Your use of an ancient language of the Chroniech is an insult to us. We do not know how you came to know our language but you will not speak it again." The connection snapped with an audible click.

"That was an interesting response," Doug said. "One minute until they can open fire. I detect no defense shield around the construction yard."

"Receiving a message from sector command," an operator said.

"Ken? I'm assuming that's you inside that monster. Don't worry about the orbital yards; they were evacuated a long time ago. All of the non-military population have been moved to deep shelters, so the only people you have to worry about are us military. The Chroniech have not yet had a taste of our planetary based weapons. They're in for a bit of a surprise! We will be opening fire any second now."

Ken used his console to establish an open connection and replied, "It's me alright admiral. We are still a few minutes away. Hold them off as best as you can. Stricklen out."

Almost simultaneously, both the Chroniech and the planet-based Alliance weapons opened fire. In an instant, one of the valuable space construction docks was reduced to a floating pile of vaporized metal. In that same instant, the planetary assault ships found themselves fighting for their existence. Five enormous rods of force had reached up from the surface of Almaranus and were pitting their strength against the incredibly resilient shields of the assault ships. The passage of these inconceivably powerful force beams through the atmosphere caused the air itself to literally explode. With the force of a thousand bolts of lightning, the beams of energy caused thunderous booms so loud and powerful that unprotected buildings would have been damaged by the shockwaves. Weapons of this power had never before been fired within an atmosphere.

The Chroniech responded by returning fire toward the planet. The weapon installations, however, were protected by powerful defense shields of their own. The energy which deflected off these shields caused tremendous damage to the surrounding area. Luckily, the defense stations were built in remote areas of the planet so no loss of civilian property resulted. Within the first fifteen seconds of the battle, the ground surrounding the defense stations outside the protective defense shield was glowing an angry red.

During this brief time period, Trel'mara had considered the Chroniech response to his first message and had prepared a reply. He opened a channel and said, "Chroniech vessels: The Kyrra know your language because our two races have had conflict with each other in the distant past. We knew you first as the Slavers when you tried to enslave our race. During our last encounter we destroyed many of your planets along with those of several other races. We are almost within weapons range of your attacking ships. You will withdraw immediately or we shall take whatever action is required."

The reply was instantaneous and completely unexpected. "Kyrra! After thousands of years the legendary Kyrra finally return. The ancients will be avenged!" All Chroniech ships immediately broke off their attacks against the Alliance and raced toward the incoming Kyrra world ship at maximum acceleration.

"Chroniech warships vectoring in," an operator stated matter-of-factly. "Suggest holding here as this will afford the Alliance with the greatest possible protection."

"All drive systems disengaged," the helm announced.

"Good Lord, what did we say?" Scarboro exclaimed.

"Apparently," Ken said after a moment. "The Chroniech remember the Kyrra for what they did to them thousands of years ago. The story must have been passed down from generation to generation until it became legend. I believe we may have just started a holy war. Trel'mara, what is your defense status?"

Trel'mara consulted a screen and replied, "Defense shield up and stable. Weapon systems are charged and ready, however, I do not think we shall need them. The Chroniech appear to be interested only in us and are no longer engaged in battle with the Alliance. Since this ship cannot be harmed by them there is no need to destroy their ships."

"Are you nuts!" Doug burst out. "You have the ability to wipe these creatures out. Why don't you use it?"

Trel'mara backpedaled a bit in the wake of Doug's overzealous remark. Recovering, he explained, "We will not fire upon any ship unless absolutely required. I agree with your opinion of the Chroniech in that they are an aggressive, repulsive, and easily hated race, but that does not mean we shall seek to destroy them at every opportunity. Such behavior may be common in the Alliance, but it is not the way of the Kyrra."

"Incoming message," an operator announced as he put it on the speakers. "Captain Stricklen, I'm not too sure how you did it, but all Chroniech ships in the area have ceased their attacks on us. You, however, now have a big problem. Our sensors show that all Chroniech ships are now on an intercept with you. If I were you I would get the hell out of there."

Stricklen opened a channel and replied, "The Kyrra assure me that this ship can withstand any conceivable attack by the Chroniech. Their response to one of our messages was unexpected. I thought we were going to have to duke it out with them but something we said really pissed them off. How are things on the surface?"

"The surrounding countryside is in ruins," the Admiral replied. "Maintown reports several buildings damaged from the concussion effects of the weapons. No civilian casualties. We lost one orbital construction platform. Not bad considering."

"Glad to hear it. I'll keep you informed on our situation. Stricklen out." Ken broke the communications link then turned to his console. The tactical display showed that four Chroniech ships had already opened fire on the world ship and hundreds more were on the way. "What are you going to do now?" he asked Trel'mara.

"This response was unexpected," his friend replied. "I will consult with the council as to our next action concerning the ships which are attacking us. We have taken care of the first problem; the Chroniech are no longer attacking Almaranus. We must now deal with the two remaining problems facing the Alliance. The removal of all hostile Chroniech forces from Alliance space, and establishing a method of preventing their return."

While Trel'mara spoke to the council, the number of attacking Chroniech ships rose. After twenty minutes the world ship was fending off the attacks of over 200 Chroniech ships including three planetary assault ships. Trel'mara finished his discussion and came over to talk to Ken. "The council has decided that it would be in our best interest to disable all of the Chroniech ships in this area. We are to do so with minimum loss of life. I intend to give them one final warning before we open fire."

Without waiting for a reply, Trel'mara walked over to his console and told the other operators what the council had decided. After opening a channel to the Chroniech, he said, "Attention Chroniech vessels. As you can see, your weapons are useless against us. This is your final warning. Cease your attacks and return to your own space immediately or we shall open fire."

"I am detecting a trans-dimensional matrix field forming between the three planetary assault ships," a Kyrra operator reported. "All other attacking ships are moving into position to charge the matrix."

"What is a trans-dimensional matrix field?" Doug asked.

Ken had never heard the term before, Trel'mara explained it to him. "It is a very energy intensive field which, if properly developed, can potentially penetrate our defense screen. I am surprised the Chroniech know of it since it involves a rather detailed knowledge of hyperdimensional physics and requires a tremendous amount of energy to generate. The field will require some time to establish but, once stable, it can be adjusted to form a transdimensional tunnel through which an energy beam can be directed. If the hyperdimensional matrix is setup properly, the energy beam could impact on the surface of the world ship. To my knowledge, there is no defense against this form of attack."

"You mean the Chroniech can shoot through your shields?" Doug exclaimed.

"Figuratively speaking, yes. You will note that it is taking the full power output of three planetary assault ships to generate the field and several other ships to control the matrix field formation. This is one reason why this form of attack is not used. We will take action to disrupt the formation of the field."

Stricklen watched and listened as the self directed team of Kyrra initiated their first combat action. "Activating analysis beam," the Kyrra at the main weapons console announced. Numbers, symbols, and graphs appeared on one of the screens. "Shield analysis completed. Transferring data to weapon control. Configuring primary weapons for shield penetration . . . Configuration complete . . . Targeting . . . Firing."

Three intensely bright blue spheres of energy traveled from the Kyrra world ship and struck the impenetrable shields of the planetary assault ships. With barely a flicker of resistance, each sphere passed through a Chroniech shield and impacted on the now unprotected hull of one of the previously invulnerable assault ships. Instead of creating a massive explosion, as Ken had expected, the blue spheres seemed to pass over each ship. It was difficult for Ken to see what was happening beyond the Chroniech shield since the shield itself was reflective. What he did see though as that the sphere of bluish energy seemed to be elongated on the other side of the shield, almost as if part of it were sticking to the ship's hull. It then snapped backward and vanished inside the shield.

Unbelievably, no earth shattering explosions occurred to destroy the assault ships. As Ken watched, the shields of the Chroniech ships wavered, became cloudy and then suddenly blinked into oblivion. Ken looked closer and saw that the hull of each ship now crawled with electrical discharges. Enormous, errie electrical arcs completely covered the surface of each ship. Several puffs of gas accompanied by minor explosions occurred as external sensors and other devices failed under the intense electrical discharge.

Several large areas of the hull glowed red. The electrical discharges continued for many seconds as the blue sphere grew weaker and weaker. Eventually, the blue glow of the weapon dissipated along with the electrical discharges.

When the display was over, Ken looked at his tactical monitor and was surprised to discover that all three assault ships had been rendered inoperable. Power output had dropped to near zero; the defense shield was down; and all weapon systems had been disabled. Ken was turning to ask Trel'mara a question when the Kyrra said, "Attention Chroniech ships. As you can see, our weapons are far more advanced than your own. Your shields are useless and your ships impotent against this vessel. I will tell you one more time to leave this area immediately or the remainder of your fleet will be rendered harmless. You have two minutes to comply."

After Trel'mara had finished addressing the Chroniech, Ken asked, "What kind of weapon was that? What did it do? How did it penetrate the Chroniech shield?"

"It is a terra-gauss magnetic field," Trel'mara replied. "The Chroniech shield was analyzed for a resonance frequency of proper phase and orientation which would allow the magnetic bubble to pass through. The magnetic bubble was created with this exact pattern, allowing it to pass through the shield with little trouble. The terra-gauss magnetic field then reacted with the hull of the assault ships, resulting in the generation of circulating electric currents. The effect is similar to that used to produce the electric currents in a generator."

Stricklen was familiar with how an electric generator worked. Basically, any conductor that moves within a magnetic field will generate an electric current. The Kyrra must have turned the entire assault ship into a gigantic generator. Ken also knew that most electric generators employed magnetic fields measured in hundreds of thousands of gauss. A terra-gauss field was something unheard of. The damage to the Chroniech ship must have been extensive.

As if reading his thoughts, Trel'mara continued, "The circulating currents generated from the effect of the terra-gauss field burn out control circuits, computers, sensors, and any other electronic components and devices within the ship. The crew are mostly unharmed because the currents tend to stay within the confines of the ship's structure. The weapon renders a ship useless without much risk of causing the crew any harm."

"Incredible," Doug finally said. "Hey! Look!"

POWER STRUGGLE

Ken turned his attention to the main tactical display and was surprised to see that all of the Chroniech ships were leaving. The three planetary assault ships, of course, were now dead in space and drifting. "I'll be damned!" Scarboro exclaimed. "Show them a little of what you can do and they turn tail and run."

"They'll be back," Stricklen said. "And it won't be with a hundred, two hundred, or even a thousand ships. From what I've seen of the Chroniech and their reaction to the Kyrra I think they'll be back with every ship that they can spare."

"Captain Stricklen!" the voice of Admiral Singth blared over the speaker. "On behalf of the Alliance and especially Almaranus, I want to thank both you and your Kyrra friends. I have received word from the Almaranus civilian government that they want to throw a welcoming party for as many Kyrra as would like to join. I don't think they realize that an entire planetary population might be attending. I would, however, like to invite you and the Kyrra leaders to the surface so they can be officially thanked."

"The thought is appreciated," Stricklen replied. "But, we have some other business to attend to. This battle is not over yet. I would like permission for the *Dragon* and her crew to remain behind. I think most of my crew would like to contact their families."

"Understood. Permission is granted. Your crew may land at the main starport at any time. Before you go, there is someone in my office who insists on speaking with you."

The Admiral stepped away from the video pickup and Sorbith moved into view. "Congratulations Captain! Your mission was far more successful than anticipated. I take it you have returned Falnath in one piece?"

Ken chuckled a bit before answering. "Oh yes. You might have a hard time getting her to leave though. She has been in the Rouldian equivalent of heaven since we encountered the Kyrra. She spends her every waking hour wandering around their research labs. Frankly, I'm surprised they have not thrown her out."

"Glad to hear it. What's this other business you're talking about?"

"We may have chased the Chroniech away from Almaranus, but the rest of the Alliance is still in jeopardy. The Kyrra cannot be bouncing from system to system chasing Chroniech ships away only to have them come back as soon as they leave. Something must be done to pull the Chroniech back to their space and keep them there. I intend on going to one of the Chroniech home worlds and threatening to destroy the entire planet unless they stop their attacks on the Alliance and recall their ships."

"Sounds risky. I can't imagine the Chroniech allowing you to approach any of their capital worlds without a challenge. Just how do the Kyrra expect to keep the Chroniech contained?"

"I have not the foggiest idea," Ken replied shrugging his shoulders. "The Kyrra have been tight-lipped about that. Don't worry about us. This ship is about as close to indestructible as you can get. The Chroniech are about to receive a lesson in extreme power. As soon as the *Dragon* is clear we will be leaving."

While Ken had been talking to the Admiral, Trel'mara had been speaking to the Kyrra council. Both conversations ended at about the same time. Trel'mara turned to Ken and said, "The council has requested that all Alliance personnel leave the world ship. A general recall of your ship's compliment has been put out."

"That's exactly what I was about to do. I think our best approach to get the Chroniech out of Alliance space is to take the battle to their home worlds. Threatening to destroy one of their major planets should convince them to recall all of their ships."

Ken then noticed the look on Trel'mara's face. "You're not telling me I have to leave also, are you?"

The alien placed a hand on Ken's right shoulder and replied, "Yes. I do not know why the council has ordered this, but I must ask you to leave. You have been a good friend, Ken Stricklen. I will miss you."

Ken was confused. "This is not a final good bye, Trel'mara. I don't know what the council plans on doing after we leave but I do know that you will be back. Talk to them, ask them to let me stay on the world ship."

"I am sorry, but the council's decision is final. All Alliance personnel, including yourself, must leave immediately."

Stricklen was about to offer further argument but after seeing the look in his friend's eyes decided against it. Trel'mara was having a difficult time saying good bye and he did not want to make it any worse. Reaching out and placing his right hand on Trel'mara's shoulder, Ken said, "All right. Just promise me that you will look me up when you get back."

"If I am able, I will do so," Trel'mara replied.

Ken took one last look around the control room, spun around on his heel, and left. A transport was waiting for him outside the control center. Twenty minutes later, he was once again seated in his familiar command chair aboard the *Komodo Dragon*. As soon as the ship was ready, the immense docking hatch opened and the heavy-cruiser once again found itself floating in its natural element.

"Good Lord, look at the size of that thing!" Doug remarked as the ship accelerated away from the Kyrra world ship.

"Helm," Stricklen ordered. "Set course for Almaranus, maximum speed." He then punched up a tactical display just in time to see the world ship as it engaged its stardrive and blasted toward Chroniech space. A sense of loss swept over Ken as he watched the world ship until it finally disappeared off his screen.

"What do you think they are going to do?" Doug asked.

"I have no idea," Ken replied. "But I have this awful feeling that we will never see them again."

"I wouldn't bet on that," Doug replied as he turned and walked off the bridge.

Chapter 19

The master's clawed fist slammed into the table top with an earth-shattering crash. The other members of the council growled in agreement of their leader's anger. "Three planetary assault platforms destroyed with one shot to each!" he raged. "These Kyrra are indeed the ones spoken of in our legends. If the legends predict the behavior of the Kyrra accurately then they will come here next to destroy us. The legends tell of how the Kyrra attacked and nearly destroyed the ancients. Despite the incredible power of their weapons, the ancients massed all their strength and overcame the Kyrra. I am ordering the immediate recall of all ships. While our forces gather, we will develop an attack plan to stop the Kyrra."

* * * * *

The crew of the *Komodo Dragon* were welcomed to Almaranus by as much celebration as could be achieved in a domed city. The atmosphere of the planet was inhospitable to life and thus all cities and structures were either domed or air-tight. Stricklen attended several banquets before he finally, but politely, told the officials that he had had enough. Throughout all this, Stricklen kept in touch with the strategic situation. Amazingly, all Chroniech ships had withdrawn from Alliance space. The damage they left behind was considerable.

Eleven planets, two of them heavily populated, had been laid to waste. Nearly three thousand Alliance ships had been destroyed. The total loss of life was still being compiled but so far the number had risen beyond fifteen million. It was believed that only twelve hundred or so Chroniech ships had been destroyed. The Alliance had been hit hard by the Chroniech and it would take years before they fully recovered.

The Kyrra had refused to respond to any attempts at communication. Stricklen had no idea what they were up to and he could not keep them out of his mind. Several times, he had sent personal messages toward the world ship but had never received a reply. By now, the Kyrra were outside the communications range of even the Hess provided transmitters.

POWER STRUGGLE

After a week of celebrations, banquets, and speeches, Tasha convinced Ken that they needed to take some time to themselves. Ken applied for and received one month of leave. Being Tasha's superior officer, Ken also approved her leave request. A prominent local businessman heard of their plans to take a vacation and, in appreciation for ridding the Alliance of the Chroniech, allowed them to use one of the company's small superluminal Leer's. Ken tried to refuse but in the end gave in. At long last Tash and Ken had some time to themselves. Their private ship spent most of the three day trip on autopilot.

Their first stop was an Omel world fifteen light years from Almaranus known by Humans as Oceanus. The planet consisted of thousands of small islands dotted around the planet's equatorial region. The vast majority of the world was covered with water. "Tell me," Tasha whispered into Ken's ear as they lay together in a hammock. "Have you decided if you're going to put in your resignation?"

The two lovers had not discussed their future since beginning their vacation. They had been too involved in enjoying and exploring each other. Ken looked up at the clear star-studded sky and took in a deep breath. He knew this question had been on Tasha's mind for some time. He adjusted his shoulder a bit then replied, "I have been in the military since I was eighteen. My father, and my father's father were all in the military. It's in my blood. Do you think I would be happy being retired?"

Tash reached down, absentmindedly stroking his thigh, and said, "I think I could keep you happy!" Relaxing her hand she continued, "Seriously, I don't know. The decision is yours to make, not mine. Whatever you decided though, I want to be able to see you more often than once a year. We will either stay in the military together and remain assigned to the same command or you will have to think about retiring. You did mention your father's sailboat back on Earth."

"Yes I did, and the more I think about it, the better retirement sounds."

"How far is Earth from here?" she asked.

"I believe it's just over seventy light years. We could make the trip in under two weeks, why?"

"I have a deal to make with you. Talk to your superior and ask for a leave of absence. Take me to Earth and show me this boat you keep talking about. After two weeks you can decide if you want to retire or not. I will respect whatever decision you make."

Ken thought about it for a moment. He then rolled out of the hammock and took a drink from his rum which had been patiently waiting for him on the table. He looked at his lovely wife and said, "I'll call the Admiral in the morning. If he approves, I'll tell Mr. Taylor that we will be keeping his private ship a little bit longer than originally anticipated."

Tash rolled out of the hammock and embraced her husband. "Great! Let's celebrate," she said in a voice Ken had grown to love.

"Again? You're going to wear me out before my time," he said jokingly.

"Maybe," she said, leading him into the cottage. "But at least we will have fun doing it."

In the age of advanced communications, nobody was more than a phone-call away. Ken, however, was still surprised to find a message waiting for him in the morning. Tasha was still sleeping so he decided to go ahead and play the message. It was from Admiral Singh.

"Sorry to bother you on your honeymoon Captain, but a situation has developed which has forced us to issue a recall of all available military personnel. I cannot give specifics over an unsecured channel so you will have to be in the dark until you arrive. I have dispatched the *Komodo Dragon* to your location to pick you up and return you to Almaranus since she is still the fastest ship in the fleet. The *Dragon* should be arriving at your location by 0800 local time. Someone else will be responsible for piloting your private ship back to its owner. Sector command out."

Stricklen uttered an explicative and glanced at the clock. It was already 0740. Cursing under his breath he turned around and almost collided with Tasha. The look in her eyes told him that she had overheard the message. "What does he mean by 'a situation'?" she asked.

"I have no idea," Ken replied. "But, it must be bad if they are issuing a recall. The *Dragon* will be here soon, we had better get packed."

Ken and Tasha were enjoying an after-breakfast cup of coffee when a knock sounded at the cottage door. The couple looked at each other and Ken yelled out, "Come in!"

The door opened and Doug Scarboro strode into the room. "Your taxi is here!" he announced.

Ken stood up and shook hands with his friend. "We were beginning to wonder what was taking you so long. Why didn't you call us as soon as you arrived?"

"I thought you two could use the time together. Besides, we still had to send a shuttle down to pick you up. A good old-fashioned knock on the door works just as well as a com-link."

"I thought you and Cheryl would be going on a honeymoon together?" Tasha remarked.

"We decided to wait until you two returned," Scarboro replied. "I did not want both the Captain and myself to be away from the *Dragon* at the same time. Speaking of a honeymoon, did you enjoy yours?"

"Too short," Ken answered. "But relaxing never-the-less."

"I'll bet!" Doug replied with a sly look in his eyes.

"As long as you're here," Ken said, finishing the last of his coffee. "Why the recall? What's happened?"

"There's a transport outside. I'll explain as we load up your things," Doug said, picking up a waiting suitcase.

As they loaded the transport, Doug quickly told Ken all that he knew. Ever since the Kyrra had left, the Alliance had been sending probes into Chroniech space. Eighteen hours ago contact with all of the probes except two had been lost. The data collected by one of the operational probes seemed to indicate that all of Chroniech space has simply ceased to exist. It was not known if this was some sort of Chroniech deception to hide a massive attack or some other phenomenon. As a precautionary measure the Alliance was recalling all military personnel and is putting the fleet on high alert.

As soon as they had transferred their bags and boarded the shuttle, Ken asked to see the data from the probe. Doug activated a computer terminal and said, "Display probe C189 data from time index previously marked as event one minus sixty seconds."

One part of the screen showed a star field as it was observed through the electronic eye of the probe while the other part of the screen displayed a series of graphs and numbers representing the non-visual information which the probe collected. Suddenly, the star field shifted – several stars seemed to grow brighter and others vanished entirely. The effect was so fast that it was difficult to see.

"What was that?" Ken asked the first time he saw it.

"Hard to see, isn't it?" Doug replied. "Watch this. Computer: Loopback replay of event one over a five-second interval at one-half normal speed."

Once again, Ken watched the stars shift. This time the computer repeatedly displayed the shift over and over again. Ken could now pick out which stars had disappeared and which ones had brightened. He stared at the computer screen for thirty seconds before turning away. "What the hell is it?"

"We don't know," Doug replied. "There is something else. Computer: Isolate energy spectrum spike associated with event one and display."

The screen now showed an energy spectrum. The complex series of graphs reminded Ken of something but he could not quite make the connection. The time-line showed that the spike lasted a mear ten millionth of a second. Shaking his head, Ken asked, "Which stars brightened and which ones vanished?"

"Now that is the most interesting part of this entire mystery," Doug replied. He glanced out the window of the shuttle to take a look at the *Komodo Dragon* which had just come into view. Still staring out the window he continued. "According to the computer, all of the stars which have disappeared are those which are located within Chroniech space. Those which have become brighter are those located beyond Chroniech space. It's as if all of Chroniech space has ceased to exist and the rest of the universe has shifted to close the hole."

"That's impossible!" Stricklen said not believing what Doug had just said.

"Not according to Falnath," Doug replied turning around.

"Falnath has seen this?" Ken asked incredulously.

"You can ask her about it yourself after we dock. She's onboard. Since the *Dragon* is the fastest and most powerful ship in the Alliance, we have been tasked with investigating this phenomenon. We'll be leaving as soon as we dock."

Stricklen sat in his seat in silence. Scarboro loved to spring little surprises on his Captain now and again, but this was too many too fast. Nothing he had just heard seemed to make sense. Stricklen was still trying to make heads or tails of it all when the shuttle docked with the heavy-cruiser. Before he had even exited the shuttle, Ken felt the familiar sensation as the ship engaged its stardrive.

Falnath was waiting for them on the bridge. Ignoring her for the moment, Ken took his place in the command chair and said, "Status!" He needed to get up to speed on what was going on with his ship.

The officer he had just relieved replied, "All systems on-line. Course has been set for the heart of Chroniech space. Ship's speed now nine-kay-cee and accelerating. All sensors clear. ETA to Chroniech border is roughly six days."

After looking over the status screens, Ken finally felt comfortable enough to address Falnath. Turning to the Rouldian he asked, "Explain to me how a piece of space over twelve hundred light-years in diameter could simply vanish."

Falnath maneuvered her considerable bulk until she was closer to Stricklen's command chair. "The Kyrra have most likely erected a hyperdiminsional field around the Chroniech. This would explain why their area of space has appeared to vanish."

Something clicked inside Ken's mind and a connection was made. He now remembered why the energy spike recorded by the probe looked so familiar. It was basically the same as that seen when the Chroniech were attempting to form their transdimensional matrix field. "How could they generate a field that big? Twelve hundred light-years is one hell of a big force field."

"Not in hyperdimensional space. A thousand light-years of our three-dimensional space can be crossed quite easily in a short distance if you exist in multi-space."

"I don't follow," Stricklen said. "Can you put it into simple terms. All I want to know is what happened. What will we see when we get to the Chroniech border? A force field? A hole in space? Nothing?"

"If we had never mapped this area of space," Falnath said after a moment's reflection. "We would never have known that a part of it was missing. It is very difficult to explain in physical terms. It is much easier to explain mathematically."

Falnath paused for a moment and Ken could tell that she was trying to come up with some way of explaining what was most likely unexplainable. Finally, she reached out and formed a cup with her clawed hand. "Let us say that this area of space is enclosed within a hyperdimensional field. Normal space flows around the surface of this field. To someone traveling in normal space, this curvature cannot be detected and it appears as if that person continues to travel in a straight line. This supposed straight line curves around this area of space and thus that area of space no longer exists."

Ken thought he was beginning to see a little light at the end of the tunnel. "So what we are seeing is actually the surface of a hyperdimensional shape? Doesn't this affect stardrive fields?"

"Stardrive fields affect normal space much like a hyperdimensional field does. However, there are differences. A stardrive field is also affected by the hyperdimensional field and thus the area within the hyperdimensional object is unreachable and undetectable."

"A perfect cloak," Ken said to himself. "I wonder why the Kyrra did not hide behind something like that instead of parking their world ship inside a star?"

"Because once inside a hyperdimensional field, all contact with the universe outside the field is lost. The field would also require the expenditure of tremendous amounts of power."

"Do we understand enough about hyperdimensional theory to be able to create such a force field?"

"Technically it is not a force field. It is a field-induced curvature of space. To answer your question, no we do not. Our understanding of hyperdimensional physics is limited and not complete enough for us to develop the field emitters required to generate the proper fields to fold space into a hyperdimension."

"If we can't detect this phenomenon, and we can't understand it then what do we hope to accomplish by the trip toward Chroniech space?"

Falnath cocked her head to one side in her people's expression of puzzlement. "To verify that the stars on the other side of the now vanished section of space are now closer to us. If this is found to be true, then we will know for certain that the Kyrra have encased the Chroniech within a hyperdimensional prison."

"And themselves along with them," Ken said. "Thank you, Falnath."

Stricklen sat in his chair and thought about the Kyrra, their world ship, and the friends he had made during his stay there. The more he thought about it the angrier he became. He felt as if the entire situation was his fault. If he had not offered to take the Kyrra home then the world ship would not be where it was now. Admittedly, they had done the Alliance a great good by removing the Chroniech threat, but at what expense.

"Tell me Falnath," he suddenly said. "You said that this hyperdimensional field requires a constant source of power to maintain it. Is there any way at all that we can breach it?"

Falnath turned from her science station to answer the question. "The field is artificial and will collapse as soon as the generator is turned off. As far as I know, there is no possibility of penetrating the barrier from either side. We do not have the knowledge to even detect the presence of the field. If we were in possession of Kyrra technology, we might be able to detect the field but I do not believe that it can be penetrated."

"Captain," the communications operator spoke up. "Urgent message coming in from Almaranus."

"On the main," Stricklen ordered.

The tactical plot of the main viewscreen was replaced by the image of Admiral Singh. The link indicator showed it to be a live feed with a round-trip delay of less than half a second. "Captain Stricklen here Admiral, how may I help you?"

"We've just received a message from the Kyrra," the Admiral replied. Ken's interest instantly increased. "It's from an automated beacon which was set to send a message on a time delay. It's about to repeat so I'll pipe it through to you."

Ken could see the Admiral manipulate something below the camera's field of view. The image shifted and a Kyrra appeared. Ken immediately recognized Trel'mara. The image was frozen for a few seconds and them suddenly came to life, "Attention Alliance! I am Trel'mara of the Kyrra. By now you may have discovered that all star systems belonging to the Chroniech have vanished. Be assured that they are still in existence. We are generating a hyperdimensional field which has isolated the Chroniech from the Alliance. Do not fear for our safety. We have chosen a new star near the center of the Chroniech empire for our new home. The world ship is safely within the photosphere of this star and thus protected from any possible attack.

"The council agreed that this course of action was the best for all concerned. They felt that the continued presence of the Kyrra among the various cultures of the Alliance would have resulted in increased competition between yourselves in attempting to obtain a technological advantage over each other through the acquisition of our technology. Many of our people were uncomfortable with the decision to establish relations with a group of cultures so different from our own. The actions which we have taken have served both our peoples. The Alliance is free from the Chroniech and my people are once again isolated, however we also now have a purpose which is to protect the Alliance and, if possible, attempt to guide the Chroniech toward becoming a different society.

"We shall maintain the hyperdimensional field for as long as required. It is our belief that the Chroniech will either learn how to cooperate among themselves and thus eventually mature into a society which can, at some time in the far future, be re-joined with the rest of the galaxy or, they will turn upon each other in mutual destruction. Either way, when the time is right, the hyperdimensional field will be dropped and we shall initiate contact with the Alliance once again.

"I wish to personally convey my thanks to Captain Ken Stricklen and the entire crew of the *Komodo Dragon* for their willingness to help me and my fellow Kyrra return to our people. Do not worry about me my friend, I have found a purpose for my life. I am the new head of the alien species information and cultural research organization.

"This message is being transmitted from an automated capsule. The message will repeat on multiple frequencies until an Alliance ship locates it. The concept of an alliance between your varied species shows us that your inherent aggressiveness can be controlled and that your cultures have a long future ahead of you. The Kyrra look forward to re-establishing a relationship with you in the future. Until then we wish you luck."

Trel'mara's image once again froze. After a moment, the image of Admiral Singth reappeared. "We have dispatched a ship to retrieve the message capsule. There is no reason for you to continue with your mission Captain. Return to Almaranus. I am declaring the Chroniech threat to be ended and all Alliance military units are to stand down. See you back at base. Almaranus sector command out."

Ken suddenly felt very empty. "Set course for Almaranus," he said as he stood up. "Let me know when we arrive." Ken then silently walked off the bridge and headed for Tasha's stateroom.

*****

This is how life was meant to be enjoyed, thought Ken as he stretched out on the deck of his eight meter sailboat. The pleasure craft was drifting aimlessly, the only sound being the gentle slap of the waves as they caressed the side of the ship. Ken was watching a spectacular sunset and enjoying every minute of it. The sun appeared as a gigantic reddish-orange ball sitting on top of the water's surface; it slowly sank lower as Ken watched.

The stars were beginning to peek through the darkening sky. As Ken tried to make out the constellations, Tasha came up from behind and kissed him on the forehead. "Dinner's ready."

Sitting up and returning his wife's kiss Stricklen replied, "Sorry, I didn't realize it was getting so late. I was just looking at the stars."

Tasha looked him in the eyes and said, "You're not regretting your decision to retire are you?"

Taking one last look at the darkening sky, Stricklen embraced his wife and replied, "Not on your life. Let's eat."

THE END